The Underbelly

The Underbelly

Dr. Jacquelyn and Mrs. Hyde

EVELYN COLE

authorHOUSE®

AuthorHouse™
1663 Liberty Drive
Bloomington, IN 47403
www.authorhouse.com
Phone: 1-800-839-8640

Cover design by Kristi Anderson - Kristi.Anderson.Creative@gmail.com

Published by AuthorHouse   03/26/2012

ISBN: 978-1-4685-7198-1 (sc)
ISBN: 978-1-4685-7197-4 (e)

Library of Congress Control Number: 2012905358

Dedicated to The South County Nightwriters: Dennis Young, David Georgi, Claire Gordon, Ginger Lasher, Judy Guarnera, and Susan Tuttle as well as to my tolerant husband, John F. Turrill.

CHAPTER ONE

Hailstones drummed the roof of the little house on Glendale Street in Worcester, Massachusetts on the dark night of the new moon. Jacquelyn, age two and a half, propped three teething rings and six pacifiers against the buffer on one side of her crib. She started with the smallest and arranged them by feel according to shape and size. Her skin itched with the thrill, the power. She could create her own order. She would've called herself smug if she'd known the word, for she had hidden each new pacifier along with the teething rings inside the rip in her crib mattress until she had enough to make a proper line up.

Then her bedroom door opened. A flash of light came in, followed by her father, mother and brother.

"Hey, Kiddo," her big brother said, "are you organizing again?"

"Well, my wee Jackie," her father said. "I thought I heard you scurrying about. Why are you awake?"

"Night, night, Papa." She dove onto her stomach, stretched her legs and, seeing her big brother's grin, clenched her eyes shut. *She's coming to get me.*

Her mother's narrow chin moved in closer. Jacquelyn peeked. The V crease between her mother's eyes mirrored her pursed lips.

*She's my other Mama, the light-hair one, my new Mama. She won't hit me if I go to sleep. I dint break **her** tiny elephant.*

"Tsk, tsk," her mother said. "You'll catch a death of cold." As she pulled the covers over Jacquelyn, she knocked the pacifiers and teething rings out of line.

"My word, where did all these come from?" She scooped them all up and left, taking them with her

Jacquelyn covered her head and cried herself to sleep.

*   *   *

Forty-two years later, Dr. Jacquelyn Hyde drove her BMW through a hailstorm into Worcester, back to the small house on Glendale Street where she grew up. Her parents were moving to

Florida, and much as she disliked visiting them, she felt obligated. After all, they had paid for her Ph.D. A group from their church was helping them pack Sunday afternoon, and her father wanted to show her off. It was the least she could do.

She parked opposite the house, opened her umbrella to protect her recently highlighted hair, and crossed the street. The white picket fence she'd loved as a child now tilted inward and looked out of order. She used to go outside when she was little, touch their picket fence, and run her forefinger over the top of each picket, appreciating all things that lined up. In fact, her father had told her that "in-odda" was her first word.

She entered the house now without knocking. The familiar scent of metal polish annoyed her. She wished she could be more tolerant.

Bill Nestrom, her father, cradled a trombone in his arms and bounced in place on the balls of his feet. Abby, her mother, hovered beside him. The church people stopped packing to greet her. Jacquelyn spoke to them all with a smile she did not feel.

"I'm glad you made it, Jackie. Hard to leave Worcester's hailstorms," Bill said, "but the young folks who bought this old place are eager to work on it and we're heading—"

"Bill, stop!" Abby said. "We asked Jackie to speak with our friends, so let her."

"Yes, yes, of course."

"So nice to see all of you," Jacquelyn said. "Thanks so much for your help packing." She stood on the raised hearth by the fireplace to give her some height. Looking up at an audience hurt her neck.

"You should see my wee Jackie's house," Bill said. "Near Rocky pond on three acres." He grinned. "Cold underground springs feed that pond. It's got a huge rock in the center that my grandkids—"

"Why, I remember when you were little, Jackie," said a plump woman with gray teeth interrupting Bill. "You sure did love your Madame Alexander doll collection. And now look at you, with a doctor's degree and superintendent of a whole bunch of schools."

"Assistant superintendent," Jacquelyn corrected, wishing she could end this fiasco and exit with steady hands.

"It's strange," a man with a raised hand said, "that you're so little with such tall parents, but you sure are pretty."

Jaquelyn smiled. *What a strange comment.* She wanted to say, "My grandmother was short," but managed to keep her defenses down.

"What does your husband do?" another man asked.

"My husband runs a small electronics business, *Arthur Hyde Software Solutions.*"

"How old are your kids now?" a woman asked.

"Ethan is sixteen and Sylvia's thirteen," she said, swallowing a sigh. She answered a few more questions and then said, "I'm sorry, but I really must be going. The children keep me hopping." She pictured the mess in the kitchen that would greet her and made a mental note to hire a housekeeper.

Bill Nestrom blew a few notes on his trombone and everyone except Jaquelyn applauded. How she hated his trombones. Even now, after all these years.

*   *   *

Patricia "Trishita" McCabe stepped over a man sleeping on the sidewalk in front of Russo's Bar and Grill in Worcester, Massachusetts. A pile of rags smelling of paint thinner under the guy's head caught her attention—Clark University T-shirts. The sight of those shirts unlocked her longings as she unlocked the door to Russo's. She began cleaning the place with a vengeance, plotting to escape through those ads for live-in maid.

That damn paint contractor used Clark T-shirts as rags when she would give anything to be able to wear a new one for real. That thought struck her irony-bone, since she was the illegitimate child of Dr. McCabe, a one-semester exchange professor from Scotland. He knew naught of her, yet Flossie, her mother, had forged his name on Trishita's birth certificate. Nor did she know his academic field, for Flossie had not asked. This particular unknown skewered Trishita's academic fantasies.

"I'll be at the track," Russo said when he stuck his head in the front door just before noon. "Looks good, Trish. Don't let the assholes get you down." Then the cook and dishwasher came in the back door chattering in Spanish.

The place was full by noon with hung-over guys at the long bar overlooking Beacon Street, a few law students and some older bitches at the tables. Regulars at the bar called her "The Red Amazon" as if she couldn't hear them, and "Trishita" to her face. Newcomers always asked how tall she was. At that question, she pointed to a hand-lettered sign over the bar that read, "six foot, one inch" in red ink. Men in suits spoke in hushed tones about having those long legs wrapped around them.

Older women from the campus called her "Miss".

"Miss, would you please turn down that hideous music."

"Miss, I don't believe this fork is clean. Please bring another."

"Who does your hair?" one with straight blonde hair asked. "Do you have it tinted red and then permed?" The others smiled behind their napkins.

She hated them, but continued to wait on them. She hated them, yet wished she could join them.

The place emptied by four in the afternoon, except for a couple at the bar. Trishita stretched her legs across a chair and picked up "The Grapes of Wrath" to read about a life worse than hers. But not much worse. There's supposed to be progress, she thought. These poor jerks sleeping on the streets of Worcester, Massachusetts, a city that brags about being home to ten fine colleges, are no better off than those Okies in California during the depression. And that was 75 years ago.

Sharp claps of thunder outbid the police siren that wailed down Beacon Street and stopped outside, interrupting Trishita's reading. Pellets of hail stuck to the jackets of a policeman who stormed in. Trishita looked up from her book.

"To what do we owe the honor of your visit?" she asked.

"We're looking for a Miss, uh, Ms. Patricia McCabe."

"Yours truly." Trishita stood, wary. "What do you want?"

"Is Florence Giraux your mother?" The officer, no taller than five-seven, tilted back his head to examine her face, thereby avoiding her breasts, which she knew confronted him

"Yes sir."

"I need to take you in for questioning."

Rage burned its way up Trishita's torso and exploded in her throat. She swallowed hard, stifling it. She knew better than mouth off at a cop.

"What did she do this time?" she asked.

"Painted what looked like tulips all over the inside of the city hall bell tower," the officer said, lowering his head as if to hide his smile.

"Why do you need me?" Trishita asked.

"She said you hatched the plot," he said.

"I did not. I have nothing to do with her shenanigans."

"Why not come along easy like. Save yourself some skin on your nose," the officer said.

Trishita hung up her apron, called for the cook to replace her, and followed the officer out to his patrol car. It was a familiar scene, and hailing as well. She shivered.

*   *   *

Flossie came toward her from a hallway in the station wearing a torn red and yellow pantsuit and a wobbly grin on her face.

"Thanks, Mija." She hugged Trishita, her head breast high.

Don't suck me dry, Trishita thought, and turned to the desk to pay Flossie's bail.

"Why, Ma?" She asked as they left the station.

"It seemed like such a good idea," Flossie said, "I knew it had to be yours."

Trishita just shook her head as they trudged home, wanting the storm to whip them with icy rocks. But, like Trishita, it was spent. If she could hate her tiny Canuck-French mother it would be easy to clear out, but this aging Hippie not only needed her, but loved her.

Together, they climbed the three flights of stairs of the old tenement building to their flat. Trishita's long legs skipped every other stair. Flossie scampered beside her like a child.

She ushered Flossie inside. While she waited for Flossie to come out of the bathroom, she looked around at this so-called home and pretended to be a rental agent showing the place. It was a familiar fantasy—a downtown kind of job. "The kitchen," she said to herself, rehearsing in her most suave tongue, "connects to all the other rooms in the flat and is the very heart of a web of rooms. It has impressive windows on the north side and is big enough to feed a crowd."

Of course, she thought, interrupting her role-play, the normal feast consists of hot dogs on Wonder Bread rolls with a squirt of French's mustard.

"That plaid sofa where I was born," she continued, "fills the south wall. And then, when I was almost nine, my half-brother Robert arrived on that same sofa. Three years later, Johnny. The baby girl Flossie had in between was born in a hospital. She gave her up for adoption."

Trishita retreated from her imagined role and wondered for the first time why Flossie had kept her. Now she just stared at the picnic table and benches and the refrigerator, with legs, standing between the table and rust-stained sink. The refrigerator was as old as the tenement, probably lifted into the kitchen as it was being built by that particular wave of immigrants.

She recalled a program on public radio describing the waves of desperate people that came to Beacon Street and surroundings. Since the sixteen hundreds, immigrants had clung to Worcester's center, then, gaining power, fanned out, making way for more. First were the Pilgrims followed by all manner of English and Scots. The Irish came after the potato famine. They were followed by Italians, Swedes, Jews from Eastern Europe, some few Lithuanians, and Poles. The most recent were the Puerto Ricans. That's why slums surrounded some of Worcester's finest ivy-covered universities. *Yeah, drunks sleeping on stinky Clark T-shirts.*

Although her room connected to Flossie's through the bathroom, it had a blessed fire escape out one window. *Now was the time to escape all the way.*

"You need your vegetables, Ma," she said when Flossie appeared. "Sit down." Trishita heated the stew she'd made that morning.

"If you say so, Mija," Flossie said.

"Ma, I'm job hunting." Trishita dished up the stew and handed it to her mother. "Got leads on some live-in housekeeping jobs. Soon as I land one, I'm moving out."

"No! Why Mija? Why would you do a thing like that?"

"Why do you keep calling me Mija?" Trishita asked. "You're French, for Christ's sake."

"That's what people around here call their daughters." Flossie's eyes filled. "Why're you moving?"

"Ma, I'm already twenty-five, going on fifty," Trishita said, lowering her voice. "When Johnny's Dad came and took him to California, I decided to get on with my own plans. Don't you think it's time?" The pain of losing Johnny returned, sharpened.

"Time for what?" Flossie asked. "What you need I can't give you? Besides a man. Them you can have whenever."

Trishita placed her hands on her mother's thin shoulders as if to make her words penetrate Flossie's consciousness.

"I want to learn how to drive a car, Ma, to use computers properly, to work in a downtown office. I really want to go to college someday. Shit, I could pay a semester's tuition on what I spend bailing you out."

"Ha! You spend lots more on books," Flossie said. "You need to go to high school first, you know."

"I did. When you weren't looking. Took a test." Trishita took a bite of the stew and then added some dill.

"But you get nothing as a live-in," Flossie said.

"Not much money, I guess, but I'll learn all kinds of things I need to know to get outa Russo's." Trishita pulled at a lock of her hair, straightening it. "I need to stop taking care of you, start taking care of myself."

Flossie's head snapped to the right as if Trishita had slapped her. "You don't take care of me. I take care of you. Always have."

"Yeah, Ma, I know." She picked up the classified section of the Telegram and stared at each circled name. *Ain't gonna be no toboggan ride gettin' outa here.*

The next morning she managed to use the computer at the Worcester Library, the word processing part, to forge three letters of recommendation from fictitious employers, varying the writing styles for each. She wanted out of her mother's life. Out of waiting table for drunken Puerto Ricans making passes, listening to loud rapping blacks accuse her of racism every time she put her hands to her ears.

And she wanted away from the deli where she helped Flossie work mornings, away from the whine of testy little Orthodox Jews complaining about the size of the matzo balls in the soup. Once she'd yelled at a customer, "Then put your own balls in it." Even Flossie had looked shocked.

Trishita smiled at the memory; sealed and stamped the envelopes. Which elegant family, if any, would believe her false references and hire her without checking them.

CHAPTER TWO

Jacquelyn dropped her book on the floor, turned off the light, and willed herself to sleep. Her mind would not obey. That old lady with gray teeth, whover she is, would bring up the Madame Alexander dolls. Someone stole that collection years ago.

Now why did I think of that tonight? Has it been two weeks since the full moon?

Today was a Sunday from Hell.

Although she'd practiced with the choir for two hours on Thursday, she'd sung off-key. She couldn't even get the Doxology right. Arthur had refused to go to church with her. Ethan had gone to the Catholic Church with that Kraemer girl. She certainly hoped nothing would come of that relationship. And Sylvia had defied her, refusing to change out of those grubby shorts and black T-shirt. It would be a relief to go to work tomorrow.

She shuddered remembering last Tuesday when she had gone to Clark University to address a rather large group of students interested in pursuing advanced degrees in education. Dr. Marie Arlington, head of the department, had invited her home for tea afterwards to chat with some of the more "dedicated" graduate students. The house was one of those built in the twenties in English Tudor style, white stucco with brown trim and several garrets with sloping roofs. Dr. Arlington ushered Jacquelyn and the other guests into a vaulted ceiling living room. The only thing Jacquelyn would remember about the room was one wall with shelves from floor to ceiling that held at least a hundred Lalique figurines.

Her stomach had cramped throughout the thirty-minute lecture. Mr. Arlington, the collector, babbled on about his collection, telling where he got each piece. A tall, thin, graying man with a paunch that made his belt ride high, he managed to bore the group. She hated him. When he finished, she found it hard to respond to the students who had come to admire her.

No, she told herself, *don't even think of getting revenge here. This house is professionally too close to home.* With the figurines still hovering in her mind, she cuddled against Arthur's back and let herself fall asleep.

Too soon, she awoke with a start. Her jaw ached from grinding her teeth. The clock on the bedside table, glowing in the dark, read 2:13. And it was really dark out—the first night of the new moon, and dry. Resigned, she slipped out of bed, relieved that the hailstorm had moved on. Despite all her resolutions to the contrary, she knew she'd be going out again.

Arthur's snores reassured her. She backed away from their king-sized bed and into her walk-in closet. She felt around for her navy blue sweatshirt in the back of her bottom drawer until she touched the rough texture of the burlap lining she'd sewn into it five years ago. Then she checked the drop-down gauze mask attached to its hood. She rarely washed the sweatshirt half of her costume. Now, as she pulled it over her head, she smelled the scared sweat locked into its fibers.

She put on her jeans then opened the secret compartment behind the bottom drawer of her dresser where she kept her belt and tool pouch. The pouch, lined with sheepskin, kept the tools from clinking against each other. It held wire cutters, pliers, scissors, mace—in case anyone caught her and she had to make a quick exit—a small ball-peen hammer, two screwdrivers, tweezers, a pen flashlight, dog biscuits stuffed with tranquilizers, and a magnifying glass. At forty-four, she was beginning to need glasses for close work.

She tightened the belt at her waist and pulled her sweatshirt down to cover the tool pouch while listening to Arthur's light, rhythmic snoring. She envied him. Then, with a stealth born of determination and practice, she backed down the hall to her daughter's room. She found it empty and remembered that Sylvia was staying overnight at the Jasmine's. Next, she peeked in on Ethan to make sure he wouldn't hear her. He was in as deep a sleep as Arthur, with one leg uncovered, the other wrapped in the top sheet.

The burlap scratched her bare skin as she made her way downstairs. It was just painful enough to get the job done. At least they didn't have a dog to rouse the household. She'd managed to circumvent her children's pleas for a puppy by inventing an allergy to animal fur.

She entered the garage and disengaged the automatic door opener by pulling the cord over her black BMW. She opened the door by hand, slipped into the driver's seat, and started the engine, grateful for its singular lack of noises.

The dark made her think of black holes in the universe. She backed out of the garage, left the car idling while she closed the garage door. Everything was working well and she had her alibis intact. Couldn't sleep. Decided to go for a drive. Headed toward Rocky Pond to stare at the water. And, if more were needed, she'd mention menopause, disgusting as that would be.

She drove west on 290 into Worcester, confident that she would have no trouble finding her target house near Tatnuck Hights, despite the dark night of a new moon. Her target was almost too close to her childhood home on Glendale Street.

She drove off the highway and, at 2:52 a.m. parked on a side street near Tatnuck Hights in Worcester. She pulled her folded aluminum ladder out of the trunk. Adrenaline racing, she breathed in the black air and let exhilaration command her. The land behind the house was a pine grove. The scent was more pervasive than the needles that crackled under her feet.

Soon she found herself on a brick path that led right to a back door that looked like her best entrance. With her hood on and the veil dropped, she crouched by the door lock and inserted two pieces of wire. After a few turns to the left and one to the right, she heard the click that signaled success. She opened the door a foot, peered in, listened, and sidled backwards into a game room, holding the ladder to her chest.

Dr. Arlington had shown her through the house so she knew where they slept—upstairs over the game room with its ping-pong table and about six feet away from the figurines. Awfully close. But, she'd estimated the distance and calculated the risks.

Now, she had to be careful to not bump the ladder into the ping-pong table. A mosquito buzzed her ear. She stood still for a moment, holding her breath. How she loved these moments just before the kill.

Tonight's job would be tough. She would have to open her ladder all the way and climb to the very top to reach the majority of figurines in that high ceilinged living room. No time for lolly-gagging, she told herself, and hurried to her quarry.

She opened the ladder with great care and then climbed it. Working with eyes now accustomed to the darkest of black holes, she pulled her ball-peen hammer out of her pouch and covered it with a small piece of felt to muffle the sound. Next, she knocked the heads off all the figurines within reach. She placed each head beside the body of a different figurine. Every fifteen minutes she would move the ladder. When she'd finished her work on the upper shelves, she folded the ladder and leaned it against an easy chair. It was a relief to be at floor level.

Engrossed, she saw the person coming down the staircase as if in a dream. With a sudden shock of recognition, she came to and squeezed behind an upright piano in the hallway. Fingering the can of mace in her pouch, she watched as the tall, stoop-shouldered man made his way in the darkness toward her. What if he turned on a light! She held her breath.

He was wearing nothing but a striped pajama top. His limp member swung like a tail between his legs as he walked. His pajama sleeve brushed the piano as he moved past and pushed into the kitchen, letting the door swing behind him. She heard him burp, turn on the faucet, drink, then burp again. For a second she thought of suggesting bicarbonate of soda. Instead, she got the hell out of there through a side door off a porch. She left ten figurines intact, and her ladder.

Feeling her way among the pine trees, she touched gooey sap, adding to her sense of being alive and powerful.

She started the engine of her BMW and backed down the side street to Tatnuck Square. Leaving the ladder was a nuisance, but she could replace it. Fingerprints wouldn't be a problem unless she got caught and police took her prints. She shuddered at the thought, and then smiled. It would never happen because, she promised herself, tonight's would be her last caper.

As she pulled off 290 and drove through the woods toward home, she sniffed the pinesap on her fingers and hummed the Triumphal March from Aida, picturing those large, majestic animals parading across a stage.

Closer to home she thought about her one brief spell of shoplifting after Sylvia had started kindergarten. It wasn't any good, though. She ended up spending too much time searching for safe trash barrels to dispose of the stupid stuff she'd stolen, and she still couldn't get relief from the urge that drove her to distraction. Besides, stores couldn't give her the thrill that sneaking into houses did. And collections were such a pleasure to destroy. Why the hell do people collect things? When her father started collecting trombones, she complained. Her mother shut her up.

"Don't you dare criticize your father," she'd said. "If it weren't for him you wouldn't be here." So Jaquelyn said no more.

Years later, she first began shoplifting around Boston. Then one night she broke into a house that had a collection of Betty-Boop dolls scattered all over the living room. Filled with sudden rage, she broke the arms off six or seven of them. A noise from another room sent her scurrying out. How well she slept the rest of that month.

Now, driving home to get an hour of two of sweet sleep before going to work late, she pledged tonight's caper would be her last. It was so satisfying.

She pulled into her garage, sneaked outside to ease down the garage door, and then reset the automatic door opener so Arthur would not notice anything awry. Inside the kitchen, she stopped to listen. The house was quiet, but she noticed that the sink was a mess, as usual. She vowed that tomorrow she would contact that young woman with such good letters of recommendation. A live-in maid would make their lives so much easier.

CHAPTER THREE

Trishita trudged through rain, sleet, and snow flurries for two miles—from the bus stop in Northboro center to Dr. Jacquelyn Hyde's pearl gray clapboard, two-story, neo-Colonial house surrounded by acres of young woods. A large concrete driveway lined with lilac bushes circled in front of the house and extended on one side to the garage in back. Trishita checked the address on the paper in her hand, sweaty despite the cold December air, and shook the brass knocker on the front door.

Mrs. Hyde, a tiny woman in a coral pink silk pantsuit, welcomed her into a slate-floored foyer with a spiral staircase leading to the second floor. The octagonal foyer was lined with mirrors, which made her think the family of four greeting her was a family of thirty-two. She focused on Mrs. Hyde. The woman's frown formed a distinct V in the middle of her forehead, mirroring her chin, and she didn't seem to know what to do with her tiny hands. But her smile seemed genuine.

Mrs. Hyde introduced Trishita to her husband, Arthur, a short, norm-shaped man with graying temples and a small brown mustache, trimmed. Before he could speak, their teenage daughter, taller than both of them, shook Trishita's hand.

"Hi, I'm Sylvia," she said. "This is my brother, Ethan." She nodded toward a compact little bundle of muscle with blond hair and one tiny, gold earring reflecting light in the mirror. "We won't give you any trouble, honest. What's your nationality?"

"French and Scottish." Trishita smiled, already loving the girl.

"Who's French?" Sylvia asked.

"My mother. From Montreal."

So that's why your skin is smooth, not all freckled," Sylvia said. "Looks great with your red hair."

"Sure is red," the boy said, extending his hand.

"I'd say it's as bright a red as that of a true Viking," Mr. Hyde said, beaming.

"Is your mother tall, too?" Sylvia asked.

"No," Trishita replied. *Why all these irrelevant questions?* "She's about the same size as your mother."

"Now, there's no need to discuss Miss McCabe's looks," Mrs. Hyde broke in. Then to Trishita she said, "I see you live near Oread and Benefit. I hear that's a pretty rough neighborhood. Yet so close to Clark University."

"Yes, Mrs. Hyde. It's predominantly white Puerto Rican now but has its share of black Africans, black Ricans, Jews, Maine-i-acs, Irish and Italians. My mother's the only French one I know."

"And your father?" Mrs. Hyde asked.

"He's in Scotland."

"Really?" Arthur Hyde exclaimed. "I find Scotland most fascinating. Does he live near Inverness by any chance?"

"I'm afraid I don't know." Trishita felt a another longing for a father, a felling she thought she had squelched years ago.

"Well, Patricia—what did you say your nickname was?" Mrs. Hyde asked.

"Trishita."

"Welcome, then Trishita. Come into the kitchen. I'll show you your room and go over the terms of your contract." Mrs. Hyde then led the way to the kitchen.

"Man, this is heavy." Ethan said, picking up Trishita's suitcase. What do you have in it?"

"Books."

"What kind of books?"

"I have a reading list I'm—just novels."

"Sorry," Sylvia said when she tripped over something and fell against Trishita. "Ethan can build you some bookshelves if you want. He's good at stuff like that."

Trishita felt the warmth of the household seeping through her damp shoes and clothes.

"What are you good at?" she asked Sylvia.

"Nothing yet. I'm only thirteen."

"I don't believe—" Trishita stopped in her tracks when she saw the kitchen. It sparkled in the December light, so bright were its walls and appliances. So many appliances. So many cupboards. A library of elegant cookbooks stood on a shelf above the microwave. A double convection oven snuggled into the wall next to a walk-in pantry and a central island held a five-burner ceramic stovetop, cutting board, and stainless steel sink. A window over the double sinks against the south wall looked out on a lawn sloping down to a brook that she could hear flowing through the woods. Trishita almost genuflected.

"I'm home," she whispered.

*   *   *

"The best part of being a housekeeper is you get to see the underbelly of the upper crust," Trishita said when Flossie phoned for money again in June.

"Well I still don't see why you took a cut. You useta make twice as much as you do now just in tips."

"I'll send you twenty on Friday, okay?" Trishita hung up the laundry room extension that reached into her bedroom. *I'm outa that hell hole.* Grinning, she pulled on her shorts and Grateful Dead T-shirt. She wasn't a Deadhead, but she liked to let her employers think she was. And the weather was hot. Steamy hot.

She placed one long, bare foot onto the threshold of the adjacent room. With a grunt of elation, she catapulted into her employer's home office and in the process spilled a bag of old slide rules that Mr. Hyde was collecting.

June fourteenth, Flag day and Trishita's birthday, was coming up soon. She would turn twenty-six and celebrate, if that's the right word, her first six months as live-in at the Hyde's. Now, ready to tackle the computer in Arthur Hyde's office, she tucked a clump of her thick red hair under her plaid sweat-band and struggled to tune out the sounds of television commentators commenting on race relations. She'd had it all the way up to her sweatband with problems that were skin deep. Skin had nothing to do with who she or anyone else was.

It would be strange celebrating her birthday here. Not that she'd ever celebrated it. She wondered if Northboro had a parade on Flag Day. Some towns did. More likely it would be Independence Day or Patriot's. Tears sprang to her eyes at the memory of one Patriot's Day parade when she was ten.

*   *   *

The base of the flagpole in front of city hall gave Trishita a dandy vantage point for the parade. Some kids in her class spotted her and rushed over.

"Got room for us up there?" one asked.

"Sure. Climb up."

Soon five kids were on the base with her, clinging to each other and the pole. Trishita watched the parade over their heads.

A veteran's band came by playing "Yankee Doodle Dandy." One of the kids on the pole shouted, "Hey, Dad, go for it." He turned to Trishita. "See that guy on the tuba? That's my dad."

Another said, "My dad's marching with the Shriners."

"Mine, too," said a third.

The next group of marchers wore plaid kilts and played bagpipes. The mournful sounds were unfamiliar to Trishita, yet comforting. They tugged at her, burned her eyes. She jumped down and said, "Later alligator." She took off running, longing for a father in her very bones.

*   *   *

Trishita blinked away the tears and stared at Arthur's computer set-up, demanding that she concentrate. This wholesome, country environment stirred up a whole pot-full of longings and with them, some bitterness.

When Ethan first started popping into the kitchen for visits, she'd told him about Johnny, her little half-brother who had to move to California.

"Johnny used to call me "Three T's" for Too-Tall-Trish, "she told Ethan. "He said I didn't belong in our neighborhood. He was right in more ways than one. It's a damn shame, but all communities are for the look-alikes. Otherwise you're a freak."

"I guess real beauty is kinda freaky," Ethan said.

Smart kid.

Trishita flipped a switch that turned on Arthur Hyde's electronic work station, aware of her good fortune. Although the Hydes paid slave wages, a hundred and thirty-five per week, plus room and

board, she was getting a free education in computer use from both
Ethan and Arthur, in the language and graces of the suburbs from
Jacquelyn, and best of all, "real" cooking. The Hydes gave Trishita
the green light to experiment with their magnificent collection of
cookbooks.

Arthur's office was an add-on adjacent to Trishita's bedroom
and the kitchen. It served also as Trishita's access to the kitchen.
Large windows provided an expansive view of a huge lawn, dotted
with ash and oak trees. She loved the sound of the brook trickling
down from Rocky Pond.

While she waited for his Dell to boot up, Trishita watched Arthur
maneuver around the trees on the Deere mini-tractor he rode to mow
the grass. Sitting erect yet at ease, he drove it as if it were a golf cart.
He looked cool in his orange shorts, green pastel jersey and John
Deere cap, despite the heat and humidity.

Trishita turned back to the Dell. She preferred to practice on the
son's Macintosh, but he didn't have any accounting programs. Since
it was Saturday, the whole family was home to interrupt her, and she
had much to learn before she could pursue her dreams.

Concentrating, she flipped her eyes back and forth from the
screen to the manual in her lap. Her long legs straddled a pedestal
that held the keyboard and monitor. She slouched around it, almost
obscene, but she didn't care. The accounting program was easy to
use for manipulating the numbers under the assets' column, but she
was lost on the debit side.

"Hey Trishita," she heard Ethan Hyde call, and knew he'd jump
at her from somewhere. The son: sixteen, a grown replica of her
brother Johnny when he was six.

*   *   *

On her birthday that year, Johnny came into Russo's Bar & Grill
after the lunch bunch had gone and before the regulars showed up.
He stood in the doorway, light ringing him like a full body halo. His
blond hair sprouted to the left from a distinctive cowlick. Freckles
sprinkled his face and arms. His little six-year-old body gave off
hints of the short, compact, neat little macho package he would
become.

The crowd at the bar wasn't so bad early in the afternoon. They tipped well and weren't shit-faced. She didn't mind if Johnny came to Russo's after school, but she hated it when, feeling lonely or scared, he came in the evening. Then, any small spark could ignite the crowd. Protecting him became her reason for being.

"Happy birthday, Trish," he said and ran into her arms. "I brought you a present." He pulled a long, narrow cardboard box out his hip pocket and handed it to her. "I couldn't find any wrapping paper."

Trishita pretended to untie a fancy bow and tear off wrapping. When she opened the box, her pretense evaporated. There, cushioned on tissue, was a shiny wire whisk. It took her breath away.

"My Johnny, my prince," she crooned. She started the jukebox and danced him around the bar tables.

*   *   *

Now here came Ethan Hyde. Sixteen, bright and shining. Baseball catcher thighs. Good, all-around athlete. B-plus GPA. Tiny Catholic girlfriend who wouldn't put out.

"Where's the peanut butter, Trishita?" the shining son asked as if on cue.

"In the cupboard over the refrigerator." Trishita stared at the computer monitor. "How do you change the figures in the debit column once they're entered?"

He leaned against her shoulder and peered at the screen. She smelled his deodorized sweat.

"That's dad's program. Ask him. Why did you put it up so high?" A small whine piped through his recently deepened voice.

"Put what up so high, the debit column?" She turned to look at his face. He sure was a cute kid, styled blond hair shaved up the sides, poofing out on top. That loop of gold adorning one ear. So tasteful. Even adolescent rebellion was muted in suburbia. Still, at five-foot-seven and a hundred and thirty-five pounds, Ethan Hyde was a tasty little package.

"No, the peanut butter. I can't reach it up there."

"Go on, Ethan. Get your sweet little cojones outa here so I can concentrate." She turned back to the screen to hide her grin

"I wish you'd quit moving the step stool, then."

"I thought you were a rock climber." She stuck her tongue out at him. "Climb for it."

He giggled and tripped into the kitchen.

The manual slipped off her sweaty lap onto the floor. Cursing the humidity and the user directions that led her step-by-step on a circular trail, she didn't notice for several minutes that the engine noise from Arthur's tractor had stopped. When she became aware of the songs of bluebirds, she glanced around. He'd be in any moment now, looking for something.

"Trishita?" The interruption, though, came from Jacquelyn. A knock on the kitchen doorjamb preceded a tight, high-pitched voice. "Sorry to bother you, Dear, but could you tell me where you put the espresso roast?"

"The what?" Trishita pulled back from the monitor and looked hard at her employer entering Arthur's office.

Jacquelyn glanced at the toppled paper bag with Arthur's old slide rules spilling out. The V in her forehead darkened.

Trishita studied her. Mrs. Hyde, at five-foot-two and ninety-eight pounds, made all her own silk dresses. Sylvia had told her people often said that her mother really knew color. Now the tiny woman in rose silk backed into the kitchen.

"Coffee," Mrs. Hyde said, "the espresso roast. I can't find it."

"It's in the top left hand cupboard over the sink," Trishita said.

"Oh, that's where it is. Thanks."

Trishita gloated. The poor little lady knew no more about relating to a maid than Trishita knew about being one. The nuances escaped them both. Mrs. Hyde would never be able to reach the cupboard where Trishita had stashed the coffee. Feeling a rare touch of guilt, Trishita closed the manual and entered the kitchen to fetch the coffee. She made a hasty retreat before Mrs. Hyde had a chance to thank her.

Every once in a while she had to fight off creeping affection for her little employers. Such feelings could interfere with her plans to milk them for all the direct training in computer use and business management she could get, plus indirect coaching in the social graces. She figured her momentary lapses into affection came from seeing too much of Worcester's underbelly.

Mrs. Hyde had a Ph.D. in reading and a high mucky-muck job in the local school district. Made more money than Arthur, he'd once told Trishita in a moment of candor. All the teachers adored her and asked for "Dr. Jacquelyn" when they called. Townsfolk respected her, too. She sang in the choir of the Congregational Church, supported local charities. Often locals asked her to give lectures on reading, although she never read a book beyond the first chapter.

Trishita caught this particular view of the up-country underbelly by looking at the books Dr. Jacquelyn left lying around, splayed open for weeks at the same page. The more impressive the book to their intellectual guests, the sooner Jacquelyn stopped reading it. Ishmael never got out to sea in MOBY DICK. Thanks to that bastard Jacobsen, English professor at Clark University and her last lover, Trishita had read all the way to the chapter on the whiteness of the whale before she gave up. But, since it was a major book in the reading program he'd prescribed, she knew she'd get back to it.

Jacquelyn knocked on the door jamb again. "I'm going to run some errands. Is there anything we need for dinner?"

"Nope. I'm all set."

"Did I tell you the children are going elsewhere tonight? You won't have to make as much as usual. By the way, what are we having?"

"Chicken fajitas." Trishita swallowed a sigh and opened the manual.

"Wonderful. I'll get some ripe avocados to go with them."

"Good idea." Trishita punched in a few numbers. She heard Jacquelyn backing into the kitchen. The woman backed out of situations often. *Probably born breech.*

Before Trishita could figure out her next step, Arthur came in, smelling of fresh cut grass.

"How you doing with that stuff?" he asked.

"Man, am I glad to see you. I keep going around in circles with this damn accounting program."

He glanced at the pedestal between her stretched out legs. His eyes registered both shock and amusement.

"I guess when you're six-foot-one," he said, "it doesn't matter how slender you are. There's just not enough space in here." Leaning forward, he inspected the screen. "Do you want me to shower first or should I explain it now?" His shirt armpits were damp circles and his narrow brown mustache glistened.

"You smell of chlorophyll and fecundity—is that the right word?" Trishita asked. "Stay and help me."

"I see you've been playing with the thesaurus again. Yes, it's an appropriate word, especially this time of year." He leaned over her left shoulder, his damp pectorals just brushing it, and showed her each step for setting up and varying the equations. She concentrated; he taught. An hour went by.

"I need to take a shower now. You practice some more." He headed toward the kitchen, but stopped to pick up the slide rules. "I'd like to hang these on the wall in here. What do you think, Trishita?"

"Nice. It'll give the room some class."

"Do you know where my golf clubs are?" he asked when he came back smelling of after-shave lotion.

"They're on the top shelf on the window side of the garage."

He disappeared for five minutes and then returned.

"Trishita," Arthur asked, "where's the step stool?"

"I think Ethan used it to find the peanut butter. Look in the kitchen." She sighed and shut down the computer. With all the interruptions, there was no point in going on any longer, and the girl hadn't pestered her yet. Trishita went back to her room, tore off her sweat-band, and stretched. Her fingertips brushed the overhead light. She let her hair swing loose and tugged at her shorts, which had worked their way too far up for comfort. She knew he was watching her through the hole she'd discovered in the pantry wall. Which "he" had drilled the hole and was watching now didn't matter. She could feel the eyes of either father or son. They were so genteel, these educated shorties, not a bit grabby like the ones she used to wait on. These guys didn't dare look at her body straight on. Had to use the peephole. The very subtlety of their watching gave her a new and happy challenge. She got a kick out of giving them something worthwhile to watch.

CHAPTER FOUR

A sweet, cool breeze blew in the one window of Trishita's room as she stepped into it from the shower. Eight by fourteen feet in size, her room was a wedge between the kitchen and laundry. It included a private bathroom that used to be a lavatory until Arthur installed the shower for her. And Ethan had built floor-to-ceiling shelves along one wall of the bedroom to hold her books. Flossie had always resented them, but the Hydes were impressed and often told their friends in hushed, almost reverent tones about their housekeeper who reads.

The first few months she lived with them, Jacquelyn and Arthur maintained a semi-formal relationship with her. Although they asked her to call them by their first names, they responded to Mr. and Mrs. Hyde. Then Trishita began creating household problems that only she could solve. She re-arranged things; they had to ask her to find them. Then she started planning the meals. It wasn't long before she got them to realize their need for her. She continued to pay lip service to her original deferential formality, though, always in front of company.

As she turned in the breeze coming in the window, letting it blow dry her dripping body, she smiled, contented. Storm clouds were gathering fast in the late afternoon sky. She watched them, and herself, in the full-length mirror on her closet door, a gift from Arthur.

"Trishita, can I come in?" Sylvia, called from her father's office.

"Sure." Trishita pulled on a white cotton shift and opened the door. "Hi, Sylvia. Did you break the heat wave?"

"Naw." Sylvia held her head tilted forward in the manner of tall girls who don't quite fit into their bodies yet. Her straight, dark brown hair, parted in the middle, fell forward and hid her oval, freckled face. At thirteen and a half, she was taller than her mother and brother and the same height as her father. Still a shrimp compared to Trishita, however. Jumping like a young kangaroo into Trishita's bedroom, Sylvia hit her elbow on the doorjamb and let out a small cry.

"Hit your funny bone?" Trishita asked.

"Ow, yes. It hurts God-awful. Nothing funny about that bone." She rubbed her elbow and sat cross-legged on Trishita's bed.

The girl tilted her head to look at Trishita. Her hair fell away from her face like a curtain opening. She had two zits on her chin, sunlight bounced off the braces that stretched her cupid bow lips out of shape, and her brown eyes were rimmed in red from a cold or a crying jag. Trishita couldn't tell which.

"Well, Sylvia, what are *you* looking for?"

"Did I lose something?" Sylvia asked.

"Not yet, I hope." Trishita laughed. Sylvia was, like many tall, pubescent girls, an ugly duckling and yet, beautiful. The kid was ruining Trishita's shtick out here in the country. She could use the others, put their favorite things out of reach, learn enough computer shit to get a downtown kind of job, make all kinds of trade-offs. But Sylvia got to her just as Johnny had. Trishita wanted to serve her the choicest parts of this world, or the whole world itself, flambé, on a silver platter. The girl twanged a familiar chord, a placental chord.

"I'm gonna stay over at Anita Jasmine's house tonight," Sylvia said with a self-conscious smirk. "We're having pizza and popcorn and we get to watch an old movie called Silence of the Sheep."

"The Lambs. Close your eyes in the gross parts." Trishita tossed her discarded clothes into the laundry room and sat on a chair with her legs stretched onto the bed.

"I love your hair." Sylvia chewed on her own hair. "Do you?" she asked.

"No . . . . Now isn't that silly? I've always hated my hair and it's just hair."

"Guess you got your father's hair. Does that mean you might go bald?"

"I doubt it," Trishita replied, smiling. "I got his brains, too, but a lot of good they've done me."

"And you got my brown eyes." Sylvia grinned. Her lips caught on her braces.

"I didn't get my eyes from you, silly goose."

"I wish I had even teeth like yours. Did you ever wear braces?" Sylvia asked.

"Ha. Lucky for me I didn't have to. I sure as hell didn't have the money to get them."

"Your birthday's coming soon, isn't it?" Sylvia leaned back against the wall and squinted. "How old will you be?"

"Twenty-six."

"Wow, that's old. How come you're not married?"

"When you're as tall as I am," Trishita said, "men just want to score with you for the novelty of it, to brag to the other guys. They don't want to marry you. Not that I care. I've known some mighty rotten husbands."

"Do you think I'll get that tall?"

"Naw. You might have your full height now," Trishita said, "you little shrimp. I did when I was your age."

"I hate being taller than all the boys in my class."

"<u>Tell</u> me about it. At least no one calls you 'Amazon' every time you walk by."

"I want to know all about you." Sylvia leaned forward and looked straight at Trishita. "Please? What was it like for you growing up in Worcester? Which high school did you go to?"

"You know I didn't go to high school."

"But I remember seeing your diploma when you first came here." Sylvia's eyes widened. "Oh, that's right. I remember now. You took a test. But isn't it against the law to stay out of school?"

"That wasn't anyone's concern." Trishita laughed. "When I finished the eighth grade—graduating with straight A's, mind you—I was just twelve. My mother forged my birth certificate so I could get a social security number and a work permit. I started waiting on tables full time."

"Wo—you were younger than me." Sylvia looked at the muscles in each of her upper arms and flexed them.

Trishita remembered, too well.

*   *   *

"Wake up, Ma. Mrs. Mayberry asked me to give the speech for our eighth grade graduation." Trishita had run up the three flights of stairs and burst into the living room.

"Tha's nice." Flossie groaned and covered her eyes. "When is it?"

"Noon on Flag day. Will you come?"

Flossie sat up. Her straight brown hair fell into place. This time Trishita didn't envy her mother's easy untangled hair.

"I don't know why they have graduation for little kids," Flossie whined. "But I'll go listen to those la-de-da teachers talk on and on. I swear, that's all teachers can do—yak, yak, yak."

"Never mind." Trishita opened the curtains and let in the daylight.

"I'd go listen to you speak any day," Flossie said. "Ain't nobody talks like you."

Trishita smiled despite herself.

"Did you ever go through a graduation ceremony?" Trishita asked.

"They didn't have them for grade schools. I woulda gone in high school but we came to the states before I made it that far." Flossie put on a pair of sunglasses. "Man, it's bright in here."

"Well, I'm going to graduate as many times as I want. Maybe I'll even get advanced degrees. Why did Grandmaman go back to Montreal?"

"Thought she could do better than here, I guess."

"How come you didn't go with her?"

"Montreal's a hick town." Flossie headed for the kitchen.

"And Worcester isn't?" Trishita asked, following Flossie.

"They're too serious in Montreal. They <u>drink</u> their tea." Flossie smirked, tilted her head back to eye Trishita. "You ain't my pretty one no more. You're a beauty now. Looking more like your papa every day. Almost as tall."

Then, the morning of graduation, stomach jumping, Trishita leaned out her window over the fire escape and watched a robin flying around. She stared for a long time, searching for a robin's nest.

"Hey, Ma," she called, "Yesterday was cold, but feel this air. It's gonna be steamy today!"

"I got bad news, Mija." Flossie entered and sat on the pile of rumpled bedding at the foot of Trishita's bed.

"What now?" Trishita pulled inside with a jolt.

"What d'ya mean, now? I got good news, too." Flossie smiled at her.

"Well?"

"That bastard Feinwold fired me and the landlord raised the rent again."

"That the end of it?" Trishita felt her muscles harden.

"Want to hear the good news?" Flossie asked in her most seductive voice.

"Yeah, sure."

"You're gonna have a new brother or sister come December."

"You call that good news? Why not get an abortion?"

"Too late. I'm three months gone. But there's more good news. I know who the father is. Maybe he'll help out. Besides, Barney said he'd hire you full time at Russo's."

"Ma, that's a bar. I'm only twelve."

"But, Mija, you look twenty-one and that's all he cares about. We'll be so rich, we'll keep this baby." She lowered her head and wept. "It was so bad giving up the others, especially Robert."

Trishita softened. "Okay, Ma. This one you have in a hospital. And I'm naming it Johnny, or maybe Joanna."

* * *

"I gave a speech at my eighth grade graduation and everyone applauded." She looked now at Sylvia and her heart felt like mush in her chest.

"What did you call it?" Sylvia lifted her head, clearing the hair from her face.

"My speech? The true meanings of freedom," Trishita replied.

"Meanings?" Sylvia frowned, looking like her mother in expression if not in features. "How come the plural on meaning?"

"Has to be plural. There's more than one meaning to most everything. I want to learn as many as I can."

"Sylvia, where are you?" Jacquelyn's sharp voice pierced the door.

Sylvia jumped and ran toward it.

Trishita heard Jacquelyn scolding Sylvia in a harsh whisper. She couldn't make out the words, just the harsh tone. It continued for five minutes. She felt her first inkling that something was wrong with Dr. Jacquelyn Hyde. Something festered beneath the woman's elegant veneer.

CHAPTER FIVE

In five minutes Sylvia was back. She trailed her fingers across Trishita's books.

"Are you gonna go to college?" Sylvia asked.

"Don't I wish," Trishita replied with a laugh. "You need plenty of money to do that and my mother keeps me broke. Besides, you have to have the right color blood in your veins to know how to act. Now, you were born and bred for college."

"I hate school. Was it fun being a waitress?"

"Not at the joints I worked. That's why I'm here now. I hated it. Guys feeling you up all the time, making dumb comments like, 'Hey Trish, where do you play basketball?' or boring the shit out of you with their bragging or ever-so-savvy paternal advice. And then the other waiters slipping your tips into their grubby little hands. Or the big shot lawyers would come in, slumming, you know, condescending—"

"I forget what that means. It was one of our vocabulary words last month, too."

"It means looking down your nose at somebody," Trishita said, tilting her head back to illustrate. How well she remembered subtle insults from suits in Russo's and rich women in grocery stores near Clark University. "There are three ways to look at people, up, down, or straight in the eye. I hope you always look 'em straight in the eye, meaning you're neither better nor worse than them—I mean they."

"Ethan won't look me in the eye. He doesn't like me anymore. I don't know what I did."

"Nothing you did." Trishita pretended to yawn to cover her smile. "Just hormones distracting him." She grabbed Sylvia's foot and gave it a shake. "Remember, he's your brother anyway, for the rest of your life."

"I don't know whether that's good or bad." Sylvia wrinkled her brow, and then smiled. "He has a mean streak, you know."

"Ethan? There's not a mean bone in his body."

"You'll see," Sylvia said in a low tone. "Do you have any brothers or sisters?"

"Yeah. Bunch of younger ones, but they're scattered all over. Different fathers. I didn't live with any of them except Johnny." She looked away. "And Robert for three years. I couldn't make enough money to support 'em."

"Why would you have to support them?"

"My mother is, well, sorta sick. She can't take care of herself, let alone the kids she keeps having."

"Maybe she should be fixed."

"You got one there, kid. Fixed. She is broken, in a way." Trishita realized that she, Robert and Johnny were the only children her mother had kept. She hadn't thought of herself as her mother's child. Goose bumps sprang up on her thighs. She'd witnessed, first hand, Flossie's determination in delivering a baby—her courage.

*　　*　　*

"Push, Ma, keep pushing." Trishita had dipped a washcloth into a bowl of ice water and placed it on her mother's forehead. Another bowl she filled with boiled water. She had read several novels where the father boiled water when the baby was due, but they never showed how to use it. She didn't want to scald the infant.

Flossie planned to keep this one. The last two she had given up for adoption. But now Flossie declared that Trishita, at nine, was old enough to manage a baby.

Flossie screamed.

Where was that midwife? Trishita had called her right after the water broke. Frantic, she shifted her eyes from Flossie to the open textbook, then back to Flossie's anguished face.

An hour later, while Flossie's screams reverberated in the high-ceilinged kitchen, a baby's head came out—just as the book said it would. Trishita guided the baby the rest of the way, and handed the little boy to Flossie. After Flossie cut the umbilical cord, Trishita washed him with a cloth full of lukewarm water.

Because Flossie had no idea who the father was, Trishita named the boy Robert Giraux. And fell in love with him.

Three years later the welfare lady came after him. She said Trishita was much too young to have sole responsibility for a child. Trishita watched the young, big-chinned woman pack Robert's few clothes in her briefcase. When she took Robert by the hand, Trishita grabbed the boy's arm and screamed, "No, No."

"Come now, Patricia, let go," the welfare lady said. "We're placing him in a good home. Don't you want him to have a nice home with adult parents who will love him?" She pried Trishita's fingers off Robert's arm.

Trishita did let go because she wanted grown-ups to protect Robert. A piece of her heart went with him.

*　　*　　*

"You look weird all of a sudden, Trishita," Sylvia said. "what're you thinking about?"

"My first heartbreak." Trishita gave her head a little shake. "Also, it just came to me that my mother loved me. She couldn't protect me or take care of me, but she did—does love me."

"Don't all mothers?"

"At least they claim to." Trishita smiled. She glanced at the clock on her dresser. She wouldn't have to start dinner until after six tonight since fajitas only take ten minutes to prepare. She pulled a package of gum out of her top drawer and offered a stick to Sylvia.

"No thanks."

"Sorry, Syl. I forgot you can't chew with braces."

"Mom says I shouldn't chew, ever," Sylvia said. "What's wrong with chewing gum?"

"Looks tacky, I guess."

"If I don't go to college, I want to be a maid in a family—just like you." Sylvia's brace-extended upper lip stretched some more in a glowing smile.

"No way." Trishita said, softening the stick of gum in her mouth. "You're starting high school in September where you'll swing—get top grades, and then you're going to a good college. Maybe I'll go with you. We'll study together."

"Sylvia, Sylv-i-a? Where are you?" Jacquelyn's voice pierced the bookcase wall this time. Sylvia jumped.

"Darn. I gotta go. Don't tell her I'm in here."

"Why not?"

"She told me not to hang around you so much." Sylvia stood and moved toward the door. "Why is she afraid of you?"

"What makes you think that? Did she say she was?"

"No, course not," Sylvia whispered. "She just acts scared. Her voice gets all high pitched and jumpy."

Trishita stifled her triumphant feelings before they crawled out her pores and danced a jig.

"She's not afraid of me," she said to Sylvia, but thought, <u>herself, maybe</u>.

"I think she is. Will you tell me more tomorrow?"

"But your mother doesn't want me to."

"Yeah. So what. Can we be secret friends?"

"Sure. Here, sneak out this way to the back yard." Trishita pointed toward her bathroom.

Sylvia ducked into it and slipped out through the laundry room.

"Mrs. Hyde thinks I might influence her daughter," Trishita said to herself with a voice of tempered steel. "My coarse manners might rub off." She stood tall in the middle of her little room and clenched her fists. "My height might make Sylvia taller. Fuck Dr. Jacquelyn."

*   *   *

That evening, with both children gone, the dining room seemed almost dead. Trishita's repeated entries to serve and pour wine broke the silence. They drank more wine than usual. Arthur complimented Trishita on the fajitas, and then lapsed into silence.

Behind the swinging door leading from the kitchen, Trishita sat on a stool to rest and eavesdrop. She heard Jacquelyn say, "Don't you think it's ridiculous to collect slide rules? Collect anything, for that matter."

Trishita pulled back in surprise. She'd never heard Jacquelyn criticize Arthur so directly.

"What's ridiculous about it?" Arthur retorted, his words beginning to fuzz. "I like slide rules. Dad gave me my first one when I took algebra—freshman year of high school. Sure helped. The other kids thought I was cheating."

"Well, having one slide rule is okay, I suppose, but a collection of them? Besides, with calculators extant and PC's ubiquitous, slide rules are passé."

Extant? Ubiquitous? Trishita jotted these words on a loose piece of paper. Someday she, too, would be able to toss out words like that in everyday conversation. After all, she was supposed to be an autodidact. Remembering, she smiled.

*   *   *

Trishita had stood by the window of the counselor's office watching raindrops do a square dance on the panes. Her mother sat facing the counselor, pushing and pulling a cigarette in and out of the package.

"She's an autodidact, Ms. Giraux," The counselor said. "Nothing to be afraid of. It means she memorizes everything she hears and teaches herself. Granted, it's unusual to see a child read and comprehend text on human reproduction, but it's nothing to worry about."

"She's only five and she can cook, too. What did you call her?"

"You don't need to worry about the name."

"Does it mean she's gonna be smart?"

"Brilliant."

"Man, what'll I do with her?"

"Let her be," she said. The counselor hesitated a moment, studying the mother. "Just let her be."

Flossie pulled Trishita out of the counselor's office and shut the door behind her. She shook her head and lit a cigarette.

"You go play, now," Flossie said. "I need a drink. But, don't you ever forget, you're ma petite belle. You come home to me!"

*   *   *

Arthur's voice brought her back to the present.

"That's just the point," he said to his wife. "Slide rules are old fashioned, wonderful tools, and I like to look at them and think about the problems they helped solve. I thought I'd hang my collection on my office wall."

"Oh Arthur, Dear, don't you see that collections are for ego-trippers, people who identify with their collections because they don't have enough going for themselves without one. You have your own identity. You don't need a collection of slide rules to give you one."

This comment of Jacquelyn's was one in a series of intriguing clues she'd been dropping. Trishita was beginning to realize that Jacquelyn disliked, no, hated collections of all kinds. It was the only thing Jacquelyn hated, being so damn tolerant and sweet about everything else.

Trishita returned to the dining room to pour more wine when she felt the moment was right. As she suspected, their glasses were dry.

"I wish you'd get off that pseudo-psycho crap." Arthur shook his head, tilting it to the right as was his habit. "You smile all the while, but suggest that I'm either too rigid, too passive, or is it too aggressive? Or I'm an INFP from that stupid Myers-Briggs test, meaning I'm an introverted dreamer or something like that. When are you going to measure the bumps on my skull?" He took a large swallow of the cabernet Trishita had just poured. "Slide rules don't create my identity. I just plain like them. What's your problem?" He smoothed his mustache with his forefinger as if to control his mouth.

"I'm sorry, Dear," Jacquelyn said. She glanced at Trishita who was wearing her best blank face. "I was just afraid you might clutter up the house with a collection of old slide rules."

"They're going up on the wall of my office. No clutter."

Trishita hid her smile as she stacked the plates at the sideboard. She could hardly contain herself with this new idea for clutter. One slide rule placed right—and she could start her own collection of—of what, teddy bears? No, ceramic cows would be just crass enough.

Jacquelyn excused herself from the table and averted her eyes, but not before Trishita caught a glimpse of the rage in them—a rage so deep and powerful it almost bubbled out. As it was, it rattled the stack of Wedgwood plates in Trishita's arms.

CHAPTER SIX

Jacquelyn broke up a collection of garden gnomes on an early June, new-moon raid in Southboro. The next day she survived six back-to-back meetings where she subdued the wrath of three teachers per meeting, met the objectives of each curriculum strand, and followed state and union guidelines. She paid lip service to directives from the superintendent whose goal, stated in public, was to undermine state and union guidelines.

"Dr. Jacquelyn," her secretary, said at the end of one stormy session, "how do you stay so calm?"

"I just appear that way, Dorothy." Jacquelyn said, smiling.

She sat at her desk propped by two pillows on her swivel-chair, musing after all her employees had left. She ranked the meetings of the day according to degrees of success and felt generally satisfied with all of them. She'd done the right thing, steered the right course, though she doubted her boss, the entrenched superintendent, would agree. Ballman was of the old school. He didn't believe in change. "If it works, keep it," he'd shouted during a recent cabinet meeting. Of course, she thought with a smile, he doesn't keep up with educational research.

The walls of her office held bound journals with articles she used for Dorothy to send to appropriate people in the school district. She hoped to educate the educators. It was her mission, if not her job description.

Though weary, she felt purged by last night's raid and satisfied by the day's meetings. She surveyed her office with pleasure. The lavender rose, her trademark in its crystal bud vase, shed one petal. The rest would fall soon, but she would replace them with a fresh rose in the morning.

A large shadow spilled into her office, startling her, followed by the bulk of Superintendent Ballman. He had loosened his tie and unbuttoned his suitcoat.

"Good evening, Jacquelyn," he said. "I thought you might still be here, hard worker that you are. Got time for a chat?" He held his huge palm flat out towards her. "Don't get up. I'll just sit here." He grabbed another swivel chair on wheels and pulled it to the left of Jacquelyn's desk. His round face bore a smile, but his gray-green eyes examined her without levity or mirth.

"How are you, Jonathan?"

"Fine, fine," he said fast. "I heard about the science meeting today. Guess you pulled that one off."

"What do you mean?" Jacquelyn asked.

"You got those teachers to agree to some basic changes in the curriculum, and, worse yet, to begin as early as this fall semester. That's quite a feat."

"Not too many changes, Jonathan. They need some training, of course, but they're willing, even eager, to get students to comprehend abstractions once in a while."

"What I really want to talk to you about is the Language Arts meeting." Ballman smiled again. His long front teeth now reminded her of Bugs Bunny. "What's this 'whole language' shit you're promoting?"

"Didn't you get the literature? I had Dorothy send you—"

"It's all bullshit."

"Au contraire, Jon." Jacquelyn straightened her neck. "When people learn a language, even a native one, they learn in spirals, picking up all the pieces at once."

"I learned to read apart from listening and writing," Ballman roared. "And speaking, of all things! Now they're saying kids have to talk before they write. They talk too much as it is. And you. You have your doctorate in reading. That's a separate discipline."

"That was before we knew what we know now," she replied, pleased by her lack of fear today. She felt condescending, as if she had to explain why the sky was blue to a four-year-old. "You can't separate the language functions—"

"Worked before."

"True. We just think it will work better when we integrate all facets of language development."

"Which asshole from the state has your ear?" He leaned both arms on her desk. The rest of the petals fell from the rose.

"No <u>other</u> asshole has my ear, Jonathan." Withholding a smirk, Jacquelyn reached over and touched Ballman's forearm. "Why does the whole language approach bother you?"

"Bottom line, Miss Curriculum Queen." He stood and towered over her. His face was flushed and she wondered if he'd been drinking again. "Where do you think the money's coming from to make such vast changes?"

"It won't cost the district a cent, Jonathan.," she said, grateful that she'd vented her own rage. "The state provides the textbooks and teacher training. All we need to do is convince the teachers and parents—and the superintendent, I might add—that the change is valid. Come on. Walk me to my car."

"Okay, Jacquelyn, go ahead with this nonsense if you must. But I warn you, if this breaks your budget, the following year you'll be out begging on the streets."

She led him out to the parking lot. The sun was low, elongating their shadows. Jacquelyn realized that Ballman was as tall as Trishita, if not taller. She decided she must have him over for cocktails at the close of the school year just to see his eyes when he first encountered her live-in maid. The old lech.

"Christ, it's hot and muggy," Ballman said. He wiped his forehead with his monogrammed handkerchief. "I thought the heat wave broke with that storm yesterday."

"Guess it came back," Jacquelyn said, hoping to convey sympathy in her voice. "Say, I'm thinking of having a small cocktail party some time after the last of our graduation ceremonies. How does your calendar look for late June?"

"You'll have to call my secretary, I'm afraid. But do organize it on an evening I can make. I've never been to your house, you know."

"Nor have I been to yours."

"No kidding? I just had a staff party last Christmas."

"I had the flu. Missed it." She unlocked the door of her BMW and caught a glimpse of her ball-peen hammer on the floor of the passenger side. It must have fallen from her tool pouch. Her heart pounded.

"Well, we'll have to rectify that," he said. "Perhaps you and Arthur could come for dinner soon. I'd like you to see our collection of porcelain clowns. It's quite extensive now."

"Interesting," she managed to say. "How did you happen to collect clowns?" You clown.

"Years ago, in Atlantic City, I won a cheap little clown at one of those carnival booths—you know, about six inches long, porcelain head. My wife loved it so I started picking up collectibles, numbered pieces and such, in little shops in New York and Boston. Since then I've always known what to get her for birthday or anniversary presents. They're quite an art form, you know."

Jacquelyn drove away so awash in thought she missed the turn leading to her house. Art form! Ridiculous. She knew she couldn't do anything to Ballman's collection, but what a temptation it would be to tear those stupid porcelain heads off their silk bodies.

The idea of using collections to simplify gift giving annoyed her. If she let Arthur collect slide rules, she'd never have to wonder what to get him for his birthday. She could simplify him, simplify love, never have to think about him beyond his collection, never have to care at all.

He might even like that.

She pulled into the driveway and pushed the button on her console to open the garage door. Nothing happened. She took a deep breath to forestall the panic. When she had come home just before dawn, she'd opened the door by hand but forgot to put it back on automatic. She struggled now to remember the morning. The door had been open when she left for work. Who opened it? Damn, she was getting careless. That and the ball-peen hammer.

The garage door opened now as she was pushing the hammer back under the seat. Arthur waved her in. "Sorry about this," he said. "I guess I put it on manual for some reason and forgot to change it back."

"Thanks, Sweetheart." Arthur would think he was responsible for a bicycle accident in Bangladesh. So dear. So spaced. She drove in, slipped out of the car and into his arms. "I'm bushed."

"Come in and rest. Trishita has created a new pasta recipe and it smells wonderful. I hope you're hungry."

"I will be as soon as I have a short nap." Jacquelyn caught whiffs of garlic and mingling herbs when Arthur opened the door. She bypassed the kitchen, though, and went straight to the stairs. She didn't feel up to Trishita's presence just yet. But she was grateful for her cooking. They all ate so well now. In peace. Before Trishita, the daily decisions on what to eat, how to cook it, who would cook it, consumed the whole family. Yet, that woman's presence was just too much sometimes.

"I'll lie down for just a little while." Jacquelyn headed up the spiral staircase. "Call me when dinner's ready," she said to Arthur, then ducked as Ethan came flying down the stairs.

"Hi, Ma." He came to a dead stop on the step above of her. The mirrors on the walls reflected him over and over like those Russian dolls that fit inside each other. An endless collection of Ethan dolls.

"What's the matter?" he asked her. "Are you sick, Ma?"

"No. Just tired. I'll see you at dinner." She hugged him.

Now alone, she checked the bottom drawer of her dresser. Everything except the hammer was well hidden, not that Arthur would notice anything amiss even if she'd left the tool pouch out on the bed. As she closed her eyes and tried to block out the sounds of her family in the kitchen watching Trishita cook, she pictured Ballman's clown collection and said NO to her heart's base desire.

In that zone between waking and sleeping she remembered her own collection . . .

*   *   *

It was a snow-flurry day in February. Her father had attached six white shelves to the wall adjacent to the window in Jacquelyn's bedroom. Jacquelyn spent the rest of the day arranging and re-arranging her dolls according to the color of their dresses.

Then her father's brother, Roger, showed up with a new doll for her. Its dress was a shade of peach like the sky in October just after sunset. Uncle Roger said, "See how fine this doll's hair is—gossamer fine like yours."

"More hair on that thing than Jacquelyn and I have put together," her mother grunted.

"You both have pretty hair," her father said.

"Both who?" her mother asked, "me and the doll or me and Jacquelyn?"

Her father just turned away, shaking his head.

Jacquelyn felt her own brown hair. It was smooth and silky. Easy to comb. Why didn't her mother like it? But her biggest concern was where to place the new doll in relation to the others. That night she spent a long time trying out new arrangements. She hadn't realized how long.

"What are you doing, Jacquelyn? It's after midnight." Abby shouted in her shrill voice.

.Jacquelyn's heart raced. She jumped into bed. "Nothing, Mama."

"Don't let me catch you playing with those dolls again after bedtime or I'll make your Dad take down the shelves."

"Oh, no. Please, Mama. I'll be good." She stared up at her mother and tensed as Abby approached the bed.

"You're hot." Abby touched Jacquelyn's forehead. "Don't tell me you have a fever again."

"No. I'm okay."

"You don't get enough sleep. I'm leaving your door open. Now you keep the lights out, do you hear?"

"Yes, Mama." Jacquelyn closed her eyes and slowed her breathing. When Abby left, Jacquelyn stared in the dark and waited until she thought they'd be asleep. The doll in the peach dress was out of place. When the house was quiet, she sneaked out of bed and, guessing which doll wore peach, shifted it one doll to the left.

Now, she tensed and let her mind jump to when she turned into a woman. She'd become aware of the moon's cycles at thirteen and much ashamed of her own body's response. Her blood flowed, but her breasts refused to grow.

The day her brother Billy moved out on his own, he said, "You're going to be a pretty woman, Jackie, even if you are a smart ass."

Then he died in Vietnam. Jacquelyn felt his loss from the top of her head to the high arches of her size five feet. To her dismay, his room became a storage bin—a new challenge for her to keep in order. She spent many hours arranging the room and suffered many disappointments when she discovered yet another trombone left by her father or more sewing debris from her mother.

* * *

Jacquelyn's eyes popped open. Whatever happened to those dolls? Her eyes closed again. She remembered arranging her bridesmaids dressed in the same colors as the dolls. Then the photographer had to retake one shot and her bridesmaids were out of order. She shuddered.

Next she remembered placing the silk roses for Billy's shrine in the exact same order as the dolls.

She had protested that stupid war just once. It was the day he dropped by Glendale Street for a visit while Jacquelyn was studying for a Latin test. He gave the top of her head a light punch and said, "Gimme that stuff, I'll quiz you."

Jumping up, she said, "I'll be right back," and ran into the bathroom to screw up her courage. She stared into the mirror and tried to make her face look more like Abby's. Marching back to the living room she kicked aside a trombone and said, "Billy, go to Canada. Don't let them send you to Vietnam."

"Jacquelyn, where did you get such an idea. I don't want to go to jail."

"You don't have to. Just move to Canada. You can drive rigs there, too."

"Veni, vidi, vici," he said. "I'm not a coward. Besides, by the time I finish training the action in Vietnam will be over. C'mon, conjugate these verbs."

Two years later he was killed. She turned off to a world that could do such a thing. In Billy's trombone-filled room, she cleared space for a shrine of six roses—silk of varying hues. Where were the dolls?

*   *   *

"Come on, Ma, we're stahved," Sylvia yelled from the foot of the stairs.

Jacquelyn opened her eyes; tears spilled out. She splashed some water on her face, and, still wearing the orange and magenta silk dress she'd worn to work, her favorite "power" dress, she went down to the dining room.

"It's starved, Sylvia," she said, "not stahved. It's time you started pronouncing your r's.

"I don't want to sound like a New Yawkka." Sylvia took her place across from Ethan who stood behind his chair, chewing on a piece of bread he'd snitched.

"You won't sound like a New Yorker just because you pronounce your r's, Sylvia. Heck, they don't pronounce them either, at least not like the Californians." Arthur held the chair for Jacquelyn. She sat and inhaled the aroma coming from a steaming platter of pasta.

"I wonder," Arthur said. "Don't you think the speech of the whole country is becoming homogenized'? I rather like the Boston accent."

Jacquelyn thought of her mother's almost unintelligible, flat speech that used to embarrass her. It was as toneless as the sounds her father's trombones made.

"Aw, Dad," Ethan said with his mouth full. "You pronounce your r's most of the time."

Trishita came in with a salad bowl brimming with bright greens that glistened, Jacquelyn had recently learned, with virgin olive oil. This was followed by a platter of broccoli, zucchini and mushrooms sautéed in garlic butter.

Sylvia asked Trishita if she liked the Boston accent.

"Yes, but tempered," Trishita said. "Too much accent is like salt on corned beef."

"Right," Jacquelyn agreed. "Too much of anything, for that matter." *Or too many slide rules.* "Besides, a strong accent sounds uneducated."

"I am uneducated," Sylvia replied, heaping her plate with pasta. "Hey, Trishita, what do you call this stuff?"

"Capellini with artichoke hearts," Trishita replied. "Tonight's vegetarian night. It's made with a little crème fraîche."

"It's terrific," Ethan said.

"To the chef-ess," Arthur said and lifted his wine glass.

"Chef, Daddy," Sylvia cried. "A chef is a chef. Doesn't matter which sex."

"Gender, Dear," Jacquelyn said. She wished Trishita would hurry up and leave the room. Her family was becoming a bit too enamored of the hired help.

As if by wish alone, Trishita departed. Ethan ate so fast Jacquelyn mentioned he must be in training for Olympic eating. He grinned at Jacquelyn and her heart melted. If only Sylvia . . . weren't so abrasive.

Arthur chewed each mouthful as if counting each chew. His eyes looked glazed in pleasure.

"Some real mail came today among the junk," he said, returning to focus.

"I'll get it," Sylvia yelped, jumping up from the table. Something fell from her lap and clattered on the hardwood floor. She bent to pick it up. Jacquelyn wondered what it could be.

"A letter from Grampa Nestrom postmarked South Carolina," Sylvia said. "That means they're coming no'th. I mean north."

Jacquelyn felt her skin prickle as it often did with thoughts of her parents–love them though she was sure she did.

Sylvia set a small, black and white ceramic cow on the table and ran out of the room, returning with an unopened envelope. Trishita almost bumped into Sylvia when she came in for her mid-meal check. Sylvia hugged Trishita in the near collision, and then delivered the letter to her mother.

Jacquelyn's stomach churned. "What's that cow?"

"Trishita gave it to me. Her mother gave it to her when she was my age. Isn't it neat? She's going to help me start a collection."

Jacquelyn put a lid on all her reactions. She placed her fork across the top of her plate and stared at her father's large, rickety handwriting. Not only did she have to do something about Sylvia and Trishita, she had to deal with her parents showing up. Arthur was no help. He thought everyone was just fine. And summer vacation loomed. She much preferred to go to work every day.

"What's wrong, Mom?" Ethan asked. "You look like you've been goosed by a ghost. Open the letter. When are they coming?"

She smiled at them all, including Trishita who had busied herself with the salad plates. Jacquelyn opened the envelope and read, "My Darling Wee Jackie and family," then started a coughing fit. Trishita gave her a glass of water and Arthur pounded her back.

Still coughing, she excused herself. Between Sylvia's collection of cows and her parents impending visit, she had to take in more than she could stomach. Upstairs she put her finger down her throat and purged the artichoke capellini. For an instant, she saw an image of her father's face in the water, contorted in horror. She flushed it away. Her triumphs of the previous night and following day evaporated.

"Cows," she whispered. "Ceramic cows."

CHAPTER SEVEN

"I love Jersey cows," Sylvia said a week later. She was lying on her back on Trishita's bed, holding a brown and white ceramic cow at arm's length above her face. "They have such beautiful eyes. Where did you get this one?"

"Near the bus station in Worcester. On my day off last week I took the bus in. My mother needed cash—"

"The bus! I bet Ethan would've loaned you his Rabbit."

"I don't know how to drive," she said. Trishita hated to admit she couldn't drive, but thought she might as well tell the truth just to keep her hand in. If you get to lying too much to others, you start lying to yourself.

"Does anybody else know that?" Sylvia asked as she bolted upright.

"No, not that it matters."

"Wow. I won't tell. I don't know how to drive yet, but Ethan has sneaked me a couple of lessons in his car. Do you want to learn?"

"Sure." She picked up her hairbrush and began the daily process of untangling red curls. "I wonder what it would be like to have hair you can comb."

"How come you didn't get your license when you were sixteen?"

Trishita smiled at her and kept on brushing.

"That's right you didn't go to high school and take driver's ed," Sylvia said with a whistle through her braces.

"No car to drive, anyway," Trishita said.

"Oh." Sylvia stretched out on the bed again, clutching the cow in both hands. Trishita watched the thoughts parade across the girl's face. They were easy to read, running the gamut from incredulousness to sympathy.

"Sylvia? Syl-vi-a. Where are you?" Jacquelyn's voice came from the garage.

"Gotta split." Sylvia jumped off the bed and whispered, "Thanks for the cow." She kissed Trishita's cheek and hurried into Arthur's office. Trishita could hear her trip over the threshold into the kitchen. Poor kid couldn't keep up with her growing feet.

Soon after, Trishita heard a knock on her door connecting to the laundry room and garage. It came as no surprise.

"Come in Mrs. Hyde," she said in a deep tone of voice.

Jacquelyn opened the door and took one tiny timid step inside. She looked all around the room.

"My, you have a lot of books, Trishita. Have you read them all?"

"Maybe two-thirds of 'em. Stendahl throws me. Can't get into him at all. Turgenev, though, is terrific." She sat on the edge of her bed and gestured toward the chair.

"Yes, I suppose so." Jacquelyn ignored it and eyed the books. "I've never read either author. Someday, I'll have time." She turned to face Trishita. "Have you seen Sylvia?"

"This morning when we set up the croquet wickets."

"I've been thinking—wondering if you'd like two days off a week—Saturday and Sunday. We could manage dinner ourselves those two nights, I should think."

"Cut in pay?" Trishita asked.

"Well, maybe half a day," Jacquelyn said, looking at the floor.

"No."

"I guess it wouldn't be necessary to cut your salary. "Jacquelyn smoothed the already smooth white silk pant-suit she was wearing, accented by a turquoise and lavender scarf. "Heaven knows you do wonders around here." She touched the edge of her straight brown hair and smiled. "Just take the extra day anyway. Weekends would be best, normally, although some weekend soon I intend to have a small party for the administrators and will need your help for that."

"Is it okay if I stay here at night?" Trishita wondered where she would go. She didn't make enough to afford her mother <u>and</u> a motel, even a cheap one. Staying with her mother on a Saturday night would be hell.

"Actually, it would be better if you went to visit friends or something." Jacquelyn cleared her throat. "You see, Trish, we've all become so dependent on you we need time to learn to cope for ourselves. After all, you won't be with us forever. The weekends you're not here we can practice."

"Yeah. Damage control," Trishita said.

"What's that?"

"Ethan will have to learn to move through the kitchen without breaking something."

"Sylvia, too," Jacquelyn agreed. "Arthur and I—." She smiled. "Arthur's just as bad, or worse."

For a second Trishita felt a sense of kinship with Jacquelyn, a sisterhood, but it dissipated when she spoke to her in a business-manager tone.

"Do you have a pocket calendar handy?" Jacquelyn asked. "I've got some dates to clear with you." She pulled her own calendar out of her pants pocket.

"I don't have one."

"Oh? A wall calendar, then?" Jaquelyn asked.

"Sorry."

"My goodness. We'll have to get you one." She started backing into the laundry room.

"Do I have to start this weekend?" Trishita stood and towered over her. "Today?"

"Oh no. Besides, you've already started fixing what looks like a complicated menu for tonight. Take tomorrow."

"When are your folks coming? You may need me then, or would you rather I get out of the way?"

"I don't know." Jacquelyn grabbed the door jamb and frowned.

"Don't know when they're coming?"

Jacquelyn looked up at Trishita with such a perplexed, pained looked on her face, Trishita backed off and sat on her bed.

"They'll be here for the Fourth of July weekend," Jacquelyn answered in a rush, "and I will need you that weekend if you can arrange it."

"I'll pencil it in." She smiled at the door closing behind Jacquelyn. "Yes, pencil it in on my crowded calendar." She knew today was Saturday without a damn calendar. Her day on Arthur's Dell. Sundays she practiced on Ethan's Macintosh. Now what would she do about that? Do the housework faster, plan easy meals and practice those two short hours a day when she had the house to herself. And where the hell would she go tomorrow?

*   *   *

Trishita rolled out the buttery dough, folded it in thirds, turned it, and rolled it out again. This was the sixth turn so she wouldn't have to process any more until she was ready to bake. Why did she tackle a recipe for beef in puff pastry? Because it was there, she answered herself.

She went into the pantry to find the dried morel mushrooms. The pantry was a large walk-in with a ceiling light that she turned on by pulling a chain. She couldn't remember where she'd stored the mushrooms. While moving a box of cornmeal, she noticed the peephole again, right at eye level for short people. She had forgotten about it. Now she bent over and examined it. The size of a pea, it opened a view directly to her bed. The hole had been drilled with care and was not there by accident or the endeavors of a mouse. She almost laughed out loud.

*   *   *

"This is exquisite, Trishita," Arthur said after one bite of his beef in puff pastry. "Isn't this too much?" he asked Jacquelyn. "She has really outdone herself this time."

"It is wonderful," Jacquelyn said. "Ethan, slow down. It would be a crime to eat this heavenly meal fast."

Trishita stifled her satisfied smile.

"I'm chewing each bite forty times, Mom," Ethan replied with a beatific look on his face. He grinned up at Trishita as she refilled his water glass.

"Did you see the local news today, Darling?" Arthur asked as reached for the sauce and added a little more to his plate. "That college professor who invited you to speak, you know, Dr. Arlington—well, she and her husband were on TV today, some Worcester station along with a family from Southboro."

"Really? What on earth for?" Jacquelyn lifted her wine glass to her face. The wine, an Australian claret, made her face look red.

"Bizarre story. Seems a burglar jimmied a lock on a back door and got into their house. Didn't steal anything." He interrupted himself with a laugh. "But he broke the heads off about thirty

Lalique figurines. And the couple said some guy broke all their garden gnomes. It was one of those human interest programs, you know."

Both Ethan and Sylvia giggled. Sylvia knocked over her milk glass but caught it before it spilled. She shot Trishita a triumphant look. <u>Damage control.</u>

After Trishita re-filled Arthur's wine glass, she went back to the kitchen to sit on her stool, sip her own glass of the rich claret, and listen to the rest of the conversation. It was a bit more interesting than usual.

"What's even funnier," Arthur continued, "is the thief at Arlingtons placed each head beside the body of a different figurine. He left an aluminum ladder with fingerprints all over it, so it's only a matter of time."

"I sure hope they catch him so we can find out why he did it," Sylvia said.

"Poor Mr. Arlington," Jacquelyn said. "He was so proud of that collection. That day I went there for tea he bored us for a good half hour, explaining each piece."

"If the guy doesn't have a record," Ethan said to Sylvia, "they won't catch him. They won't have any fingerprints to match up with."

"Ethan," Jacquelyn exclaimed, "it's bad enough to dangle one preposition, but two?"

"Let's see if we can dangle four, Syl, what do you say?" Ethan said.

Trishita could almost feel Sylvia's flush of pleasure that Ethan spoke to her.

"I remember a similar case about three months ago," Arthur said, "west end of Boston. Some people there had one of those Franklin Mint Collector's Treasury of fancy, hand painted eggs from countries all over the world. Expensive things. A thief broke into that house and stole all the eggs from the Ukraine. He left a big hole in that collection."

Ethan and Sylvia giggled again. Ethan dropped his fork. Trishita heard it bounce on the hardwood floor and brought him another one. She gave him the clean fork and stooped to pick up the one he'd dropped, pinching his ankle en route. He let out a little squeal, much like that of a baby pig. He covered it by talking fast about the day's Red Sox game.

With a pained expression on her face, Jacquelyn excused herself, leaving her filet in puff pastry half-eaten.

"Are you feeling okay?" Arthur asked.

"I'm fine, Honey. I'll be back in a minute for coffee."

Trishita wondered if Jacquelyn had stomach ulcers. She rarely finished a meal, even the bland ones. Still, she asked Trishita to make all the decisions on food and seemed to trust her. Jacquelyn often told Trishita she liked being surprised at dinner.

While Trishita cleaned up the kitchen, her momentary concern for Jacquelyn's stomach gave way to anger. Where would she go tomorrow? She'd have to walk into town and take the bus somewhere. She could go to the library until it closed at five, grab a hamburger at a diner and linger over it until she'd heard fifteen comments about her height, and then take the bus back to Northboro and walk home in the dark. Mosquitoes would eat her alive. Shit.

A brief squall cooled the air. When she went to bed, she had to cover herself with both sheet and blanket. Some time after midnight, she dropped the book on the floor, turned off her lamp, and fell into a deep sleep. Five hours later she awoke with a start, covered with sweat. The humid heat had returned—God's revenge on New England Puritans. She tossed off the covers and her nightgown. After a while she realized someone was watching her from the pantry peep hole. Perhaps he'd knocked over a box and the muffled sound had twanged her antennae. She turned on her night light to give him a better view.

It had to be a he. Sylvia was too young and open to spy on her, and Jacquelyn too closed and scared. Who, then, was watching her? She decided to find out. She stretched out on her back, aware that the angle of vision from the pantry was on her opened legs, and began rubbing her torso in long, lazy strokes. Then she pulled her knees up, opened her legs wider, and covered herself with her sheet to conceal the fact that she wasn't doing what she pretended to be doing. After all, she did have some modesty. She made the sheet move faster and faster, and then let out a little gasp.

A moan from the pantry rewarded her. Naked and nonchalant, she moved into her bathroom. Then she slipped through the laundry room and garage into the hall between the kitchen and den, into the kitchen and then the pantry. She pulled the cord that turned on the light and said, "Well, Ethan! What a surprise."

"Hi, Trishita. Just getting some cereal." He grabbed a cereal box and held it in front of him. "I'm hungry." He was wearing striped pajama pants and a white T-shirt. He scanned the length of her naked body then turned his head to study the pantry shelves. "Let's see, what kind of cereal should I have?"

"Why don't you come to my room, Ethan?" she whispered. "With such a large salary as mine, I should be prepared to feed any hunger."

"You only make a hundred and forty a week," Ethan answered.

"Thirty-five, not forty." She smiled. He often missed her attempts at sarcasm. "I'm not paying room, board, or tuition. Hurry up, it'll be light soon." She turned off the pantry light and headed toward her room via Arthur's office.

"I'm scared my parents will catch us," he said, following her.

"Suit yourself. I'll be in my room."

"You won't tell, then?" He stood in her doorway.

"You think I'm crazy?" she asked, wondering if it was a rhetorical question.

He shuffled to the foot of Trishita's bed.

"Come talk to me," Trishita said, curled on her side. She patted the space near her waist for him to sit.

Moving as if the bed wore twigs, Ethan sat. His glance raced across her naked body once again and then held still as he gazed at the floor.

"You out with Judy Kraemer tonight?"

"Yes."

"You got horny—"

"It hurts, Trishita. My balls were killing me."

"I'm sure they were. Listen, I've got a deal for you. You can fuck me whenever your cojones are killing you as long as no one else ever knows, as long as you wear a condom, and if you teach me how to drive."

"Drive? Drive what?"

"A car. Your car."

"You don't know how to drive?"

"No." She started stroking his neck and back. "And your mother wants me to clear out of here on weekends. If you meet me in secret—where it's safe—when I'm supposed to be décampée as my mother would say, and give me driving lessons, you can have all the pussy you want. What do you say?"

"I'd do anything for you, Trishita." He buried his face in her breasts.

"Then it's a deal. Stand up." She reached into her make-up case under the bed. It had been so many years since Trishita had indulged in sex, it took her a while to find the condoms among her small treasures. When she found the package, she said, "Drop your pajamas. I'll help you. Ever use one of these?"

"Not really." He shook his head.

The first light of dawn sneaked into her room making the glare from her night light seem as garish as neon. She turned it off. Ethan stood by the bed. His body shook with little convulsive bursts of energy. Trishita calmed him with her hands and proceeded to stretch the condom over the end of his penis. He filled it before she got it half way on. She wiped him off with a tissue and had him lie down beside her. "It's okay, Ethan. Next time will be easier."

"I want to make you feel good," he said. "Tell me how."

"That's for another lesson." She kissed his neck. "It's a deal, then. You teach me how to drive and I'll show you how to dive. By the way, when did you find that hole in the pantry and start watching me?"

"About a month ago when I was looking for the peanut butter that you keep hiding." He grinned. "I haven't been watching you forever, honest."

A loud knock on the door connecting her room to Arthur's office made them both jump. Trishita covered Ethan's mouth with her hand.

"Who is it?" she asked, motioning Ethan to crawl under her bed. It would be too risky to send him through the laundry room without checking it first.

"Sorry to bother you, Trishita," Arthur said through the door, but I can't find Ethan. He's not in his bed, yet his car's out front. Do you have any idea where he might be?"

"Hang on a second, I'll get my robe." She didn't own a robe, but she liked the sound of that line. Instead, she donned a full length, demure, blue cotton nightgown she'd bought during a fit of rebellious chastity four years ago. She opened the door and saw Arthur standing near his computer.

"I haven't seen Ethan," she said. "Maybe he's gone for a swim. It got awful hot during the night."

"I thought I heard voices." Arthur looked at her with greater intensity than was his custom.

"I was reading aloud," she said.

"Oh. Guess I'll go check the brook. Okay if I cut through your room to the garage?"

Trishita's thoughts raced as she tried to untangle her hair with her fingers. How well was Ethan hidden? How could she refuse Arthur's request without a plausible explanation? He could get to the brook by way of the kitchen, but through her room was simpler. She took a chance.

"Sure. Excuse the mess."

Arthur entered and then went straight into the laundry room without looking around. If he weren't so spaced, he could smell his son's spilled seeds. What was Arthur doing up so early?

Trishita ripped a page from a pad of paper and wrote, "Leave what you're wearing under the bed. I'll slip you a towel. Tell everyone you went skinny dipping. I'll knock twice on the wall when the coast is clear."

She slipped the note under the bed when she heard Jacquelyn calling her from the kitchen.

"Coming," she answered and tore off the nightgown, replacing it with her white cotton shift. She tried to brush her hair, but gave up when the brush got caught, dropped it on her bed, and raced through the office to the kitchen.

"I couldn't find the coffee," Jacquelyn said. "Hope I didn't wake you."

"I'll make the coffee."

"My hair looked so limp this morning," Jacquelyn said, "I called Alice to see if she could fix it before church. She's going to sneak me into the beauty parlor. I have to leave in ten minutes so I'll just have some cereal for breakfast. Do you know where Ethan is?"

"Haven't seen him. Mr. Hyde went down to the brook to look for him."

"Mawning, Ma," Sylvia said as she came into the kitchen rubbing her eyes. "Hi, Trishita, what's for breakfast?"

"Good morning, Sylvia," Jacquelyn answered. I have to rush off so I'm having cereal."

"How about waffles?" Sylvia said. "You know, those light puffy ones Trishita makes with sour cream?"

"Let me get your mother going first, then I'll make waffles," Trishita said. She turned on the electric coffee maker, having readied it the night before.

"Oh dear," Jacquelyn said. "I just remembered this is your day off. We'll get our own cereal."

Arthur came in through the kitchen door. "Can't find him. I wonder where he went. Usually he sleeps half the day on Saturday."

"Shoo, all of you," Trishita said, making sweeping motion with her hands. "Go sit down in the dining room. I'll do breakfast. The coffee is almost ready."

Obedient, they left. She grabbed a towel from the linen closet in the hall and shoved it under her bed. Then she checked on the others by setting the dining room table. Arthur was reading the newspaper, Sylvia was staring out the window, and Jacquelyn filed her nails.

Trishita went into the pantry for the cereal. She knocked twice on the wall. Why did Arthur come to her room so early? Had he been watching through the peephole? If he had, she'd lose her job for sure.

She hurried back to the dining room and poured the coffee. In a few minutes she saw Ethan running across the lawn dripping wet. He came into the kitchen, flashed a grin, and then pounced like Tarzan into the dining room. *The son,* she thought. *The shining son.*

Trishita brought him a cereal bowl and some milk, curious to see their reactions. Jacquelyn sent him upstairs to get dressed and Arthur said, "When I discovered he wasn't in his room this morning I thought I heard voices from Trishita's room and knocked on her door a bit early." He gave Trishita a lame smile. "Did I wake you?"

"No. Remember, I told you I was reading aloud."

Sylvia shot Trishita a look that said, *You're lying.*

"Do you often read aloud?" Jacquelyn asked. She had finished her cereal and stood.

"No. Sometimes, though, I pick up the complete works of Shakespeare and let it fall open any old place. This morning it fell open in Richard the Third when he says he would give his kingdom for a horse. You have to read that aloud." She needed a horse this morning.

"I can hardly wait until my boss meets you," Jacquelyn said. "I hope you knock his socks off."

"Ma," Sylvia called out in a shocked tone of voice. "I've never heard you talk like that." She clapped her hands.

Trishita gloated when Jacquelyn blushed and made a quick exit.

"Huh?" Arthur said and Ethan returned, saying "I'm stahved."

Trishita made waffles, worrying all the while. Sylvia seemed suspicious but didn't know anything for sure. Ethan looked innocent enough, though a bit more confident somehow. Jacquelyn had seemed preoccupied, but maybe Arthur wasn't as spaced as he appeared. Somebody had drilled that hole in the pantry to spy on her. Jacquelyn wanted her out of the house in one breath then wanted her there to impress her guests with the other. As much as Trishita wanted to learn how to drive, she didn't want to lose this job before she was ready to tackle what she called real employment. Seducing the shining son could get her into trouble with the law, and she'd had enough of that with Flossie.

Yet, the possibility that Sylvia would find out worried her the most.

CHAPTER EIGHT

At least this Sunday morning Jacquelyn was able to sing on key. She'd managed to avoid detection, to come up with some creative solutions at work, and to solve a few problems at home without causing any unpleasant scenes. Except, of course, the problem of sex with Arthur. He was getting a bit edgy. Now that she'd taken care of the figurines and garden gnomes and Trishita's influence on her family—somewhat—perhaps she could relax for Arthur. There was always so much to do, though.

A man stood in the middle of the church and began videotaping the choir. Jacquelyn was glad she had Alice do her hair before church. And glad, too, that she was able to stay on key. Nowadays you could end up on nationwide TV when you least expected it. Not much in the Northboro Congregational Church would merit such coverage, though, unless she became careless. The Arlington house gave her a mighty close call. Jacquelyn shivered despite her black robe and the wet June heat.

The hymn ended. The Reverend MacKenna raised his arms like bat wings and lowered them like a swan landing. The members of the choir sat. A flurry of soft coughs scurried throughout the congregation like church mice.

"And Moses counseled the people to hear God and keep his commandments," MacKenna boomed in his deep, rich voice. It's their voices, Jacquelyn thought, that keep men in power. Voice alone. Superintendent Ballman would never have the power and prestige, which he now used to full advantage, without that booming voice of his. For sure, his actions would not warrant accolades of any kind.

"Moses," MacKenna sang out, "warned the people of Israel to destroy everything idolatrous."

Idols, Jacquelyn thought, that's what most collections were. The Arlingtons were collecting idols. It wasn't just ego-tripping after all, it was blasphemous. She determined to speak to Trishita about those ceramic cows she gave Sylvia.

"Thou shalt have none other gods before me. Thou shalt not make thee any graven image."

Clowns. Ballman collects clowns. Graven images.

"Neither shalt thou desire thy neighbor's wife—or anything that is thy neighbor's," MacKenna said with a benign smile. "Some ladies have asked me why Moses did not say, 'Neither shalt thou desire thy neighbor's husband.' He did not address the wives thusly, my friends, because there was no need to. Some few women today may need such a commandment, but only those who emulate men. The God-given natures of men and women do not change no matter how much society changes."

Jacquelyn saw two of the younger women in the choir smirk at one another. MacKenna's right, she wanted to say to them. What normal woman would covet her neighbor's husband? Heck, she didn't even covet her own most of the time.

She knew Ethan's hormones were raging but she could let Arthur deal with that problem.

"Honor thy father and thy mother. Think on these commandments this week. Reflect on the meaning of each one. For example, how do you honor your parents?" He placed his hand over his heart.

Jacquelyn wondered, despite her wandering attention, how MacKenna got the commandments so jumbled. He didn't even mention the one against killing. Moses never explained who thou shalt not kill. Thy neighbor, but not his dog. Millions of people who thought they were obeying God's laws did plenty of killing. Medical researchers alone kill all kinds of animals.

"Yes, honor they father and thy mother in thy heart. Let us pray."

Instead of a prayer, a scene came to mind. Jacquelyn was ten years old.

*   *   *

The blare of trombone notes off key came blasting from the shed. In the kitchen her mother was teaching Jacquelyn how to make a dress on the sewing machine. At the sounds of the trombone, Jackie let go of the cloth and put her hands over her ears. The machine continued sewing, zig-zagging across the dark gray fabric.

Jackie grabbed the material and burst into tears. "Why doesn't he give up? He'll never learn how to play that thing."

"You're too sensitive for your own good. Come now, let's cut out the ruined piece and start over. There's room to spare on this yardage."

"I don't want a dress out of this material."

"Why on earth not?" Abby frowned at her.

"Color's ugly." Another blast of notes grated Jacquelyn's nerves.

"It's a practical color," Abby Nestrom said over the sound of Bill's notes. "Dark gray hides a multitude of spills."

"Ma, why does Dad play them now? He used to just coll—"

"Never you mind. Let him have his relaxation. After all, he works hard all week at the garage. He needs a little music on weekends."

"You call that music?"

Abby slapped her face, and then looked as shocked as Jackie felt, cowering on the floor. Abby hadn't ever slapped her before, but Jackie felt really scared.

"Don't hit her, Ma!" Billy yelled from the doorway. "For God's sake, did you forget?"

"You keep out of this, Billy. She has to learn to respect her father."

*   *   *

Jacquelyn tried to pray but even the Lord's Prayer eluded her. She hated to think about her parents, let alone honor them. Where did it say that parents have to earn that honor? She had no trouble respecting Arthur's parents. In fact, she loved them. And Arthur respected her folks. He seemed pleased that they were coming for a visit. Why couldn't she be pleased, too?

Would Sylvia honor her? She used to. Before Trishita.

Jacquelyn released her troublesome thoughts during the closing hymn. She let the music transport her to the dunes near Cape Cod where she had run as a young girl, rolling in the soft marsh grass, luxuriating in the sun beaming down that brought all the little creatures in the sand to miraculous life, infusing her with the expansive spirit of the universe. And, she had thanked God as she lay face down, arms spread out to embrace the earth and its sandy grass, grateful for that spirit in the deepest regions of her heart.

The last time she felt such gratitude was almost fourteen years ago, when Sylvia was born. She drove home from church determined to feel it once again.

Instead of going around to the garage, she parked on the first curve in the driveway and went in the front door. She found Sylvia and her little blonde friend, the Jasmine girl, running at top speed, taking a circular route through the house from living room to dining room to kitchen to Arthur's office and Trishita's room through the laundry room and garage back to the hall, the den, and front foyer.

"Sylvia, stop!" Jacquelyn yelled.

Both girls came to a sudden stop at the foot of the spiral staircase. Sylvia tripped over her feet and went sprawling part way up the stairs.

"Heavens to Betsy," Jacquelyn said, "What <u>are</u> you doing?"

"Running," Sylvia answered between short breaths.

"Well, run outside, not through the house. Where's your father?"

Sylvia pulled herself off the steps to stand in front of her mother. She stared down at the slate tiles of the floor. Jacquelyn's eyes followed her gaze. Light from the mirrored walls bounced off the crystal chandelier and made the slate dance.

"He went to play golf with Mr. Sullivan," Sylvia said.

"Oh? When?"

"He just left. It took him forever to find his golf shoes." She giggled. "He was in a real snit about them."

"And Ethan, my other heathen?"

"He's gone somewhere. I heard him tell Dad he'd be home for supper."

"Okay." She patted Sylvia's shoulder. Reaching up to pat her head would feel awkward now that Sylvia was so tall. "Did you two Indians have lunch?"

Without waiting for an answer, Jacquelyn went into the kitchen and let out a gasp of horror. The counter tops were covered with dirty dishes and jars from the refrigerator, all uncovered and drawing flies, which clouded in through the side door. The screen door was wide open.

"Sylvia," she screamed. "Come here this instant."

"What's the matta, Ma?" Sylvia entered from the dining room.

"Look at this mess. Start cleaning up this minute." Jacquelyn slammed the screen door shut and grabbed a fly swatter. Thou shalt not kill flashed through her mind.

"I didn't do it. Dad and Ethan did it packing picnic lunches. I shouldn't have to clean it up."

"You were here then. You are here now. Clean it up."

"It's not fair," Sylvia shouted and stormed up to her room. The Jasmine girl made a hasty exit. Jacquelyn caught a glimpse of her running down the side yard. She sighed and began cleaning. She knew she should make Sylvia do it, but she just didn't have the energy.

When she finished loading the dishwasher, putting the food away and shooing those flies out that she hadn't killed, she realized two things. One, she didn't know where to put things in her own kitchen anymore, and two, she didn't want to know.

Jacquelyn changed into her teal and purple silk tank top and shorts and went into the living room to read. She had wanted to read all of Deuteronomy but couldn't find her Bible so settled on Moby Dick. The opening paragraph always comforted her. Whenever Ishmael got to the point of wanting to knock people's hats off, he took to sea. Whenever she felt that "damp, drizzly November" in her soul, the need to "drive off the spleen, regulate the circulation," she destroyed people's collections.

She was contemplating the strange needs of human nature when Arthur came home, smiling and sweating.

"I hit a thirty-eight today at Juniper Hill. We just went nine holes because of the heat and the horse flies. Man, they bite." He bent down and kissed her cheek. "How are you? You look cool and lovely."

"I'm all right." She smiled up at him. He never needed to drive off his spleen. "A little tired. I had to clean up a horrendous mess in the kitchen. Sylvia defied me and I just didn't have the strength to make her do it. She said you and Ethan made that mess."

"Sorry about that. I couldn't find my golf shoes and thought Trishita would clean it up. Where is she?"

"She won't be back until sometime tonight."

"No kidding. Since when?"

"Yesterday. I told her to start taking weekends off so we can learn to manage on our own. Now I'm not so sure it was a good idea."

He looked at her with his head tilted to the right for a moment, then righted it. His eyes glazed over.

"We'll do fine," he said, returning to the problem at hand. "What shall we have tonight? Should I barbecue something?"

"Oh dear. I forgot to look and see what we have in the way of food." She put the book on the end table face down so she wouldn't lose her place, determined to find a book mark before Trishita got to it and closed it. Every time she found a moment to read, she had to re-read several pages that sounded familiar, and she hadn't even met Captain Ahab yet.

"Barbecue's a good idea," she said to Arthur. "Set it up and I'll see what I can find to thaw in the micro." She moved into the kitchen and peered into the freezer. When she noticed she was getting chilled, she pulled out what looked like a package of ground beef. Without her glasses she couldn't read the label. "Here we go, Arthur. We'll have hamburgers tonight. It'll be fun."

Ethan waltzed into the kitchen chewing on a piece of field grass.

"What are we having for supper?" Ethan asked.

"Hamburgers," Jacquelyn said. "Hello Honey. Where've you been?"

"Out and about."

Sylvia stuck her head in and looked around. Then she came all the way in and put her arm around her mother's shoulder in an awkward embrace.

"I would've helped, Ma," Sylvia said. "I just didn't think it was fair to do it all by myself when I hadn't made the mess." She glared at Ethan.

"It's okay, Sweetheart," Jacquelyn said. "Next time we'll both know better." She took the meat out of the microwave oven and started making patties.

"The meat looks funny," Ethan said.

"Nonsense, it's fine. Here, take this platter out to Dad. Sylvia, you find the condiments and bread and put them on the dining room table, then, *voilà*, we shall eat like the children of royalty."

"Ethan has grass stains all over his white shorts," Sylvia said. She stopped in front of Ethan and asked, "What have you been doing, rolling down the aqueduct slopes?"

Ethan sidestepped her and took the platter out back. Jacquelyn watched from the window. His shorts were grass stained. She saw Arthur smile at Ethan and placed several patties onto the Grill. She relaxed. This was going to work out just fine.

"Where's the fire extinguisher?" shouted Ethan rushing into the kitchen.

"Oh my God. I don't know." She looked out the window and saw tall flames shooting up from the barbecue. Under the kitchen sink she found a spray bottle. "Here, Ethan. Quick. Put out the fire."

He grabbed the bottle and sprayed until the flames went down. Soon Arthur came in carrying the platter on his upraised forearm, looking like a waiter in a cartoon. He placed the platter, with ceremony, in the middle of the dining room table.

"They look like miniature cow pies," Sylvia said. "Let 'em harden and I'll put a couple next to my ceramic cows."

"Hush," Jacquelyn said. "They'll be fine." She began passing the mustard and relish around. "Fix your bread, I'll get the drinks." She poured Arthur a glass of wine and brought the carton of milk in for the children. She couldn't figure out where to put the milk carton and carried it back to the kitchen.

"Hey, Ma, can't we have some milk to wash these things down?" Sylvia asked.

"You shouldn't drink milk for that reason, Sylvia. I'll get you a glass." When she returned with two glasses and the carton, she saw that the others were waiting for her to sit before taking a bite. It pleased her that she had been able to convince them to say Grace, at least on Sundays.

She sat and prayed, "We thank thee O Lord for thy protection and this wonderful food. Amen."

The other three picked up their hamburgers. Each took a big bite then spit it out. In unison.

"It's soapy," Ethan said.

"And ground pork, not beef," Sylvia said. "Pork sausage."

"Burnt crap," Arthur said. "Sylvia was right. Cow pies. Don't try it, Jacquelyn."

"Tastes just like soap," Ethan said. "I remember when you washed my mouth out years ago."

"That's because you sprayed them with soap, dope." That came from Sylvia.

"What was in that spray bottle you gave me, Mom?" Ethan asked.

"I don't know. It may have been soap. Oh, dear, what should we do?"

"I'll call for pizza," Sylvia said as she jumped up. "Do you want pepperoni?"

"No anchovies," Ethan said.

"Italian sausage? I don't care for pepperoni," Arthur said, looking at Jacquelyn for permission.

"Tell them no anchovies," Ethan repeated.

While Sylvia made the call, Ethan and Arthur picked at the bread around their meat.

"We might as well wait in the den," Jacquelyn said. "It may take a while. Where would Trishita keep the crackers? I guess we should've known that pink, fatty meat wasn't ground beef."

* * *

Not too long after they devoured the cardboard tasting pizza, Jacquelyn put on her earphones and stretched out beside Arthur on their king-sized bed. Arthur was already wearing his headphones. He liked to listen to radio talk shows and she liked a little soft rock to ease her into sleep. Once in a while, Arthur would shake his head in disbelief or grin in agreement. Then she would close her eyes and hope the madness would not come again tonight, or ever. And the moon was almost full. It never came over her except during the new moon.

She tore off her ear plugs when she realized the new moon would coincide with her parents' arrival, a double whammy. Either alone agitated her almost to a breaking point. What could she do? Tranquilizers made her ill. So did Scotch or Vodka. But she had no targets in mind. Maybe that's how she'd get through it.

It used to be so simple when she was in college. Everyone else was wacky in those days. Therefore, she could be sane. Thanks to Billy's urging throughout high school, she'd earned a four-year scholarship to U. Mass at Amherst. The two years after high school that she'd worked at Filene's Boston store provided four years worth of room, board and sorority fees. If she'd stayed with the store she could've been a buyer for their better clothes. But instead, she started U.Mass at twenty where she met Arthur.

She'd had a series of disastrous dates with long-haired dopers expecting and advocating free sex. To her, sex was expensive and messy—no order to it at all. She soon found a corner of the library seldom used because all the books were on reserve. That's where she met Arthur.

Deep in to his electrical engineering major, he did not seem to care about anything else. Not only was he short-haired, compact and neat, he kept his circuits in order. All of them. One day he noticed her and asked her to go with him to the student cafeteria for lunch. Lunches progressed to dinners and long walks up the hill behind the dormitories. She decided he liked her because she was shorter than he was, even when she wore high heels. She decided that she loved him after he said that he loved her.

She and Arthur were among the few students who ran counter to the counter-culture movement of the seventies. They ignored politics and tie-dyed T-shirts. They passed on marijuana and turned down the more raucous sounds of rock and roll. They had no professed ideals. All either wanted was order. And they got it. She didn't feel the need to sneak into people's houses after she met Arthur. If only she could regain that peace.

She heard a crash downstairs and sat up.

Arthur squinted at her and pulled down his earphones.

"Listen. Are those kids running through the house?"

"Sounds like it," he said. "I'll shoo 'em to bed."

No, I'll go." She got up and put on her royal blue silk robe, one she'd made by hand and adorned with her own monogram in silver thread.

Sew! That's what she'd do this summer. Make a new wardrobe for fall. She glanced at her sewing machine in the north corner of the bedroom. It had been lying idle too long. Sewing might get her through the next new moon.

At the head of the stairs she heard Ethan yell, "Give me that, you brat."

"Not until you tell me why you have them. Or should I ask Judy Kraemer?"

"Come on, hand them over."

"I bet you carry them to show off, you show-off. Bet you never even used one."

"That's what you think, brat."

Jacquelyn heard a scuffle coming from the den. Sylvia raced into the foyer with Ethan at her heels.

"Children, stop that!" She yelled down the stairs.

They both stopped dead and looked up.

"Sylvia, what do you have of Ethan's?"

"Nothing." She held up both bare hands.

"Why is he chasing you, then? Ethan? What do you have to say for yourself?"

"She's just being a pest, Mom." Ethan shoved his hands in his pockets.

"What did she take that belongs to you? I heard—"

"Nothing, Mom. She was messing with a picture of Judy in my wallet."

"He's such an old fuddy-duddy!" Sylvia said. She stood on one foot with the other resting on her ankle and held onto the railing for balance.

Even as she attempted to mediate, Jacquelyn knew everything she said was wrong. Yet she felt compelled to play it out as if it were a well-memorized script. Knowing how ineffective she was but going on anyway gave her a strange sense of watching herself perform.

"There's more to this than either one of you is letting on." Jacquelyn stared down at them. A soft knock on the front door startled them all. Jacquelyn said, "See who it is."

Sylvia peeked through the peep-hole then opened the door wide.

"Trishita!" Sylvia threw her arms around Trishita. "Where have you been? It was awful here today. We had soapburgers for supper, then lousy pizza and I hate Ethan."

"Sorry to bother you this late," Trishita said. "I don't have a house key." She held Jacquelyn's daughter in her arms and waved at her son. She looked up and saw Jacquelyn.

"Evening, Mrs. Hyde. What time do you want breakfast tomorrow?"

"The usual. Children, go to bed. No more fighting. Good night, Trishita. I'll get you a house key tomorrow."

Jacquelyn climbed back into bed and put on her earphones. Arthur smiled at her and removed his headphones. Just as she was beginning to relax, she felt his hand on her thigh, moving down then up under her nightgown. His hand felt rough on her skin. She tensed and closed her legs tight. He stroked her stomach with such intensity, it hurt. She moved his hand back out above the sheet.

"Come on, Jackie? It's been three months."

"I know, Dear. I'm sorry, but I just don't feel like it. It hurts." She heard Arthur's exasperation in every breath he took. "Honey," she said, "let's go to the Cape this summer instead of Maine."

"Your folks are expecting us to rent the cabin next to theirs," he said.

"They won't mind if we don't go."

"The kids will," he said. "You know how they love to go to Bar Harbor with their grandparents."

"Let my folks take the children with them to Maine and we can go to the Cape alone." She turned on her side and leaned on one elbow. "I want to run through the dunes again. Maybe then I can relax. My body is too tense lately for you know what."

"We couldn't get on the dunes, remember? Everything's fenced off now." He sighed and gave her a quick kiss on her lips. "But I'm willing to try anything." He put on his earphones again.

Jacquelyn put hers away and turned on her side with her back to him. What did Sylvia take that belonged to Ethan, and why? Why does she love Trishita? Why does Trishita bring her those stupid cows? Why does Arthur hang slide rules all over the walls of his office? He knows how I feel about them.

Tears filled her eyes. She could not make love to Arthur, nor could she honor her father and mother, and they would arrive right around the new moon.

"Dear God," she prayed, "How can I keep my family, my career, and my life together in this beautiful home when all I can think about is revenge against idolaters? What's wrong with me, Dear God?"

CHAPTER NINE

By eight o'clock Monday morning Trishita had the house to herself. Arthur came home to work in his office around ten, which gave Trishita two hours to practice. *Which computer should she use today?*

Feeling lighthearted, she went up to Ethan's room to play with his graphics. Becoming a desktop publisher was a pleasant fantasy for her. People would call her Miss McCabe and admire the newsletters and brochures she designed, wrote, and produced with nary a word about her height or her curly red hair. She remembered Miss Aarons, her fifth grade teacher.

*   *   *

"You need to brush your hair often, Patricia. It's such a bright red and so wiry, it makes you look even taller," Miss Aarons said. "And stand up straight," she added, sounding like a drill sergeant from an old war movie.

Trishita pulled at a lock of her hair and lifted one shoulder.

The school secretary came into the fifth grade classroom with a note. Miss Aaron read it and sighed.

"Go home, Patricia. Your mother needs you," she said.

Outside, the wind was blowing so hard abandoned toys became dangerous missiles. Trishita bent double into the wind and kept her eye out for flying objects.

Refuse plastered the chain link fence enclosing an empty lot. A large baby doll in a long white dress, caught against the fence, looked trapped and sad. Trishita turned her back to it and gazed at the sky. Over the roofs of the tenements, she could see the skyscrapers of another world—a world of future careers—Miss Aaron had told them when she had taken the class on a field trip.

Trishita pictured herself, brown-haired and seven inches shorter, entering a suite of offices overlooking the city commons, sinking into plush carpeting, unlocking the door to her own private office.

All communication would come to her through her computer. No one could reach her against her will.

*   *   *

This, her first dream of working alone, returned often. Now it seemed possible. Some day she'd make enough to buy her own condo in a town like Northboro, and a car, too. Driving Ethan's Rabbit yesterday was fun. She'd buy a bigger car, though, with an automatic transmission. Trying to let out the clutch with one foot and put the right amount of pressure on the gas pedal with the other was tricky. She'd sent that Rabbit bouncing down the dirt road into the woods like a real rabbit.

Then Ethan became the rabbit. They'd found a grassy clearing in the woods and stopped for his lesson. He was cute rolling around his white shorts afterwards, staining them in the grass. It was a pleasant way to spend a summer Sunday afternoon despite the pesky horse flies. Going to the movies after Ethan left was not bad either. Popcorn and candy for supper, with two movies just about as meaty as her meal, prolonged her enforced day off and made it palatable.

Trishita believed that no prince charming would be forthcoming for her in this lifetime. Living in the suburbs, though, was not only possible, but already familiar. She whistled "Ain't Misbehavin" as she climbed the stairs, two at a time, on her way to Ethan's room. *Just keep your nose clean,* she told herself.

Ethan's room was so all-American boyish it depressed her. Pictures of the high school football, basketball, and baseball teams hung on his walls along with a Celtics poster and a Red Sox banner. A blurred prom picture of himself in a blue tux with his arm around Judy Kraemer in a red gown stood in its frame on his maple chest of drawers. A manly brown plaid bedspread covered his bed, under which he hid his "Playboy Magazine." Poor kid wouldn't risk "Penthouse."

But the Macintosh on his maple desk was magic. Ethan's laser printer would spit out her designs on day-glo orange or purple paper. She began playing. First, she created a file called "Advertisements for Myself." She headlined her first document, a Matisse-like line drawing of a very tall woman, in Garamond bold, "NO JOB IS TOO

TALL FOR McCabe." It was printing when Ethan bounded into his room and put his hands over her eyes.

"Hey, you're supposed to be in school," she said.

"I ditched first period."

She removed his hands from her eyes and looked at him. He was smitten.

"Judy came up to me before class." He kneeled beside her and put his head on her lap. "I didn't want to see her. I couldn't talk to her. All I could think of was you."

"Hang on a minute, Ethan," she said. She lifted his head and extricated her knees from his embrace. She had to be careful. "Listen to me while I pace." She turned off the computer, ignoring all "save" commands and walked over to the dormer window that overlooked the front yard. The super sweet smell of lilacs floated in.

"You started teaching me how to drive yesterday, Ethan," she said, her back to him. "The basics. I hate the word 'empowered' that your mother bandies about, but that's what I felt. In fact, I fell in love with your car." She turned around and leaned against the window sill. "It's just a car."

Ethan seemed to be listening. His eyes were bright and his jeans bulged.

"I want you to have as much control over your love life," she continued, "as you do driving your car. I'm just a car to you. Drive me once a week into the woods where no one can see us, but don't crash me into your father's Mercedes, or worse, your mother's BMW."

She started moving around the room. He stayed where she left him, on his knees.

"I don't want to lose my job here. I have too much to learn. You're adorable, but only a car to me—my transportation to another world. Go back to Judy Kraemer and other girls your own age. Shit, I could be your mother if I'd screwed up at fourteen, instead of just screwed. But I'm not. I'm a car. Go back to school. I'll meet you Sunday."

"You're a Rolls Royce." Ethan's face broke into a grin. He blew her a kiss and headed down the stairs. "Hey, Trishita," he called as he went out the front door. "You need to learn reverse. We can practice after dinner every night, too. Save my lessons for Sundays."

With mixed feelings, she watched him drive away. Relieved by Ethan's response, she still worried that it was all too easy. No matter how clean the deal, sex was perilous. Then she heard the sound of a car coming toward the house. "Oh, no!" she said as Arthur's car turned into the driveway and headed toward the garage. *Now, the father.* She went downstairs and met him in the hall.

"Hi Trishita," he said holding his brief case in front of his chest like a suit of armor. "I just saw Ethan's car. What was he doing home?"

"Forgot his term paper that was due today." *How was she going to get to Ethan in time to tell him that lie?* "Or, I think that's what he said. He came in and out so fast I couldn't be sure."

"That's Ethan for you, in and out fast."

"Right." Unable to contain her amusement, she averted her face and headed into the kitchen. "Would you like some coffee? I'll make a fresh pot."

"Yes, I'd like a cup." He headed into his office. "Bring it here when it's ready."

While the coffee brewed, Trishita took stock of the freezer. She pulled out some fish fillets and perused the fish cookbook. The braised fish Italian style with porcini mushroom, pancetta, and Italian seasonings looked beautiful, and she had all the ingredients. If she had a driver's license she could go to the market for fresh fish, but the Hydes weren't that fussy anyway. The frozen fish would do after she'd finished dressing it up with fresh basil from her herb garden in the cellar window.

Carrying Arthur's coffee, she stood at the open door of his office. He had his back to her. She admired the shape of his shoulders under his shirt, his strong arms covered with thick brown hair. She wanted to touch him, but she knocked on the doorjamb instead. He swiveled around; she gazed at the wall.

"The slide rules look terrific the way you have them hanging there," she said. "Here's your coffee."

"Thanks Trishita. Guess I'll take a little break. I can't seem to concentrate today." He smiled. "Have a seat."

She got herself a cup of coffee and sat in a recliner beside his desk. He looked peaked. His lips were white, just visible under his mustache, and he seemed to frown even when he smiled. Trishita knew he ran some kind of business with two employees in Southboro. She wanted to express the concern she felt for his sad face, but trusted her reticence.

"How's business?" she asked.

"We're scraping by. I'm glad you like the slide rules. Jacquelyn doesn't. Maybe they remind her of Bill's trombones." His voice trailed off like one in a dream.

"What did you say? Who's Bill?"

"Nothing important. Bill Nestrom—Jacquelyn's father. By the way, we're going away for a couple of weeks in July after her parents come for their annual visit. If you don't have any plans, I'd like you to stay here and keep an eye on things. Not all the time of course. You don't get much of a life of your own, do you?"

"I'll be happy to stay here. Besides, I want to get proficient with your accounting program and Ethan's desk-top publishing."

"What do you plan to do with this proficiency?" He studied her.

"Get an office job someday that pays enough so I can buy a condominium and a car. The American dream, right?"

"I think you could make more money cooking." He laughed.

"I hate the restaurant business, Mr. Hyde."

"Now Trishita, I've asked you many times to call me Arthur. I'm uncomfortable with the Mr." He handed her his empty cup and sighed. "Back to work. I've got lots of calls to make, and, I hope, some money."

"See you later, Arthur," Trishita said with a smile. She spent the rest of the day vacuuming, washing, cooking, and listening to Italian opera. Jacquelyn bought compact disc sets of operas, but Trishita was the only one who played them. Fascinated by the unfamiliar sounds, she liked the challenge of trying to figure out what was happening in the stories from the dips and swells of the music and voices alone. She couldn't decide whether to read the librettos. She felt curious to know how close she could come, but didn't want to end the game.

Arthur left round three o'clock. Soon afterward Sylvia came home. A sweet, cool breeze came in with her. The weather was changing again. Trishita scanned the sky but the skimpy clouds withheld a forecast.

"Two whole weeks more of school." Sylvia said as she dropped a thick, worn textbook on the kitchen table. "This year is never going to end."

"Seems like it, I bet. Then you'll graduate from grade school. Will your grandparents be here for the ceremony?"

"I dunno. They may not get here until July. Will you come?"

"I'd like to, but I doubt it."

Sylvia shot her a look of admiration. <u>What for</u>, Trishita wondered, <u>the truth?</u>

When Sylvia picked up her textbook, an old, beat-up mahogany slide rule fell out on the table.

"Oh, look, Trish. Harold Johnson gave me this to give to Daddy. It was his great uncle's."

"Your father will like that a lot."

"Ma won't. She hates grandpa's collection of trombones, too."

"Ah, why's that?"

Sylvia went into Arthur's office and put the slide rule on his desk then returned, dropping onto a chair with a thud that amused Trishita. She, herself, moved the same way before she learned to accommodate her height.

"Don't know why," Sylvia answered. "She claims she likes them fine, but I don't believe her."

"Slide rules and trombones do have something in common," Trishita said, arranging cutting boards and knives on the countertop.

"Yeah, they slide. What're you doing?"

"Fixing to fix fish."

"Can I watch?"

"Sure." Trishita unwrapped the Italian bacon and began dicing it. "Just think, Sylvia, next fall you'll be going to high school. You can ride to school with Ethan."

"I hate Ethan."

"How come?"

"He thinks he's such a big shot. Yesterday I found a package of those things—you know, condoms—in his wallet. He came unglued. I thought he was going to hit me."

"Sometimes, in fact, quite often," Trishita said as she sat on a stool to bring herself into eye contact with Sylvia, "people hit people who look in wallets that don't belong to them. You were lucky."

"Well, why does he carry those things?" Sylvia glanced away.

"Most boys do. Nowadays some girls do. It's macho in some cases and sensible in others."

"What if he gets AIDS? We saw a movie at school that scared me. It said AIDS was moving into the heterosexual community and nothing but abstinence can prevent it."

"When I was your age nobody had even heard about AIDS. It's good to be a little scared, I guess." Trishita grinned. The kid sounded so sophisticated.

"I started the virgins club at school," Sylvia said. "Seven of us belong. We all swore to stay virgins until we're twenty-one."

"What do you do at your club meetings?"

Sylvia reached into the refrigerator and pointed at the fish fillets floating in a bowl of milk.

"Looks like a milky aquarium," Sylvia said. "Why are you thawing them in the refrigerator? Ma always defrosts stuff in the micro."

"Fish stays fresher tasting when it thaws in milk."

"Wow. Where did you learn to cook, Trishita? In those restaurants you worked at?"

"Ha! In a way, you might say so. The food was so bad in those joints I learned how to cook in self-defense. Actually, I began to learn for real when I came to work here and discovered all these cookbooks." She pointed to the shelf of books over the built-in food processor. "You didn't answer my question. What do you do at your club meetings?"

"We only meet once a month. We follow Roberts' Rules of Order—read the minutes from the last meeting, the treasurer's report—stuff like that. Then we talk about sex and how to avoid it."

"Do any of the boys know about this club?" Trishita asked.

"God, no. It's top secret. Don't tell Ethan."

"Don't worry, Sylvia, I won't," Trishita said, looking straight into Sylvia's brown eyes. "Cross my heart."

"I believe you," Sylvia said and put her empty milk glass in the dishwasher. "How old were you when you lost your virginity."

"Twelve."

"Geez, Trishita, that's almost two years younger than me. How did it happen?"

"I was raped."

Sylvia rushed over and put her arms around Trishita's waist, and then moved away turning her back. She crossed her forearms on top of her head as if she didn't know where else to put them.

"How awful. Who was it?"

"Don't know," Trishita said. "It was your classic rape. Guy wearing a stocking over his head broke into my room from the fire escape and held a knife at my neck."

"Didn't your mother call the police?"

"She wasn't home."

"How about when she got home?" Sylvia asked with a catch in her voice. "Did she take you to the hospital?"

"My mother just said she was glad he didn't kill me." The old pain stung the corners of Trishita's eyes. She figured it was like arthritis or an old knee injury, always there and ready to flare up at any provocation.

"That's terrible, Trishita!" Sylvia turned and looked up at Trishita with a shocked expression on her sun-splotched face. "She didn't even call the police?"

"My mother doesn't call the police; they call her. When I complained, she told me to be brave. She said all girls get raped and that the first time was the worst."

"First one! There are more? She's wrong isn't she? All girls don't get raped, do they?"

"Yeah, she's wrong, generally speaking, but she had had the same experience. Colors your thinking." Trishita felt her heart beating. *Jesus, how did I get into this conversation?*

"Did it happen again to you?"

"Only once more, then I learned how to defend myself."

"I need to learn, too. Will you teach me?" Sylvia pleaded.

"No need to scare you with all that." Trishita shook her head and moved into the hall. "Come down to the cellar with me, Syl. I'll show you how to cultivate fresh herbs and how to cook with courage and finesse. You don't need to learn self-defense. In your world, most men are gentlemen."

"Ethan's not."

"Ha! Listen, if any man ever tried to rape you, I would beat him to a pulp, and so would Ethan."

"You just don't know Ethan," Sylvia said under her breath. Then she stopped under the skylight in the hall and smiled. Sunlight glinted on her braces. "You think he'd care?"

"You bet." Trishita opened the cellar door. The cool, damp air calmed her. Talk of rape always agitated her. The way she figured it, you need to get your adrenaline going for real danger. Wasting it on memories and imaginary situations could rob you of it when you needed it for real. No point in pumping Sylvia's adrenaline with self-defense tactics too early.

Instead, Trishita spent a good half hour showing Sylvia how and when to plant and care for herbs, gratified by Sylvia's genuine interest. Trishita began to breathe easy again. She noticed that Sylvia seemed calmer too. The healing power of herbs. Sylvia was such a quick study, Trishita wondered why the kid hated school.

Ethan came home all sweaty and red-faced from playing baseball. Sylvia followed him into the foyer and apologized for raiding his wallet. Trishita overheard her words as well as Ethan's silence. She guessed that he was as dumbfounded as Trishita—and as pleased. Later, when they both came back to the kitchen, he was teasing Sylvia about her throwing arm.

"Hi Trishita," he said with a false air of nonchalance. "We came in to watch you cook, okay?"

"Sure. Just don't break my concentration." She had her back to them and heard scraping sounds of moving furniture. She looked back over her shoulder and saw that they were moving the picnic bench in from the side yard. Arthur showed up and helped with a smile so wide his thin mustache seemed to stretch like a rubber band across his upper lip.

Ethan carried letter-sized sheets of white cardboard with a black number printed on each. After one perfunctory glance, Trishita returned to her tasks. She put the homemade chicken stock on to boil with a cup of rice and heard Ethan whisper.

"That's at least a seven," he said.

"But it's only rice. I'd say a five," Sylvia said.

"Rice made with chicken stock and flavored with fresh grated pecorino," Arthur said, "is more than ordinary rice. I'd give it a nine."

Curiosity crept up Trishita's back. She turned to look at them. They sat side by side on the bench, each holding up a numbered card.

"What are you guys doing?" she asked.

"We're cooking judges," Sylvia answered. "We rate your performance by number and hold up our judgment on each thing you do for our make-believe audience."

Trishita smiled and went back to work. She sliced the artichoke hearts and put them aside. Then she heated the olive oil and sautéed the diced pancetta with the chopped porcini mushrooms. The pungent smell of the wild mushrooms, mixed with the sweet scent of the Italian bacon, brought a cheer from her judges. She turned to look. Each was holding a card bearing the number ten.

"What's this all about?" Jacquelyn asked as she came through the swinging door from the dining room.

"You're home early tonight." Arthur said. He jumped up and gave her a quick kiss on the cheek. "Good for you. We were watching Trishita cook and rating each of her activities."

"I don't get it." Jacquelyn frowned.

"You know, Ma," Ethan said, "how judges rate athletic events like the high dive or gymnastics? We're just pretending Trishita's in a cooking contest—"

"Like we're training her for the cooking Olympics," Sylvia said.

"Well, I don't think you should bother her this way." Jacquelyn made a sweeping motion with her left arm. "Come on everyone, clear out and put that picnic bench back where it belongs."

Trishita started to say they weren't bothering her, but Jacquelyn's face did not look open to alternative points of view. She decided instead to keep her eyes on the cookbook and let her anger at Jacquelyn for kicking her out on weekends smolder. Her day would come.

An hour later, she pulled the fish and its elaborate dressing out of the oven. She was decorating it with shredded fresh basil and toasted pine nuts when Jacquelyn entered.

"Looks gorgeous, Trishita." Jacquelyn glanced around the kitchen. "Will it hold a minute?"

"It keeps hot a long time." Trishita sat on a stool so as not to tower over her diminutive boss.

"I've been meaning to talk to you for some time now. Lately I've noticed you've been wearing shorts and that T-shirt a lot. You didn't before."

"It wasn't hot until this month."

"Ah. I see. Well, uh, I was wondering if you would like some sort of uniform—cool, of course."

Trishita pictured the little black and white maid's costumes in racy cartoons with the maid's bare ass showing in the back under a lacy bow. She didn't think Jacquelyn had that uniform in mind, but Ethan and Arthur wouldn't protest too much.

"Whatever you like, Mrs. Hyde."

"It's just, uh, I simply don't want you to entice—Ethan's so young. Well, I'm sure you understand."

"Of course. I'll wear something more appropriate. Forgive me, I wasn't thinking." *My second lie of the week*, Trishita thought. She changed into her demure white shift and served dinner. When she knew each one had tasted the fish, she re-entered the dining room to get their reactions.

Ethan pulled a card from under the table and held it over his head. "A ten, Trishita."

"Hear, hear," Arthur said, clapping his hands.

"Even I like it," Sylvia said, "and I hate fish."

Trishita bowed. Not waiting for Jacquelyn's response, she returned to her eavesdropping post behind the swinging door.

"When I came home this morning around nine," she heard Arthur say to Ethan, "you were just driving to school. How come?"

"Forgot something," Ethan answered. "Had to ditch first period and come home." Trishita tensed.

"That's right, now, I remember," Arthur said. "Your term paper. Trishita told me you forgot it. What was your paper on?"

"The relationship between people and cars. How cars can be metaphors for other aspects of people's lives," Ethan said.

"What course was that for, Dear?" Jacquelyn asked.

"Chemistry," Ethan answered. No one disputed him and Trishita muffled her laugh.

CHAPTER TEN

Trishita's life resumed its illusion of safety during the next three days and her mother did not phone for money. Arthur came home every morning at ten and worked in his office until noon. Trishita would use his computer between eight and ten and then go up to play with Ethan's graphics. She enjoyed this life and wanted to keep it a while longer.

Jacquelyn, too, seemed pleased with her. Thursday she brought Trishita a pocket calendar decorated with flowers from the Seventeenth Century Flemish School of flower painting. She seemed unaware of Trishita's seething anger at her weekend banishment and asked her to plan a party for Jacquelyn's "colleagues" on June 20th.

"The invitations went out yesterday," Jacquelyn said.

"How many are you expecting?"

"No more than twenty, Jacquelyn replied. "It's just a cocktail party between five and eight. Hors d'oeuvres. Can you think of something appropriate to serve?"

"It'll be fun." Trishita said. "Can I knock their socks off?"

"You mean with canapés and such?" Jacquelyn looked scared.

"Sure." Trishita shrugged. "What else?"

*　　*　　*

Trishita moped a while on Friday, the day before her birthday. She would have to spend that day alone in the Worcester City Library since she couldn't stay at the Hydes. Jacquelyn had gone to work so Trishita put on her her shorts and Grateful Dead T-shirt to vacuum the house. Arthur came home at eleven, an hour later than usual. To her dismay, he went straight to his office without speaking. She made a fresh pot of coffee anyway, and brought him a cup. He looked ill. His face had no color and his shoulders sagged.

"Are you all right, Mr. Hyde? I mean, Arthur?" She longed to comfort him somehow.

"Thanks. I'll live." He took the cup from her with a weak smile and then turned his back to her. "Have you mastered the accounting program yet?" he asked.

"I think so. It's a powerful program, but I've got a handle on it," Trishita said.

"Did you bring a cup of this rich brew for yourself?" he asked, still staring at the blank screen of the monitor.

"No, but I'll get some." She stared at his back. The cords in his neck showed his tension. She wanted to massage his neck and shoulders. Instead, she said, "By the way, tomorrow's my birthday."

"No kidding. Why didn't you say so? Hell, you won't even be here tomorrow." He jumped up and hurried through her room and into the garage. "This calls for champagne." His voice echoed back to her from the refrigerator in the garage.

He returned with a bottle of champagne and two chilled glasses. Still without looking at her, he opened and poured. He toasted her birthday and had to look at her. She noticed his eyes were tight, smaller than usual as if someone had taken a vise to them.

"Thank you, Arthur," she said and took a sip of the champagne that was dryer and smoother than any she had ever tasted. "Are you all right? Has something happened?"

He punched the keyboard and opened a file that looked like a list.

"See these names?" he asked.

"Yes."

"I'm deleting half of them." He swigged the rest of his champagne. "I just lost the Digital account to a competitor. The rest of these will follow as soon as they learn about it." He turned his back to the screen and said with a sob, "I've lost the business." He burst into tears.

Forgetting who she was and who he was, Trishita knelt in front of him and put her arms around him. Holding him, she rocked him and whispered, "Go ahead, Arthur. Cry your heart out."

His tears soaked her Grateful Dead T-shirt. He slipped to the floor between his desk and chair and pulled her down beside him. Later, after his sobbing subsided, he touched her T-shirt.

"I got you all wet," he said and began ironing the front of her shirt with his hand, touching her erect nipples. Next, he kissed her neck and ear. His tongue penetrated her ear and sent shivers the full length of her body. Then he kissed her eyes and her mouth, letting his tongue slide in and out of her opened lips.

She felt his hand on her thigh, fingers inside the edge of her shorts tugging at the crotch of her underpants which was now as wet as her T-shirt. She felt out of control, dumfounded, and entranced as he removed her shorts and underpants, slowly pulling them down her long legs and over her feet.

He lifted her T-shirt to her neck and kissed her nipples and belly button. Then he kneeled between her legs and caressed her inner thighs, eyes roaming her body all the while. "Lovely. So lovely."

When he removed his trousers, she regained her senses.

"Wait. What am I doing?" she cried.

"It's okay, Trish, we're safe now." He touched her lips with his forefinger and then caressed her shoulder.

She had never known such a gentle touch and melted.

"Condom," she said.

"Don't need one. I had a vasectomy years ago and have had no other lovers. Not even Jacquelyn. And you?"

"I'm clean." She said with relief and such desire she vacuumed him in. He began a gentle pushing in and pulling out, kissing her mouth all the while. His tongue mirrored the action of his cock. She wrapped her legs around his back and tilted her pelvis up to meet his. This was the missionary position, she thought during one wild moment, and she was on one hell of a mission.

She stayed in rhythm with him as he moved faster, feeling his thrusts in every inch of her body. She felt tidal waves roll through her, over her, lifting her and dropping her. She crested and screamed. Involuntary. Incredible.

Two slide rules from Arthur's collection fell off the wall behind the desk.

His tongue caressed the roof of her mouth and his fingers became tangled in her hair. His sweat mingled with hers and caused sucking noises when he moved. She laughed at the sound. So did he. His lips were now blood red and his frown all gone. Her breathing returned to normal.

Arthur half crawled to make a languid reach through the kitchen doorway. He picked up and then shuffled through the stack of white cards he and the kids had used to rate Trishita's cooking. He pulled one out and held it up for her to see. It was a ten.

"I need a much higher number now," he said.

She smiled, pleased with the gesture. Then she remembered the kids. "Jesus, we could get caught. What time is it?"

"Don't worry. It's not quite lunch time," he said. "The kids won't be home for hours."

She helped him untangle his fingers from her hair.

"I don't know how this happened," she said, "but it was wonderful." She felt the blood rush to her face and knew she was blushing, a first for her. "You drilled the hole in the pantry, didn't you?"

"No." Now he blushed. "I discovered it accidentally, thought it was natural, you know, just there. I didn't think you'd know that I could see you through it."

"Weren't you worried Jacquelyn might—"

"She never goes into the pantry," he said.

"Right."

"Trishita? Arthur? Where are you?" Jacquelyn's voice came from the front hall, singing, as if she were practicing for the choir. "I've got some fresh cherrystone clams here."

CHAPTER ELEVEN

"Oh, my God!" Trishita whispered. "It's Jacquelyn."

Although she was looking at Arthur, it took several blinks for her to see him. Naked, he covered himself in a half crouch. He looked like a statue of a discus thrower. The sight shocked her out of her own paralysis.

"Arthur, get dressed." Trishita grabbed her clothes and ran to her shower.

A few minutes later, she wrapped her wet hair in a towel and put on her white shift. Her stomach ran out of control, rumbling, cursing the juices bombarding it. Undaunted, she entered the kitchen from the hall, humming a refrain from Verdi's <u>Ernani</u>.

Arthur, somehow all dressed, stood beside Jacquelyn at the sink admiring the clams.

"Hi, Mrs. Hyde," Trishita said. "What are you doing home? Playing hooky from reading?"

"Hello Trishita. Look at these. My secretary's husband went clamming before dawn in Buzzard's Bay. He came by the office and gave me a bucketful. I thought I should bring them home right away so they wouldn't spoil. Do you know how to prepare them?"

"Sure. They'll make a perfect appetizer for tonight," Trishita replied.

"Good." Jacquelyn clapped her hands like an excited little girl. "Now I must run. Luncheon meeting with Jonathan Ballman and the new accountant." She kissed Arthur's cheek and left.

Trishita collapsed into a chair as soon as she was sure she heard Jacquelyn's car on the driveway. She looked up at Arthur who stood leaning against the refrigerator.

"We gotta talk, man," she said, and the phone rang.

Arthur answered and listened for what seemed an interminable time. His hair, still damp, looked pasted to his forehead. He nodded at the receiver.

"I'm sorry, Trish," he said when he hung up, "I have to go to Southboro right away. We'll talk later." He shook his head. "Whew, that was close." He turned and said as he hurried out the door, "Trish. You are wonderful in every way."

The next day Trishita sat at a study carrel in the library with a book on Japanese business management techniques open in front of her. She'd decided to take a break from Dr. Jacobsen's reading list. The Worcester City Library was a lonely place to spend a birthday, she thought, right after you'd had great sex for the first time in years. After Jacobsen left, she'd sworn off except for her deal with Ethan. She'd even thought about becoming a nun at one time, but she had too much trouble believing in anything. Her heart ached, remembering.

*　*　*

Trishita had been wiping down the bar at Russo's when Flossie came in.

"Gimme that, Mija," Flossie said, reaching for the bar rag. "Your Dr. Jacobsen's out there in the alley. Wants to talk to you."

"Ah? Here you go." She handed her mother the bar rag. "Wonder why he didn't come in." She hurried outside.

The long, thin frame of her professor-lover curved like a scythe as he leaned against the back of the building next to the trash cans. His shoulders and head drooped forward. He looked weighted down.

"Jack," Trishita called, and hurried toward him.

"Can't see you tonight," he said.

She reached out and touched his cheek. "You okay?"

"No, I'm not." He jerked away from her touch. "I can't see you any more. Marian's getting suspicious. Besides, I was offered a job at Berkeley. We'll be moving soon."

The news weakened her knees. She leaned against the building beside him.

"Here's your reading list." He pulled a mimeographed stack of papers out of his pocket. "Go through all these and you'll have a better education than most college professors."

Frozen, she just stared at him.

"This is damn hard, I know." He cleared his throat. "I should never have gotten involved in the first place. This is for the best, I suppose. Now you can get a life of your own."

"What the fuck are you talking about? I can't get a life of my own." Trishita glared at him.

"Sure you can," he said. "Christ, you're almost twenty-one. Just move out."

"And leave Johnny? 'Fraid not." Trishita shook her head. "Can't leave my mother either."

"I don't know about the child, but I do know why you can't leave Flossie. I've seen how seductive she is with you. She's living off of you, trapping you with her professed adoration and equally professed desperation. She's sucking you dry. You need to join Al-anon."

His harsh voice felt like a barrage of sharp rocks against her face. He shoved the reading list toward her.

"Thanks," she said, taking the list.

"No problem. Well, Trishita, I have to go now. You were really important to me, you know." He slipped down the alley and turned the corner.

Tears ran down her face. He had come into her life a year ago. Her ticket to the outside world, she'd thought, but he never took her beyond the local motel or Russo's. Now all she had was a reading list. She opened it up and scanned the titles. It was a long list. Better than nothing, she supposed. Yet her heart felt cut so clearly, she could almost see the pieces separate.

*   *   *

She closed the book on Japanese management and took inventory of her life. Here she was, twenty-six years old with a game plan that included at least two more years as live-in maid before she'd be ready for the "real world" and maybe a chance at college part time. She needed to keep her job. Seducing both father and son was no way to do that. Worse was letting her affections run wild. She wouldn't mind a repeat of yesterday's action, even the giddy illusion of love, but how much would it cost? Far too much. First and last for you Arthur Baby, she thought as a huge lump formed in her throat.

She stood up fast, checked out the book, and started walking in the afternoon heat. Sweat dripped down her face and trickled between her breasts. She paid no heed to streets signs nor direction, but did notice there were hardly any other pedestrians around. Others had better sense than to stray too far from air conditioning or swimming holes.

At one intersection she stopped to read the street signs. Salisbury and Park. She had walked almost to her old neighborhood and decided to risk visiting her mother. Maybe Flossie would be coherent enough to talk and listen. She wanted to cry in a mother's arms. She never had, but those rare movie scenes where the daughter comes home in tears to a loving and sympathetic mother hovered in Trishita's fantasies of life in the suburbs.

"Well, look who's here." A tawny skinned little man appeared from an alley. "Where the hell have you been hiding out, Trish?"

"Hi Manuel. You seen my mother lately?"

"Not today. Try Russo's Grill." He moved up to Trishita and stood toe to toe. "You still growing girl? You're mighty pretty and mighty tall—a beanstalk if I ever seen one, and I'm Jack."

She gave him a friendly shove and headed toward mother territory, a squalid bunch of dark brown three-deckers on streets where the people competed to see how ugly everything could be. Patches of weeds grew on bleached soil planted with plastic flowers and fenced by dirty white pickets, most of which were broken or missing. Everything wore a gray haze like the film some old folks get on their teeth.

The smell of rotting garbage came crawling out an open door like a snake, not dangerous, but something you wanted to avoid. The closer Trishita got to the Public Inebriate Shelter on Main Street, the more she held her breath against the stench of urine. Past that, she felt cheered by a whiff of burning hot dogs and spilled beer. Down the street she could see the new gym and the old Gothic, ivy-covered buildings of Clark University—lilies floating in the city's cesspool.

She wiped her wet forehead with her arm and peered between the iron gratings of the dirty windows of Russo's Bar & Grill, the main hot spot she'd worked for six dollars an hour plus tips and a few fanny pats on the side. She opened the door.

"Trishita," a chorus of voices greeted her. She had to wait until her eyes adjusted to the dark before she could recognize any of the folks calling out her name.

She waved and then scanned the room. A familiar little woman with short, straight, blonde hair and black roots came from the hall leading to the rest rooms. When Flossie came under a light Trishita could see that Flossie's coffee and cream complexion was marred by make-up applied in a hurry. Eye-liner smudged onto her right cheek, mascara dripped into the bags beneath her eyes, and blush went beyond her cheeks to the top of her ears. She wore a pale yellow spaghetti-strap sundress and blue high-heeled shoes. One strap fell off her bony shoulder revealing the top of a small breast. She held a cigarette between her middle and third fingers. Her fingernails, lengthened with acrylic and polished bright red, reminded Trishita of posters for blood drives. Flossie coughed without covering her mouth.

"Hi, Ma." she said, realizing that Flossie was the same age as Arthur and may outlive him. The irony annoyed her.

"Well, well, Patricia McCabe." Flossie kept her erratic approach toward Trishita. Flossie stopped when she came within two feet of her, raised her chin to look, and said, "Happy birthday, Mija. Let me buy you a drink."

It wasn't much, but it was home.

"Come on, Ma," Trishita said three beers later. "Let's go get something to eat." The gang at the bar responded with slurred voices of protest.

"Lemme finish my cig first," her mother said, coughing.

"Sure." Trishita managed a smile and leaned on the bar. Weariness nipped at her elbows and heels. Boredom. Obligation.

The bartender flicked a rag across the shiny, cigarette-scarred wood. History in that wood, Trishita thought. So many dumb jokes, so many sad, angry stories. So few variations. Starving people making babies just to feel alive for five minutes.

"Hey, did you hear the one about the African witch doctor," a fat man asked, "that tried to perform a clitorectomy—"

"A what? Jeb, you're too drunk to pronounce anything with three syllables," the bartender said.

Five syllables, Trishita thought, disgusted.

"What's that?" a toothless woman asked.

"It's where they cut the girls' clits so they can't feel no pleasure fucking," a man in shadows said. "Keeps the women home."

"Sorta like circumcision," another said.

"Not at all, Roberto," Trishita said, grabbing her mother's arm. "Let's go, Ma."

"Like a vasectomy?" her mother asked.

"Just what you need, Flossie," the fat man said. "Keep you home barefoot and sterile."

"Coming, Ma?" Trishita asked. The misogyny infuriated her and the sheer stupidity of the conversation drove her nuts. She opened the door and braved the sunlight.

Trishita had to bend down to steady her mother as they walked. Flossie's narrow two-inch heels caught in all the crevices in the sidewalk. Trishita wondered how her mother managed to walk without someone along to lead her over every crack and grating.

She maneuvered Flossie up the three flights of stairs to their apartment by pushing her ahead and catching her when she fell back. By the third flight, Flossie had sobered up a little. She made the last flight without Trishita's help.

The door was unlocked. Trishita followed her mother into the dark, square room that smelled of dust and mildew. The window shades were down. Trishita flipped the light switch, but nothing happened.

"Bulb's burned out," Flossie said.

They felt their way between the old stuffed couch and a Laz-E-Boy into the dining room that Flossie now used as her bedroom. Beyond it was the kitchen. The light over the sink came on when Flossie pulled a chain.

"Go see your room, Mija. It's just as you left it—waiting for you to come home." Flossie pulled two hot dogs out of the refrigerator and put them in the microwave oven that Trishita had bought for her last Christmas.

"Shouldn't we cook those on the stove?" Trishita asked. "They'll curdle in there."

"Stove don't work. Go see your room."

"Okay, Ma." She opened the bathroom door and went through to her old bedroom on the other side. The air was stale. She opened the window and looked out at the fire escape that she never used for escape. It took her almost twenty-five years to develop the attitude that permitted escape.

The old, torn poster of Albert Einstein was still taped to the ceiling over her bed. Nothing had changed, all right. Even the sheets on the bed were ones she'd bought at a thrift shop nearby, along with the scratched maple, four-post bedstead.

The bell rang on the microwave oven, the signal that their feast was ready. Trishita opened the bathroom door to return to the kitchen and found her mother sitting on the toilet. She hurried through.

"Damn two-door bathrooms never let people have any privacy," Trishita said.

"Since when d'you need privacy?" Flossie asked.

Trishita ignored her.

Later, over shriveled hot dogs with French's mustard and beer, Flossie grinned. She still had all her own tobacco-stained teeth. "Goddam, it's good to see you, Mija. Happy birthday. If I'd known you was coming, I'da baked you a cake."

"Well, I didn't know myself."

"Robert was by to see me a couple of weeks ago," Flossie said. "Looks real good. Says he going to enlist as soon as he's eighteen."

"Robert Giraux? Our Robert?"

"Yep. He said to say Hi if I saw you."

Trishita felt her body soften. She hadn't thought about this little half-brother for years—not as often as she thought of Johnny. She used to sit with Robert on the fire escape outside her room and sing to him so he wouldn't hear some jerk slapping their mother.

Flossie finished her hot dog. "That was good. You gonna stay the night? Your bed's still clean. Nobody's slept in it."

"Don't know. What are your plans?" Trishita asked.

"You know me. I don't make plans."

"Ma, when you entertain men do you take precautions?" Trishita stared at her mother's tiny hands topped by long red fingernails.

"Like what? I don't mess around with pills. I don't get pregnant no more. Don't do drugs, neither." She looked up at Trishita sideways, her shoulders up to her neck.

"What I mean—" Trishita laughed. "Are you being careful so you don't get AIDS?"

"Oh, I won't ever get that disease," Flossie said with a snort.

"Why not?"

"Mary protects me."

"Mary?" Trishita asked. "You don't mean the Virgin Mary, do you?" Trishita reached into the refrigerator and handed Flossie another beer.

"Who else?" Flossie said. "I pray to her every day that I don't get AIDS and I don't. So, will you stay overnight? Maybe we can go to Cohen's for breakfast. I could sure go for some lox and eggs the way you used to make them when you worked there."

"I'll stay." Trishita nodded. Flossie hadn't changed, wouldn't change. The painless leech keeps the blood circulating.

In her old bedroom, she flashed on the scene between Flossie and Mrs. Mayberry when Trishita was sixteen.

*   *   *

Trishita had climbed out on the fire escape outside her window to read an essay by John Kenneth Galbraith. She finished it and then gazed at the gray November sky, dreaming of talking to someone—anyone—who had read it, or read anything else, for that matter. Her little brother Johnny was sound asleep on her bed just inside. She looked in at him and smiled. He made up for no friends who liked to read.

She heard what sounded like a knock on the front door of their flat and climbed inside. She made her way through the web of rooms to the kitchen sink where she stopped to see what her mother would do.

Flossie was still sober for so late in the day and opened the front door. Trishita's last schoolteacher, Mrs. Mayberry stood there wearing a grimace caused either by the climb up the stairs or by ill-disguised distaste

"Is Patricia McCabe in?" she asked Flossie.

Trishita grabbed the edge of the sink. Torn, she wanted to run to her teacher, hug her, and talk about books and ideas. And she wanted to hide in shame. Mrs. Mayberry had expected Trishita to breeze through high school in three years, and here Trishita was, at sixteen, a drop-out cocktail waitress.

"What are you selling?" she heard her mother ask.

"Selling? Nothing," Mrs. Mayberry said. "I was Patricia's teacher a few years ago. I couldn't find her name on the roll at any of the high schools in the city. Wondered if you'd moved away. Such a brilliant child."

"She's out," Flossie said.

Trishita felt her face burn, yet she didn't move.

"What school did she—"

"Not in school."

Trishita pulled herself away from the sink and headed toward the front door on leaden feet.

"She has to go to school." Mrs. Mayberry said. "I'll do anything—"

"She's pregnant," Flossie said. "I'm busy now." Flossie shut the door, but not before Trishita saw the startled expression on Mrs. Mayberry's face and the smirk on Flossie's.

She heard Mrs. Mayberry's familiar footsteps running down the last flight of stairs and screamed in rage.

"Don't hate me, Trishita." Flossie crumpled into a ball at the door. "I had to lie. She'd take you away from us." Tears streamed down Flossie's face.

Johnny came running into Trishita's arms, wailing. She swallowed her rage and rocked him.

*   *   *

Thinking about Johnny, she went to sleep. Light gushed into her room when the sun rose over the top of the neighboring buildings the next morning. She squinted and stretched. What should she fix for breakfast? The kids love waffles, but Jacquelyn—. She saw Albert Einstein's soft eyes looking down at her and remembered where she was.

Trishita groaned her way out of bed feeling heavy, headachy, and hung over. Cup of water in the microwave. Instant coffee on the dead stove, crystals of it spilling down the outside of the jar, crusted onto the coils. Loud snoring from the next room.

She opened the door and peeked in. The smell made her gag. Some drunk old geezer was in bed with her mother, breathing out foul fumes like an old diesel Mercedes.

Trishita slammed the door, grabbed her coffee cup and climbed out on the fire escape. A soft rain started falling from one dew-heavy cloud. She wanted it to rain hard, clean her off. When it stopped raining, she went inside and took a hot shower.

She climbed out to the fire escape again, dressed in yesterday's shift. More light rain made the corrugated metal glisten. A clap of thunder warned her that lightning could come in closer. She tensed—alert, angry, determined.

Flossie came to the window, coughing hard. "Trishita? What are you doing out there in the rain?"

"Thinking."

"About what?" Flossie asked.

"You gotta start charging those guys you sleep with." Trishita's eyes burned looking at her mother's swollen eyes and pillow-wrinkled little face.

"I ain't no whore." A gush of Flossie's bad-smelling breath came through the open window.

"Didn't say you were," Trishita said, "I'm talking rent, Ma, not sex. Hell, they're so drunk by the time they get to bed they can't raise a finger, let alone anything else." Trishita climbed back into the bedroom. "I just want you to collect rent money from them. I'm tired of paying it."

"You pay my rent?" Flossie asked, surprised

"Who else?"

"I thought the welfare lady—"

"They don't pay rent, Ma," Trishita said. "I want to maybe go to college someday. Need to start socking money away."

"College? That's right—I remember. I'll get a job. Right away." Flossie danced around the room. "I'll put you through college."

"Where you gonna get a job, Ma?"

"Hey, I know the restaurant biz inside and out. I'll be a waitress," Flossie said.

"Ma, no one will hire you around here. They know you."

"Just you wait, Mija." Flossie reached up and patted Trishita's cheek. I'll get a job in one of the swank houses uptown. This time I won't drink on the job." She twirled. "My baby's going to college. You got your daddy's brains, all right."

"Do you know where he is?"

"No. Once, years ago, I looked up McCabe in a Scottish phone book in the library, but there was a bunch of them and I wasn't sure what his first name was," Flossie said. "We just called him 'Red.' Never mind. I'll send you to college."

"Just cover your rent, okay? That'll help a lot."

"Sure, Mija. Let's go get some bagels and lox. Birthday breakfast." Flossie wiggled her hips. "Got any cash on you?"

"Ma," Trishita screamed, "this eagle is wrung dry. I quit. You've got to get money on your own for a change."

Flossie moved in and stood almost toe-to-toe. She tilted back her head and looked up, her eyes wet with tears. Church bells began ringing, calling the faithful to come confess their sins. Flossie blocked her ears.

"I try. But you are my strength, Mija," Flossie said. "Without you, I die a tortuous death before I am fifty years old."

Trishita had heard this speech before. It carried the Yiddish lilt Flossie picked up from hanging around the delicatessen where Trishita had worked. It was phony, she knew, but it always worked. Trishita pulled two twenties out of her purse and handed them to her mother. "Here, you take us out to breakfast."

"Thanks, Dear." Flossie stuffed the bills into her bra. "We'll be careful what we order, okay?"

CHAPTER TWELVE

"Trishita, you're not paying attention," Ethan hollered at her. "You have to move the gearshift all the way to the right and then pull down. You're in fourth, not reverse."

"You're right." She lifted her slippery palm off the shift and looked over at Ethan. "I'm not paying attention. Guess I had too much to drink last night."

"You? Where were you?"

"At a bar in Worcester. Ran into some old friends."

"Okay." He looked doubtful. "Wanna try reverse again?"

"Sure." This time she got the hang of it. Ethan cheered and made her drive back and forth on that bumpy dirt road fifteen times before he spread out an old bedspread at the base of an oak tree and said, "Now, you teach me."

Trishita felt robbed. By Arthur. He'd stripped her of her cynicism, her calculated plans, her revenge against short people who have it all. She not only wanted more sex with him, she wanted to give all she had to him. Affection she couldn't afford, especially with Arthur. Teaching Ethan how to make love was easy enough, but as people say, quoting Nixon, "It would be wrong." Yet, she'd made a deal. It would be wrong to renege on the deal. *Too late for second thoughts.* She pulled off her sweat-stained shift.

She stretched out naked on the bedspread, inhaled the scent of rich soil underneath, and taught Ethan how to save his ching for greater duration. Then she showed him how to do everything Arthur had done two days ago. He was, as they used to say about her, a quick study.

*   *   *

Ethan dropped her off at Chet's Diner on the highway. She had a piece of blueberry pie and a cup of coffee while she read about Japanese management techniques and the life-long loyalty of Japanese employees. Then she walked the two miles to the Hydes' house, planning her own management techniques.

The sun had just set when she unlocked the front door. Someone, she supposed Jacquelyn, was in the den watching Masterpiece Theater.

Sylvia came running down the stairs and threw her arms around Trishita.

"Shh. Come with me." Sylvia put her fingers to her lips and beckoned toward the kitchen. Trishita followed by way of the den. She waved at Jacquelyn to let her know she was home. Ethan was sound asleep on the couch. Poor baby wore himself out. Teaching and learning was hard work. Arthur had his back to her. She was glad to avoid his eyes.

In the kitchen, Sylvia was busy making two root beer floats. After blueberry pie, a float lost much of its appeal, but Trishita sipped hers and listened.

"Ma and Dad had a big fight over you tonight."

"Oh? Who won?" Trishita chewed on her straw, willing down the flares she felt rushing to her face.

"No one ever wins a fight in a family. Don't you know that?" Sylvia said with pride lining her voice.

"You're right. I forgot," Trishita said. "Well, then, did I lose?"

"Naw." Sylvia grinned through ice cream dabbled braces. "Actually, the fight was over what we'd have to eat for supper and who would get it together. Dad wondered why you couldn't be here to feed us 'in the manner to which we had become accustomed.' Ma went on and on about self-reliance and I said I was getting hungry. I think I yelled that I'd do the meal if they'd let me."

"Did shouting at them work?" Trishita asked.

"No. Dad was too busy yelling at Ma about not letting you do what you were hired to do and Ma was too busy explaining her position to notice anything I yelled."

"Time for you to learn the art of soft-speak."

"Hunh?" Sylvia asked and then said, "Anyway, in all that mess, Ethan came home with four hamburgers from Chet's diner, ice cream, and root beer. Things settled down then." She nodded toward Trishita's book on the table. "What're you reading now?"

"Library book on Japanese management techniques."

"Jeez, you read weird stuff," Sylvia said. "How come?"

"I'm hungry, sweetheart. Hungry for information. Your mother's right about self-reliance. I have no one to rely on except myself, so I read weird stuff."

"You can always rely on me," Sylvia said.

Trishita's eyes stung. If she weren't careful, she'd not only lose her cynicism, she'd lose her job.

"Thanks, Sylvia. I believe you, although I know there will be times when I can't rely on you, times when you'll be disappointed in me. But on the whole, you and I will be friends for life."

"Swear to God?" Sylvia asked, eyes shining.

"I swear to God. When I was your age I had a friend. An old man. Janitor at Clark University. He used to sneak me into the classrooms on weekends. I wandered around while he worked, sat in the front row center of each classroom, smelled the chalk dust. He used to say he kept good thoughts about me even if I was a tall drink of water."

"What happened? Is he still your friend?"

"He's dead. When I first met him he was on the wagon. Then one day when I was fifteen he started drinking again and making passes at me. I ran away from him. Let him down, I suppose he thought. One night when he was real drunk, he fell into Lake Quinsigamond and drowned. As it turned out, he couldn't rely on me, though I'd told him he could."

Arthur pushed through the swinging door from the dining room. His eyes were mother-of-pearl-shiny. Trishita greeted him, feigning a calm she didn't feel.

"Hi, Arthur," she said. "You been snooping on us?"

"Sure. Beats Masterpiece Theater," he said, sounding just like Ethan.

"Well. I'm off now. Goodnight." Everything was getting too lovey-dovey for comfort. Trishita inhaled one more swallow of root beer, mumbled, and made a quick exit through Arthur's office to her room. She wondered if the shining son and the adoring father would bump into each other in the pantry. She felt a sudden nostalgia for the simplicity of her life before she discovered that hole in the wall. The sweetest feeling, though, came from her relief that she'd once again escaped Flossies clutches. "Put me through college," she said under her breath. "What a joke."

A timid knock heralded Jacquelyn. Trishita opened the door and smiled down at Mrs. Hyde who backed into Arthur's office a couple of steps.

"Sorry to bother you, Trish, but I just wanted to remind you that my party is this coming Saturday. I'd appreciate it if you could stay here next weekend. That is, if it's okay with you."

"I'd be glad to," Trishita said, "Will you help me decide what—"

"Oh, you're much better at choosing the right food—"

"—to wear?" Trishita asked.

"Ah. Certainly. Goodnight, dear. By the way, did you have a nice weekend?" Jacquelyn asked.

"It was okay. Goodnight." She closed the door. Later, she drifted off to sleep with the smell of chalk dust permeating her dreams.

*   *   *

Trishita felt feisty in her white nautical pantsuit and seaman's cap clipped to her tangled hair. When Jacquelyn first gave her the outfit, she spent a good ten minutes looking at herself in the mirror, trying to see herself from a stranger's perspective. When she sat down, she could appreciate her beauty. Standing, she was formidable. She couldn't do her job from a wheelchair, though the idea amused her.

Each time the doorbell rang, she answered it with an extra wide opening of the door. She welcomed in the guests, asked their names, and then led them to the living room where she announced them to the Hyde family. The Hydes sat or stood arranged in front of the fireplace. This procedure had been Trishita's idea. She called it her Masterpiece Theater mock. Jacquelyn loved it; Sylvia detested it. Ethan hammed it up and Arthur looked like he was trying to see the humor in it.

Trishita not only introduced the guests, she played bartender, mixing drinks with the flair she'd learned in her barmaid days. In addition, she served exotic tidbits she'd been preparing all week: gorgonzola stuffed artichoke hearts, marinated mushrooms, smoked salmon and brie mini pizzas. As she observed this staid, middle-aged group in their tailored outfits, she had the feeling that she was knocking their silk socks off.

When Superintendent Ballman arrived wearing a gray worsted suit, the party was well into its anticipatory set. Trishita thought as she pulled the strings, that some people liked the limelight, others liked to hide out alone or with one another, while a few, like her, wanted to control events from the sidelines, secretly. She loved operating from the fringes, and there was no way she could explain that to Sylvia.

"Superintendent and Mrs. Ballman," she announced, aware that he was an inch taller than she was and unable to take his eyes off her for more than thirty seconds. Mrs. Ballman was short and round with a Barbara Bush hairdo.

Ballman, road map eyes, jelly-like jowls, potbelly and all, followed Trishita when she went into the kitchen to replenish the food trays. She wondered if guys like him ever saw what mirrors reflected. They often acted as if they were still their mothers' hot potatoes when they were really their wives' okra. With a momentary twinge of guilt, she wondered if anyone there saw her as Worcester garbage recycled into white plastic.

"My, you are an eyeful," Ballman said.

She just nodded and went about her business.

"Do you need some help?" He closed in on her by the sink, brushed her hip.

"No, thanks." She swiveled away, picked up a tray of stuffed grape leaves and headed toward the door.

"Trishita. Nice." He blocked her exit with his bulk. "Where did you get that nickname?"

"From Patricia. That's my name."

"I get the Trish part. Who gave you the ita suffix?"

"My mother." Trishita feigned a civility she didn't feel. "It's a Spanish diminutive. I was little once."

"Spanish? Is your mother Puerto Rican?"

"No. She lives in a Rican neighborhood, but she's French Canadian."

"Ah, that's where you get your brown eyes and lovely complexion. Unusual on a redhead."

"Right." She swerved around him like a quarterback, leaving him jumping back to get out of the way of the swinging door.

Throughout the evening Ballman followed her into the kitchen each time she went in, copping feels at every opportunity. One time he goosed her. She shot him a dirty look. He just grinned. She hadn't been goosed since women started goosing back. This guy was old fashioned and a definite pain.

At seven-fifteen she prepared two pots of coffee, one decaffeinated, and checked the timing on the final baking of the baklava. It was time to shut down on the booze so they could drive home okay. Ballman appeared, and in a ministerial voice, said, "Let me help you, my dear."

"Please do." She smiled at him. "Go ask Mr. Hyde if he can come in here a minute."

"I can do anything he can do," Ballman said.

"Better? Afraid not in this case. I need some signs I left on Ethan's printer."

Trishita remembered reading in a book on effective management that you can get people to do what you want if you give them a reason, no matter how illogical the reason. Ballman said he'd send Ethan after the signs.

"Please don't, Sir," she said. "You see, Ethan needs to learn how to fit into an adult social scene. He's doing so well it would be a shame to disturb him."

"Your hair smells as good as it looks and feels." Ballman held a handful of her hair and sniffed it. I'll go get Arthur for you." He didn't move or let go of her hair.

"I need those signs." Trishita looked him straight in his bloodshot eyes.

"What for? What's on them?"

"Caff and de-caff." She gave her head a quick twist. Her sailor's cap fell off.

"Clever," he said as he released his hold on her hair and headed out.

Arthur came in and picked up her cap.

"You okay, Trish?" he asked.

"Sure," she lied. She wanted to drop to her knees so she'd be short enough to ask him to fence her in, protect her from the likes of Ballman. "Will you get the coffee signs? They're on Ethan's printer. I can't leave the baklava right now."

"I'll be right back." He studied her, touched her hand.

After he left, she bent over at the waist to turn the two trays of baklava in the lower oven. As she was re-arranging the trays, she felt a worsted covered dick rubbing against her ass. She let him rub for a few seconds, then, in one swift move, grabbed a fistful of worsted and his balls, and squeezed hard. Ballman doubled over with a groan.

"Trishita," Jacquelyn said from the doorway, "we're just about ready for coff—my God, what happened to Jonathan?"

"He dropped a stuffed grape leaf and bent over to pick it up. I think his back went out."

"Oh dear. Go get Mrs. Ballman. Jonathan, let me help you to a couch."

"No," he gasped. "I'll be okay soon."

"Here," Jacquelyn said. "Lean on me."

Arthur returned with the signs. He took in the scene with a glance and shot Trishita a questioning look. She shrugged and left the kitchen.

Mrs. Ballman was talking about her clown collection. Trishita had to be quite forceful to get her attention. Also, it took a while to get her out of the chair. A lot of good she'll do her jerk of a husband, Trishita thought.

She got Mrs. Ballman into the crowded kitchen just in time to rescue the baklava. Only those on the edge burned.

Ballman straightened his back. Trishita gave him a drink of water and Jacquelyn helped him into the living room. Arthur held Mrs. Ballman's arm and steered her in behind them.

Sylvia looked morose sitting on the edge of the raised hearth. Trishita beckoned her and she jumped up so fast she knocked over a man's glass. Luckily it was empty. Trishita picked it up.

"Let's get him a fresh drink," she said to Sylvia Scotch?" she asked the guest.

He nodded and continued his conversation with Ethan.

"Thanks for the rescue," Sylvia said in the kitchen. "What a drag this is. But they all keep raving about you."

"Boring," Trishita said in sympathy. "Means the party is a big success."

"Hunh?"

"Here, help me serve the coffee."

As the party ended, Trishita handed guests their summer wraps. Ballman kept his distance.

"This was such a wonderful party," Mrs. Ballman said to Jacquelyn, "thanks to your marvelous maid. I wonder, do you loan her out? Could we hire her to do a soirée for us sometime?"

"You'll have to ask her."

Mrs. Ballman then looked up at Trishita's smiling face. "What do you say? Would you be available Trish?"

"Sure, but only on weekends."

"We'll be in touch, won't we, dear?" she asked her husband. He was slipping his bulk out the door and didn't respond.

"Wasn't that a wonderful party?" You were superb, all of you." Jacquelyn said, hugging Arthur and Ethan after the last guest left. They were standing in the front hall. Sylvia leaned on the banister.

"I wasn't," she said.

"You were fine, dear," Jacquelyn said. "Just a little clumsy, that's all."

"You were pretty good yourself, Jackie." Arthur put his arm around Jacquelyn. "I'm glad you had a good time."

"Don't forget our star maid," Ethan said. He shot a lusty look at Trishita.

Trishita saw Sylvia studying Ethan and realized she needed to show Ethan how to disguise his eyes. Arthur, too, looked at her with desire, but only when they were alone.

"We couldn't forget Trish." Jacquelyn leaned her head on Arthur's shoulder and looked up at Trishita. "Everyone wanted to hire you."

"Might be a pretty good business for you, Trish," Arthur said with disguised eyes.

"Maybe," she answered, but she knew she'd hate it.

"No, no," Sylvia cried, running up the stairs. "Trishita's going to college." Her words seemed to echo as her figure multiplied in the mirrored walls of the foyer.

The others looked at Trishita in surprise.

"Sylvia dreams for me." She shrugged.

Trishita lay down for the night, exhausted yet exhilarated. She wondered how educated people decided what to do in their lives.

How did they get around their passions? Their obligations? Their guilt? Their mothers?

Her career plans were tumbling down around her like buildings in an eight-point earthquake, exacerbated by her passions. The more she felt that tender, maternal love for Sylvia, the more she hated Jacquelyn Hyde. But, she didn't hate her enough to diddle with Arthur, much as she wanted to. Dangerous territory.

CHAPTER THIRTEEN

Jacquelyn held her mother's old soft beige lace against her cheek. It smelled of Woolworth's and its hints of popcorn and candy. Abby had given it to her when Sylvia was born and told her to dress her in lace.

"Don't ever let Sylvia know poverty," Abby had said, "for it's especially ugly for children. I know too well."

She wished she could feel grateful toward Abby, or at least understanding. All she felt was bitter towards her mother and she did not know why. Battles with Abby over her father's collection of trombones had ended many years ago. She really had no current reason to feel bitter. She hoped Sylvia, at least, would like the lace on the collar of her graduation dress.

The bark of a dog startled her and she dropped the lace. There was just too much going on this time of year.

Arthur rushed into their bedroom and shut the windows on the east side.

"It's raining in, Jackie," he said. "Didn't you hear the storm?"

"No. I was—I don't know."

A sudden flash of lightning, followed by a quick clap of thunder, made her jump again. Arthur came over to her and put his hand on her shoulder.

"You okay?" he asked.

"Just jumpy." She smiled at him. "I need to finish Sylvia's dress today because I have back to back meetings in the morning and two high school graduation ceremonies tomorrow afternoon."

"I'll be in my office if you need me." He patted her shoulder. "I love you, Jackie." He disappeared down the stairs.

"Thanks, Hon," she said after he'd gone. Why didn't she believe him? When he lost his business, she expected him to moan and carry on about it, but he'd been almost manic instead. Running errands for everyone. Helping Ethan teach Trishita how to drive. Whistling—too much.

Arthur was the least of her problems, now, though. First came Sylvia and her damn collection of ceramic cows, second came her own parents' impending visit. They had called from Delaware and would arrive far too soon. Third, the new moon would coincide with their visit. Lightning flashed and its thunder filled the house, shaking the very eaves. Jonathan Edwards' sermon, "Sinners in the Hands of an Angry God," came to mind.

She finished sewing the lace along the edge of the Peter Pan collar. The dress was lovely, if she did say so herself. One by one, she bit off the loose threads and hung the dress on a hanger. She hoped it was long enough. Sylvia was getting to be so tall.

The rain let up. Sunlight poured in at a slant. Five o'clock already. She heard a strange male voice, laughing. It boomed from the kitchen. She went down to see who could generate that much noise. Trishita was at the sink chopping vegetables, wearing the white pantsuit Jacquelyn had made for her. Sylvia, Ethan, Arthur and a young man with a crew cut and a full, dark brown beard sat at the kitchen table. The man stood when Jacquelyn entered.

"Hi, Mrs. Hyde," he said. "Remember me? Mickey Careggio." He held out his hand.

"Oh, yes." Jacquelyn shook hands with him. Her movements felt stiff. "I didn't recognize you with that beard. Good to see you. You've been gone quite a while, haven't you?" She remembered that his parents divorced and moved out of town the year Mickey graduated. They kept their old fifteen-room house beside the river and didn't even bother to rent it out, a sore spot with the townspeople who called it a "terrible waste."

As the sun disappeared again and the gathering clouds darkened the room, Trishita ran the garbage disposal. Mickey waited to respond to Jacquelyn, but watched her striking maid.

"I've been traveling for the past two years—getting a hard knocks education," he said to Jacquelyn after Trishita turned off the disposal. "Now I'm ready for U. Mass. This summer I'm recruiting for a local baseball team. That's why I'm here today." He nodded toward Ethan who couldn't stop grinning. "We used to call your son here, 'Little Hyde-bound,' but he's loosened up a lot. I've been watching some of the high school kids play. He's the best."

"Well, that's impressive." Jacquelyn sat beside Sylvia on the chair Arthur vacated for her.

"It's terrific, Ma," Sylvia said. She walked a ceramic cow across the end of the table. "He'll be playing with pros."

"Not exactly," Mickey said stifling his explosive laugh with the back of his hand.

"Mickey's staying all by himself in his folks' house," Ethan said. "Can he stay for dinner? I told him Trishita got us to eat pasta instead of spaghetti and how—"

"Sure," Jacquelyn said. "You're welcome, Mickey." She turned and asked, "Trish, okay with you?"

"Fine with me." Trishita said without looking up from her chopping. "We have more than enough to go around." Lightning flashed again and the white of Trishita's pantsuit reflecting the sudden light made Jacquelyn blink. She wished she'd made the suit out of beige or blue instead.

"Mickey's got a super collection of beer bottles from all over the world," Ethan said when the thunder subsided. "In his front parlor. You oughtta see it, Ma."

"That's nice." Jacquelyn's stomach dropped as if she were riding the down side of a roller coaster hill. She'd been in his folks' old yellow farmhouse several times and remembered most of the fifteen rooms.

"Well, you know how it is, Mrs. Hyde. You gotta try the beer in every country just to be polite. I started sending the empties home for the fun of it. In two years you can collect a bunch of bottles."

"I imagine so," Jacquelyn said.

"At least you have enough room for them in that house," Arthur said, standing behind Jacquelyn with his hands on her shoulders. "I'm running out of space here to hang my collection of slide rules."

"Yeah," Sylvia blurted, "and Harold Johnson told me he found another one for you. He's bringing it over today, I think."

"Good," Arthur said. "He's my favorite nerd."

Jacquelyn thought she saw Trishita smiling. Gave her a chill.

"It's been a blast," Mickey said, popping his knuckles, "coming home to so many bottles, and then setting them up. I put up narrow shelves on three walls of the old parlor that overlooks the river, sorted the bottles by country. It's like reading a diary of my travels, you know. The best ones came from Austria and Sri Lanka."

"How interesting," Jacquelyn said as carefully as possible. She wanted to strangle him. Lightning flashed, followed too soon by a huge clap of thunder, then a downpour.

Underneath all that noise Jacquelyn heard a timid knock on the door leading to the side yard. She got out of her chair and opened the door. There stood a gangly kid—all legs, braces, glasses and pimples—dripping wet. She recoiled in horror—something about his eyes. But, when she looked at him again she was confused by her reaction to him.

"I brought this over for Mr. Hyde." The boy held up a mahogany slide rule. His voice squeaked, obviously in the throes of change.

"Come on in, Harold, Arthur said. "Hey, thanks, that's a beauty." To Jacquelyn he said, "Honey, do you know Harold Johnson, Sylvia's friend?"

"Not another slide rule, Arthur," Jacquelyn said, then called over to Sylvia, "Get a towel, Dear. He's soaking wet."

Sylvia toppled her chair when she stood. Jacquelyn felt a headache coming on, but she finally managed to greet Harold.

"I can't stay," the boy croaked. He reached around Jacquelyn and handed Arthur the slide rule. "Here you are, Sir. It was my grandfather's." Then he turned and disappeared out the door.

Jacquelyn peered after him, worried. There was something wrong with that boy. She decided to ask Ethan about him, but looking back inside, she saw Ethan and Trishita laughing so hard they were both red in the face. A slow rage crawled up her torso.

Sylvia had returned with one of Jacquelyn's best towels.

"Not that one," Jacquelyn shouted in a nasal voice that she deplored. "How can you be so stupid!"

"S'okay Jackie," Arthur said.

Sylvia ran upstairs crying, leaving the towel on the table with everyone staring at it.

"She's only a little kid," Arthur said softly.

"She'll be all right." Jacquelyn frowned at him. But, she regretted being so harsh with Sylvia.

Mickey and Ethan kept staring at the towel. Mickey popped his knuckles.

"If you'll excuse me," Jacquelyn said, "I'll go take a rest before dinner." She picked up the towel, folded it, and made as graceful an exit as possible under the circumstances.

*   *   *

"When will Grandpa and Grandma Nestrom get here?" Sylvia asked. She leaned over and peered down into the foyer where sunlight danced from mirror to mirror. Jacquelyn was on her knees marking the hem on Sylvia's graduation dress. They were in Jacquelyn's bedroom near the open doorway.

"Hold still, Sylvia." Jacquelyn said. "I'll never get your hem straight if you don't stand still."

"Okay . . . . Well, when will they get here?"

"Any minute." Jacquelyn had some pins in her mouth and spoke around them.

"That's beautiful," Trishita said as she came up the stairs carrying a basket of laundry. She tilted her head and studied Sylvia. "You'll be the best dressed one in your class."

"Thank you, Trish," Jacquelyn answered. Sylvia twisted around, grinning. "Hold still, young lady."

"Mrs. Hyde," Trishita said and set the basket on the top step. "I was wondering if it would be okay with you if I went to Sylvia's graduation."

"Coo-ool!" Sylvia sang out.

Jacquelyn finished pinning the hem and stood, eye-level with Trishita still standing on the stairs.

"I'm sure that would be all right," Jacquelyn said, "except my parents will be going, too, and we won't have enough room in the car—"

"Then take two cars," Sylvia said, rather sarcastically, Jacquelyn thought.

"I'm sure we can work something out," Jacquelyn said. Damn Trishita. She would ask in front of Sylvia. The crass beeping of a horn announced the arrival of her parents. It felt like a ball-peen hammer on the top of Jacquelyn's head. "Nothing ever changes," she said to herself as Trishita and Sylvia rushed down the stairs with girlish glee. When Sylvia has her own home, will she dread our visits?

Jacquelyn leaned on the banister at the top of the stairs and watched her father come in the front door. Tall, thin, and stooped, he walked on the balls of his feet as if the flagstone flooring were hot coals. He wore loud plaid shorts and a striped blue and white T-shirt that stretched across his small potbelly. He glanced up at her and waved.

"Hi, Dad. How are you?" Jacquelyn moved down the stairs slowly, wishing she had wanted to rush into his arms.

"Pretty spry for seventy-five," he replied. The age changed each year but the phrase varied in no other way.

Her mother came through the door with Sylvia, who towered over the little white-haired lady with the pretty face and awful voice. Feeling robotic, Jacquelyn hugged and kissed her father and then her mother. Trishita came in carrying three suitcases. Jacquelyn gestured toward her.

"This is our housekeeper, Trish McCabe, and these are my parents," she said to Trishita, "Bill and Abby Nestrom." Jacquelyn wished she'd remembered to say Mr. and Mrs. Nestrom. Sometimes having a maid was more trouble than not.

"Sylvia introduced us outside," her mother said, rolling her eyes at Jacquelyn.

"Yes, yes, indeed," her father said. "Imagine that. A maid. Tall as a tree, but mighty pretty. Where's Arthur?"

Jacquelyn realized she had no idea where Arthur was. "He's around somewhere."

"And Ethan?"

"Playing semi-pro baseball," Sylvia said, pride ringing her voice.

"I used to play pro ball myself," Nestrom said, patting his belly. "Third base. One time down in Hartford just before the war we got up a game against—"

"Now, Bill, don't start in on one of your stories," Abby said. Her mother's words seemed normal enough but her voice reminded Jacquelyn of the feel of a Styrofoam cup.

"Come upstairs, Grandpa," Sylvia said. "Let's put your suitcases in Ethan's room and get you settled." She took two suitcases and headed up the stairs. "Trishita has a yummy menu planned for tonight—"

"Where will Ethan sleep?" Abby asked.

"In the den," Jacquelyn answered. "He doesn't mind."

"I used to sleep in my tree house when the old folks came to visit," Bill said. "One time there was this bat in the tree house and I scared it right into the house—"

"This way, Dad," Jacquelyn said, leading him up the stairs.

Bill put his hand on the banister and started up. "We be-bopped all over New York City last night. Heard some pretty good horns, too. Not a one could hold a candle to Tommy Dorsey, though." He put his hand on the railing and pranced up a few stairs. Jacquelyn couldn't fathom his rhythm.

"Careful, Bill," Abby called.

"When I was in gay Paree, I heard a trombone outside the Gare d'Orleans that grabbed me by the short hairs—"

"Get going, Bill," Abby said. "We need to clean up for dinner. Sylvia says Trishita's a marvelous cook."

He's harmless, Jacquelyn thought, just ego-starved. Why do I want to bury him in sand, or gag him? Why can't I be tolerant?

Abby pulled herself up the stairs fast. When she came abreast of Jacquelyn at the top, she leaned against her and panted.

Jacquelyn waited, softening.

"Sylvia tells me Arthur lost his business," Abby said in a harsh whisper. "How can you afford a maid?"

"Oh, Ma, I make enough to cover all our expenses. Don't worry," Jacquelyn said. How had Sylvia managed to tell them so much in such a short time?

"But doesn't that do something to Arthur? How can he stand it?"

"I don't know." Jacquelyn looked straight at her mother and said, "Why don't you ask him?"

Sylvia and her grandfather came toward them from Ethan's bedroom. He was telling her some long-winded story about Billy's big rig. Jacquelyn knew her folks visited his name on the wall in Washington D.C. every fall. Jacquelyn had seen it just once.

"Not now, Bill." Abby closed in on him and put her fingers against his lips.

"But, Grandma, this is interesting. Ma never talks about him." Sylvia's brown eyes widened as she looked from one face to the next.

"I have no objection to talking about him," Jacquelyn lied. "He did what he had to do." How she had begged Billy to go to Canada.

"You're damn tooting," Bill said. "Come with me, Sylvia. I'll tell you all about your uncle. He was a hero of the first order."

Jacquelyn watched the bald spot on the top of his head go down the stairs like a bouncing ball. She remembered her brother in the one striking scene that always came to mind when his name was mentioned. Billy was twenty-one at the time, she sixteen. He had dropped by for his usual prodding. It was a miserably cold afternoon, dark and wet with half snow, half rain pouring down. She and Billy were in the kitchen. They'd finished her trig homework and were playing Gin rummy, wearing gloves to keep their fingers warm enough to shuffle the cards. The side door opened. Their father's breath came through the doorway in small clouds. He followed, cradling a long black case as if it were a newborn baby.

Billy, normally mild mannered, threw the cards on the floor and shouted, "Not another God damn trombone! There's no heat in this dump, yet you keep filling it with horns and you can't even play them worth a damn."

She'd forgotten her father's response. Certainly Billy's diatribe had had no lasting effect. Bill Sr. continued to buy trombones. But Jacquelyn knew every word and inflection of Billy's outburst by heart. She made it into a mantra of sorts.

Later, when they gave Billy a full military funeral, Jacquelyn, dry-eyed, promised him at the gravesite that she would someday destroy those trombones. How silly, sad, and young she'd been. Luckily she'd outgrown that promise. Trombones were out of her life and no longer a problem. Now they were just ridiculous. She pictured them hanging on every wall and from the ceiling in every room of her parents' Florida condo—even the bathroom.

She helped her mother unpack a few things, and then headed downstairs with her. Arthur and Ethan burst in through the front entrance. Their faces were flushed and dripping with sweat. They greeted Jacquelyn's parents with far more warmth than she could muster, and headed for the showers. Their meteor like appearances brightened the house. She breathed all the way in, then out, now aware of this simple, vital function. This wasn't going to be as bad as she feared. And dinner would appear on the table as usual, miraculous and beautiful. In that sense, Trish was worth her height in gold.

*   *   *

The morning of Sylvia's graduation ceremony Trishita served sour cream waffles with homemade blueberry sauce just sweetened—sweet enough for Bill Nestrom, yet subtle enough for Jacquelyn. Sylvia plopped into her chair at the dining room table. She carried a pink ceramic cow shaped to look asleep when placed on a shelf.

"Look what Trishita gave me for graduation," Sylvia said." She was wearing her new beige dress with the lace collar. Her brushed brown hair had a nice sheen.

"You look lovely, Sylvia." Jacquelyn said, ignoring the cow.

"Thanks. Dad brushed my hair."

"Here's a present from me." Ethan said to Sylvia when he came in from the kitchen, red in the face. Jacquelyn wondered why.

"Thanks Ethan." Sylvia opened the box and pulled out a black and white coffee mug on three cow legs with an udder on its base. "Neato, Ethan," Sylvia said with a squeak.

Arthur arrived from the side yard carrying a hair-brush. Jacquelyn smiled at him. Maybe, she thought, she could make it through the family scene today.

"Be careful you don't spill blueberry sauce on your dress," she said to Sylvia, Abby tied a napkin around Sylvia's neck as Trishita served regular coffee to Arthur, Bill, and Abby and gave Jacquelyn a small cup of espresso.

"What are you drinking, my wee one?" Bill asked, raising his eyebrows.

"She likes coffee you can eat with a fork," Arthur said, grinning.

Jacquelyn wondered how he managed to stay in such a good mood all the time. He wasn't angry or even disappointed at the failure of his business. Didn't even brood. She smoothed the frown out of her forehead with her fingertips.

"I remember coffee like that in North Africa," Bill said to Ethan. "We were out in the middle of the frigging desert when this A-rab shows up selling stuff so thick—"

"Now, Bill, don't get started," Abby said. "These waffles are wonderful."

"Sylvia, let's you and me go for a walk after breakfast," Bill said. "There won't be so many interruptions."

"Sorry, Dad," Jacquelyn said. "I need to take Sylvia shopping for shoes before graduation.

"Aw, Ma, I don't need shoes. These are fine." She lifted one leg and showed her flat sandal-shod foot.

"You can't wear those with that dress, Honey. We'll get you some nice pumps."

"I don't want to wear high heels to graduation."

"We'll get low heeled ones, of course." Jacquelyn wanted to stamp her own heels.

Trishita came in with another platter of waffles. Sylvia looked up at her, eyes begging. Trishita stopped still and cocked her head.

"I <u>won't</u> wear heels of any kind." Sylvia said, turning to Jacquelyn. "I want to wear these." She pointed to her feet.

"Be reasonable, dear," Jacquelyn said. "You can't wear sandals with that dress."

"You be reasonable! I'm too tall. I don't want to stand on stage looking like a fucking bean pole."

"Sylvia! You sound like a fishwife." Jacquelyn stood. "Go to your room this instant."

Sylvia darted out, knocking over her chair in the process. Ethan and Trishita reached to pick it up at the same time.

"My, my," Abby said. "Jacquelyn, she's just nervous. This is a big day for her."

"Don't be too hard on her," Bill said. "Kids hear that kind of language every day now. Why I remember when only grown men in the service said that word." He laughed. "In fact, we said it so much we used to joke about coming home on leave and asking our mothers to pass the you-know-what-ing butter."

"I'll go to her." Arthur stood. "She doesn't need new shoes, Jackie."

Jacquelyn could feel the rage in her belly. Then, when she saw the smirk on Trishita's face, she exploded.

"How can I teach her anything with all of you subverting me. You and your damn collections. You're all against me. Who the hell pays the bills around here?" She ran out of the room, hot tears blinding her. They all hated her and loved Trishita. She slammed her bedroom door behind her.

"Don't bother, Arthur," she said without opening her eyes when Arthur came in. "I'll be okay as soon as I fire Trishita. I'll give her notice today. She can look for another job while we're on vacation. I'm sure Ballman would love to hire her."

Arthur left as quietly as he came in.

CHAPTER FOURTEEN

Jacquelyn still felt at odds with her handling of her conflict with Sylvia when they were ready to leave for the graduation ceremony. She had conceded to Sylvia's wishes and they had made up. Sylvia rode to the ceremony wearing her sandals in Bill's car with Trishita. Jacquelyn and Arthur took Abby and Ethan in the BMW. They all had ice cream at the malt shop afterwards. Jacquelyn and Arthur gave Sylvia her own Macintosh PC and printer without expecting as much enthusiasm for the gift as Sylvia expressed.

Jacquelyn couldn't find the right time to speak to Trishita, but she was determined to let her go. She realized that her headache was gone when she went to bed and put on her earphones. Arthur lay like a board beside her. When she touched him, he didn't move. She removed her earphones and studied him. He was staring at the ceiling.

"What's wrong, Arthur?"

"Nothing," he said with a small smile. "I'm just thinking, that's all."

"About what?"

"The business."

"What <u>do</u> you think about it?" she asked.

"That it's just as well it went belly up," he said. "I'll start job hunting when we get back from the Cape."

"Good. Okay, goodnight, Darling. All's well that ends well."

His breathing deepened, rippled. Jacquelyn was amazed at how fast he fell asleep, and wondered how she felt about him. Struggling to recall her early feelings for Arthur, she thought about their meeting in the student union in Amherst—on the empty side of the room.

She remembered how Arthur lived in his head, barely aware of anything beyond the immediate application of mathematical theory. This suited Jacquelyn. They courted for five years as Eisenhower-era lovers during the Nixon and Ford years. Finally, in 1979, they married. By then Jacquelyn was well on her way to a doctorate from Boston University and Arthur was designing mainframe computers.

*   *   *

The wedding ceremony fulfilled her dreams. She spent a full year planning every detail. Six of her sorority sisters agreed to be bridesmaids and wear dresses of six different colors. Jacquelyn made each of their dresses. They promised to arrange themselves throughout the day of the wedding in Jacquelyn's prescribed color order.

The reception was held at the Tatnuck Country Club. Jacquelyn had chosen the table flowers to match the colors in the bridesmaids' dresses, and had seen to it that they were placed around the clubhouse in the same color order. She insisted that mauve be adjacent to peach and a darker shade of peach to lime green although no one could understand why. She knew what was most effective.

The official photograph session lasted far too long. After the guests had traversed the line and kissed the bride, Arthur lifted the train of Jacquelyn's pearl-studded white satin gown and escorted her onto the dance floor. Jacquelyn glowed. The orchestra played a waltz which Arthur, leaden-footed, gamely endured.

Next the ushers, on cue, brought the bridesmaids onto the dance floor.

"There's something strangely familiar about those bridesmaids. Jacquelyn heard her father say to Uncle Roger. "And they sure are pretty!"

"Right so, brother. They're all dolled up." Uncle Roger's explosive laughter echoed throughout the club room. Jacquelyn's stomach cramped.

Then the photographer, a skinny young man with cold hands, interrupted the dance to whisper to Jacquelyn that he had to re-take the wedding party.

"I'm so sorry," he said, "but I'm afraid the flash didn't work on one of my cameras. I don't want to take any chances."

Abby Nestrom hastily gathered the members of the wedding party for retakes. The photographer finished shooting the group in a hurry and said, "Wonderful. I'm out of film now, but I have these for sure. Come, beautiful bride, take a look at this presentation."

When Jacquelyn stepped out of the line-up and faced it, she saw that two of her bridesmaids were out of order. They'd destroyed

Jacquelyn's color arrangement! The fire in her belly flared. She ran to the ladies room and vomited bile. She was so sick Abby had to take her home, leaving Arthur in charge of the guests.

"Tsk, tsk," Abby said, as she drove Jacquelyn home. "You've soiled your gown. Not a good omen."

*   *   *

What a terrible thing to say, Jacquelyn thought, listening to Arthur's soft snoring. We may not have much of a sex life now but everything else is fine between us.

With that thought, she drifted off to sleep. When she awoke at two, she was surprised. She'd assumed she'd licked it this month, but no such luck. The dark, dark night reminded her it was new moon. She sighed and got out of bed.

She slipped out of the room as soon as she had her outfit on. The burlap scratched her back just enough. Tonight she had to check on two more sleepers before she could drive off. Her parents were snoring peacefully in Ethan's room. Sylvia didn't move when she peeked in on her. Ethan wasn't in the den. Where was he? Motionless, she listened hard. Someone was in the kitchen. No, in the pantry. She ducked into the living room and hid behind the couch. Pretty soon she heard Ethan enter the den and yawn. She gave him ten minutes to fall into a deep sleep then slipped down the hall and into the garage. She didn't bother to listen for Trishita.

She disengaged the garage door opener with quiet care and lifted the door. The tools in her belt clanked. She rearranged the cotton padding around the hammer before starting her car and then backed out of the garage. No lights came on in the house and she left her headlights off until she'd reached the road. It was three o'clock. What if Mickey Carregio closed the local bars and then got hungry? He might still be up. Or worse, he might have a girl with him. Where would they go in that huge house? She knew where the beer bottles were, but not where he might be.

The trip to Mickey's house took five minutes. She drove slowly by, gratified to find it completely dark. Where to hide the car? She had never raided a house in Northboro. Some late reveler might see and recognize her car.

She drove to the school district parking garage, amazed at how quickly she could find solutions when energized by a raid. She used her electronic opener to get in, and parked in the first stall. If an early janitor saw her car he would assume she'd left it overnight. Besides, not a soul was around.

From the garage, she walked along the river's edge back to Mickey's house, pushing her way through tall bushes, listening for barking dogs, judging their proximity and danger.

In the back of the long yellow house there was an entrance to a cold cellar where previous owners who farmed the land stored their root vegetables and canned goods. She had no trouble entering the cellar, but it turned out to be a dead end. She felt along the damp, musty smelling walls for a door. Not one speck of light helped her out. She could hear mice scurrying on the floor. She jumped when she heard the gong of a grandfather's clock in a room overhead signifying the half hour. It had to be three-thirty. She wished she knew which of the fifteen rooms Mickey slept in.

Giving up on the cellar, she went back outside and made her way along the river to the front of the house. Okay, genius, she thought, solve this problem. The only entrance she knew was the front door and that would be locked. In the faint light of a distant streetlight, she was able to scan the side of the house. A window was open about ten feet above. She climbed a nearby oak tree, crawled out on one branch and studied the possibilities. She could jump for the sill, but might make a lot of noise or worse, fall into the river with a big splash. Deciding against those risks, she climbed down and continued around to the front.

On sudden impulse, she went up on the porch and tried the door. It was unlocked! She should have known Mickey wouldn't bother to lock up. The grandfather clock struck four. She'd been messing around with that tree too long. The sun would come up in an hour or so.

She slipped inside and went right to the parlor Mickey had talked about. She listened hard for five minutes, and then turned on her flashlight. The room held wall-to-wall beer bottles. It took her a few minutes of intense searching, but she soon found all the bottles from Austria on a shelf she could easily reach. She pulled on her gloves and wrapped each bottle in a rag before giving it a hard enough blow with the hammer to break it. Then she unwrapped it and covered the next one. She broke twenty-two of them. The ones from Sri Lanka were on a shelf too high to reach, and she hadn't replaced the ladder she'd lost on her last caper. She managed to push an overstuffed chair close to the shelves and climbed up on its arms. It was hard to balance, wrap, and break the bottles, but she managed. On the last bottle, she lost her balance and had to jump. A loud screech startled her. She had landed on a cat's tail. The cat's eyes glowed staring at her. Had Mickey heard it? Her heart pounded so loud she could hear nothing else. She crouched behind the chair, certain that Mickey would wake up and investigate.

The cat curled up on the floor beside the chair. She had to get out, now that she'd finished the job. When the pounding of her heart subsided to a Bellson drum roll, she headed for the parlor door only to stop at the sound of giggles on the front porch. Two voices. She dove behind the sofa.

The hall light came on. Mickey giggled and turned it off. Whoever was with him tripped and swore. They were both quite drunk. Jacquelyn hoped they were blind drunk. She peered at the hall from under the sofa. She could see their feet. He had a girl with him. They were embracing, periodically losing balance. Oh, go upstairs and fuck, will you? She repeated the thought, hoping they would get the subliminal message.

They obeyed her after several tense minutes. She slipped out the front door and ran down the street to the school district's parking garage. She drove home feeling truly contented for the first time in weeks.

When she climbed back into bed, Arthur startled her by asking, "Where were you?"

Goose pimples raised the hair on her arms and legs. "I couldn't sleep and went for a drive around Rocky Pond. Arthur, let's make love."

"Now?" he asked.

"Why not?"

"You smell like beer," he said.

"So what?"

He was less than enthusiastic for one who had gone without so long, but she had a great time.

CHAPTER FIFTEEN

Trishita awoke at the sound of a box toppling over. The night was darker than usual. She had to hold her watch in close to read the time. It was two in the morning. Who was in the pantry?

"Are you watching me again?" she asked softly, not sure who might answer.

"It's me," Ethan said. "Couldn't sleep. I need some, Trishita."

"Not now, Ethan. It's too risky here, especially with your grandparents in the house. I'll see you Sunday if you're still here by then. When are you leaving for Maine?"

"Hope I won't have to go. Mickey's going to try and talk my Mom into letting me stay. We've got some tough games scheduled."

Trishita worried about that. She wanted her driver's license badly, but wondered how the price would jump if Ethan stayed home with her.

"Hey, kid, I made doughnuts tonight. They're in the cookie canister right near you. Have a doughnut and go back to sleep."

"Homemade doughnuts? Wow." He rustled around. "I found 'em. Sweet. Better than nothin'."

She heard him close the canister.

"Thanks, Trishita," he said with a mouthful. "Sunday, if not sooner."

She listened to him make his way in the dark back to the den. Just as she was drifting off to sleep, she heard the garage door opening. She tensed. Now what?

The engine started on the BMW and then the garage door closed. Trishita went to her window and peered out. Sure enough, Jacquelyn's car was backing down the driving, headlights off. Strange. Lucky thing she'd kept Ethan out of her room tonight. Did Jacquelyn hear any of their conversation? The thought made her so nervous she slept fitfully and awoke completely at four-thirty.

It was too early to make noise in the kitchen. She thought she might read until daybreak. But, since she'd finished the book on Japanese management, she left the lights off and let her mind wander.

Then she heard the garage door open and the BMW return. Where the hell had Jacquelyn been?

The garage door closed, quietly. It sounded as if Jacquelyn entered the house by way of the hall between the kitchen and den. Trishita heard her stop at the entrance to the den. Probably checking on Ethan. Then she heard her sneaking up the stairs. Weird. Could that woman have a lover? No. But she wished that were a possibility just to loosen Jacquelyn up a bit.

The morning broke sunny and clear. Everyone's routine had broken, too. Sylvia and Ethan had been released from school and Jacquelyn, too, would be through for the summer any day. Arthur no longer pretended to work. And the parents were in town. Yet, there was a solidity to these broken routines that Trishita had never known. Change for her meant big change—move to a cheaper apartment, mother in jail, new job, give up another baby brother or sister. Now she lived in a place where a break in routine was no more threatening or disruptive than a rainstorm.

She loved the quiet moderation of everything in this suburban world, from Ethan's one earring to Jacquelyn's backing down the driveway with her lights out at two in the morning. The tension at breakfast yesterday was so brief! An argument over shoes, one swear word, quick, embarrassed exits. Nobody hit anybody. No blood shed. In Trishita's neighborhood, when they slung the shit it was real shit.

No wonder she found Jacquelyn's operas fascinating. The melodrama was familiar if the music wasn't. Trishita mused as she cooked.

This morning she was making date omelets when Bill Nestrom came into the kitchen wearing red and green plaid Bermuda shorts and a blue T-shirt. She smiled, genuinely amused by him. He'd been hanging around her ever since he'd arrived. He liked to tease her about her feet.

"Hey Trishita, don't you know I hates you cuz your feets too big?" he said, quoting Fats Waller.

"Just look at you, Bill Nestrom," she retorted. "Your clothes don't match and your pot belly makes you look like you're pregnant with a mouse."

"It's a kitten, Kitten." He patted his belly. "Not a mouse. A red-haired kitten." He stood next to her and placed his left foot beside her right one. "Man, look at that."

"Lucky thing you got tiny little feet, Billy boy. Your gaunt ankles would look mighty funny over normal feet."

"You call this gaunt?" He lifted his foot and stared at his ankle. "Why, you shoulda seen those guys in North Africa—hey, what's that you're cooking." He was so used to being interrupted he interrupted himself.

"Date omelets," she answered.

"What's in 'em?"

"Just dates and eggs. I pitted the dates first. They add just the right amount of salt and sweet to perk up the eggs. Don't need any other seasoning."

"Do the kids eat this stuff?"

"They love it. So will you."

"How did you happen to come up with that combination?"

"It's a common dish in the Middle East. Persian, I think."

"Stop bothering her, Bill," Abby said, opening the kitchen door. "Besides, Sylvia wants you to help her set up her new printer." To Trishita she asked, "How soon before breakfast? Should I call Sylvia down or send Bill up?"

"I'll have everything on the table in five minutes." She popped some bagels into the toaster oven.

Bill followed Abby out to the foyer and called Sylvia down. Soon the whole clan assembled in the dining room. The mood was festive. They had finally reached agreement about their vacations. Bill and Abby would take Sylvia and Ethan, despite his wrangling to stay home, to Bar Harbor, Maine, where plenty of second cousins would entertain them. Jacquelyn and Arthur would go to Cape Cod for a week and then join the others in Maine.

Trishita was relieved that she would be left home alone. She could get to the spring cleaning. Besides, her growing desire for Arthur complicated her deal with Ethan, much as her affection for Sylvia screwed up the detachment she needed to be ruthless. In fact, she wished Sylvia were staying home. She wondered what it would be like to have a vote on family issues.

"This is <u>not</u> your family, idiot," she told herself under her breath. Whisking the eggs harder than necessary, she fixed another batch of date omelets. She was serving espresso to Jacquelyn when Mickey Careggio appeared at the side door. Trishita saw the blood drain out of Jacquelyn's face.

Ethan welcomed him in and asked Arthur if he could join them for breakfast. Arthur set another place. Sylvia blushed. Bill started on a WWII story, Abby stopped him, and Jacquelyn got the hiccups so bad she had to leave the table. Head bent, she rushed out of the dining room.

The festive mood had been shattered by Jacquelyn's reaction to Mickey. Why? He certainly was pleasant enough. Grateful for the breakfast. Complimented Trishita's cooking. Listened attentively to Bill, talked to Ethan about today's baseball game. He had told Arthur and Jacquelyn he was glad to be back in Northboro even though he really rattled around that old house all by himself. How could Mickey cause such a gut reaction in Jacquelyn? No one else seemed to notice.

The generational switch in Mickey's rhythm fascinated Trishita, He used a rapid-fire staccato with Ethan and Sylvia, a lyrical lilt with Trishita, a fox-trot melody with Arthur and Jacquelyn and a slow waltz with Bill and Abby. All without using a whole lot of words. Trishita thought his visit was nothing but innocuous. Then why Jacquelyn's reaction? Where did she go that night? To Mickey's house for romance? No, that didn't fit. There was something else. Mickey didn't seem aware of whatever it was.

Mickey asked Arthur if he'd give up Ethan for two weeks for the "glory of the home team." He said Ethan could stay at his house with no problem. They were in training, after all.

"It's okay by me," Arthur said, "but you should speak to Jacquelyn. I'll see where she is."

The family scattered, leaving Mickey alone at the table. Trishita began clearing away the dishes, but started toward the kitchen when Arthur returned.

"I don't know where she went," he said to Mickey.

Then Jacquelyn came into the dining room from the side yard. Her face was ashen.

"My God, Jackie, what's the matter?" Arthur asked.

"Sylvia said you wanted to see me, Mickey," she said, and then turned to Arthur. "Perhaps we should talk alone. Would you mind, Dear?"

"Not at all, but tell me, are you ill?"

"I shouldn't eat such rich food. I'll be okay soon. Go on, now."

By now, Trishita stood safely ensconced behind the kitchen door. She heard the outside door close, presumably on Arthur.

"What is it you want, Mickey?" she heard Jacquelyn ask,

"I was hoping you'd let Ethan stay home while you're on vacation. He can stay with me—safely—because we're in training. He's our best catcher, Mrs. Hyde. The team really needs him."

"Is that all you wanted?" She heard Jacquelyn sit down with a thud, surprising from one so light.

"Yeah, sure."

"Well, Sylvia will be disappointed, but it's fine with me."

"Thanks, Mrs. Hyde. You won't regret it."

"Arthur?" Jacquelyn opened the back door. "Ethan's going to stay here with Mickey while we're on vacation."

"You and Ethan won't add to your beer bottle collection, will you?" Arthur asked from the doorway.

"Naw. Like I said, we're in training."

Trishita heard Jacquelyn calling for Ethan with a joyful lilt in her voice. That was some quick recovery from the problematic digestion of rich food.

*   *   *

Sylvia came in to help Trishita load the dishwasher after the word spread that Ethan would be staying with Mickey. She didn't seem disappointed. Instead, she chatted about going to Bar Harbor, seeing her cousins, Harold Johnson hiding under the bleachers at graduation, nerdiness in general, and Mickey Careggio. As she jumped from topic to topic, she spoke faster and faster until she dropped a cup on the floor. The cup didn't break, but Sylvia did. She crouched to pick it up and burst into tears.

Trishita knelt beside her and put her arms around her. Sylvia buried her head on Trishita's shoulder and sobbed. Realizing this was a reverse of her suburban mother fantasy Trishita rocked Sylvia and patted her back.

"There, there," Trishita crooned. *Harold was hiding under the bleachers?*

Looking up, Trishita saw Arthur peering in through the window over the sink. His facial expression was warm, tender. She gestured at him with her head, telling him to disappear, which he did. The moment didn't call for a third party. Then she stood and helped Sylvia disentangle herself.

"What's wrong, Syl? Are you disappointed about Ethan staying home?"

"No. I dunno. Something's weird about Ma. She acts like she hates me." Sylvia put the cup in the dishwasher. "I know she hates Harold Johnson."

"Your mother doesn't hate you," she said. "Nobody could. Maybe she just needs a vacation." Privately, Trishita agreed with Jacquelyn on the subject of the nerd. The kid gave her the creeps.

"Yeah, I guess so. I'm going to miss you a whole lot."

"And I'll miss you, too. It's going to be lonely around here, but two weeks will fly by and I'll get hours of practice on the computers."

"That's right. Then you can teach me word processing." Sylvia's brown eyes sparkled as bright as her braces in sunlight. Her face looked freshly washed. Now that I'm going to be in high school—"

"I have a little notebook I want you to take with you," Trishita said, interrupting. "Every day in Maine, write in it whatever you would've told me if I'd been there. Not a whole lot, necessarily, just the important stuff, okay? I'll read it when you come back. If you let me, that is."

"Where is it? I'll pack it now."

Trishita went to her room and pulled a little red leather accounting book out of her top drawer.

"Never mind the vertical lines," she told Sylvia. "Write in it as if the pages were blank. That's what I did." She opened the book in the middle. "I wrote in it up to here, but the rest is waiting for your thoughts."

"Can I read what you wrote?"

"Would I give it to you to take to Bar Harbor and tell you not to read it?"

"No, you wouldn't." Sylvia grinned, clutching the book to her chest. "I'll bring it back full." Then she dashed down the hall and up the stairs.

Trishita worried that the notebook would come back full of thoughts about Harold Johnson. That kid reminded her of the weird types she used to see hanging around the bars where she worked in Worcester. They never came in for a drink. Instead, they leaned against the outside wall and stared at the women walking by. Their eyes bulged like Harold's. How could she warn Sylvia? Should she?

*   *   *

In preparation for her vacation in Maine, Jacquelyn and Arthur took Sylvia shopping for a new bathing suit. The Nestroms went into the den to watch the soaps and Ethan was out practicing for the big game that evening with Boylston. That left Trishita free to change into her old cut-off jeans and knit tank top, appropriate attire for cleaning the oven. Since the family had been invited to their friends' house for dinner, Trishita was free to do as she pleased.

By evening, she had finished all her tasks and decided to walk into town and watch the game with Boylston. It was still hot, so she didn't bother to change her clothes. Her tank top, a fading Kelly green, had shrunk the last time she washed it. It bared her midriff and clung to her breasts. She realized halfway into town that she should have changed and tried to stretch it back to its former shape as she walked.

At the baseball field, she slipped into the nearly empty bleachers. Ethan ran over to greet her, and then deliberately slowed his pace. "Hi, Trishita. You here to cheer the home team on?"

"I decided to see for myself if Mickey's judgment is any good."

"Is that so?" A voice with a familiar rhythm blasted her left ear. "That judge knows who the best cook in town is. Ain't that enough?"

Trishita turned toward Mickey and smiled, feeling the pinpricks of pleasure that came from her interactions with these strange, rich, clean people. The rest of the team surrounded them. Ethan introduced her as if she were a distant cousin, but she caught the lust in his eyes—and something more: genuine affection.

The sun was low in the sky, the air warm and mercifully dry. The smell of these young jocks, who were so studiously not drooling over her, was mild and pleasant. She inhaled deeply so she could take the scent with her.

Trishita cheered with abandon. Mickey's team won four to three, thanks to Ethan's home run with one man on. Afterwards, she drove the Rabbit home—smoothly. Ethan and Mickey chatted about the game and ignored her driving.

"So," Ethan said when she got out of the car, "let's go get your driver's license tomorrow. Mickey and I will go with you."

"Terrific. I'll be a nervous wreck."

*   *   *

While the Hydes and Nestroms were running around and packing both their cars, Ethan and Mickey, with Trishita driving the Rabbit, headed for the Registry of Motor Vehicles for Trishita's driving test.

"Okay, Trishita, when can you cross a double yellow line?" Ethan asked. A steady sprinkle of rain started to fall.

"You don't need to quiz me. The written test will be a snap. It's the driving that scares me. Will they make me parallel park?"

"Depends on who you get," Ethan answered. "Dad says they're all old, fat curmudgeons anyway."

"That's for sure," Mickey agreed.

"The streets can get real slick in rain," Trishita said, worrying.

"If you start to slide, just turn the steering wheel into the slide." Mickey patted her shoulder.

"Don't worry," Ethan said. "You'll make out fine. Just remember the trick I showed you for parallel parking."

Trishita rehearsed the procedure in her mind. Pull forward all the way beside the car in front of the parking space, back up straight until you can see the left headlight of the car behind in your rear-view mirror, then turn the steering wheel and back in. It seemed simple enough, and she'd done it a couple of times last week.

The rain stopped. Bright sunlight made them blink and reach for sunglasses.

"Get a load of this sun," Mickey said. "It's a good omen, Trish."

She stood in line to take the written test and watched Mickey and Ethan outside talking with a Registry inspector who looked like a football coach. The butch-cut, gray-haired man had a huge belly, and despite the sunshine, wore a yellow slicker. He carried a clipboard and moved slowly, deliberately—as if he would mow down, without remorse, anyone in his way.

The line inside moved slowly. Nervous sweat was the pervading scent. Ethan was right—the Registry employees were fat, old, and cranky. A scowling employee shoved a "closed" sign in her face when she finally reached the counter and waddled off for a break. Trishita moved to another line. A half hour later, a woman handed the exam. She quickly answered the questions and then waited for her score. Next, she followed the arrows outside to the parking lot. The big inspector stood beside Ethan's car, dwarfing it. Ethan introduced him as his former driver's ed teacher. Trishita sat behind the wheel and prepared herself by reviewing the more difficult routines Ethan had taught her. When the inspector climbed into the passenger side, Ethan's Rabbit tilted and shook. Trishita's mouth felt as if she had been sucking rocks.

"Did you pass the written test okay?" Mickey asked

"Sure."

"What did you score?' Ethan asked.

"A hundred."

The inspector turned to look at her in astonishment. She didn't think she'd be able to drive out of the parking lot with his bulk spilling over the gearshift and her left knee practically brushing her boobs each time she let the clutch out.

"That's incredible," she heard Mickey shout.

"Ready?" Trishita glanced at the inspector.

He nodded, frowning.

"I think she's got one of those photogenic minds," Ethan said to Mickey, Trishita smiled at that and started the engine. *So far so good.*

"Doesn't he mean photographic memory?" the inspector asked.

"Yes, but I don't have one." She concentrated on her feet and prayed they would work in synch.

The inspector took her on a route that included a stoplight at the top of a steep hill, a traffic circle, and a toll road with several choices of tollbooths and directions. Periodically he made check marks on the form attached to his clipboard. She hadn't stalled the engine once—yet. But the sun went under a cloud and the cloud unloaded a torrent of rain just as she came to an intersection.

Trishita was sure she'd go into a slide. *Which way should I turn the wheel?* She could barely see out the window, so slowed to a crawl. Drivers behind her leaned on their horns.

"Hey," the inspector barked, "speed up."

She forgot to downshift. The car lurched forward.

"Can't ya see it's raining? Turn on the windshield wipers. And your lights."

Mortified, she turned everything on. A trickle of sweat ran down between her breasts making her skin itch. She felt incredibly stupid. Somehow, miserably, she managed to drive back to the Registry.

"Wait. I'll go in and check my figures." The inspector struggled and grunted his way out of the car. He nodded at his clipboard. "Back in a minute."

"How did it go?" Ethan and Mickey both asked.

"I failed. Forgot to turn on the windshield wipers when it started raining. Couldn't see and slowed down. Got all the cars behind me honking at me."

"Oh, Jeez," Ethan said.

"It's just as well," she said. They sat still listening to the rain. Trishita scratched the itch between her breasts. "Humbling."

"It was close," the inspector said to Ethan when he returned. "I didn't think she'd make it, but she got just enough points." He turned and said to Trishita, "You passed by one point. Remember, you gotta react to weather. You know how often it changes in this part of the country."

Ethan and Mickey danced with Trishita around the parking lot in the downpour until they were completely soaked. The inspector stood under the eaves, scowling.

Trishita went inside to have her picture taken for the license. Her wet hair sent rivulets down her cheeks.

"Stop crying, will ya? The fat lady with the camera said. "The picture won't come out right. Can't you sit a little lower?"

"I'm not crying," Trishita answered, wiping her face. "It's the rain." She slouched in the seat, looked up at the camera, and burst into tears. The camera clicked, and then she smiled.

CHAPTER SIXTEEN

"I got my license!" Trishita shouted as she ran toward the house followed by Ethan and Mickey, both laughing and poking each other.

Inside, she found Sylvia and Arthur playing cribbage with the Nestroms.

"I got my license," she repeated.

"Goody for you! Was it hard?" Sylvia jumped up, knocking over the cribbage board.

"Yeah. I didn't think I'd make it." Trishita glanced at the board game. "How come you're playing cribbage? Where's your mother?"

"Aw, she had to go to work. Somebody on her staff has been caught embezzling lots of money. Grampa and Grandma and I are leaving early tomorrow anyway. Who knows when Ma and Dad will get to go."

"Congratulations, Trishita," Arthur said as he folded the cribbage board. To Sylvia he said, "And you were winning, silly girl. No matter. Your mother and I will be taking off right after you guys leave."

Bill Nestrom stood and stretched his arms. "You get a driver's license and our wee Jackie gets an embezzler. I remember once when I was working for this machine shop in Worcester there was this guy who came in to do the books—"

"See you later, Gramps," Ethan said. "Gotta practice." He and Mickey made a quick exit.

"Anybody hungry?" Trishita asked and headed for the kitchen.

*   *   *

Trishita changed into her shorts and Grateful Dead T-shirt after lunch and slipped through the garage down to the brook for some precious moments alone. The weather, dry for a change, made the shade in the woods cool and inviting. Crickets were hard at work, along with four species of birds Trishita could name and five she couldn't.

She crossed the brook and headed deeper into the woods, squishing across the mulch of dead leaves and admiring new shoots on the branches that blocked her path. Arthur had once told her that the woods in New England had a will of their own. "If you clear away the trees," he'd said, "to raise crops, you can't turn your back for more than a day or two or the forest will reclaim the land."

She couldn't believe her luck at being able to walk in a forest, having the opportunity and time to wonder when these skinny little saplings had reclaimed a less than watchful farmer's land. Stone walls deep in the woods were evidence of early farming, meaningless now except for their beauty. The flat rocks piled on top of each other seemed held together by moss. Lichen gave each rock a pattern, a leitmotif of some overall design.

She sat on a mattress of mulch, leaned against the cool stone wall and pictured the young farmer a hundred years ago clearing the land and building this wall. Wiggling side to side, she made herself comfortable, closed her eyes, and inhaled the mild scent of naturally decaying vegetable matter. And mixed greens. Soon she was asleep.

"Arthur!" His soft kiss on her cheek awakened her.

"You looked so beautiful sleeping out here I hated to wake you, yet I had to." He was kneeling beside her.

"How did you find me?"

"Your footprints," he answered. He lifted her hand and kissed her palm. "I've got bad news." He sat beside her and leaned against the wall. "Jacquelyn said she was going to give you two weeks' notice today to find another job. I haven't been able to talk her out of it, and she pays your salary."

His words were a hammer blow on her solar plexus. She felt her heart breaking and wanted to wail, but was dammed if she'd give into that.

"Does Sylvia know?"

"I don't think so. When I saw her crying in your arms yesterday, I assumed she did, but she hasn't said anything to me."

"Does Jacquelyn suspect us?"

"No."

"Then why is she firing me?"

"She says she can't afford you, but I don't believe that. She says, too, that she wants the summertime off from work to reclaim her family. That I do believe. The truth is, she has lost us to you. I don't know what to do about that."

Just like the trees reclaim the land, Trishita thought. She could not remember when she had ever felt so forlorn. She put her head on her knees. Arthur lifted her face, caressed her forehead.

His tenderness infuriated her. She shook him away. "I don't need your fucking sympathy."

He pulled his hand away as if she'd slapped it.

"Hey, I'll help you get a job nearby," he said. "I must see you."

"I don't want another damn maid's job. This will have to be my first and last."

"Your first?"

"Yes." She didn't mind admitting that lie, especially to him. "I made up those letters of recommendation from former employees."

"You mean you never cooked for a family before?" Arthur slapped his forehead and laughed.

"Right."

"You are the most amazing woman I've ever known. How did you learn to cook so well?"

"Jacquelyn's cookbooks. I figured if she had them, that was the kind of food you were used to."

Arthur rolled onto his back, laughing hard. He sat up suddenly. "My God, we can't let you go. We'll starve to death or die from too much junk food."

She smiled. As her anger dissipated, a sense of betrayal brought tears to her eyes. She blinked them away. Nobody had betrayed her. She was the one who had cheated on them, traded off them and lied to them.

"Our food doesn't matter," he said, suddenly serious. "Are you ready for office work?"

"Hell, I don't know. I've barely seen what an office looks like and I don't know anyone who works in one besides Jacquelyn. I used to wait on office workers at lunchtime. They'd come in wearing high heels and carrying tennis shoes in a gym bag."

"What do you imagine yourself doing?" He stroked her hair.

"Sitting in the front row of a college classroom listening to a fascinating lecture, then discussing ideas with classmates in a coffee house. Remember that British movie about the working class wife and the drunk literature professor?" She shook her head. "Shit, it was just a movie. I'm too old for college."

"No one's too old for college." He stood and began pacing back and forth along the stone wall. "Tell you what, I'll be getting a full time job somewhere soon. It's not hard for circuit board designers to find work. Then I'll send you to college."

"Yeah. Sure. You and my mother."

"I tell you, I'm not going to abandon you."

"Listen Arthur, you've got to get your marriage back on track."

"You're right," he said, rubbing his eyes. "I suppose I should try to find out what's eating Jacquelyn alive." He looked over at Trishita with damp eyes. "Oh, Trish, I can't let you go."

That did it. The thought of moving back to Worcester, leaving the woods, the cookbooks, the gentleness was more than her heart could bear. She lowered her head and wept.

He pulled her into his arms, stroked her face and ears, and rocked her. She relaxed into him. He kissed her lips, pulled up her Grateful Dead T-shirt and fingered her nipples. Then he helped her lie back on a bed of mulch and kissed her with increasing passion.

A sudden crack of a breaking branch made them both jump. Someone else nearby. Trishita stood and listened for more evidence, but heard only the crickets and frogs.

"Just a dead branch," Arthur said. "C'mere."

She shook her head and moved through the trees even though she wanted him in every inch of her body. That one time was a big mistake, she knew. It shouldn't have happened. Did happen. She thought that her heart would escape her chest and run wildly around the woods. She felt like a little girl caught in a maelstrom of mysterious forces. Why did she want him?

Dead branch? Could that be true? The woods were strange, exotic and dangerous. She hugged a young hemlock a few futile minutes and then returned to Arthur.

"No, Arthur," she said, "As much as I want you, I can't. You can't."

He dropped his arms and pulled his knees to his chest with a groan.

"I'll hang out here awhile," she said with new authority. "You go back. I'm sure someone is looking for you by now."

"You're right, damn it." He stood, grabbed her hand. "I may not see you alone before we go on vacation. Remember my promise to you. Once I get a job, I might be able to make Jackie change her mind. No matter what happens, you keep in touch. Okay?"

She smiled at him. "Sure, I'll remember." She backed away and waved.

"Wait. What will you do? Where will I find you?"

"Don't know. I'm my mother's daughter after all and don't make plans."

After he left, she hugged the hemlock again. She had never before known sex to be sweet. In her affair with Dr. Jacobsen it was passionate and hasty. She knew he craved her and that gave her courage to enter his world. But he'd caved. No better than the guys at Russo's after all.

She remembered how bitter she used to feel toward the "upper class," how much she'd wanted to screw them, get back at them, prove that she was as good as they were.

And then they—Arthur, Ethan and Sylvia—loved her as she had never before felt loved. She, the Amazon from the underbelly of this world, had seduced the upper-crust into loving her. And there was no way she could tell that to the judge.

She released the hemlock and headed back to the house, not home. By then the sun was off to the side as if resting. So were Bill, Abby, and Jacquelyn in their respective rooms. Sylvia lay on the floor of the den watching television and Ethan was just getting into his car out front. She waved at him; he nodded and drove off. Everything seemed so normal, yet she couldn't shake the sense that someone else besides Arthur was in the woods.

She took a shower. When she was drying off she noticed an envelope on her pillow addressed to her in Jacquelyn's fancy script. Her heart dropped to her stomach. She wandered around for a while and looked at it, half expecting it to leap off the pillow and strangle her. In a sudden rush, she grabbed it and tore into it. She took a deep breath and sat down. The letter read,

"Dear Trishita,

    This is the hardest thing I've ever had to do. We can no longer keep you in our employ. The uncertain economy plus Arthur's business failure means we can no longer afford the luxury of a housekeeper.

    We want you to stay here while we're on vacation, and we'll give you your regular salary plus a bonus to help you find another job."

Trishita laughed bitterly. What kind of bonus? Fifty bucks?

    "We hope you will stay and do the spring cleaning as we planned, but we want you to be situated elsewhere by the time we return July fifteenth. I'll be home for the rest of the summer and will take over your duties.

    I've put in a word to Superintendent and Mrs. Ballman. I'm sure they'll consider hiring you. We have nothing but the highest recommendations for your work.

    It would be best if you didn't tell Sylvia or see her when we return. We will all miss you.

Sincerely,
Jacquelyn Hyde."

    The cunt had to do it by letter. "It would be best if you didn't tell Sylvia." That was the key. She wasn't worried about Arthur or Ethan. Just Sylvia. What irony! She crumpled the letter, threw it in her wastebasket, and walked into town for dinner. Let Jacquelyn eat shit!

    The next morning she served breakfast as usual. Bill came in for his morning teasing, Abby interrupted him, Sylvia rushed around clutching Trishita's little red notebook and got into an argument with Jacquelyn about taking her ceramic cows with her to Maine. Arthur looked more spaced than usual and Jacquelyn wouldn't look her in the eye. The strangest thing, though, was the fact that Ethan hadn't come home all night and no one seemed worried.

When the Nestroms drove off with Sylvia, Trishita finally asked, "Where's Ethan?" They were standing next to the BMW out front, near the lilac bush that overwhelmed them with its sweet scent.

"He called from Mickey's. He's staying there while we're gone." Jacquelyn handed Trishita a check. "Here's your pay for the last two weeks plus an advance for the next two weeks and a fifty dollar bonus. I gather you got my sad note."

"Yes." She took the check. "Thanks. I'll find something."

Arthur was putting their luggage in the trunk. He looked like he was going to cry.

Pull yourself together, Man. Trishita shot her thought at him.

They drove away without looking back. Trishita went inside to answer the ringing phone. It was Ethan sounding strange. "They just left, Ethan."

"I figured."

"I've been fired. I have two weeks to do the spring cleaning and clear out of here."

There was no sound.

What the hell? "Ethan? Are you there?"

"I saw you with my father in the woods yesterday," he said, then slammed down the receiver.

CHAPTER SEVENTEEN

Trishita heard the screech of tires in the driveway. That and the acrid smell of burning rubber told her Ethan was home. She had already steeled herself. Ethan's fury couldn't touch her. Nothing could now. She stayed still, sprawled on the living room floor, finally reading that chapter in <u>Moby Dick</u> called "The Whiteness of the Whale," where Melville goes on and on about white as a symbol of purity.

Ethan burst in. He was wearing his grass-stained shorts and holding his catcher's mitt. He looked like Hell. Like Flossie in the morning. Like Jacquelyn when she was so uptight she was about to vomit. Ethan's short blond hair had a streak of grease in it. His eyes were bloodshot, his expression grim. The shining son was tarnished. With regret, Trishita realized she had done most of the tarnishing.

"What are you?" he shouted, his face read, contorted. "How could you fuck both of us?" He threw his mitt onto the coffee table. "Don't you have any feeling, any sense of decency?"

"I'm not sure," she answered without moving from her prone position on the floor other than to lean on one elbow and look up at him, determined to keep her cool.

"How's my father in bed, anyway? I mean in the woods. Does he need lessons in saving his ching? Is this why he comes with us when you practice driving?" He stopped his frantic arm flailing and glared at her. "No. He's teaching you his accounting program. Is that your deal with him? Is that why Mom fired you, you fucking whore?"

"I made no deals with him—"

"Does my mother know what you've done? I think she should. She has a right to know." He kicked the base of the couch. "Or were you just trying to get back at her?"

He didn't hear all of Trishita's responses, but she made them, anyway, giving him enough counterpoint to rave on until he was spent.

"No," she said, "she doesn't know, and no, I wasn't trying to get back at her. What happened, didn't happen in the woods. If you'd stayed, you would—ah, never mind. I sure as hell didn't plan any of it."

"She may have to get a divorce because of you. You realize that? Is that fair to Sylvia?"

Low blow. It almost connected.

He threw himself around the room like a baseball on infield warm-up, nearly knocking over a lamp and hitting his shin on the hearth so hard he winced.

Trishita pulled herself up off the floor, stood still a moment, and made sure she felt her weight solidly on her feet. Then she raised her voice.

"Ethan, stop! You're whirling yourself into a tornado." She caught his arm and grabbed his shoulders. "Sit down and shut up. Your life as well as mine depends on how we act now. It's not a huge crisis in terms of the rest of the world, but for us it's pretty big."

Ethan twisted away from her touch, but slowly wound down. He perched on the back of a couch. She sat facing him eye to eye. "Let me talk for a while. Will you listen?"

"Yeah. I guess so." He began hitting the palm of his hand with his fist.

"I wish I didn't have a conscience. God knows I've tried to unload it. Sex does weird things to people. That's why I gave it up five years ago. Then, when I got here, I relaxed too much. As you well know. Afterwards I convinced myself there wouldn't be any trouble if I was careful." A glimmer of shame worked its way through her defenses. "I was wrong."

His eyes widened. The blue turned to dark gray. She could see the rage in his neck and the struggle for control in the twitch of his cheek muscles.

"Sex, without feeling, is rare," she said, hoping to soften potential blows. "But if you open to the feelings, you can have a hellava time and then regret it later. I have some regrets. But I do and did love you and your Dad—in different ways, of course, but far more than I should have—or would've if I'd kept my guard up."

"Bullshit. How can you love two men at once?"

"Easy when both of you are so lovable." She watched his jaw muscles relax and wondered if she were telling the truth or just protecting herself. She decided to blunder on anyway. "Think about sex in general. People need it—like food, except we can survive without sex. Come to think of it, the species can't survive without it, but individuals can." She felt a constriction in her throat and turned her neck just to loosen up. "Hey, sex is a lot like eating. Eating attitudes and habits, anyway. If you like to eat with family and friends, that says one thing. Alone at the diner or in front of TV says another. If you like sensuous pleasures, you prefer filet in puff pastry to Kraft's macaroni and cheese."

He stopped hitting the palm of his hand.

"Think about it," she said, continuing. The concept excited her. She spoke fast, gestured broadly. "Is a meal a sacrament or a hog feed? Most likely somewhere in between. Is sex a loving, sensual, slow building ¡Caramba! experience or a quickie for relief like jacking off?" She saw the confusion on his face. "Now, you, Ethan, are unusual. You're willing to try new foods, unusual flavors and new combinations. In other words, you're un-Puritan in your approach to food—and to sex. You've learned the Tao of sex and love." She flashed on skinny Dr. Jacobsen who was so generous with book lore and so stingy in bed. And he wouldn't try any new foods.

Scowling, Ethan asked, "What the hell are you getting at?" His voice hit a high pitch. He hastily cleared his throat.

"Well, you know the word Puritan means pure, separate, unmixed, clean. Our New England heritage." She pointed at the opened copy of <u>Moby Dick</u>. "We got it all through grade school. How many kids do you know who like hot, spicy, food? And mixed together so the flavors blend?"

He stopped hitting his palm, dropped his hands to his side and thought for a minute.

"Sylvia," he said.

"Yes. You and Sylvia."

"So?"

"So, people go at food like they go at sex. New England Puritans eat for fuel to live, not for fun. There's no passion in a plain carrot, but sauté that baby in Pernod, add orange zest and fresh dill, and you have all kinds of sensual pleasure."

"You're putting me on."

"I swear, I'm not," she said. "Look, you needed me for sex, and not like you might need hamburgers and fries to fuel your batting average, and not like you might need a passing pussy. We had much more than that. We have a special, if un-pure, kind of relationship."

"You can say that again." His voice hit a much lower pitch with a touch of sarcasm this time.

"And you didn't want me as a lifelong sex partner. We both knew that. You were experimenting, exploring, bravely. The way you try new foods. And I needed you. I made a deal with you because I trusted you and respected you. I wouldn't make such a deal with any old horny kid with a car."

"Then Goddammit, why did you fuck my father?"

"After it happened—and believe me, it only happened once and it surprised me—I realized I wanted to be the child. He fathered me. When I realized how dangerous it was, I refused him—after you broke that branch in the woods."

"Well, you don't need _me_ anymore." He picked up his mitt and headed for the front door. "Is Dad in love with you?"

"No. He loves your mother. Something's bothering her. They're in trouble now, but he won't leave her. I wouldn't want him if he did. You got that?"

"I'm just a pip-squeak to you."

"One hell of a pip-squeak, Ethan, with the ability to contain yourself. Not many people your age can do that. My mother can't. Shoot, all her sexual experiences are like eating old hot dogs on stale buns washed down with gin."

A smile wobbled Ethan's lips. "I guess containing yourself is like waiting for just the right second to pick the runner off first."

Thinking about her mother, she had to refocus on Ethan to respond.

"Right," she finally said, "like keeping our mouths shut about anyone having sex with the wrong person, whether it's you or your father or mother or sister."

"Sylvia? She's still a little kid." He set his mitt on the banister newel.

"Not by much. She'll be acting out sooner than any of us want. Talk to her, Ethan. I worry about that Johnson kid. She'll need you a lot this year."

He squinted at Trishita and began popping his knuckles. "She talk to you?"

"Yes—not about him."

The muscles in his face relaxed. "Yeah, he's a nut case. I talked to her once. Told her to nix it on that nerd."

"What did she say?"

"She said he was harmless. The only reason she let him hang around was he added some neat slide rules to Dad's collection. You have to move outa here before she comes home?"

"Right." Tears burned her eyes.

His face tightened. He picked up the mitt and opened the front door. "Okay. I listened to you. And I'll keep my mouth shut, but I'm still pissed so I'm outa here till you split."

She gave him a limp wave. He drove away—without burning rubber. Goose flesh raised the hairs on her arms. She sighed with relief. This was the first time she'd ever come out of a conflict over sex without any black and blue marks.

*   *   *

Several days went by and she didn't see Ethan. That made her apprehensive. What was he feeling? She wasn't out of the woods with him yet, so to speak. She despaired of finding a decent job, of having to live with her mother again. She considered packing it all in, but only for a moment. She still had much to read.

Early one morning she heard the putt-putt of a motor scooter in the driveway. She went outside and saw Mickey Careggio pulling up. A plastic sack hanging from his handlebars made a clinking sound, as if it were full of glass. She smiled at him; he turned off the engine and nodded at her, an unusually serious response for Mickey.

"Hi Mick," she said. "Come have a cup of coffee with me. I need some company."

"Hi." He untied the bag and opened it. "Get a load of this. Some asshole broke up my beer bottle collection—destroyed all the ones from Austria and Sri Lanka. I'm driving these around town hoping to catch someone with a guilty look."

"Oh, man, that's shitty. Do you think it was someone from around here?" Trishita peered into the bag then flashed on the scene in the kitchen the day she met Mickey. Jacquelyn had looked like she was going to faint when Mickey talked about his beer bottle collection. Arthur said he was running out of space for his slide rules just as that creepy Johnson kid showed up. Then Jacquelyn really came unglued. Trishita distinctly remembered Mickey telling Jacquelyn that his favorite bottles came from Austria and Sri Lanka. Could it be Jacquelyn?

"Must be someone local," Mickey said.

"What a shame," she said. "When did this happen?"

"I don't know. I just found them a few days ago. Haven't gone into in the parlor much lately."

"Why do you suppose anyone would do such a thing?" Trishita asked, thinking still about Jacquelyn's reaction to Mickey when he'd shown up at breakfast.

"Some prick's out to get me, I guess. I can't remember pissing anyone off, though."

"Strange," she said. "How would anyone know which ones were your favorites?"

"My big mouth. I've shown them to lots of people."

"Well, I'm sorry to hear it, Mick. Maybe it's that crazy guy who broke up a Lalique figurine collection in Tatnuck a while back."

"What? Never heard of it." Mickey's eyes widened.

"It was in the paper," Trishita said. "Did you call the police?"

"Naw. The less I have to do with them, the better." He followed her out of the sun into the cool of the kitchen.

She handed him a cup of coffee and a doughnut. "What's with Ethan?" he asked with his mouth full. "He's been raging and sulking for a week and he won't talk. It's affecting his game."

"I'm afraid I—I let him down."

"How?"

"That doesn't matter. I'll be gone in another week." She peered out the window at the sloping lawn that now needed mowing.

"Whatever you did, hoo boy, he's sure a basket case."

"He'll come out of it."

"Man, I hope so. He can't even catch a straight pitch anymore."

She followed him outside and waved him off. The cloying scent of the lilacs reminded her of Jacquelyn. The rest of the day she puzzled about Mickey's broken beer bottles. After dark, she went for a walk along the brook. Its gentle ripple, though soothing, reminded her that she was only a tenant in this world. It was the owners who had collections. Not that she wanted to collect anything. She just wanted to be able to own her own living space. Maybe if she did own it, she would start collecting useless shit just to add new goals. As she thought about people always striving for some dumb thing, she recalled a quote from William James about the various, extravagant wants of people, far in excess of need.

"The quest for the superfluous," she said, remembering. "Man's wants are to be trusted. They are the best guide of his life. "Prune down his extravaganzas, sober him, and you undo him."

Who knows what Jacquelyn wants?

Heading back, she looked up at the crescent moon among the stars. Why <u>did</u> Jacquelyn fire her? Arthur wouldn't confess. Ethan hadn't. And Sylvia would've blurted all, if she knew. And why did Jacquelyn hate Arthur's slide rules and Sylvia's cows?

"There are more things in heaven and earth, Horatio, than are dreamt of in your philosophy," she whispered to the summer sky.

The next day she spent deep cleaning the rooms while listening to Italian opera. Her heart was breaking right along with the soprano's in each opera. She not only dusted the furniture, she caressed it and faced the fact she wanted the Hyde family to adopt her. She wouldn't want to leave even to go to a better situation. Despite Jacquelyn. What a fool she'd been to fool around! Sex was a two-headed monster, beautiful and ugly.

As Desdemona's willow song slid into its soft closing notes, she heard the side door into the kitchen close. Someone was in the house! She grabbed the wrought iron poker from the fireplace and moved toward the kitchen. Heart pounding, she pushed open the swinging door. It was Ethan pouring a glass of water at the sink. Of course! Why would she suspect otherwise out here in the suburbs?

"Hi, Ethan," she said, feeling a foolish smile on her lips as she propped the poker against the kitchen table.

He twirled around facing her. His forehead looked strange, almost bulging. His smile was as cold as his voice when he said, "I miss your cooking—you know, all those sexy spices blending together." He moved in close, reached up and grabbed her neck. "No, this won't do. Hold still."

He pulled out a kitchen chair from the table and stood on it. "Come here, Trishita. Let me be taller than you for a change."

Warily, she approached him. "What's up?"

He smiled again. "The usual." He grabbed a hunk of her hair and pulled her close.

The pull hurt. This wasn't like Ethan. She stiffened.

He kissed her lips hard. "I'm hungry, Maid. Aren't you gonna feed me?"

She backed away. "What the hell are you on?"

"Just a few shots of gin and a dose of betrayal."

She straight-armed him. "I didn't betray you. I made no promises to you."

His eyes flashed. He jumped off the chair and pulled an apron out of a drawer.

She stared at him and backed away. He looked more like the guys she grew up with than Ethan.

With a flick of his wrist he lassoed her neck with the apron and pulled the strings tight. "Lie down," he barked.

"Come on, Kid," she said, feigning a light heart. "What are you doing here?"

"I told you I'm hungry. Lie down and spread your legs. Final payment for that driver's license."

"How about on my bed? Like the first time," she asked, hoping she could gain the upper hand by cooperating,

"Down on the floor," he growled. He tugged at the apron strings so hard she choked.

"Okay, okay." She did owe him. She took off her shorts and underpants and lay on the floor. The tile felt cool and hard.

Ethan held onto the apron as she arranged herself. He let go of the strings to rip off his T-shirt and undo his shorts. Rage darkened his eyes. When she started to move he kicked her thigh.

The pain brought tears to her eyes. "Sylvia was right. You do have a mean streak."

"Look who's talking." Naked, he stood over her, feet planted just outside her thighs. "Take off your dumb T-shirt."

She started to sit up to take it off and he shoved her breasts. That did it. She came up fighting and biting. She knew the dirty tricks well. Although she missed his balls she gave him a nasty bite on the knee that made him scream and gave her the chance to get to her feet. He rushed her; she ducked and he hit the sink. Hard. He picked up a chair and she grabbed the fireplace poker. When he swung the

---

---

chair at her, she hit his hands with the poker, knocking the chair out of them. It went flying across the table, breaking a bowl of fruit. He came at her again, wielding a huge cookbook. She didn't dare hit him with the poker. It could kill him. But she was able to fend him off.

He threw the cookbook at her. It hit the cord in her neck and hurt so bad her knees collapsed. She dropped the poker and fell to the floor on her hands and knees. Helpless, not caring anymore, she wept.

She felt his kisses on her hair, his trembling hands caressing her back. She relaxed and rolled onto her back. He gazed at her with wet, soft eyes that were blue once again. The gin-crazed rage was gone. She sat up, opened her arms and pulled him close. He leaned down and kissed her lips.

As he continued kissing her, her heart opened to him. She wanted to give and forgive. Gently, she pushed him back to standing and took his dick in her hand. He spasmed and almost immediately ejaculated. His eyes widened in astonishment.

"Oh God, Trishita," he whispered in a hoarse voice, "did I hurt you? I'm so sorry."

She held him close to her and said, "I am, too."

He got up and dressed, twitching his shoulders as he moved, regaining his manhood, she thought. It wouldn't occur to him to offer her sexual satisfaction now. He was too young, and she wasn't about to remind him of that lesson. Besides, he wore his shame on his face like a scarlet letter. Her heart ached for him.

At the front door he smiled with closed lips. "I've got a game this afternoon. Mickey will be relieved to see my eye on the ball for a change."

"Good luck." She went upstairs and watched him leave from his bedroom window, reflecting on her strange reactions. Shame kept her from protecting herself from the minute she saw him at the kitchen sink. Shame made her acquiesce to rape.

When she took this job she thought that she could toy with these rich people, get back at them for having everything she wanted, make a few deals to learn some of the things they take for granted, screw 'em if need be. She had never felt that weak before. Why now? She never suspected she'd end up screwed, craving their affection, even Jacquelyn's.

And she had to duck out on Sylvia, another cruel twist to the irony of her life.

Goddamn them. They'd made her vulnerable. Just like that bastard Jacobsen and his reading list.

She opened the window and leaned out. Choking on the thick, sweet smell of lilacs, she let out a long painful wail from her bruised throat, ending with "Fuck 'em all, the long and the short and the tall."

CHAPTER EIGHTEEN

While Trishita was washing the windows in Sylvia's room, the final touch of her spring cleaning there, the phone rang. She ran into Jacquelyn's and Arthur's room and answered on the gold lamé phone on Jacquelyn's desk. It was Flossie asking to borrow twenty dollars.

"I've got news for you, Ma." Trishita said. "I lost my job here. I'll give you the twenty, but that's gotta be it until I find another job."

"What happened? Did you get fired?"

"Yup."

"Whoo, boy. I bet you fucked the old man and his old lady found out."

Life was so simple to Flossie. "Not exactly. Anyway, is it okay with you if I come home for a while?"

"Mija, my place is yours. You know that."

"Yeah."

"You can always work at Russo's. They've been losing money since you left."

"Yeah." Trishita had to be careful. She could turn into a fatalist just like her mother. One moment of self-pity could do it.

"I'll get a job," Flossie said, "and you can go to Clark and get a degree. What will you be, a lawyer or social worker?"

"It's okay, Ma." Trishita smiled. Her mother knew those professions too well. "I'll find something. I'd rather not work at Russo's."

"You'd be among friends and make good tips."

"I'll see you when I finish up here—in a couple of days." Trishita shook her head at the thought of those friends.

"That's the best news I've had in ages. You wait and see. I'll get me a job tomorrow and send you off to college."

"Sure, Ma. Bye, now." She replaced the ornate gold receiver on its cradle and looked around. This was the last room she had to clean, and then she could kiss her suburban job good-bye. The part she would miss the most was just being alone, able to read her books and listen to opera in these elegant surroundings. No, she would miss Sylvia more.

She finished Sylvia's windows and wrote her a quick note. If she took too much time with it, she'd start bawling.

Instead, she left the note on Sylvia's pillow and started in on Jacquelyn's walk-in closet, washing down the woodwork. She pulled the chest of drawers out from the wall to wash behind it and discovered a false bottom drawer that didn't move with the chest. "Well, I'll be damned," she said, holding her breath against the suddenly released, unpleasant smell, and knelt down to examine its contents.

She picked up a particularly stinky blob of material that turned out to be, on closer examination, a navy blue sweatshirt. It was stiff from old sweat. *So unlike Jacquelyn,* she thought. The sweatshirt was lined with burlap and its hood had a gauze veil attached. *Weird.*

She next examined a leather tool belt containing a ball-peen hammer, pliers, wire cutters, rags, dog biscuits, and a spray can of mace. What was the point of all this stuff?

Slowly, gingerly, she replaced the tool and sweatshirt. Her thoughts raced. Did Jacquelyn break Mickey's beer bottles? Is that where she went when she backed out with her headlights off? Why on earth would she? Did Jacquelyn invade that professor's house near Tatnuck Square and break off all those Lalique heads? Trishita remembered a dinner conversation about that house. Jacquelyn had been a guest there for tea. Arthur had read about the break-in in the paper or heard it on TV. The kids laughed about it, but Jacquelyn ran upstairs, leaving a particularly good dinner uneaten.

"Man, do these things add up," she said to herself. "Add up and shout that our wee Dr. Jacquelyn, the darling of the school district, turns into a monstrous, collection-busting Mrs. Hyde!" Trishita felt so crazy and profound, she laughed out loud. What an underbelly!

*   *   *

The next day, in a frenzy of energy, Trishita finished cleaning all the rooms. No more opera. Instead, she played Ethan's <u>Metallica</u> discs.

After the sun set she calmed down, slowed her thoughts. Crazy as it seemed, it had to be true. Jacquelyn was this cat burglar. She'd be vicious if she knew Trishita even suspected her. Jacquelyn had so much to lose if anyone found out.

Trishita's discovery felt like pieces of hot coal she had to juggle. Or hot gold. The possibilities were endless, but she had to think them through. If she threatened Jacquelyn into keeping her on as their maid, she wouldn't be able to look Sylvia in the eye or turn her back on Jacquelyn. She decided to do nothing for a while, except a little sleuthing at the library.

Meanwhile, Mrs. Ballman called offering her a two-week job at the end of August and first week of September. Five hundred bucks "under the table." What the hell, Trishita thought. Most of her life was either over or under a table. She accepted and asked Mrs. Ballman to say nothing about their arrangement to anyone.

"I agree," Mrs. Ballman replied. "I'd just as soon Jonathan didn't know until you get here."

"Good. Then I'll call you towards the end of August—during the day." Trishita trusted her inclination toward secrecy about this job, but when she hung up, she thought about it. It would be best if the Hydes didn't know she would be in town those two weeks. She decided there was an advantage to making a clean break from a messy situation even if she couldn't put her finger on why.

Early the next morning Trishita took the bus into Worcester and went straight to the library. She spent a couple of hours scanning two years' worth of back issues of the Worcester Telegram and found three items on break-ins where nothing was stolen, but collections were destroyed. Evidently, Jacquelyn didn't have many victims in the Worcester area. She then searched two years' worth of the Boston Globe and found four isolated cases in and around Boston that matched Jacquelyn's method of operation. She decided she had enough to go on without researching all the local rags, although she was sure she would find isolated cases in any of the neighboring towns.

She wrote a brief summary of each break-in then searched for a common thread. Other than the fact Jacquelyn attacked personal collections, she could find no other connection. One was a collection of crystal doll houses, another Raggedy Andy dolls. Obviously the collections themselves weren't related. Using the calendar Jacquelyn had given her and one she found in the library for the previous year, she marked the date of each break-in to see if they had anything in common. The days didn't fall on the same day of the month or on any particular day of the week. Puzzled, she studied the fine print at the bottom of the library calendar page that gave the dates for the phases of the moon. Feeling the excitement that comes with the verge of discovery, she compared the dates of the break-ins. Sure enough, Jacquelyn's capers coincided with the new moon every time. Was Jacquelyn using the darkness that comes with the new moon for cover, or was the pull deeper? Primal?

In the Reader's Guide to Periodical Literature she looked up articles on obsession, discovered that they could be treated. The articles described a high percentage of cures whether or not the obsessions were caused psychologically or biologically. In fact, the most recent research showed that people with obsessive behaviors had identical patterns of brain waves in a specific part of the brain.

But to be cured, you must first admit that you are sick. What did Jacquelyn think about her obsession? Jacquelyn's response to idle conversation about collections showed that she was aware of her problem. What started this particular obsession? Revenge? Some sort of twisted and unsatisfactory revenge, if that. What might Jacquelyn do to Arthur's collection of slide rules? And to Sylvia's cows? How could she warn Arthur and Sylvia without hurting them? There was no way. Inaction seemed the wisest course for now. *Make a clean break.*

At three o'clock Trishita took the bus back to Northboro, getting off the bus at the only stop in town. Ethan was nearby, hanging around the Town Hall steps with the usual group of high school kids. He approached her with a nonchalant swagger. "Ride home?" He walked her to his car and opened the door for her. "Where've you been?"

"What are you doing here?"

"Waiting for you. I drove out to the house, discovered you were gone. Figured you took the bus somewhere, so came back here. Now that you have your license I thought you might want to borrow my car to move your books."

She grinned at him. "That's wonderful, Ethan. God I'm glad you're beginning to for—"

"So, where've you been?"

"Worcester library. Job search."

He looked at her sorrowfully. "Shit." He ground the gears and drove hard. "Any leads?"

"Not yet."

"Where will you live?"

"With my mother. Temporarily, I hope."

"Why not find another job in Northboro? Then Sylvia could still see you once in a while."

"No, I don't think so. Ethan, why did you tell Sylvia to stay away from Harold Johnson. What do you know about him?"

"Not much. He's pretty much a loner. But once I saw him sniffing the seats on the girls' bicycle seats in the bike rack."

"Jesus. Watch out for Sylvia, will you?" Trishita inhaled. The smell of the Rabbit's greasy gearshift made her nostalgic already.

"Sure. I think you should get a job around here."

"Ha! Your mother mentioned the Ballmans were interested. Maybe Mrs. Ballman would be, but that lech of a superintendent wouldn't ever want me around."

"What makes you say that?" Ethan's eyes brightened.

"The night of your mother's party he kept copping feels. I squeezed his balls so hard he doubled over and had to pretend his back went out."

"So that's what happened." Ethan laughed out loud. "I noticed he spent a lot of time in the kitchen. Man, what an actor. His name sure fit him that night. What did Mom say?"

"She didn't—doesn't know."

"Dad?"

"He doesn't either."

Ethan smiled and drove the rest of the way home in silence. He looked pleased.

*   *   *

"T. S. Elliot has a line he keeps repeating," she said to Ethan when she handed him the keys to his Rabbit. "It goes, 'Hurry up, please, it's time.' Thanks for the driver's license. And for the use of your car. It was fun driving all by myself, even if it was just to move my books. Now, it's time."

She had been cleaning her way to the front foyer, and giving the mirrors there a final inspection when Ethan appeared.

"How come you sound like an English teacher half the time?" He took the keys.

"Years ago when I was an underage, under-the-table bar maid at Russo's, I fell for an English professor at Clark who used to come in every afternoon at three for a gin toddy. I agreed to sleep with him if he'd direct my reading. Man, did he ever give me a list! Then he got a job at Berkeley, California and I never saw him again. Always wanted to let him know where I was on the list, though."

"Wow, you swap your body for the weirdest things. Maybe not so weird after all—sorta logical. Did you get all your stuff moved okay?"

"Yes. I packed all my books in your father's old electronics boxes. My room at my mother's is stacked with boxes that say HYDE CIRCUIT BOARDS. They'll make it tough for me to forget you guys. Now, if you'll give me a ride to the bus stop—"

"Wait a sec." He went to the kitchen. She followed to clean up after him. A matter of silly pride, she knew, but she wanted Jacquelyn to realize she'd earned that fifty dollar bonus.

Ethan went into the pantry, moved the box of cereal and said, "Oh," when he discovered she had filled the peep hole with spackle.

"You won't need that anymore. If you get a new maid, it would be unfair to the memory of me to peek at her. Or maybe the maid will be a man."

"I—I just wanted to see your room empty so I could realize—" Ethan turned to face her. His eyes were soggy.

"Let's go." She hurried outside.

"Did you think my father drilled that hole in the pantry?" Ethan asked on the way into town.

I asked him. He thought it was a natural hole. Don't mention it even when you're furious with him. Promise? You'll find other ways to compete with him."

He nodded with the serious face of attempted maturity and pulled up behind the bus stop.

"Let me take you into Worcester," Ethan begged. "I don't even know where you live."

"No. This is it. I told Sylvia we would be friends for life. I probably won't see either of you again, but you'll be in my heart for life. Got that? You don't need to know where I live. Now go before I lose it altogether."

He looked like a little boy again, blinking back tears. He drove off staring straight ahead.

She sat in the rear of the bus and lost it altogether. With a rush of anger she commanded herself to stop blubbering. Why did she think she could be part of a family like the Hyde's? What right had she to be hurt? Her only family, such as it was, lived in Worcester, most likely in Russo's Bar & Grill.

When she trudged past the sparkling new gymnasium and the old ivy covered buildings of Clark University, she had a brainstorm. Now that she was "computer literate" and "suburban literate," she could apply for an office job in the university. She knew exactly how to fabricate an appropriate résumé. Good old Worcester library. Or was that just wishful thinking—Flossie thinking?

"I'm home, Ma," she said into the dark cavern of Russo's.

"Mija. Come give me a kiss."

"Hey, Trishita! Want a job?" The bartender asked.

"Maybe. Give me a couple of days." She bent down and kissed her mother's cheek. Flossie almost toppled off the barstool. She introduced Trishita to a wizened old man beside her. His eyeglasses were lopsided on his face.

"This is my good friend, Mr. Blockenspiel," she said. "He's going to get me a job at his posh restaurant up town so you can go to college."

"Is that so?" Trishita raised her eyebrows. "Nice to meet you, Mr. Blockenspiel." She held out her hand to shake and he fell to the floor.

The bartender said, "He's passed out again. I'll put him in the alley. We can't have no drunks lying around in here." He came around and threw the skinny little man over his shoulder.

"Wait," Trishita said. "You can't leave him in there. Cars speed down that alley."

"I've put him there before."

Trishita felt her mother pulling her in by her hair, gently. It was Flossie's way of getting Trishita's head down for a private conversation.

"Can you carry him to our place?" Flossie asked.

"Yeah, I guess so." *Here we go again.* She said to the bartender, "Toss him over my shoulder will you? I can't leave him in the alley."

"Suit yourself."

Trishita nearly gagged at the smell. The old guy had peed his pants. Although he weighed not much more than a hundred pounds, she really had to struggle to get him up the three flights of stairs and into Flossie's tenement. Luckily, Flossie was able to make it home on her own.

The shower worked. Trishita took a long one. First day home and she knew she had to leave or join, and she wasn't about to join them.

CHAPTER NINETEEN

"Watch out for those dogs," Sylvia cried out.

Jacquelyn swerved to avoid two mid-size, brown mongrels stuck to each other limping to the side of the road. Arthur dozed in the back seat; Jacquelyn was driving the last leg of their trip home. At Sylvia's cry, Arthur sat up and looked out the rear window.

"We gotta stop and help them, Mom," Sylvia said.

"They're all right," Jacquelyn replied.

"They're stuck together, Ma. They can't walk."

Jacquelyn glanced at Arthur in the rear view mirror. He was smiling as he lay down, and not about to help her out.

"They'll be okay in a little while," Jacquelyn said.

"Do you s'pose they sat on some gum?" asked Sylvia.

"No, they were mating." Jacquelyn took a deep breath.

"Ma, I've seen lots of dogs mating," Sylvia said. "They don't get their butts stuck together."

"It's relatively rare. The male dog was probably too big for the female. When detumescence occurs, they'll separate with no problem."

From the back seat came Arthur's voice.

"Do you know what that means, Sylvia?" he asked.

"Sure." She slouched low in the seat. "I wonder what Trishita's fixing for dinner. She knows we're coming home today, doesn't she?"

Here it comes, Jacquelyn thought. Their vacation had been wonderfully free of tension. Sylvia spent most of it romping with her cousins and Bill and Abby hung out with the old folks. She didn't have to listen to her father's interminable stories. She and Arthur had enjoyed long hikes through the woods. How he'd surprised her with his passion and tenderness. Making love in the woods was a first—and so romantic—followed by picnics on giant, sun-drenched rocks at the shore. But, with the mention of Trishita's name, all Jacquelyn's worries came cascading down. The problem used to be Trishita's overwhelming presence. Now it would be her absence.

Arthur's absolute quiet in the back seat rang in her ears. *The coward.*

"Trishita won't be there, Honey," Jacquelyn said. "We had to let her go."

"What?" Sylvia bolted upright and glared at Jacquelyn.

"I gave her severance pay before we left. With your father's business—"

"Trishita knew?" Sylvia's voice rasped.

"I asked her not to say anything to you," Jacquelyn said. "I didn't want to spoil your vacation."

"You mean *your* vacation. Where did she go?"

"I don't know. I guess we'll find out when we get home. I tried to find her another job in Northboro."

"She's my best friend, Ma. I've gotta find her." Sylvia waved a red notebook at Jacquelyn. "This is her personal journal! She gave it to me to write in."

Jacquelyn slowed to get on to the Massachusetts Turnpike. "We'll be home in an hour or so." She glanced over at Sylvia huddled in the corner and saw tears in her eyes. Oh, dear, she thought, this was going to be much harder than she'd expected. That Trishita was a conniver, all right. Good riddance.

*   *   *

Ethan stood in the front doorway wearing nothing but a pair of shorts, holding his catcher's mitt in both hands. Sylvia jumped out of the car and ran to him. "Where's Trishita, Ethan?"

"I don't know."

"You have to know!" She stood facing him, hands on her hips.

He looked at her with sad eyes.

"Maybe she left me a note," Sylvia said and barged into the house.

"You okay?" Jacquelyn asked Ethan and kissed him on the cheek. He seemed wooden.

"Sure."

"Did you have some good games?" Arthur asked. He shook Ethan's hand then gave him an awkward hug around the mitt.

"Yeah, pretty good." His voice was tense and his face masked. "How was Maine?"

"Wonderful." Jacquelyn answered as if nothing were wrong, matching Ethan's mask. "We missed you, but had a lovely, relaxing time. I take it Trishita's gone."

"Moved out yesterday," Ethan said. "She did all the spring cleaning. I was afraid to go inside, it was so clean."

"Well, that's a surprise," Jacquelyn said.

"Nothing surprising about that," Arthur snapped. "You told her that's what you wanted for her big fifty dollar bonus."

"Oh, dear. Let's just get beyond this, shall we?" She moved around Ethan and went inside. The mirrors in the foyer shined. As she looked around, she realized this was the first time they had ever come home from a vacation to a clean house. She vowed to keep it up. In September, when she went back to work, she'd consider hiring another maid. An uglier one.

Sylvia came running down the stairs clutching the little red notebook and a piece of paper. Her eyes were swollen.

"She did leave me a note," Sylvia said, "but she didn't say where she was going. Ma, do you have a phone number or address? Anything?"

"I assumed she'd leave a forwarding address. Ethan?"

"She wouldn't tell me where she was going. Took the bus outa Northboro."

"Did the Ballmans call?"

"Not that I know of. I've been staying at Mickey's."

Sylvia ran into Trishita's room then back to the foyer where they all seemed to be stuck to their spots. Jacquelyn saw their suitcases mirrored over and over, growing smaller with each reflection. What looked like the shell of a lobster's claw poked through a hole in Sylvia's duffel bag.

"Is that a lobster in your suitcase, Sylvia?" Jacquelyn pointed at the reflections in the mirror.

"All her books are gone," Sylvia wailed.

"Of course, Jacquelyn said, "she moved out. Now answer me. Did you pack a dead lobster? The smell will—"

"You fired her. Why?" Sylvia's eyes blazed. Her braces looked like barbed wire.

"Calm down, Honey," Arthur said. "Your mother had to let her go."

"Why?"

"She told you. As you know, my business failed and we have to live on your mother's salary—"

"That's not the real reason. It's got to do with Ethan, hasn't it?"

Arthur blanched. "What do you mean?"

"She was afraid Ethan would want to fuck Trishita."

"Sylvia, that's enough," Jacquelyn snapped. "You are way out of line."

Ethan moved closer to Sylvia. He opened his mouth, and then covered his face with his mitt.

"You're just jealous, that's all," Sylvia flashed at Jacquelyn.

"No, kid," Ethan said. "You got it wrong about me."

"Then she was afraid Dad would go for her."

"Naw." Ethan grinned and put his arm around Sylvia. "Go easy on Ma, Syl. It's hard for all of us—"

"Hush, both of you," Jacquelyn said. She glared at Arthur, commanding him to speak.

Arthur had been leaning on the banister looking like overcooked fettuccine. He straightened and cleared his throat.

"Enough of this bullshit," he said. "We can't afford a maid and that's all there is to it. Attacking your mother isn't going to change anything. In fact, it will make everything worse." He headed up the stairs.

Sylvia and Ethan moved sideways, like identical twins, and disappeared. Jacquelyn knew their exit would give her only a moment's peace. But, she needed that moment. She connected with Ethan more or less. Everything she did or said was off the mark with Sylvia. She had vowed when Sylvia was born that she would not be like Abby and all those women who love their sons and are so jealous of their daughters they're mean to them. She wasn't jealous of Sylvia, but seemed to be always off center with her.

* * *

Puzzled by the shape of the Clark library, Trishita wandered all the way around it. An imposing structure built thirty years ago, it still looked like the architecture of the avant garde with its granite and glass reading rooms jutting out over the streets like outspread wings of a giant seagull. The Human Resources office of the university was in the basement of the library. Trishita entered feeling timid as she went downstairs to apply for secretarial positions. She loved the smell of bookbindings that permeated the building. If she ever got into glue sniffing, that would be her glue of choice.

"What you looking for, Honey?" a round, black woman wearing a red headband and large purple earrings asked.

"Is this where I apply for a job?"

"Yo's in the right place for sure. Faculty or slave?" She cackled, flashing white and gold teeth.

"Genus slave, species, secretary," Trishita said with a smile.

"The form you need is over there on that shelf. Fill it out and give it to the head woman when she comes back. I'm the cleaning lady." She went out the door, cackling.

Trishita began filling out the application form. First, she had to decide which ethnic heritage to check. She finally checked "other" and wrote in Scottish/French. It took some creative lying to account for the last ten years of her life. They wanted such detail she wondered why they didn't also request the name of her last lover and the exact measurement of his dick—in repose. She re-read her résumé to make sure she kept her stories straight. She had written that Arthur Hyde, her most recent employer, was the CEO of a fictitious accounting firm. She did give his real telephone number. She next wrote in Mickey Careggio's real number as manager of a fictitious software firm. The rest of the former employers she made up completely, hoping nobody would check any of them.

The "head woman" in personnel sent her to the math department where Mrs. Linneus, a short, soft-faced woman in her fifties who had squired the math department for the past fifteen years, interviewed her.

"You are an unusual young lady." Mrs. Linneus said, perusing Trishita's application and résumé.

"That I am, I guess," Trishita simply said, surprised by that comment

"You say here," Mrs. Linneus said, pointing to her application, "that you're familiar with a wide variety of computer programs."

"That's right."

"Why did you leave your last job?"

Trishita tried to remember what she'd written as her reason for leaving the accounting firm. "Sexual harassment," she said, "but I didn't write that. I'm not a troublemaker."

"Your application is impressive." Mrs. Linneus cleared her tiny throat. "We'll check your references and get back to you."

Trishita's muscles twitched. She'd have to call Mickey and ask him to warn Arthur. She doubted either one had any talent for lying.

Mrs. Linneus stood. "We'll call you soon, Miss McCabe. There's one thing that puzzles me. Why, with your experience and expertise, are you applying for such a low paying job?"

"I want to work here so I can take a class." Trishita stood and put her purse strap over her shoulder.

"A class? In what?"

"Anything."

Mrs. Linneus smiled. "We'll be calling you."

Gambling that her prospective employers wouldn't bother to check her references, Trishita didn't call Mickey to warn him. She was afraid Sylvia would find out and come looking for her.

The gamble paid off, and she landed the job as adjunct secretary to the math department. She wouldn't get paid for a month, and wouldn't get health benefits because she was part time and temporary, two adjectives she found most apt to describe her life, but she could audit classes free, on her own time, of course. When her ship came in, she'd take a course for credit. Meanwhile, reading the schedule of classes, she felt like an immigrant kid in a See's candy store.

After an extensive search of the schedule, Trishita found a one o'clock class on Mondays, Wednesdays, and Fridays called Cultural Anthropology 103. It appealed to her as soon as she found the meaning of the course title in the dictionary. First, she would have to complete her gig at the Ballman's. Then she'd be able to take her first college course. The anticipation of actually belonging at Clark University made living with Flossie again bearable.

Her eyes burned when she thought about Sylvia and Ethan. She had mixed feelings about Jacquelyn, mainly negative. And, aside from occasional sexual longing and his name on her résumé, she didn't think about Arthur. He faded first in her memory—the blur in the family photograph. She missed the landscape a lot, the town, the house she'd cleaned so well, the elegant beauty that made waking up every morning a wonder. Too bad she'd fucked that up. But, if she hadn't, she wouldn't be able to take her first college course. All of life involved trading one thing for another—a gigantic swap meet. She planned to upgrade the merchandise.

In late August, when no classes were in session, she began her job in the math department. Mrs. Linneus showed Trishita how to answer the phone, file old dissertations, and type on a computer keyboard with almost as many math symbols as letters. She then learned how to type scholarly articles written by the local professors, wishing she understood what she typed. Here was a whole new language.

But the job wore her out. It wasn't like waiting table or cleaning house where you moved around a lot. This was a new kind of tension even though the people she worked for were really nice. She hated that word, but could think of none that fit them. They were not at all abrasive and they were patient with her as she learned the ropes. One old, stooped professor with glasses sliding down his nose and an Einstein hairdo said, "You are a quick study, Patricia. I wish you were one of my students."

That compliment cushioned her for days. She, too, wished she were one of his students but wondered if she'd get this strange exhaustion if she were. By the time she finished the dinner shift at Russo's, such as it was, she was so tired she didn't hear Flossie and her drunken friends in the next room.

She was too tired, also, to hang up her clothes or unpack her books. They sat in their HYDE CIRCUIT BOARDS boxes piled one on top of the other, almost up to the torn print of Einstein on her ceiling, and her clothes draped over all four posts of her old, scratched maple bed frame. She figured she'd be moving the books to her own place as soon as she could earn enough money to rent a "room of one's own." After the gig at Ballman's she'd have enough for first and last month's rent. The timing was perfect. She could take two weeks off from the math department because it was between sessions. And fuck Russo's. She could always find work in a bar.

Just before she left both jobs to go to the Ballman's, she asked Mrs. Linneus how she should go about signing up for the class in Cultural Anthropology.

Mrs. Linneus said, "You have to ask the professor for permission to audit his class, but you're in luck because I just saw Dr. McLaren coming down the hall. He's not usually in this time of year. Come, I'll introduce you."

Trishita hadn't thought about getting the professor's permission. She had nothing to offer him. He might refuse, but timing was on her side. She sensed that the rhythm of a university was unlike that of the regular world. It had seasons of its own. Now, between seasons, the pace was slower.

Mrs. Linneus said, "I think you'll like Dr. McLaren. He and his wife, our other Dr. McLaren in the English Department, hold annual luncheons for all the classified staff. They don't look down their noses at us."

When they arrived at his office, Mrs. Linneus introduced her to Dr. McLaren then clattered away down the empty hallway. Trishita found herself shaking hands across a littered desk with a man taller than she was. He had a face rich in freckles and kindness—blue eyes, a big nose, a long, skinny jaw, large white teeth, and thinning red hair cut short. He made no attempt to hide his ugliness, nor his craggy handsomeness. Red-haired men, she thought, really show that dichotomy.

"Why do you want to audit my class?" Dr. McLaren asked. He pointed to the chair facing his desk. "Have a seat."

"To tell you the truth, I want to audit any class at this school and yours is offered at a time I can take it." She sat.

His whole face smiled. All his responses to her said he was concentrating on her. She trusted him.

"What do you know about cultural anthropology?" he asked.

"Outside my experiences with varying nationalities and social classes, nothing. That's another reason why I want to take your class." She gazed at his book-lined walls, noting that the titles were unfamiliar.

He reached behind him and handed her a book by Edward T. Hall opened to an essay entitled, "Proxemics in the Arab World." He said, "Here, read this. It'll give you an idea what we're about."

"What does 'proxemics' mean?"

"I wish my other students would ask that question," he said. His blue eyes shone. "They read blithely on, skipping over words they don't know as if they were no more than polish on a hardwood floor and not the floor itself. Proxemics is the study of people's responses to spatial relationships."

"Thank you. I know all about polishing hardwood floors, and I love your metaphor."

The professor blushed. She'd overstepped her bounds. She could seduce him and she wasn't about to seduce anyone again.

"Well, then, fine" he said with a little cough. "I'll expect to see you in my one o'clock class." He stood and handed her a sheet of paper. "Here's my syllabus. It lists reading assignments and research papers. Of course, since you'll be auditing, you won't have to write the papers."

"But I want to," she blurted.

He raised his bushy red eyebrows and stared at her.

"Oh, you won't need to read them. I mean, since I'm not taking credit—"

"I'd be happy to read them. I don't come by an heuristic learner very often."

"Whooristic?" Trishita stood and began backing out of his office. He smiled warmly; weak, she leaned against the door.

"Heuristic—from the Greek word for discovery—loosely means learning for the sake of learning." He joined her in the hall.

"That's what I thought school was for."

"What did you say your name was?"

"Patricia McCabe. Most people call me Trishita."

"Would that I lived in a world where even fifty per cent of the people thought like you." He shook her hand and headed down the hall at a brisk pace.

She stood in his wake, glowing and confused.

CHAPTER TWENTY

Jacquelyn brooded about Sylvia as the last days of summer burned into one another, washed by occasional thunderstorms. After her initial outburst, Sylvia had turned silent. She went swimming at Rocky Pond as usual, watched television, cheered at some of Ethan's baseball games, cleaned up after herself and did all her designated chores without complaint. She didn't mention Trishita's name again. Jacquelyn thought such behavior was too good to be true. Something was brewing.

It began percolating one night before the new moon. Jacquelyn had been feeling jumpy all day. Arthur, luckily, was job hunting in Boston. And she, foolishly as it turned out, decided to fix a Greek meal to surprise them all. When she discovered that she'd boiled the orzo to mush and had added too much lemon juice to the broth, she started all over again, only to discover she didn't have enough chicken stock.

"Hey, Ma, something's burning." Ethan burst into the kitchen, shouting.

Jacquelyn opened the oven door. The moussaka had spilled over the side of the baking dish onto the coils. She pulled it out of the oven, set it on the counter, and then, with a sigh, wiped her forehead with the oven mitt.

"Kinda hot for cooking." Ethan shot her a quizzical look.

"I thought it would be easier than it is."

"Smells good anyway," he said, grinning. "Hey, Ma, where's the peanut butter?"

"On the bottom shelf of the pantry."

"Bottom shelf? You've been moving things around."

"Yes. Just putting things within reach."

Sylvia pushed hard through the swinging door, letting it fan the air behind her. Jacquelyn recalled stock scenes in cowboy movies and half expected a challenge to a gun-fight.

"Want me to set the table?" Sylvia asked, instead.

"Sure. How was swimming today? I should take you shopping for another bathing suit so you don't have to wait for yours to dry. In Maine you had to get into a wet suit every day."

"It's okay. I don't need another suit." Sylvia carried a stack of plates into the dining room.

Suddenly Jacquelyn realized she hadn't seen Sylvia's bathing suit in days, nor a wet towel. She wasn't going swimming every day. She looked at Ethan.

"Where's Sylvia's bathing suit?" she asked Ethan.

Ethan shrugged.

Arthur showed up looking wan. His face belied his cheerful words. Jacquelyn realized they were all lying to each other.

The soup tasted unpleasantly sour. The moussaka was burned on the edges and cold on the inside, yet Ethan and Arthur gamely ate both and requested seconds on the moussaka. Jacquelyn noticed that their conversation was forced. She realized she rarely saw them doing things together anymore. Now her own throat barely contained her scream.

She escaped into the kitchen, found the corkscrew where Trishita had hung it by the swinging door, and opened the bottle of Retsina she'd bought for this Greek feast, but forgot to serve. What did she want to scream at them? Stop lying? Then she had to stop lying, too. She filled four liqueur glasses, put them on a tray, and pushed through the swinging door with as much flourish as she could muster. Sylvia and Ethan registered surprise, but each took a glass of the yellow wine and sniffed it.

"To Trishita." Jacquelyn raised her glass for a toast and clinked it against each of theirs. They drank in shocked silence. No one made a face at the strange taste.

"In a way you were right, Sylvia," Jacquelyn said, breaking the silence. "I fired Trishita because we can't afford her, but also because I was jealous. You were wrong, though, about the focus of my jealousy. I wasn't worried about Trishita stealing Ethan or your Dad's affection away from me. But I did know I was losing you. I hated to lose you."

Sylvia stared at her with damp eyes. Arthur's eyes widened and his jaw dropped. Ethan kept his head down.

Jacquelyn wanted to tell all of them to close their mouths, but knew better this time. She took another sip of the strange resin-flavored wine and decided it would taste better in Athens.

"Where have you been going every day?" she asked, aiming her words at Sylvia. "You haven't been swimming at Rocky Pond, have you?"

"No." Sylvia lowered her head.

"Then where?"

"Worcester."

"Did you find her?" Ethan asked,

"Not yet."

"How and where are you looking?" Arthur leaned forward and lifted Sylvia's chin.

"Places near Clark," Sylvia replied. "She told me she used to work in a bar and restaurant around there. And a deli."

"You go there by yourself?" Arthur asked. "That's dangerous territory."

"Wait a minute," Jacquelyn said. "Why are you looking in restaurants? She was a maid before she came here. We read her references."

"I'm afraid they were false," Arthur said. "She wrote them herself."

"Impossible. I studied those letters. Why, the sentence structure alone," she said and then shifted. "You knew?" She heard her voice rising to razor sharp. And she'd thought she had the rage under control this month.

"Not until recently," Arthur replied in a weary voice.

Jacquelyn's stomach muscles tightened unbearably. God, she was sick of being sick. She looked down at her hands. Her fingers clenched around her knife and fork. Her knuckles were turning white. If she could just let go!

She felt a hand on her shoulder and looked up. Sylvia was trying to comfort her. That one tentative touch was a crescendo, a full orchestra, the Mormon Tabernacle Choir celebrating Easter.

That night Jacquelyn took two sleeping pills and managed to stay asleep until daylight. It was the first time in a year she had slept through the night of a new moon.

The next day she taught Sylvia a systematic approach to problem solving. Without leaving the house, they were able to find Trishita's neighborhood, if not her actual address, by adding all the clues she'd given them to the name of the bank that cashed Jacquelyn's last check to her. They pulled Ethan into the search so he would drive Sylvia to Worcester in his car. Jacquelyn felt her BMW would be too conspicuous, if not an actual invitation to danger.

Since Arthur was job hunting and more spaced than usual, he had little to offer on the subject of Trishita. Jacquelyn thought this was just as well.

Then later that week a bit of good news came in the mail. An international educational journal published a research article Jacquelyn had written the previous winter on whole language learning. Subsequently, Ballman acted as if he had told her to write it. Still, he convinced the school board that anyone who was able to publish internationally should be rewarded financially. "Otherwise," he said, repeating his pitch to Jacquelyn, "that person might accept the better job offers coming in as a result of such publication."

Dr. Jacquelyn, then, got a hefty raise. Her family cheered.

"Now we can get Trishita back," the children said.

That was the last thing Jacquelyn wanted. Trishita could be worshipped from afar as long as it was afar. Jacquelyn found herself in the tricky position of helping her children find the housekeeper of their dreams and hoping they wouldn't find her.

Meanwhile, Arthur landed a challenging job with a small electronics firm. The money was good, but he'd have to travel overnight frequently.

*   *   *

Mrs. Ballman met Trishita at the Westboro bus stop. Rather furtively, she hurried her into a dark green Volvo.

There began two weeks of Purgatory for Trishita. The superintendent greeted her formally then studiously avoided her. Trishita figured his balls were still sore. But Mrs. Ballman was the kind of woman who feared silence, particularly her own. She filled potential voids with interminable, vacuous stories about people Trishita had never met and wouldn't care to meet. The strain of constant listening counteracted Trishita's pleasure at cooking again and seeing the beauty of the countryside.

Jacquelyn's father's stories were about himself, at least, and he rarely finished one. Mrs. Ballman's tales lasted a half hour each and died off at the end, pointlessly. But the clown collection was a Jacquelyn-baiting doozy. Trishita dusted each clown, polished the old wide-plank wooden floors, re-arranged the kitchen and, best of all, cooked with abandon. Mrs. Ballman was generous with the food budget, and, since she lived to eat, happy with the results.

Trishita dreamed about having a kitchen of her own and enough money to stock it properly. Meanwhile, she concocted sauces and dishes close enough to the Ballman's pedestrian palates to please them, yet stretched enough to educate them. She relished the challenge and pretended she heard resounding applause when both Ballmans raved about her sweetbreads.

From the dormer window in her room on the third floor, she could see for miles. The maple leaves were beginning to turn, igniting the woods with patches of red. Their reflections in the pond shimmered and deepened the reds.

The Ballman's old house had a secret back stairway hidden by closet doors. The stairs started in the basement and went up to a laundry room on the first floor. Then another flight went to the closet of a bedroom Mrs. Ballman used to store her unfinished sewing and needlepoint projects. From there the stairs led into the closet of Trishita's room. She loved the extravagance of rooms, the cupola with its widow's walk overlooking the pond where, supposedly, the widow stood peering for the return of her husband lost at sea, in this case, pond.

Here in Westboro, Trishita missed Sylvia beyond understanding, but resisted the temptation to call her. Trishita knew Jacquelyn would be tempted by the clowns when Mrs. Ballman mentioned the party for Jacquelyn. She wouldn't dare go after them, would she? Trishita ran through several scenarios before telling herself to let go of the Hydes.

"Hide from the Hydes," she chanted to herself as she cooked.

*   *   *

In late August, when the nights following the new moon took on a familiar chill and the foliage developed a slightly pungent scent, Jacquelyn was able to stay asleep until daylight. On one of these brisk evenings, the Ballmans held a reception in her honor. The date conflicted with Arthur's first trip to New York City for his new company. Jacquelyn was just as happy to go to the reception alone. She knew Arthur couldn't stand Jonathan Ballman and would be bored with the politics of education.

For the occasion, she made herself a dress out of silk with an abstract print in orange, red, and purple. In Boston, she'd found Italian shoes and purse to complement the dress, and had her hair styled on Beacon Hill. Ethan and Sylvia raved about her looks, promised to stay home, alone, and call out for pizza.

Jacquelyn drove off, pleased with Arthur, her children, her dress, her published article, and her raise. Ballman had hinted that a state senator might be at the reception. What a long way she had come from that two bedroom, trombone-laden bungalow in Worcester!

The Ballmans lived just over the town line in Westboro. She had never been in their home, but she'd seen it from the street often enough. A white, three-story mansion with a cupola, it was built in the early 1800's and presided over neighboring farms from its perch atop a high hill. Jonathan Ballman grew up in that house. He spoke often of his first memory there during a World War II blackout when he was three. His parents took him up to the cupola to watch the lights go out all over the area. Jacquelyn expected to hear the story again this evening.

As she drove up the steep driveway lined with maple trees, she tried to like her boss and host, and almost succeeded. But she dreaded seeing his clown collection. She knew he would insist on showing her every stupid clown he owned. When she approached the front door, he appeared. His big, hot hands wrapped hers, and he pulled her into a large parlor crowded with antiques. She was tempted to ask Mrs. Ballman how she could stand living with her in-laws' old, dark furniture.

Soon Jacquelyn stood engulfed in low-keyed praise for her article—and for her dress. The state senator was unable to come, but an impressive number of people from the State Department of Education did show, as well as members of the local school board.

Mrs. Ballman offered her some exquisite smoked bluefish pâté. It was strangely familiar. Dishes of elegant hors d'oeuvres sat on every antique table throughout the house, on all three floors and in the cupola—along with strategically placed ceramic and silk clowns. Jonathan led the guests on a tour. He pointed out the clowns on each step of each stairway, and in the rooms on the third floor, which were full of them. The guests sidestepped the clowns and ate their way to the cupola where they took turns looking through an ancient telescope at the pond below.

Despite the clowns, Jacquelyn was impressed. This party was more than she ever expected from the Ballmans. Jacquelyn excused herself as the party drew to a close and went to a guest bathroom on the first floor. When she came out, she was disoriented in the dark hallway and headed toward the light, only to find herself in a huge, high-ceilinged kitchen. A familiar figure clothed in a white pantsuit hovered over the kitchen sink. "Trishita," she gasped. She should have known when she tasted the bluefish paté that Trishita had made it.

"Congratulations Mrs. Hyde." Trishita turned around, her voice rimmed with sarcasm.

"How long have you been here?" Jacquelyn controlled her bristle.

"Two weeks. It's temporary. I'm leaving tomorrow."

"Where do you live?"

"In Worcester, at my mother's. Why did you fire me? Really."

"I told you. There's nothing more to say." Jacquelyn felt slapped.

"Were you satisfied with the condition of the house?"

"Oh, yes. Very much." Suddenly Jacquelyn wanted to beg her to come back. She needed her help. And she did feel guilty about firing her so peremptorily. Yet she hated Trishita and wanted to shout, "Stay out of our lives." Instead, she just stood there and wrung her hands.

"There you are, Jacquelyn," Mrs. Ballman said, entering. "So, you discovered our little secret. We figured you would once you tasted the food. Isn't she wonderful? But do come. The guests are getting ready to leave and want to say good-bye to you." She steered Jacquelyn out of the kitchen.

"Don't touch the clowns," Trishita called after her,

Jacquelyn whirled around.

"What did you say?"

"I just said I thought you'd like the clowns." Trishita stood there smiling.

Mrs. Ballman seemed unaware of the tension that the mere swish of a clown could build, and continued moving down the dark hallway.

"Jonathan had a fit when he discovered I'd hired her." she whispered behind her hand. "I can't imagine why, since I'm paying her out of my own money." She sighed. "I'll miss the luxury. He just doesn't want her around."

Neither do I. Jacquelyn put her hand on the older woman's fleshy arm and peered down the hall to make sure no one was in earshot.

"Who knows she's here?" she asked.

"No one else. Jonathan was adamant about that."

"Let's keep it that way, okay?"

"Of course, Jacquelyn." A funny little smiled wormed across her face. "She's going back to Worcester tomorrow."

*   *   *

The week school opened for Jacquelyn, Ethan, and Sylvia, the dull comfort of routine settled on them like fine silt over the land. Although Jacquelyn still worried now and then why Trishita made that remark about the clowns, the woman soon became a distant memory. Jacquelyn's workdays filled with new-school-year tasks, training sessions, and diplomacies.

Both Sylvia and Ethan went to the high school, she a freshman, he a senior. Jacquelyn noticed that her children had developed a new, congenial intimacy. Trishita's absence had far-reaching benefits.

But the problem of meals, shopping, washing, and cleaning increased geometrically. Ethan and Sylvia stepped up the pressure to find Trishita. There could no longer be a financial excuse for not hiring her again—with a substantial raise.

"She's got to be able to save up for college," Sylvia said. She, herself, was saving five dollars a week and had her college fund almost up to two hundred already. At that, Jacquelyn held her tongue and her smile. It had cost her parents twenty thousand dollars of their inheritance from Jacquelyn's grandfather Nostrum for her Ph.D. degree alone. Jacquelyn reminded herself to be grateful, for that degree had really paid off in the end.

Jacquelyn had begun to notice physical changes in Sylvia. She was taller than Arthur and Ethan, and her breasts were fuller than most girls her age, fuller than Jacquelyn's ever were, even when she was nursing. Sylvia's skin had cleared up, and in a few days she would be out of the braces that had fenced her teeth for three and a half years.

Sylvia still made the sudden jumpy movements of a colt and her posture was terrible as she tried to shorten herself, but Jacquelyn knew a startling kind of beauty was emerging with all its inherent danger. That slide rule nerd, Harold Johnson, appeared now and then. He had grown at least six inches over the summer and was as tall as Trishita. The afternoon of the first day of school, Jacquelyn saw Sylvia and Harold walking up Church Street. She stopped and offered them a ride. He nearly jumped out of his pimply skin. Sylvia got into the car and said, "Later, Harold."

"Doesn't he want a ride?"

"Naw."

"What do you see in that boy?"

"Nothing. Am I supposed to see something?"

Nevertheless, Jacquelyn worried. There was something not quite right about him, but she couldn't say what. Also, she wondered what she would do if the kids actually found Trishita. At some point, Trishita would certainly say she'd been working for the Ballmans and that she was there the night of Jacquelyn's reception. Could she explain her secrecy, her jealousy with benign results a second time? And how many sleeping pills would it take to resist, in the next new moon, the temptation of Ballman's clown collection? Resist it, she must. She had far too much to lose.

Each night she lay awake for hours, wearing earphones to listen to music that could not drown out her thoughts. When she did sleep, the Johnson kid haunted her dreams. Tonight, at the blast of a trombone played off key, she awoke and jumped out of bed, heart beating in alarm. She ran into Sylvia's room and found her safe, and fast asleep.

"Must've been a dream," she said to Arthur when she came back to bed. But she didn't fully believe herself.

CHAPTER TWENTY-ONE

Trishita made it through Purgatory. After the one delicious encounter with Jacquelyn, she headed back to Worcester with a check for five hundred dollars, a low paying job in a college atmosphere, and a plan. She didn't earn enough from both jobs to rent an apartment, but a room of her own and a hot plate would be a start.

"Mija, you came back. I miss you so!" Flossie acted as if Trishita would stay with her forever. She tugged at Trishita's hair to bring her cheek within kissing range.

"Yep, I'm back, but I'll be moving again as soon as I find a place."

Flossie's cigarette cough was worse than usual. Trishita tried to ignore it. They were standing in the kitchen near the defunct stove.

"Why?" Flossie asked. "What's wrong with your room?"

"Ma, I'm twenty-six years old. On my own. I can still see you now and then, but I want a place where I can cook—"

"You can cook here."

"Let me go, Ma, please. Let me go." Trishita put her hands on Flossie's tiny shoulders.

"Suit yourself." Flossie backed up two steps and turned away. She bent double in a fit of coughing.

Trishita poured her a glass of water and touched Flossie's face. It was burning hot. She knew Flossie's fever wasn't intended, but she reacted in her guts as if it were another ploy. In any event, it worked.

Intense heat radiated from Flossie's tiny body. Trishita half dragged, half carried her mother two blocks to a medical clinic. After a two hour wait, a doctor examined Flossie and prescribed antibiotics. By the time Flossie's pneumonia had receded, Trishita had spent two hundred and fifty dollars.

Russo re-hired Trishita and she stopped reading the rental ads.

When the big day came, first day of classes, she was as nervous as a vocalist at an audition. She knew she had the requisite intelligence, but she didn't know the protocol. When her old janitor buddy used to take her into the classrooms on weekends she would sit front row, center. But there had been no other students around.

The weather was cool and dry. White clouds striped across a clear blue sky. The smell of burning firewood added to the pleasure of the crisp air. Trishita wore a knee length black skirt, a gray pullover, gray knee socks and black moccasins. She wanted to be as inconspicuous as possible.

Students surrounded Dr. McLaren in his classroom. Most of them wore oversized T-shirts advertising musical groups or environmental causes. Untucked, they hung like sacks over stonewashed jeans. She headed toward the back and slipped into a chair with a wide right arm. When she looked around, she noticed that the students had lots of equipment: pens, pencils, backpacks full of books, three ring notebooks, spiral notebooks, folders. Trishita had come to class empty-handed. She hoped no one would notice.

Dr. McLaren ushered the students into seats, took roll, and passed out his syllabus. A couple of young men, one on each side of Trishita, eyed her with open curiosity. She was an anomaly, as usual, but she shrugged off that thought in the pleasure of listening to McLaren's introductory lecture. She didn't need to take notes; she remembered every word.

"Wow," she said to Dr. McLaren after the other students left. "That was fascinating."

"I'm glad you enjoyed it." He blushed and smiled.

"I can hardly wait until Wednesday," she said, feeling so tongue-tied and stupid she hurried away.

"Man," she said to Russo's bartender when she showed up for work, "my class at Clark is gonna be fuckin' interesting. I get to study my Scottish heritage as well as the others, but the best part is I'll learn how people are alike all over the world, how I'm like the Aztecs or the Amazons—"

"Amazons for sure."

"Eskimos, too, asshole," Trishita said.

"You're weird, Trish. I can't figure why Russo keeps hiring you."

"I can." She grinned and started clearing lunch dishes from tables. "Nobody else'll work here. Hell, Russo won't even come into his own place to check on it."

The evening regulars started drifting in around four. Flossie giggled in on the arm of the guy Trishita had carried up three flights of stairs just so he wouldn't get run over in the alley. Flossie introduced him again. He didn't remember Trishita, of course.

With awe in his voice, he said, "She's <u>your</u> daughter?"

Flossie glowed, and then began the familiar narrative on Trishita's birth, strange red hair and phenomenal height. When the little guy staggered off to the head, Trishita brought them fresh beers.

"I forgot to tell you, Flossie said. "Some kids came around looking for you a couple hours ago. Rich kids. They prolly gone by now."

Trishita's hackles went up.

"Who were the kids?" Trishita stared at her mother. "Did you get their names?"

"Yeah. Horace or Harold or something was the boy's name. Can't remember the girl's."

"Oh my God—that freak! Where were they? Near our place?" Trishita shouted, resisting the impulse to shake her mother's shoulders.

"I came across them wandering down Oread Street looking real scared. A couple of black Ricans was taunting 'em. They asked me if I knew you, so I took 'em home—said I'd find you sooner or later."

"Where are they now?"

"Like I said, prolly gone home. I left them in your room. They recognized the boxes of books." She took a swallow of beer. "How was your first class?"

Trishita grabbed Flossie's shoulders. "Was the girl named Sylvia?"

"Maybe. Sounds right. She was tall and pretty with brown hair and rich clothes."

Alarmed, Trishita tore off her apron and ran out the door, dodging traffic to cross the streets. She wasn't sure why her adrenaline was pumping like a Kuwaiti oil well, but she trusted it. When she reached the front door of her tenement building, she stopped to catch her breath. If she ran up the stairs, Harold might hear her coming.

Following her gut, she decided to go up the fire escape and peek in. She backed up and made a running jump to catch the bottom rung. A police siren wailed nearby. She was grateful for the sound cover as she climbed. When she reached the top, she tried to peer in her bedroom window, but the setting sun sent bright rays that obscured her vision. She shaded her eyes with her hand and looked again. They were there!

She gasped. Sylvia lay on her back, naked, arms and legs tied to each post of Trishita's old bed. Harold knelt beside her wearing a T-shirt but bare-assed. He held a knife in one hand and his engorged dick in the other.

CHAPTER TWENTY-TWO

Trishita pulled open the window and jumped in, releasing a gutteral roar.

"You pervert!" She grabbed Harold by his balls, and yanked him to the floor. He let out a wild scream and doubled up, wailing in agony. His knife went flying. She lunged for it, cut the rope off one box of books and wrapped it on her arm. Harold huddled in a corner.

Sylvia's terror-filled eyes flashed at Trishita over the pillowcase that gagged her mouth. She was alive! Trishita's hands shook as she untied the gag.

Sylvia coughed and then began to cry.

Trishita cut the ropes tying the poor girl's limbs to the bedposts.

"How bad did he hurt you?" she asked, touching Sylvia's cheek.

Trishita twirled at the faint sound of movement near the window. Harold was trying to climb out. She dove, tackling him at the thighs. He struggled, clinging to the windowsill; she pulled him back inside and kicked him in the balls. He collapsed and sobbed.

"Fucking bastard," she said as she trussed him and tied him to the leg of the radiator. Then she went back to examine Sylvia.

"How bad are you hurt?" she asked again, wondering if the girl could talk.

"Where is he? He's got a knife!" Sylvia whispered. "Oh God, keep him away!" Her eyes rolled and her head fell to the side. She passed out.

Trishita rushed toward the kitchen to call emergency but a chair propped under the doorknob to her room stopped her. Lucky thing she had come up the fire escape! She kicked away the chair with more force than needed and ran to the phone. She heard a sigh when the police dispatcher repeated Flossie's address and imagined the dispatcher winking at the guys on duty. The cops would be in no hurry to come to Flossie's place again. They'd avoided domestic disputes and the neighborhood altogether since one woman shot at them when they tried to restrain her husband. Trishita pulled herself together and barked, "Send the paramedics STAT! We have a rape of a fourteen-year-old girl and a jerk with a knife about to carve her up. I've got him tied up but need help now!" She hung up, checked on Harold who hadn't moved, and then called Jacquelyn Hyde.

"Mrs. Hyde, this is Trishita and . . . I don't know how to tell . . . oh damn, I have awful news. Sylvia is here with Harold Johnson. He had her tied up at knife point on my bed when I found them."

"Oh my God! Is she . . . was she . . . ?"

"She's alive. She seems unharmed, physically, that is, but she'd better see a doctor. I tied Harold to the radiator and called the police."

"We'll be right there." Jacquelyn's voice broke. "What's your address?"

She gave Jacquelyn directions and hung up. Tears burned her eyes as she tried to revive Sylvia with a damp washcloth. She examined her to see if he'd cut her anywhere. Finding no wounds, she covered her with a sheet.

Sylvia opened her eyes and grabbed Trishita's arm. "I thought I'd never find you." She looked at Trishita with eyes full of relief. "Where's Harold?"

"Over there, hog tied." She pointed at the trussed figure by the radiator. His eyes were bulging like a gigged frog's. "Did he . . . ?"

"No. You got here just in time. He was going to carve his name on my stomach so I'd be his forever. You know what happened to his thing? It got real big! He said he was going to put it in me. That's rape isn't it? That thing couldn't fit inside me. No way." She started to cry.

"Poor babe." She stroked Sylvia's hair. "We've got to get you to a hospital anyway. Have a doctor check you over. I just called the police—and your mother."

Sylvia stopped crying; opened her eyes wide. "She'll be too tired to come all the way in to Worcester. She'll be mad at me."

"No she won't. She loves you and will be here right away."

"She never liked Harold."

"Did you?"

"No. I wasn't thinking about him. I just wanted to find you and he offered to help look. Never thought he'd tie me up and gag me. Jeez, we were just sitting on the edge of your bed talking and wondering about your books. I didn't think a thing about it. Then all of a sudden he pulls this knife on me. His whole face changed. I don't know what I did." She gazed at Trishita. "God, Trish, if you hadn't stopped him I couldn't be a, you know, couldn't see my friends in the club anymore."

"It's okay, kid. And nothing is your fault! Got that?" Trishita stroked Sylvia's face. I'm real glad to see you. You're not wearing braces anymore—oh, shit." She started to cry and choked it back. This waiting was damn hard. Would the cops ever show?

Harold moaned again. Trishita glanced at him. He was no longer a threat. She studied Sylvia's face. It was so white her freckles popped out. The intense fear must've left her in adrenaline shock.

"Where are your clothes?" she asked Sylvia.

"He kicked them under the bed."

Trishita gave Harold a quick kick in the butt then lowered herself to the floor to reach under the bed. She pulled out Sylvia's cotton underpants, limp, yellowing bra, Northboro High T-shirt and cut-off jeans. The jeans were torn at the waist and a button was missing. "Here. Do you feel like getting dressed?"

Sylvia sat up and put on her bra and T-shirt. Then she pulled the sheet over her and finished dressing under it.

"Why you run from work, Mija. Wha' happen?" Flossie showed up wide-eyed, red-eyed, but alone.

"Crazy kid over there has mixed up hormone signals. He was aiming to carve his name on my friend here. This is Sylvia Hyde. And that creep is Harold Johnson."

"Did you call the cops?" Flossie asked, closing her eyes to slits.

"Yeah, but I doubt they'll come. What kind of hex did you put on 'em?"

"Can I have some water?" Sylvia asked.

"Sure." Trishita went to the kitchen, grabbed two glasses from the cupboard, and filled them with water. She brought one to Sylvia and gave the other to Flossie.

Flossie took one sip. "This needs some gin. I think I got some under my bed."

"Not now, Ma."

Trishita and Flossie stared at each other, waiting. A distant clock struck seven. Trishita pulled a chain and turned on the overhead light. It swung, sending shadows into a slow dance.

A loud rap on the front door startled them.

"I'll be damned. Don't tell me the cops decided to show. Let 'em in, Ma."

Flossie nodded and took her half-empty glass of water with her.

It turned out to be Jacquelyn and Arthur. They rushed into Trishita's bedroom, followed by Flossie carrying a full glass.

"Sylvia!" Jacquelyn cried. "My poor little girl." She hugged Sylvia and wept.

"Where's that boy?" Arthur asked, eyes blazing. He spotted Harold on the floor, still tied to the bureau, and rushed over and pounced on him. Harold screamed as Arthur punched him in the face.

Trishita grabbed Arthur from behind and tried to pin his arms. "He's tied up, Arthur. For God's sake, you'll kill him."

Arthur relaxed a bit and Trishita let go of him.

"Where are the medics?" Arthur asked, moving over to kiss Sylvia. He whispered in her ear, stroked her hand.

"I don't know," Trishita answered. "I called, but they won't come without the cops and they're all afraid of the neighborhood."

"That's impossible" Arthur shouted at Trishita and Flossie, who had moved in close. "Police aren't afraid. They're hired to protect—"

"They afraid," Flossie said.

"Who are you?" he asked, softening his tone.

"I'm Trishita's mother. Name's Florence Giraux." She held out her hand.

"Where's the phone?" Arthur asked as he shook her hand.

Flossie pointed toward the kitchen and Arthur hurried away. Trishita followed. She heard Jaquelyn ask, "How could you be—" and Flossie reply, "I have proof." She dreaded what Flossie would show them, but felt she needed to help Arthur call the cops.

"Is this the number?" Arthur asked without looking at her.

"Yes, I'll dial it for you." She made the call and handed him the receiver.

He spoke in a normal voice at first. Then he began shouting.

Trishita returned to her bedroom and found Flossie running her old super-8 projector along with a tape in her boom box.

"I recorded the party on this tape." Flossie said to Sylvia. "Here's my Trishita at six months. Already tall."

"Oh no, not that old movie, Ma!" Trishita cried. "Turn it off."

"It's okay, Trish," Sylvia said. "I want to see it."

Flossie started the reel and the tape on the boom box. "I made a talkie," she said.

*   *   *

The scene showed Flossie running up the stairs to the tenement carrying a baby in a long christening dress, surrounded by a fluid group of "friends, neighbors, and recent acquaintances," Flossie said over a scene of her rolling Trishita onto a pallet in the middle of the kitchen floor.

"Les' drink to my redhead," she said and popped open a bottle of champagne. Then she reached into the refrigerator and pulled out a baby bottle half filled with milk. She ran some hot water over it.

"Where's the doobie, Flossie?" one guy asked.

"Right here, Man. I wouldn't have a Christening party without a decent stash, would I?" She pulled a joint out of her pocket.

"Yo, Baby, light up," he said, grinning

The baby wrinkled her nose.

"Well, here's to Patricia McCabe," Flossie cheered through her coughing and poured the champagne.

"Hey, ain't she a Gemini?" one woman asked.

"Sure is," Flossie replied. "Popped out on flag day." She turned off the faucet and handed Trishita the bottle.

"She'll be a great cook, I betcha," a man's voice said.

"Whyzzat?" the woman asked.

"Gemini's are quick and can do two things at once," he answered.

"Hey pass the doobie," a man with a cracked voice said.

"Where'd you get the kid's last name, Florence?" a woman asked.

"She's my little bundle from Scotland." Flossie beamed, took another hit.

"No shit? Who's the old man?" the guy with the cracked voice asked. "Had to a been some big dude with flaming red hair."

"And thick curls," someone else said. "Never saw a kid this young with curly hair. And her skin's so white it's almost blue."

"Her papa's six-foot-seven, freckled, red-headed, and super smart," Flossie said. She bent over and planted a sloppy kiss on Trishita's cheek.

"G'wan. How do you know he's smart?" several onlookers chimed.

"Cause," Flossie replied, "he was teaching over at the college. That's why. Exchange teacher or something like that."

"Whoa, a prof. How did you get that guy to bed—or wherever?" one woman asked.

"Short story. Long guy," Flossie said. Her voice was getting fuzzy.

"Enough, Flossie, enough," Trishita said and pulled the plug of the projector off the wall socket. The old black and white film ground to a halt, spinning.

"Were they smoking dope?" Sylvia asked.

"We were celebrating Trishita's Christening." Flossie shrugged.

Sylvia and Jacquelyn stared at Trishita just as Arthur returned from the kitchen.

"You were right," he said to Flossie. "I had to raise hell with the desk sergeant to get any action. They hadn't even called the paramedics." He moved toward Harold and glared.

Harold flinched. His eyes flitted back and forth. "I wasn't going to hurt her, Mr. Hyde, he whined. "I love her."

Trishita moved in again.

"Bullshit," Arthur said to Harold, leaning around Trishita. "You need to be locked up in an asylum." He turned away.

Harold started to cry. Arthur whirled around, fists raised.

"I'll give you something to cry about."

"Easy, Arthur. The cops will be here soon." Trishita straightened her arms toward him to hold him back. Sylvia sat up in bed with her hand over her mouth.

"Would anyone like some gin?" asked Flossie.

Sylvia dropped her hand and smiled at Trishita. Arthur saw and grinned, too. Jacquelyn relaxed her jaw and let her mouth hang open.

Trishita started to laugh, then glanced up at the Einstein poster and lost all control. She dropped to the floor and sat cross-legged, laughing and crying at the same time. Jacquelyn put her hands on Trishita's shoulders and said, "There, there."

The police and paramedics arrived. It felt like an intrusion.

*   *   *

The paramedics asked Sylvia if she could walk.

She nodded and got out of bed, but her knees collapsed. One of them picked her up and carried her out. Jacquelyn followed.

A big, gruff policeman untied Harold and handcuffed him while a young, scared looking cop questioned Trishita. Then they left with Harold.

Flossie went back to Russo's and Trishita rode with Arthur in his Mercedes to the hospital.

"Some neighborhood. I can't picture you living here," he said as he drove down Beacon Street.

"You develop blinders after a while, "Trishita said. "At least most people do. I haven't done too well at that." She ducked at a series of loud, sharp noises.

"What's that? Firecrackers?"

"No. Gunshots."

"My God, how do we get out of here?" He doubled over the wheel.

"Just keep going. We're almost to Main."

"Aren't you worried about your mother?"

"She's got bullet-proof skin. One hundred proof skin. Flossie stays mellow on the 'good juice.'" Trishita exhaled hard and shook her head. "Yeah, Flossie used to 'fine tune' her mellow—get just a little drunk, then taper off for an hour or so. Lately, she's been going over the edge, though. I hate it."

He turned right on Main Street. Trishita directed him to the city hospital.

"I think Sylvia's going to be okay," she said.

"God, I hope so. Repercussions, though, may be rough."

"The nightmares stop eventually," Trishita said.

"You know, don't you." Arthur turned to look at her.

"Sure."

"I've missed you." He reached over and touched Trishita's hand.

"It's over. I had no right—" She moved her hand.

"Nor I. If you come back, I won't see you alone. Besides, I'm pretty busy these days."

"Yeah, I heard you got a new job. When I was at the Ballmans those two weeks at the end of August—"

"You were at the Ballmans? Superintendent Ballman?" He slammed on the brakes at a red light.

"They hired me to do the party for Jacquelyn."

"You were in the next town? Jacquelyn didn't say she saw you."

"Please don't say anything to her." Trishita touched his arm. "She knew Sylvia was looking for me. Obviously, she didn't want her to find me." *And your Jackie is much worse off than you know.*

The light changed. The driver behind them honked his horn. Arthur started up. "Shit, you were at the Ballmans, I was in New York, and Sylvia was in Worcester every day looking for you on those streets back there. Jacquelyn couldn't have known how bad it was. She did send Ethan with Sylvia, though."

"She did? Wow . . . . How is Ethan?"

"Fine. He's changed, though. Something's different. More reserved. Private. Actually, I miss the kid in him." He pulled into the parking lot.

"A while back you said, 'if I come back.' What do you mean by that?" Trishita asked, relieved that Ethan had kept his mouth shut.

"We want you to come back. All of us want you. You left a big hole, you know. Jacquelyn told Sylvia she would ask you to come back if she found you."

"Yeah, well I have two jobs now and I'm taking a class I don't want to give up." *Especially to work for a weird cat burglar.*

"A class?" He came around to open her door, but she was already out of the car.

"A college class in cultural anthropology." She grinned. *A class that might study weird obsessions.*

Jacquelyn ran to greet them when they found the waiting room and said the doctor was in the ward examining Sylvia. Jacquelyn studied Trishita's face.

"How did you know Harold was dangerous?" she asked Trishita. "What made you go up the fire escape?"

"I don't know. I didn't stop to think. Actually, when Flossie told me the nerd was with her, my hackles went up. Lucky thing they did."

Jacquelyn took one of Trishita's hands. "I'll say. I had the same response to that kid. Trishita, can you forgive me? Would you consider coming back to work for us?"

"A lot of muddy water has gone under the bridge." Trishita stared at the ceiling. "I have a job now at Clark University so I can take a class there. I don't want to give up either."

"Mrs. Hyde?" The doctor said as he entered the waiting room.

"Is she going to be all right?" Jacquelyn placed her tiny, manicured hand on the doctor's arm.

She's fine." He gave her a professional smile. "She hasn't been harmed physically in any way. No need to keep her here. I've signed her release." He hurried off.

Trishita wanted to flip him off. She started toward the ward to see Sylvia, but stopped, remembering to let Arthur and Jacquelyn go first. She watched Sylvia greet them. They stood talking for a while. A long while. Then Sylvia's lanky frame folded and she collapsed onto the bed. Jacquelyn beckoned Trishita to enter.

Trishita approached with a full heart. Sylvia's brown eyes beseeched her, but she said nothing.

"Please tell Sylvia," Jacquelyn said, "that I asked you to come back but you said you have other interests now."

"It's true, I do." She looked into Sylvia's eyes. "But nothing is more important to me than you."

Sylvia dropped her head and then looked up at her mother through strands of hair. "I'm sorry, Ma."

Jacquelyn stroked Sylvia's hair back. "I am, too."

Arthur opened his mouth to speak, but closed it. Trishita caught a glimpse of a smile as he turned his head.

Sylvia looked up at Trishita and smiled.

"Come now," Jacquelyn said, what are we going to do?"

"I guess we deal," Trishita answered, torn by what McLaren would call an 'approach-approach' conflict. She wanted independence and she wanted the Hyde family, most of it, anyway.

CHAPTER TWENTY-THREE

Jacquelyn felt her back stiffen. She had to be careful not to bargain from need. She glanced at her husband. He stared at the wall in front of him and wouldn't be much help anyway.

"Arthur, would you and Sylvia go take care of the paperwork here?" she asked in a soft tone. "Bring the car around when you're finished. Trishita and I will discuss business in the waiting room. After all, it *is* between us, basically."

"Sure, Hon. Good idea." Arthur snapped to attention. He took Sylvia's arm and headed with her down a branching hallway.

Trishita sat on the plastic, waiting-room couch. A television blared commercials behind her. The ugliness of their surroundings made everything Jacquelyn planned to say seem especially crass. Nevertheless, she sat across from Trishita and began.

"Sylvia wants you to come back to live with us. So do Arthur and Ethan." She felt a tickle in her throat grow to irritating proportions and tried to clear it away.

Trishita waited, open-faced.

"They certainly miss your cooking," Jacquelyn continued, taking a deep breath. "I'm not totally in favor of it, you realize, but I do respect their attachment to you." The tickle interfered with speaking. She went to the drinking fountain for relief, finding just enough to continue.

Trishita looked calm, watching without moving.

"I miss your cooking, too," Jacquelyn continued, "as well as your good management of the household." She coughed twice more and then said with cleared vocal chords, "I'm prepared to offer you double your salary, two hundred and seventy a week, with the stipulation you don't put everything out of reach."

"No deal."

"What? That's a generous offer? What more could you expect?" *The woman's impossible!*

"I gotta admit I love Sylvia." Trishita smiled. "Ethan, too. And let's say I respect you and Mr. Hyde. At one point I wanted you guys to adopt me, for Christ's sake. I wanted a say in family matters as if I belonged."

Jacquelyn studied Trishita. Could this be another manipulation?

"Obviously," Trishita continued, "I overstepped certain boundaries. Realized it after the fact. It's probably right that you made me back off. Now things are different. I have a part time job and a college class I don't want to give up."

"Well, then, what would entice you? I won't beg, you know."

Trishita stood and began pacing the length of the room behind the couches. An old lady in a wheelchair watched, leaning in Trishita's direction as if straining to hear.

"Sylvia, of course," Trishita answered. "She's the main reason I'd consider your offer. There's something else, too. I really want to go to college and get a degree even if it takes twenty years." She sat opposite Jacquelyn, loafers square on the floor, hands resting easily in her lap.

"Why twenty years?" Jacquelyn asked. "You'd be forty-six by the time you graduated at that rate."

"I'll be forty-six anyway, if I live that long. Doesn't matter when or if I get the degree. Only matters that I go for it. Maybe you could help me get started."

Jacquelyn leaned back. Trishita's intensity sparked in her eyes and resonated in her voice. No wonder she felt jealous. Still, Trishita was playing right into her hands. If anyone knew how to maneuver through an academic maze, she did. This put her on top in the bargaining position. Besides, she had made it through the new moon in September without a raid, giving her a new strength.

"How's this, then?" Jacquelyn said. "You move back with us and do all the cooking in exchange for room and board and a meager seventy-five a week. You can use one of our cars to go to your precious job and class at Clark this semester. Next semester you quit your job and go to school full time. In exchange, I will show you how to take the necessary tests to get accepted, to win scholarships, and to use affirmative action programs to your advantage. But, you will still have to do all the cooking, some washing and cleaning, and be a positive role model for Sylvia.

"It's a done deal." Trishita jumped up and held her hands over her head in a gesture of victory.

The lady in the wheelchair clapped her hands.

Jacquelyn pulled herself into the couch corner and clung to its arm, afraid Trishita would pick her up and kiss her.

*   *   *

Trishita smiled each time she met Ethan and Arthur on the three flights of tenement stairs as their paths crossed. When she came up empty-handed, they were going down, each carrying another box of books. They grinned back and joshed about what Trishita might make for dinner.

Flossie hadn't come home by the time they finished. Trishita left her a note and a twenty-dollar bill.

Ethan drove her and her books back to Northboro in his new Toyota pick-up. He was reserved, but radiant. Something new and wonderful had come his way, something that made it easier for her to move back.

"You can have my Rabbit," he said, "now that I've got this truck for my job."

"What job? What happened to baseball?"

"Season's over in case you haven't noticed," he said, smiling at her. "Now I have a job hauling apples. Found out I could double my money if I used my own truck. Dad has a company car so he traded in his Mercedes for this. Pretty cool, huh?"

"Damn right." Trishita grinned. "I get to use the only car I know how to drive. Do you suppose I've forgotten how?"

"Ha," he exploded. Glowing still, he said, "No way. It will all come back as soon as you take the wheel."

It wasn't just the truck, and it wasn't her return to the household that caused this change in him. Something else. They drove in silence for a few miles. Trishita grew more curious by the minute.

"You still dating Judy?" Trishita asked.

"Judy who?"

"I thought her name was Judy. You know, the little Catholic girl?"

"No. She's going with Ike Bogbender now."

"So, who are you in love with? Not that it's any of my business."

Ethan punched Trishita's shoulder.

"Dunno about love," he said. "Anyway, I'm seeing Melissa Martin. She just moved into town and she's beautiful—deep down."

Deep down. Probably not very pretty, Trishita thought. She was sure Ethan meant the girl was beautiful because she loved him. New love feeds on itself until it's old and there's nothing left to eat. Reminded her of a myth that Professor McLaren had told them about a lean monster who was so hungry he started eating his feet and came chomping up his body until there was nothing left but a face.

When love is new, it's a feast; at least it looks like one. She'd had no such luck. Her extravagant crushes were not reciprocated. She'd like to know the love that fed on itself until there was nothing left but a face. Maybe she'd been lucky after all.

"This Melissa Martin," Trishita said to Ethan, "sounds terrific. I hope I get to meet her."

"You will. I've told her all about you."

"All?"

"Not quite all." He looked away.

"Good." This girl must be putting out. That would simplify Trishita's re-entry into the Hyde family, at least as far as Ethan's libido was concerned.

*   *   *

Sylvia and Trishita went into Trishita's old room between Arthur's office and the laundry room to unpack the books. The room echoed when they entered.

"I used to love this room," Sylvia said. "It's been so awfully empty. Now I can love it again."

"I feel like I've come home," Trishita said.

"You belong here more than you ever could in that awful room with Einstein on the ceiling."

"Thanks." Trishita felt her face flush. "I like to think so."

"You know, Trishita, I spent a long time staring at that poster that horrible day, praying to Einstein to keep me alive." She handed Trishita a pile of the heaviest hard cover books for the bottom shelf.

"I doubt he answered your prayers. It was plain luck, both good and bad. Random chance. Einstein certainly understood mathematical probabilities."

Sylvia stopped, tilted her head. Her eyes looked vacant, but Trishita guessed that a hell of a lot was going on behind them.

"I wonder what made Harold what he is," Sylvia said when her eyes came back to her task. She shuddered.

"I wonder, too." Trishita put her arm around Sylvia's shoulders. "I sure wouldn't want to have a kid of my own."

"Why not?"

"The chances of me being a wholesome mother are one in a thousand."

"Better odds than most mothers have," Sylvia said.

"Why do you say that?" Trishita dropped the books in her arms and stared at Sylvia.

"Most mothers don't listen to their kids. You listen. That's why your odds are better."

Ethan came whistling through from the garage, barging through the glow from Sylvia's compliment. "Hi, guys. Want some help?" he asked and began pulling books out of a box.

"Sure," Trishita said. "Just don't burn my books with your passion."

He blushed. Sylvia wrinkled her nose. The phone rang; Ethan ran to the kitchen to answer it and stayed on the line.

"That must be Melissa," Sylvia said, exaggerating each syllable of the girl's name. "I can tell by his tone of voice. He's whacko about her for no good reason."

"Have you met her?"

"Sure. She's a junior, but I'm in the same gym class with her. She practically kissed my ass when she found out I was Ethan's sister."

"I bet she's pretty."

"Hell no. She's got a big nose and greasy brown hair with no style and she wears dorky clothes out of the last century—black tights, skimpy, tied-dyed tops that don't go much below her waist, and Birkenstocks. I hate Birkenstocks!"

"No resemblance to Judy Kraemer, then. Interesting."

"Oh, they're all midget dorks."

With that, Sylvia sounded like Flossie and her drinking buddies. Trishita thought she should admonish Sylvia, warn her against making dumb, flat statements about sizes of anything, but she realized the girl was only fourteen. Did that mean Flossie's crowd hadn't developed beyond age fourteen? The people at Clark University didn't go around talking about size and body parts all the time.

She watched Sylvia unpack the next box, carefully handling each book, and felt a familiar tug on her placental chords. Sylvia was her child in spirit all right. It was easier just to love the kid and not admonish her. Probably wiser, too, at this point, given what Sylvia had just gone through.

"How can Ethan think Melissa's pretty when she isn't?" Sylvia asked.

"He sees her through love colored glasses." *Actually, through his dick.* "Distorts one's vision, you know."

"Is that why they say love is blind?" Sylvia asked laughing.

"Yeah. That among other things—like illusion. I wouldn't mind a little blindness. I'm sick of seeing."

Ethan came back and picked up a leather bound volume of Whitman's poetry.

"Nice looking book, Trish," he said.

"Ha!" Sylvia said with a smirk.

"Shit." Ethan smacked his forehead. "I forgot to tell you Trish. Your mother called a while ago and I promised you'd call back."

"How desperate did she seem?"

"I couldn't tell. She said she had some good news." He looked perplexed.

"Imagine that." Trishita went to the phone and called.

Flossie said, "I'm in love, Mija. It's a brand new man. He's handsome and rich and he's going to move in and pay the rent and fix the stove."

"Make him use condoms," she wanted to scream, but instead she said, "I'm glad, Ma." And then a sudden yearning to understand human behavior, her own included, engulfed her.

* * *

"I hear you got your amazing Amazon back," Ballman said to Jacquelyn in the administrative parking lot. He didn't conceal his smirk. "She's quite a cook."

"You ought to know, I suppose. I imagine she fed you well those two weeks she worked for you." Each time Jacquelyn saw Ballman lately she thought of his stupid clowns. She couldn't will the image away and kept seeing a damn clown on each stair for three flights. Her palms started to itch. She scratched them fast and hard.

"What's the matter with your hands?"

"Allergy." *Clowns, actually. Your clowns.* She headed toward the office ahead of him.

"Yes sir she's quite a cook." He caught up with her and patted his stomach. "I've been on a diet since." He leaned down to whisper at her. "My wife is in a dither. Do you suppose she could borrow Trishita now and then and pay you?"

"Trishita's not my slave. Your wife can call anytime she likes and ask her directly. I'd better warn you, though. She's busy. She's working part-time at Clark University as well as taking a class. Also, I've scheduled her into a full series of tests, and we're busy filling out applications for grants and scholarships."

"Is that so? She does seem rather intelligent for someone with her background."

"Yes. Apparently she's an autodidact—self taught. Tell Mrs. Ballman to catch her between semesters." Jacquelyn surprised herself with her protective response. Trishita was again part of Jacquelyn's life despite the fact the woman's presence still unnerved her. At least Trishita didn't put things out of reach any more. And Sylvia had blossomed. So had their house.

Jacquelyn had to admit that Trishita was one hell of a house-manager. Too much so, perhaps, but Jacquelyn had to remind herself that good work doesn't come out of withdrawn or passive employees.

Ballman opened the door to their office building. He pulled a ten-inch porcelain clown out of his side pocket. "Get a load of this one, Jacquelyn. I found it in a thrift shop in Worcester after the County breakfast meeting this morning. I'm going to keep it in my office. It'll make the office more homelike."

"Very nice, Jonathan." Jacquelyn's stomach cramped. "See you at the meeting this afternoon." She hurried toward her office, and then slowed with an encouraging thought. Since Ballman would leave that clown in his office, she could sneak in some night and break it there. Maybe that would satisfy her craving—safely. The new moon was due soon.

* * *

October came in all its glory. The fall colors peaked mid month. Sunday, after Jacquelyn had sung every note on key with the choir, Jacquelyn and Arthur strolled through the woods. Red maple leaves rained down on them. Jacquelyn giggled like a school-girl and chatted to Arthur. She spoke of her progress at getting Trishita admitted to Clark as a full time student and faked silly interest in Ballman's latest clown. Her hands started itching and she changed the subject.

"Let's celebrate tonight," she said. "Celebrate our lives together—toast our solved problems before any new ones stump us again."

"Sure." Arthur picked up a handful of leaves. "Let's have Ethan's buddy Mickey over if he's in town, and Ethan's new girlfriend. We can burn Harold in effigy and open the rest of our good champagne."

"Oh, yes. I'd like that." Jacquelyn hadn't seen Arthur look so vital, handsome, and present for years. And lately Ethan and Sylvia were models of lighthearted joy. Even Trishita seemed especially happy driving Ethan's old Rabbit to Worcester every morning, coming home, radiant, to plan and cook a fabulous meal, then rushing off to study her precious anthropology. "Our life is good," she said, bending over to kiss Arthur on the nose. "Let's go see what Trishita's making for dinner."

"You're right, Sweetheart. Our life is good again." Arthur tossed the leaves in the air. "Too bad your folks aren't here to see it."

Jacquelyn had crouched to re-tie the lace on one tennis shoe when he spoke, spoiling her good mood. She tried to ignore this intrusion of her parents, but failed.

"You could've gone all day without mentioning *them*." She stood. Her voice was cold to her own ears.

"I could've." He turned his neck to look at her. "Should I have?"

"Yes."

"Why?"

"I don't want to talk about them. That's all."

He grabbed her hand. "Okay, Jackie, you don't have any parents to talk about and we're going to see what Trishita's got on the menu for dinner."

"Good." She broke away and started running. She didn't want him to see the shame on her face.

"Tonight we celebrate." He ran ahead and turned to look at her.

"Right." She shielded her face against him and the branches he broke as he crashed through the woods running backwards ahead of her. "Our life is good."

If I can control myself again next week.

CHAPTER TWENTY-FOUR

Trishita drove the Rabbit into Worcester that first Monday back with the Hydes. She hoped it wouldn't rain until she had more practice driving. She tensed when she neared the university. Where to park? She'd never had that problem before. Solving it made her almost late for work.

She encountered Dr. McLaren in the hall just before class that afternoon. He stopped, greeted her warmly.

"Have you decided on a topic for your research paper?" He asked.

Her heart raced. She felt her face flush.

"Yes." Her voice cracked. Words log-jammed in her throat. Why was she so fucking shy around him? It was a new feeling for her, and a shitty one at that.

"Well?" He raised one eyebrow and smiled broadly, lighting up his long thin face, softening his craggy features.

Trishita noticed that his eyebrows needed combing. They were so wiry they would probably snag if she tried to comb them.

"Reference group behavior," she replied after chiding herself for such wild thoughts, "in former British colonies all over the world."

"Good idea, but a bit too broad. How about narrowing it to the Bahamas, say, or Calcutta?" He started walking toward the classroom. She moved along beside him, noting that he was at least an inch taller than she was. "Come to my office after class," he said. "I can steer you toward some useful books in the library as well as loan you some of mine. How did you happen to come up with that topic? I think it's brilliant in concept, by the way."

"At the beginning of the semester, when you first lectured on it, I realized that I'm prone to such behavior myself—aping the educated when I didn't even go to high school." She warmed and loosened up to his eager interest in her. "The language of my speech is quite different from the language of my thoughts."

"Well, yes. I see. I'm interested in both, you know." He stopped at the classroom door. Other students clustered around him. Trishita went to her seat wondering if the others could see the color of her glow.

*   *   *

The days of October counted off and the winds bared the maple trees and worked on the oaks. Trishita drove to Clark each day with the spirit of spring, then to the grocery stores with the spirit of harvest. The glory of her life was Dr. McLaren's class. On the last Monday of the month, Dr. McLaren lectured on the relationship of death and sex in primitive as well as modern societies. She opened her eyes wide when he introduced the topic of his lecture. There was no need to open her notebook.

"All societies have stories describing the beginning of time," he said, moving his wiry eyebrows. "Stories of death and sex—the basic correlates of temporality, of course—usually relate some event signifying man's first awareness of his own death. In Genesis, it's the eating of fruit from the tree of knowledge. Knowledge of good and evil."

He drew a simple diagram on the board. The chalk broke as he was printing "evil." He bent over to pick up the largest pieces. Trishita watched him as if he were Barishnakov dancing to the dichotomy of good and evil.

"The cannibalistic tribes of New Guinea," McLaren said returning to the podium, "used to conduct ritualistic ceremonies to re-enact the creation of the world by their gods—the Dema. Their ritual involved a sexual orgy that went on for weeks. Then, the final night of the ceremony, a young girl was led into open view of the congregation and placed beneath a platform of heavy logs."

All the students were leaning forward in their seats. No one took notes. Dr. McLaren looked up from the lectern and directly at Trishita. "Those pubescent boys," he continued, "who were being initiated into manhood, lined up to take turns fucking the girl. When the last boy in line entered the girl, the platform dropped, killing both of them. The crowd would then let out a hideous howl, drag the dead boy and girl to the fire, roast them and eat them." He looked at all the students. "I'm not telling you this to shock you. Bear with me and you'll get the point."

Trishita could tell they would bear with him until doomsday. She was surprised at first by his use of typical Russo language, but soon realized he would only use that word as a verb, never an adjective.

"These initiation rites," he said, "were typical of the cannibal gardeners throughout the South Pacific. Consider how many of our own pubescent boys and girls die in gang fights and automobile accidents. We ascribe their deaths to drinking, drugs, and other social problems—sacrifices to the gods of the city. We, in the city, are not gardeners, though."

His rich deep voice flowed through her. Trishita reminded herself that McLaren was married.

"Consider the world of plants." He flipped a page of his dog-eared notes. "We kill their fruits to eat them, yet their deaths quickly result in shoots of new life. Sex and death. Man relates his own destiny to that of the animals and plants he kills, and to the phases of the moon. The primitive cannibal gardener harvested his plants at the full moon and planted his seeds at the new moon."

Trishita heard nothing after "new moon." Jacquelyn! What day was the next new moon? She had to protect Jacquelyn or Trishita would lose everything that was sweet in her life—Sylvia, the woods, the cooking, and her studies at Clark.

She rushed to the library, postponing the visit to McLaren's office.

"Do you have a calendar that tells when the new moon is?" she asked a librarian.

"Yes, right here." The woman pulled a pocket calendar out of her desk drawer. It's the twenty-fourth at two a.m. this month."

"Oh, that's tonight! Thanks." She drove home with a heavy heart and parked the Rabbit on the street, far enough from the house for a discreet get-away in case she had to follow Jacquelyn. Meanwhile, she couldn't do anything but wait and worry.

CHAPTER TWENTY-FIVE

Trishita changed into her jeans and Grateful Dead T-shirt and began making dough for foccacia. She thought it would go well with the spinach salad. Besides, kneading the dough released some of the tension in her neck, some of her worry.

Soon Ethan and Arthur drifted into the kitchen, more nowadays to hang out where the food was, Trishita thought, than to watch a sex temptress. Sylvia breezed in and began drying those dishes and glasses that were too delicate to put in the dishwasher. Arthur hummed a tune from "Mary Poppins" as he opened the red wine and removed the stopper from the decanter. Ethan, grinning, made enough erratic moves to get in every one's way.

"Sylvia!" Jacquelyn's voice was so sharp it could cut cardboard. Trishita's scalp tingled. Abruptly, she stopped her kneading.

Ethan froze en route to the refrigerator. Arthur stopped, too, holding the bottle at pouring angle over the decanter. Sylvia clutched the dishtowel in one hand. The other hand extended forward toward the wine glasses, hovering in mid-air.

Trishita gave her head a quick shake. *Why are we all playing statue?*

"What's the problem, Mrs. Hyde?" she asked.

"It looked like Sylvia was going to drop one of our crystal goblets," Jacquelyn said in a soft voice that barely carried into the kitchen. She stood outside on the flagstone walk that led to the side yard and then started backing away. "Not that it matters, really. I'm sorry I raised my voice. Bit jumpy today, I guess." She turned and headed towards the woods.

The others began to move like cartoon characters in slow motion, slowly warming up to normal speed.

"What's with her?" Sylvia asked, to no one in particular.

Trishita worried. This night of no moonlight was going to be Mrs. Hyde's night out for sure. She vowed she would stay awake, follow Jacquelyn whenever she left. If she tried to stop Jacquelyn too soon, she'd do no more than embarrass her and arouse her hatred. If she caught her in the act, her rage would be intense, but if she saved Jacquelyn—somehow. She had to protect her in order to protect herself.

Timing. Don't pick fruit until the stems are brown. Ripeness is all. Don't even try to rush a river. Don't fall asleep and miss it all.

Trishita pulled on her new maroon and gray Clark University sweatshirt with Gothic lettering after the others had gone to bed. It felt warm—and lucky. She decided that meddling in other people's obsessions wasn't much fun, but she could keep herself awake with coffee, Shakespeare, and pacing. She perused the tragedies to find the character who said, "Ripeness is all." That killed a couple of hours. It was almost midnight when she found the line in Act Two of "King Lear."

"Men must endure their going hence, even as their coming hither: Ripeness is all."

The night was ripe, all right, for going hence.

Next, she thought about her research paper currently focused, with McLaren's blessing, on British acculturation in the Bahamas. She paced her little room and pictured Professor McLaren watching her through the former peephole in the pantry wall. He would be intensely curious, but not judgmental. Someone like him, she decided, would be happily married to a plain speaking, educated lady with short gray hair and sinewy calves, noticeable under the short skirt of a white tennis outfit. Maybe her own father was like Dr. McLaren. Someday she would go to Scotland and find her father. She grinned thinking about what a shock that would be to the poor guy.

Her eyelids weighed so heavily they reminded her of velvet drapery. She sat on her bed and leaned back against the headboard, letting her muscles relax and then shook herself awake with a start. Sleep would be so sweet, staying awake, pure torture. Maybe Jacquelyn wouldn't go out tonight. Did she go out in September? Did she raid a collection every month? Even if she did go tonight, maybe her mission would be successful. Maybe she wouldn't even need Trishita.

"No!" She stood and resumed pacing. If Jacquelyn went after Ballman's clowns, her chances of being caught were dangerously high. Ballman was a light sleeper who suffered with insomnia. He roamed the house—usually after two in the morning. Several times during the two weeks Trishita had lived there, she had braced against his possible intrusion. She would hear him breathing outside her door. Then he'd shuffle away. One time she imagined she could see his breath coming through the keyhole on the old unlocked door to her room, but she realized he was afraid of her. She slept soundly after that, barely aware of his slippers shuffling in the hall.

She doubted that Jacquelyn knew Ballman was a night wanderer. Now she concentrated to recall all she knew about that old house. The backstairs might come in handy.

She stretched and looked at her watch. Ten past two. God, she wanted to sleep. Then a faint sound from the front foyer started her adrenaline pumping. She sat on the edge of her bed and listened hard.

Frogs croaked; crickets rubbed their legs together in love songs. Dogs barked and howled in the distance. Finally, the sound of footsteps, on tiptoe, came slowly down the hall toward the garage.

Trishita assumed that Jacquelyn would listen before entering the garage. She crawled under her covers and breathed audibly through her mouth. Then she heard the garage door open. Next, the engine on the BMW started its purr. Trishita made her way through the dark house to the front door. She listened for two minutes but heard no new noises. Satisfied, she slipped out the front door and ran to the Rabbit parked on the street.

She drove almost into the center of town before she caught up with Jacquelyn's BMW. Trishita knew the most direct route to the Ballmans' house in Westboro, but, to her surprise, Jacquelyn turned right on the old Post Road. Puzzled, Trishita followed—several car lengths behind. Could Jacquelyn be heading for Worcester? Some other collection?

Jacquelyn turned right again on a country road. Trishita stopped. On this road Jacquelyn might notice and recognize the car behind her. Perhaps she had noticed already and was trying to shake Trishita by going this route.

Trishita turned off the headlights and, after wiping her sweaty hands on her jeans, slowly drove up the narrow road. Jacquelyn's car was out of sight. The night was black. One faint streetlight gave off a weak light. No houses lined this street. Just light-swallowing trees.

Then, just ahead on her right, she spotted a parking lot and Jacquelyn's BMW. As soon as she saw the school district logo on the building, she backed down the street until she came to a dirt road. She pulled in and parked. Why was Jacquelyn at her own office?

She left the car and walked through the woods toward the building. A branch scratched her cheek, stinging it. She worried about poison ivy and shuddered, remembering painful bouts with it each time she'd wandered off the pavement. Perhaps nothing more would come of this night of sleeplessness and sleuthing than poison ivy.

Trishita stood still and watched thirty feet away from the building and hidden by trees. The night was so dark she strained to catch any movement in the barely visible shadows.

Jacquelyn came out of the main entrance and moved within ten feet of Trishita's hiding place en route to her car. Jacquelyn's body language pierced the dark. It spoke of angry frustration in small gestures Trishita knew well: a convulsive twist of the right shoulder, a subdued shaking of the right foot, Jacquelyn's restrained form of kicking.

Jacquelyn jumped into the driver's seat and drove off burning rubber. Trishita ran back to the Rabbit, turned the key and gunned it. Nothing happened. She turned the key again and floored the gas pedal. The engine refused to ignite. Again she tried. The smell of gasoline told her she'd flooded the engine. There was not a damn thing she could do but wait and wonder which God would be willing to grace her shoulder.

She checked the time. Her watch read two-thirty. Jacquelyn was en route to hell and Trishita couldn't follow. She was sure Jacquelyn was on her way to Ballman's.

At two-forty the engine coughed its way to life. Trishita sped to Westboro in seven minutes. She parked a quarter of a mile away from the Ballmans' house and ran the rest of the way. Was she too late?

She went by Jacquelyn's car parked a football field away from the house. If there weren't so much at stake, Trishita would smile at these ludicrous nighttime shenanigans. But, there was far too much to lose.

A quick appraisal convinced her to head for the lower slope on the pond side of the house. The cellar door was hidden by the wood-pile. She doubted Jacquelyn knew about this entrance. She opened the ancient wooden door with care. It creaked, but creaks ran rampant in that house. One more wouldn't matter.

Inside, the darkness seemed damper. She tripped against a box, releasing the scent of apples and heard a mouse scurry out of her path. Where was Jacquelyn? And worse, Ballman?

She crept up the cellar stairs and let herself into the kitchen. Under the sink, if she remembered correctly, there was a fire extinguisher. Figuring it might come in handy, she released it from its hook and put it under her arm. Then she listened. The creaking sounds were too normal. Was Ballman awake? Was Jacquelyn aware of his insomnia? Where *was* she?

Trishita started up the back stairs, pausing at each floor to listen. On the third floor, she heard a human mouse moving through the empty rooms. Trishita pictured Jacquelyn in her smelly, hooded sweatshirt tearing off the porcelain heads of Ballman's clowns, carefully setting each head beside the wrong body. There was in ironic artistry to Jacquelyn's obsession that Trishita admired.

Next Trishita heard heavy steps on the second floor. A toilet flushed. The footsteps went down the front stairs to the first floor. The human mouse stopped scurrying. Trishita concentrated on remembering Ballman's nocturnal route. After breathing through the keyhole of her room, he would climb to the cupola. He wouldn't stop at her old room tonight, though, unless they'd hired another maid. That thought shook her. What if someone else was listening to these nocturnal ramblings?

The plumbing groaned. He'd turned on the kitchen faucet. She recognized the sounds in this mausoleum and realized her two-week stint here had given her valuable information. Now, after taking two aspirins, he would be likely to head up the front stairs to the cupola.

Suddenly a long, guttural roar wound up the front staircase. Trishita knew he'd spotted the broken clowns.

Lights came on in the front stairwell before she could hide. Trishita scurried into a closet and listened to Ballman roar and to Mrs. Ballman's frightened chirps that penetrated his din.

Where was Jacquelyn now? Had she worked her way up or down? Trishita felt the fire extinguisher under her arm and knew she had to divert Ballman's attention.

She slipped down the back stairs to the kitchen. The overhead lights were on but the room was empty. Matches were still in the same drawer. She grabbed them and some newspapers and raced up the back stairs to the cupola. There she found Jacquelyn huddled in a corner with a headless clown in her hands. Ballman's heavy footsteps on the front stairs signaled his approach.

"Jacquelyn, it's me. Trishita. I'm going to start a fire to distract Ballman. We'll go down the back stairs. Take my hand—stay close behind me." She crumpled the newspapers and lit the match. The flames filled the cupola with light. Jacquelyn's eyes looked dazed.

"Come." Trishita extended her hand.

Jacquelyn didn't move.

"Now!" Trishita hissed. She put the fire extinguisher under her left arm and picked up Jacquelyn as if she were one of Flossie's drunk friends.

She felt Jacquelyn's muscles relax. Trishita carried Jacquelyn down to the third floor bedroom and sat her on the top step of the back stairway as the fire took off in the cupola. Ballman came roaring up the front stairs. Trishita hovered over Jacquelyn and whispered, "Go down this way."

Ballman rushed by them in such a panic he didn't see either one of them. She pushed ahead of Jacquelyn and led her down to the cellar. Mrs. Ballman's keening added operatic overtones to their flight. Ballman thundered back down the front stairs yelling "Fire! Call the Fire department!"

Trishita took Jacquelyn's hand and pulled her into a huddle behind the woodpile. "We need to listen for a couple of minutes to know which way to run."

Jacquelyn nodded. Her eyes were those of a trapped fawn.

"Damn! I have the fire extinguisher. You stay here. I can't let the house burn down." She ran up the cellar stairs, burst into the kitchen and ran up all three flights up the back stairs to the cupola. The fire was just beginning to ignite the stairs. She sprayed it wildly until she was sure it was out. Then she made the mistake of taking a deep breath. The smoke made her cough.

"Halt," Ballman shouted from the first floor. "Stay where you are."

I'll never make it back down those stairs again, she thought. *Which route will trap me?*

She knew the firemen were on their way at the sound of sirens. A strange calm descended on her. Maybe firewomen, too. Would police people be far behind? She thought about her fingerprints on the fire extinguisher then realized her prints were all over the house. Mrs. Hyde was wearing gloves. Besides, neither one of them had a record, yet. The cops wouldn't have anything to match the prints with.

She peered out the window of the cupola. The pond was a black hole in her universe. Then she saw the fire truck, a red vision of law and order, approaching full speed, and, as well, Jacquelyn's BMW turning down a side road. The scene was a testament to Trishita's luck—good on the one hand, rotten on the other.

She could go to jail for what she'd done tonight. She tasted bile as footsteps thundered up both the front and back stairs.

CHAPTER TWENTY-SIX

Trishita shoved open a long narrow window on the cupola and squeezed out, carefully closing the window behind her. A rusted weather vane protruded from the top peak of the roof.

She grabbed its base, pulled up onto the roof, out of sight from within. Looking down gave her vertigo. She looked up and tried to find some stars to reassure her.

The remainder of the night she listened to people stomping around only a thin roof away. Periodically she convulsed with shivers. Her Clark University sweatshirt was not intended to keep a body warm all night in late October, especially one spread-eagled on the sharp incline of a cupola roof.

At best, the fire she'd set had done little damage. At worst, there was no escape. Soon it would be daylight. She wondered if people driving to Westboro would spot her on the roof. She imagined a dialogue:

"Didja happen to look up on your way to work today?" one would ask.

"Up? No."

"Go by the Ballman place?"

"Yep."

"I looked up," a third would say. "A long-legged creature of the human variety was plastered against the Ballmans' cupola."

"Might be a murder case."

"Somebody oughtta call the police."

She clung to the weather vane first with one hand then the other as she struggled to take off her sweatshirt, turn it inside out, and put it on again. She didn't want anyone to know it was a Clark sweatshirt. Tears sprang to her eyes at the thought of police interrogations. The last one she'd endured regarding one of Flossie's drunken capers had given her the impetus to move out. Yet, here she was again, in deep guano over someone else's caper.

A scream welled up in her throat. She wanted to cry out, "No. I won't take it. I'm sick of bailing people out." She stifled the scream and watched the eastern horizon turn pink.

A black BMW moved slowly up the side road perpendicular to Ballman's street and stopped. Jacquelyn had come back for her! Of course, it was right that she should, but Trishita felt surprised, nonetheless. She wiggled her foot in a brief wave at Jacquelyn. Only from her special vantage point could she recognize the BMW. She doubted that anyone below would see it.

The last of the fire trucks and police cars finally drove away. The sun came up in a cloudless sky shedding brilliant light deep into former shadows. Trishita rounded her shoulders in a futile but automatic attempt to hide. She listened hard, heard no one moving in the cupola. Now was her chance to go back inside.

She inched open the window and was greeted by the warmth within. So far so good. Slowly she opened it wide enough to slip inside. The warmth gave her courage.

She heard the Ballmans talking. Their muffled sounds seemed to come from the first floor. She made a dash for the closet in the empty third floor bedroom. Once there, she sat hugging her knees, willing the time to fly. Her full bladder nagged for release.

An eternity later she heard a car start in the garage and assumed it was Ballman driving away. The remaining hurdle was Mrs. Ballman. Then the phone rang.

"Hello? Jacquelyn?" she heard Mrs. Ballman say. "No, he just left. We had a terrible time here last night. Someone came into our house in the middle of the night, broke the heads off Jonathan's clowns and set a fire in the cupola. Jonathan called emergency and they sent out the fire trucks. It was really strange, though. The culprit put the fire out even before—"

Trishita stopped listening. She knew Jacquelyn would provide cover by keeping Mrs. Ballman talking—an easy task the way that woman liked to talk.

Trishita slipped out of the closet and descended the back stairs on her toes. The woman's chirpy monologue came from the Ballmans' bedroom. Trishita sneaked through the kitchen then down the cellar and out to the woodpile. The bright morning light blinded her for a second.

She hid behind the woodpile until she could decide which way to go. The Ballmans' bedroom overlooked the pond, so she shouldn't pretend to be a morning pond jogger. Several cars came down the road. She straightened and walked with a determined gait across the lawn on the north side of the house, waited for the traffic to clear, then crossed the street.

Once inside the Rabbit she had to work to get the key into the ignition. A policeman in a patrol car stopped and asked her if she needed help.

She jumped, and then pulled herself together.

"No thanks," she said to him. "I just flooded the engine and had to wait a while. I'm sure it'll start okay now."

He drove off. Trishita turned the key with a shaking hand and the engine roared to life. She headed east with no plan in mind other than finding a restroom.

She spotted a Mobil station on Route 20 and pulled around to the back. When she came out of the rest-room she saw a black BMW parked beside the Rabbit. Jacquelyn opened the passenger door and beckoned.

"Man, did you ever save my ass," Trishita said, sliding in to the front seat. "Keeping Mrs. Ballman on the phone was a stroke of genius." She heard admiration in her voice.

Jacquelyn was wearing jeans still, but had changed from the smelly sweatshirt to a rose colored, cashmere pullover. Her hair had been brushed and she had make-up on. Incredible!

"I believe the rescue was yours, Trishita, she said. "Your sweatshirt's on inside out."

"I know." Trishita smiled. "I didn't want the cops to see the Clark lettering when they arrested me."

"Why did you follow me last night?" Jacquelyn's tone revealed a strange mixture of accusation and gratitude.

"To protect my interests." Trishita turned to look out her window. She didn't want to see Jacquelyn's embarrassment.

"Who else knows?"

"No one," Trishita answered, looking back at her tiny boss.

"Ah . . . . What do you intend to do?"

"Nothing. Why?" Trishita could smell the tension in the air. "We're both up to our sashaying asses in this."

Jacquelyn tried to smile despite the frown creasing her forehead, but her lips formed a straight line.

"How did you find out?" Jacquelyn asked.

"Spring cleaning, just after Mickey told me his favorite beer bottles had been broken," Trishita replied. "Then, accidentally, I came across the false bottom in the chest of drawers, saw your gear. So, I went to the library and read the articles about the cat burglar who broke up collections of things and put two and two together. Why do you do it?"

"I . . . I don't know." Tears filled Jacquelyn's eyes.

"What about Arthur and the kids? Do they suspect anything?" Trishita felt damned uncomfortable.

"No."

"Do they know where you are now?"

"No." Jacquelyn said. "When you went back to put out the fire, I went home, changed out of the sweatshirt, and left Arthur a note saying I'd gone to an early breakfast meeting and that you'd gone into school to study for a test."

"Good thinking. Were they all still asleep."

"Yes. Then I left . . . . I must admit I didn't want to go back to the Ballmans, but I felt obligated."

"Shit, you didn't have a choice. If I was caught don't think they wouldn't investigate you!" Trishita shook her head. For someone supposedly intelligent, the woman was sure stupid sometimes.

"I suppose it would be a bit awkward." Jacquelyn studied her fingernails. "Well, when I saw the police, then Jonathan, leave, I called Mrs. Ballman. I didn't actually watch you getting to your car, but I did see you drive away. And here we are."

"It's almost seven o'clock." Trishita stifled a yawn. "I'm supposed to be at work in the math department by eight. I'd better go home and change." She opened the passenger door of the BMW.

"Not until the children leave for school. Please." Jacquelyn reached over and touched Trishita's wrist with ice cold fingers.

"Right."

"Can you call in sick?" Jaquelyn asked.

"You got your cell? I'll call the tape and leave a message." Trishita said. "I could use some coffee, food, and about fifteen hours of sleep

"There's a little diner in Marlboro center," Jacquelyn said, handing Trishita her cell phone. "Meet me there after you make your call. We'll use up the hour before we can go home by having some breakfast."

"Okay by me."

Trishita made her call in a weary daze. It was a wonder she could still drive. Her arms ached and she felt a head cold coming on. Calling in sick wasn't a lie.

At the diner, she sat opposite Jacquelyn in a booth that smelled of vinyl and ketchup. A round, gray-haired waitress took their order of coffee and cheese omelets.

"How come you went to your office first last night?" Trishita asked when the waitress left.

"You followed me there?"

"Yes."

"I thought I could get it out of my system by destroying the clown Jonathan had in his office. But it wasn't there. I felt desperate. You must have had your headlights off. It was awfully dark." She spoke in a whisper.

"Yeah, new moon."

Jacquelyn blanched.

Trishita knew she'd plucked a chord. Now that she was relatively safe again, she felt intense curiosity about her boss. There was a whole lot to admire about Jacquelyn, but not much to like. Sylvia said more than a few times that her mother was weird, reflecting this sense that something was missing. Arthur and Ethan walked on eggs around her, but otherwise accepted her with the usual bewilderment educated men seemed to feel toward women.

Trishita had a new academic fascination.

The waitress slapped a plate in front of Jacquelyn. On it was a pale yellow, flat pancake of an omelet, frozen string potatoes heated in a microwave oven, and a packet of grape jelly. She slapped a similar dish in front of Trishita. Cardboard looking toast came in a paper napkin lined basket that she slid across the table.

Though the food didn't have any smell, it was hot. Trishita chewed, grateful even for rubbery food and the patty of butter that barely moistened the toast.

"How did you know about the new moon?" Jacquelyn asked in a savage whisper, squirting ketchup on her potatoes.

"As I told you before, I did some sleuthing last summer at the Worcester library. I wrote down the dates for all the news stories about the weird burglar who broke collectors' items. Two years' worth. Then I looked at a calendar and compared the dates. The raids always coincided with the new moon. Is it because it's darker on those nights or something else?"

"You said you followed me last night to protect your interests." Grimacing, Jacquelyn swallowed hard then took a sip of coffee. "Now you're just butting in. Besides, I don't want to talk about it—now or later."

The waitress refilled their coffee cups. It gave Trishita a moment to think. A grim looking blonde policewoman came in and sat at the counter.

"What do you suppose she wants?" Jacquelyn whispered.

"We better keep an eye on her." Trishita saw the cop speaking to a waitress and re-focused on Jacquelyn. "I think you need to talk about it even if it isn't any of my business. If not to me, then somebody. For your own good."

Jacquelyn ignored her and continued eating, more than Trishita had ever seen her eat.

The blonde cop at the counter was sharp-nosed and gaunt. She looked away when Trishita faced her. The uneasy feeling came back again. Trishita shook it off, but lowered her voice anyway.

"You know how gays have been coming out of the closet for the last ten years or so," Trishita said, "with lots of news coverage?"

Jacquelyn nodded and chewed.

"Well, the big deal lately is about people, women mostly, who were sexually molested as kids and don't remember any of it until they're in their thirties or forties. Then all hell breaks loose."

"That has absolutely nothing to do with me." Jacquelyn put down her fork and gazed out the window that overlooked a lot full of junk cars.

The gaunt blonde was watching Jacquelyn. Maybe it was the incongruity of Jacquelyn Hyde in this old, rusty diner now filling up with unwashed drunks, crazies, and bums. Jacquelyn's neat, smooth brown hair framed her little face, marred only by the perpetual frown. The elegance of her cashmere sweater belied her kinship with the others in the diner—her reason for being here in the first place. Trishita thought how fucking hard it was for people to come to terms with themselves.

"I bet Professor McLaren has skeletons in his closet, too," she blurted.

"The gods do have feet of clay." Jacquelyn smiled, giving off a rare burst of sunlight. "Aren't you going to finish your omelet?"

"I don't want any more. You can have it."

"Thanks." She stabbed the rest of Trishita's omelet and flipped it onto her plate. "It's not up to your standards, but I'm starved this morning."

"I wonder why." Trishita released a nervous giggle. The policewoman concentrated on her chocolate doughnut. Maybe that's all the cop wanted after all. Turning back to Jacquelyn, Trishita said, "Seriously, Mrs. Hyde, you need to weed out this obsession—pull it out by the roots. Hell, it's important to me. If you go down, I kiss my education good-bye." She caught the blonde's eye. The cop averted her eyes in a flick. Trishita's skin crawled. She wondered how much the cop could hear.

"Hush," Jacquelyn breathed. She looked toward the counter and frowned. Then asked in a cheery voice, "Have you finished filling out the Title IV scholarship application?"

"I'll mail it in as soon as I finish the personal essay." Trishita got the message. "I started it the other day."

"Good. I'll put a call into Washington. A colleague of mine is in the Department of Education. He'll keep an eye out for your application." She waved toward the waitress who brought the bill, a small, grease-splattered piece of paper.

A stoop-shouldered man needing a shave stumbled as he moved by the blonde cop, knocking aside her jacket. Trishita saw the handgun on her belt. The policewoman snapped her jacket closed and swiveled toward the counter.

Jacquelyn slipped out of the booth and went over to the cash register two stools down from the cop. Blithely, she returned to the table with change for a tip.

"You ready?" she asked.

Trishita unclenched her hands from the table edge and, with shaky knees, made it out to her car. The gaunt blonde followed.

"This is it," Trishita said, ready to make a run for it. Then two police cars, red lights flashing, drove onto the junk yard and the blonde policewoman ran right past Trishita.

"She's arresting somebody," Jacquelyn said. "Look."

Trishita's heart played a riff. Sure enough, that gaunt little woman had a man spread-eagled against an old pink Cadillac and was cuffing him. Cops from the patrol cars backed her up. Trishita stared at Jacquelyn with awe. "Did you know who she was after?"

"No, but I figured it wasn't us." Jacquelyn unlocked the driver's door of her BMW. "See you at home."

"Hey, wait." Trishita held up her arm. "You're not off the hook, Mrs. Hyde. I've got some high stakes, here."

"I understand."

*   *   *

Trishita started a pot of coffee and sat at the kitchen table. Jacquelyn sat across from her. Trishita avoided Jaquelyn's eyes for a minute or so. She took a deep breath and looked only to discover Jaquelyn looking at the ceiling. Trishita relaxed.

"You don't have to do much to beat that diner's coffee," Jacquelyn said.

"Okay, what's with the new moon?"

"I don't know." Jacquelyn rubbed her eyes. "I have trouble sleeping at the new moon. Sometimes I make it through the night. But then, other times, I want to destroy some collection of stupid things so badly, it seems like a perfectly sensible thing to do. Last night I took a sleeping pill but still woke up at quarter of two."

Trishita had never experienced insomnia herself, but she felt a brief pang of sympathy. Jacquelyn's battle with herself had to be intense.

"How long has this new moon thing been driving you?"

"At least ten years," Jacquelyn replied in a soft, embarrassed tone.

"Fuck a duck! And you never got caught?"

"I had some pretty close calls." Jacquelyn shook her head.

"Didja ever talk to anyone about it—like a shrink or a hypnotist?"

"No." Jacquelyn lowered her eyes. "I don't trust psychiatrists . . . or psychologists. They're not very bright, you know. Their logic is soft."

The coffee maker gurgled. Trishita poured out two cups on its last wheeze, and then sat down again.

"Jesus," Trishita said. You've gotta talk to somebody who can help you. Somebody who's had experience with your kind of, well, obsession. Doesn't matter how bright they are."

"I keep hoping I can conquer it myself."

"Yeah, right. Look, maybe something weird happened to you when you were a real young kid. Has to be something, for heaven's sake. How do you know you weren't molested?"

"You read too much."

"You don't read enough," Trishita said.

"This conversation is deteriorating." Jacquelyn stood, staring down at Trishita.

"You're right," Trishita said. "I'm sorry. How in hell do you expect to conquer it?"

"Somehow . . . . I take your point. My father didn't molest me, but I certainly do have difficulty in my relationship with him—in ways I can't quite fathom."

"Difficulty? How?"

"I feel awful towards him and he doesn't deserve it." Jacquelyn dropped onto her chair. She started to lift her cup and then replaced it. "I don't know why I resent him so. There are all the superficial reasons—he spent all his money on trombones, he tells interminable stories—but he has never truly hurt me."

"That's how I feel toward my mother, and she's led a pretty wild life."

"My brother—did I ever tell you about Billy? He was killed in Vietnam." Her eyes filled with tears that she blinked away. "One really cold day, when I was about seventeen, he blasted my father for spending more money on trombones than he did on heat. The next day Billy went into the army. Two years later, at Billy's funeral, I vowed that I would destroy Dad's trombones, get back at him for wasting so much money." She glanced at Trishita and said, "Of course, I never did."

Trishita propped her arms on her elbows and rested her weary head on her hands.

"I lost a few baby brothers," she said looking away from Jacquelyn. "Half brothers. Hurts like hell, but I don't think that's even in the same ballpark. Whatever got into you must have happened when you were real little. Kids don't think about the costs of things. Besides, you break figurines, bottles, and ceramic heads—stuff like that. Nothing like trombones."

The clock chimed signaling the half hour. Jacquelyn looked at her watch.

"It's eight-thirty. I'd better call the office."

"So, what is it about your Dad's trombones?" Trishita asked, staying on track.

"He bestowed an inordinate amount of affection on them. He always had a trombone on his lap, polishing, caressing—never played the darn thing."

"What a terrific phrase: 'bestowed an inordinate amount of affection.'"

"It is a bit stilted." Jacquelyn's eyebrows arched.

"I suppose . . . . I never had a dad, you know. I used to pretend I had one with really long legs who would hold me in his lap and read to me. Did your father ever do that?"

"How could he?" Jacquelyn asked in a bitter tone. "A trombone took up all his lap space." She headed toward the phone to make her call.

"That's why you hated Arthur's slide rules. And the ceramic cows I got for Sylvia." Trishita felt a twinge of remorse as waves of exhaustion flowed over her. Her muscles ached and nothing mattered anymore.

"They were just stupid collections." Jacquelyn replaced the mouthpiece of the phone without making her call.

"Like all the others—ugly weeds, proliferating," Trishita said. Is that the right word?"

"You keep making the weed comparison," she said with her back to Trishita. "Well, those proliferating weeds are my dad's trombones. I hated them. I just wanted to smash them to pieces."

"Well, why don't you?"

"What an idea!" Jacquelyn turned. Her eyes blazed. She began pacing the kitchen floor. "I could go to Florida and raid my dad's collection. The raid to end all raids . . . . I'd need a sledge hammer."

"True, those suckers would be hard to break."

"I'd be content just to dent them, I think." She studied the wall calendar. "Next month on the new moon, just before Thanksgiving." She sat on the stool by the sink and stared out the window. "They have a seventh story condo on the beach. Hutchinson's Island. It'll be hard to break in. Might have to scale down from the roof on the beach side of the building." She whirled to face Trishita and asked, "Will you go with me?"

Trishita stretched, touching the ceiling. She knew she'd be heading for trouble. This caper could do them both in, royally. Hell, Jacquelyn was really close to the edge. Whatever Trishita did could knock her over it. Including doing nothing.

"What the hell," she said, "why not? I've never been to Florida."

CHAPTER TWENTY-SEVEN

A week of good mail for Trishita followed. Tests results came in. She had scored high on all her aptitude tests and though her S.A.T. math score was just average, her verbal nearly hit the top.

"You're a shoo-in for scholarships," Jacquelyn said, her smile showing none of its usual ambiguity. "These scores make my end of the bargain quite simple."

Trishita headed toward Dr. McLaren's office on Friday when she finished her work in the math department. She couldn't decide whether or not to tell him about her scores and her high hopes for enrolling next semester, but as soon as she saw him she blurted it all, surprised again by her childish reactions to him.

"Congratulations, Trishita," he said, taking both her hands in his. It was a gesture she'd not seen nor felt before. Little nips of heat raced down her torso, meeting in a chorus line where her legs began. She sat hard.

He moved behind his desk and eased into his creaky swivel chair. Leaning forward, he clasped his hands together and rested them on a clear spot of his cluttered desktop. Trishita admired his wide, square hands sprinkled with freckles and tufts of red hair that glinted in the light. His long fingers ended in nails that had white half-moons. These were no-nonsense nails, square-cut, and clean. She had always loved clean fingernails on a man and wondered if his wife cleaned them for him. Ashamed of that thought, she focused on her research paper.

"Dr. McLaren, does climate shape mythology and custom?"

"Why, certainly—but not precisely."

"I was wondering. The British, generally speaking, are logical, analytical, and, somewhat patriarchal. They came to the tropical Bahamas from a cold climate and took over. I doubt the local folks wanted to take tea precisely at four on the dot every afternoon."

"Have you ever been there, Trishita?"

"No. I've never been south of Connecticut. But I'll be going to Florida over Thanksgiving. I'm afraid I'll have to skip classes that week."

"No problem. Knowing you, you'll have your paper completed before you go—all drafts. It certainly won't hurt you to miss two class sessions."

"I don't want to miss them, but my employer needs me to go with her on a trip."

"Well, enjoy it. I hope you can get over to the Bahamas and feel the air. It's rich and soft, sensuous, actually. Imagine the poor Brits trying to adapt to that." He laughed. "I doubt that I could adapt to it."

"How about the poor Bahamians," Trishita replied, feeling more sparks of excitement than fear of embarrassment, "trying to adapt to clock time."

"And learning how to set a proper table," he said.

"Right." She laughed. "Some Bahamians to this day do not believe that Americans landed on the moon. They say it was just a television special."

McLaren smiled, baring long, white teeth, crinkling his eyes.

"There was a Welsh comedian," he said, "who did a bit called, 'Morgan the Moon.' Practically everyone in Wales is named Morgan, by the way. Well, this particular Morgan was the first to land on the moon, according to the comedian, but he landed on the dark side." McLaren's face sparkled with mirth.

Trishita fell in love.

"I know this is besides the point of my research, she said, sobering, "but will you tell me more about moon mythology?"

He leaned back in his chair, clasped his freckled hands behind his head and began talking. He spoke for a good half hour.

Rapt, Trishita barely breathed.

"Dr. McLaren," she asked when he paused, "do you think the moon can govern our actions?"

"It's a gravitational pull. It may affect some people sometimes. Personally, I haven't felt an urge to howl at the full moon, but I can't deny it has some pull." He glanced at his watch and said, "Okay, I'll end this monologue with Ovid's tale of Tiresias. One night Zeus and Hera got into an argument. Zeus claimed that women found more joy in making love than men did." McLaren fumbled with a book. "Hera said, 'No way, Zo-ay' so they went to Tiresias to settle it because Tiresias had experienced both points of view."

"How did Tiresias get to do that?"

McLaren pointed toward a book on a top shelf. "According to Ovid, Tiresias came across two snakes mating one day, and hit them with his stick. This offended the snakes. Somehow, they managed to get Tiresias changed from a man into a woman. After seven years as a woman he—or she—saw the same two snakes mating. She hit them with her stick again. They didn't appreciate this a bit and turned her back into a man."

"I've read lots of tales like that," Trishita said.

"There are several around, that's for sure. The more you read, the more you wonder about the universality of human imagination."

"Well, did Tiresias settle the argument?"

"He took the side of Zeus," McLaren replied. "This annoyed Hera no end, and she struck Tiresias blind. I guess she felt guilty about doing that because she gave him the gift of prophecy, thereby making him wiser than Zeus or Hera."

"It's metaphor, isn't it, that unites all cultures?" Trishita asked, jumping ahead of herself.

"I'm not sure it unites them, but it's central to all mythology." He glanced at the wall clock.

"Please go on. We have five minutes before class." Trishita noticed she was sitting on the edge of her chair. She pushed back. "Tell me about the patriarchal view."

"Okay." He smiled again. "The patriarchal viewpoint—in the instance of your research—the British set apart pairs of opposites as if they were absolutes and not merely aspects: male-female; true-false; life-death; good-evil. This is a solar view versus a lunar mythic one."

"How so?" Back on the edge of her chair.

"In the solar view, darkness is opposite light. It flees from the sun. In the moon, dark and light interact like yin and yang, on one sphere. The blinding of Tiresias gave him lunar wisdom. He was blind to the sunlit world where opposites are absolute, but developed vision of the inner eye which penetrates the dark side of the moon—and the dark side of life, I might add."

"Penetrates the dark side of life," she said, feeling as if she were in a Greek chorus. A bell rang. She jumped up. "Thank you, Dr. McLaren, so much."

"My pleasure, Trishita."

She drove the Rabbit back to Northboro like a pilot soaring through the clouds. McLaren had power over her—much as her lit professor lover had years ago. She was a sucker for professors, that's for sure, and was probably lucky that McLaren was married.

"Forget him," she told herself, and pulled into the grocery parking lot. In the aisle for pastas and rice, she literally bumped into Mrs. Ballman who walked backwards into Trishita's cart.

"My dear, Trishita," Mrs. Ballman exclaimed. "what luck to run into you. Can you show me some penne. It's spelled P E N N E. Do you suppose this store carries it?"

Trishita smiled and handed her the pasta from the shelf right in front of them.

"Oh that's it. I wondered. Say, did you hear about our break in?"

"Yes, I heard all about it. Weird." Trishita backed down the aisle. "I have to run. Much to cook before I sleep." She made it through the check stand before Mrs. Ballman had the chance to expound further. With a back handed wave at her, Trishita escaped.

While loading her groceries into the Rabbit, she realized she was more tolerant of Mrs. Ballman than of her own tight-assed, brittle, employer. Yet, she and Dr. Jacquelyn were going to take a road trip together beneath the dark side of the moon. Hell, she'd seen enough of the dark side of life in Flossie's house. Time for light. College light. And Mrs. Hyde was the only one who could provide it.

*   *   *

"Someday I'll catch the dirty bastard who broke my clowns," Jonathan Ballman growled. "And when I do—" He wrung his huge hands.

Jacquelyn stood in the hallway of the administrative offices facing him. "I'm so sorry, Jonathan. Why do you suppose anyone would do such a thing?" She backed down the hall toward the exit.

"Sick. That's what. Sickos everywhere masquerading as saints!"

"Yes," she replied. "Really a shame." That tweaked her strings. Was she truly sick? "I must run, now. Meeting with social studies teachers." She turned and hurried out to the parking lot.

"Tell them to find the bastard who wrecked my clowns," he yelled after her. "Good social studies project."

Jacquelyn drove toward home, worrying. It had been three days since the raid and so far Trishita had kept their secret. Yet, what a bind. Here she was beholden to Trishita, of all people. Talk about politics making strange bedfellows.

She hadn't spoken to Trishita beyond simple greetings since that morning. The woman acted as if nothing had changed between them. How could she trust Trishita? She grew up in the worst slums of Worcester. Lied her way into jobs. Set fires. Well, one fire.

She had to trust Trishita.

The bare branches of the trees along the road saddened her. Wind whipped them against each other beneath a gray sky. She swerved to avoid a darting squirrel.

With a heavy heart, she realized she must follow through—actually destroy the trombones. At least it was worth a try. Otherwise, she might just continue on her compulsive path until she got caught. She realized, too, that she needed Trishita's height and strength to help her accomplish this task. Poor old Bill Nestrom. Oh mein papa. She wept the rest of the way home.

After she pulled into the garage, she blew her nose then powdered it. "Fuck mein papa," she said under her breath, and then put on a happy smile.

Sylvia and Trishita were cooking and chatting when Jacquelyn entered the kitchen. "Hi, there," she said. "What are you two concocting now?"

Standing at the stove, Sylvia looked up from her vigorous stirring. "Hi, Ma. Look—risotto." She smiled at Jacquelyn, flashing white teeth now so straight and unfettered. Then her pretty face darkened. "Ma, what's wrong?"

"Nothing, Dear," Jacquelyn replied. "What makes you ask?"

"I just thought . . . well, you looked kinda mad—"

"I'm not angry, dear." Jacquelyn kissed Sylvia's cheek. "A little tired, that's all." *What does my face show?*

"Keep stirring, Sylvia," Trishita said as she looked into the pot of rice. To Jacquelyn she said, "You have plenty of time for a rest before dinner. We'll call you when it's ready."

Jacquelyn didn't dare look into Trishita's eyes for fear of seeing—seeing what? Contempt? Triumph? Pity? She nodded and went upstairs, cursing herself, her father, and her housekeeper—that maid for all seasons.

*   *   *

"You won't be here for Thanksgiving?" Sylvia whined.

Jacquelyn was tempted to tell her family the truth. She toyed with the vegetables on her plate—tasty little carrots, potatoes, peas, and baby onions from Trishita's Coq-au-vin—and wished she could eat without cramping.

Arthur stared at her. "Where are you going?"

"I have a medical problem." The lie thickened her tongue. "My stomach. Something's wrong. There's a specialist in Florida that my doctor recommended. Thanksgiving week is the only week I can take off from work. I certainly don't want to leave home at Christmas."

"How bad is it, Ma?" Ethan asked. "Do you think you have ulcers?"

"No. Well, perhaps. Whatever, I need to find out. Your father can take you to a restaurant for Thanksgiving this year."

"Yuck," Sylvia said. "That would be awful. Trishita can cook the turkey."

"I'm afraid Trishita won't be here either. I've asked her to go with me."

The chorus of "What?" felt like a face slap. "Why?" followed.

Arthur stifled a smile. He looked guilty of something. For feeling amused in the first place?

"Well, Honey," Arthur said, "you could have asked me to go with you to this doctor all the way down in Florida, but since you didn't, my next choice of companion for you would be Trishita." He frowned. "Why didn't you ask me?"

"Your job's too new to just take off on a whim," she said, thinking fast. "Besides, going around to a bunch of doctors is no fun. Trishita offered to go because she's never been south of Connecticut."

He looked placated as he filled his fork with chicken. "Are you gonna fly down?"

"No. We'll take the BMW. You know how I hate airplanes. That's why we'll be gone all week."

"You could take the train," Ethan said,

Jacquelyn smiled at him. What an easy-going child he was.

"I want to have my car down there to use, she said to Ethan. The doctor may run me around for medical tests, you know, and I dislike driving strange rental cars."

"Are your folks expecting you?" Arthur asked, "or will you be going as far south as Hutchinson's Island?"

"They're not expecting me, but I may see them." Jacquelyn stabbed a carrot.

"Grandpa Nestrom would be awfully glad to have you visit them for a change," Sylvia said.

"Does he still have all those trombones?" Ethan asked. "I remember seeing his house on Glendale Street when I was real little. It was so full of trombones there was no place to sit."

"It has been about ten years since we visited them," Arthur said, wrinkling his eyebrows. "Just where are you going in Florida?"

"Orlando," Jacquelyn lied, then swallowed a piece of carrot.

Trishita entered carrying a hot dish of date pudding and a bowl of whipped cream. Jacquelyn concentrated on chewing the bites of chicken on her plate, counting each mouthful thirty times.

"Ma just told us you won't be here to cook Thanksgiving turkey," Sylvia cried out to Trishita.

"How about it, Sylvia," Trishita said as she set the dessert dishes on the sideboard and began clearing their dinner plates, "if I show you how to do it beforehand, then you can cook Thanksgiving dinner?"

"Wow! That would be fun. Show Dad and Ethan, too, so they can help."

"Dad, can we invite Melissa and Mickey?" Ethan asked.

"Sure, and Melissa's folks, too," Arthur said. "Hell, we'll round up all the strays."

"We'll get a twenty-five pound turkey and have two kinds of stuffing." Sylvia clapped her hands.

Once again, Trishita had saved the day. Jacquelyn felt the old rage burning in her stomach.

*   *   *

Jacquelyn Hyde regretted on that Sunday before the November new moon that she was not singing in the choir, was not listening to the soothing voice of the minister reading lyrical phrases from the King James Version, and was not meditating through a sermon. Instead, she was driving south on the Merritt Parkway with a far too cheerful woman whose hair alone seemed to fill her car. Trishita had pushed her seat as far back as it would go. Jacquelyn had to look over her right shoulder to see Trishita's face, not that she wanted to.

"I packed my bathing suit," Trishita said. "Do you think we'll be able to go swimming?"

"Perhaps." Jacquelyn kept her eyes on the highway and maintained a steady fifty-five. The other cars whizzed past her.

"I've never seen New York City. Will we go close enough to see it?"

"You'll see the skyline from the highway."

"Yo mama, what a blast!"

"Down, Trishita." Jacquelyn groaned. "Two days of your excitement will give me a migraine."

"Sorry. How about some music to soothe this savage beast?"

"It's soothe the savage breast, not beast. See if you can find some hymns."

Trishita turned on the radio and scanned the stations, stopping short at some wild, rocking spirituals. "I know I'm generalizing, but those black dudes sure can make music," Trishita said. "Course, the only black people I know personally are Puerto Rican. They don't make these sounds in the Catholic Church."

Jacquelyn felt the overwhelming presence of Trishita in her relatively small car, especially when Trishita leaned forward to look at her. "Sorry," Trishita said. "I'll shut up. Let me know whenever you want me to drive."

Three hours later Jacquelyn concentrated on maneuvering the lanes for the bridges and routs around Manhattan. Trishita had been mercifully quiet, but the sight of the city made her sound like a bad talk-radio show.

"My God, look at that skyline! Just like in the movies. Have you ever been to Ellis Island? My great grandmother came through there from France. At least that's what my mother used to say. Man, get a load of that crowded cemetery! What do they do, dig 'em up every hundred years to make room for more?"

"That's precisely what they do."

A double axle truck cut in front of Jacquelyn. She had to slam on the brakes.

"Asshole," Trishita said.

"You shouldn't swear at other drivers, Trishita. Someone might shoot at you."

"He couldn't hear me. Besides, it releases some negatives ions, or enzymes." She leaned forward and grinned. Her thick red hair curled all over the place.

Jacquelyn concentrated on the traffic rushing by on both sides. Why had she decided to drive to Florida?

"I've often wondered about decision-making," she said when the traffic eased into a steady flow. "Sometimes I have trouble making the right choices for myself."

"I'll say. Jeez, look at that billboard. It's like a TV commercial in 3-D."

Jacquelyn felt the presence of a huge trailer truck right on her heels. She speeded up, but the truck stayed with her, its driver blasting the horn at her. "What does he want?"

Trishita peered back. "I can't tell. Guess he wants you to go faster."

"Oh, dear, I'm already doing sixty."

"Ignore him, then."

The horn blasted again, a deep, big-man-around-town roar. Jacquelyn gripped the wheel. "I'm in the right lane. Why doesn't he pass me?"

"Because he's an asshole, that's why." Trishita leaned back.

Through the rear view window Jacquelyn could see that Trishita's hair spilled over onto the back window shelf. The horn roared again. "Oh dear, what should I do?"

"Ignore him, curse him, or both."

"Asshole," Jacquelyn whispered.

"A little louder please." The horn almost drowned out Trishita's words.

"Asshole, asshole, asshole," Jacquelyn hollered.

"Atta girl. Now slow down and let the fucker burn."

Jacquelyn's heart pounded. She slowed down to forty-five. The truck stayed behind her. It was so big she couldn't see if it was driven by a human being. Now it couldn't pass her because the other lanes were packed solid. It roared like a newly caged gorilla. The more the horn blasted, the slower she drove. Finally, when she saw an exit sign, she yelled, "Asshole!" and slipped off, waving her middle finger toward the rear window. "Time for a pit stop, anyway," she said, smiling.

Trishita applauded; the trucker leaned on his horn for one final bellow.

"Atta girl," Trishita repeated, "but you need a lesson in flipping off."

Jacquelyn pulled into a Shell station. Trishita unfolded like a photographer's tripod and stood beside the car stretching her long torso and arms. A series of catcalls came from some men leaning against nearby pick-up trucks. Jacquelyn wondered what they were saying. She came around the car where Trishita stood and handed her a twenty-dollar bill. "You get the gas, okay?"

"Get a load of Mutt and Jeff," one deep-voiced man called.

"Show us some more of those long legs, lady," another shouted.

Jacquelyn hurried inside the station. She looked out and saw Trishita calmly filling the tank.

"Those men back there," Jacquelyn asked later when Trishita was driving, "did they frighten you?"

"Naw. That's par for the course."

"What do you mean?"

"They always shout at me like that. With my height and wild hair I'm enough of a freak to make them uncomfortable, so they yell."

"Oh my. We'd better stay away from cities."

"They're worse in the country. But don't worry. If we ignore them, they won't bite."

"You talk as if they're animals."

"I bring out the best in people." Trishita took a savage bite of the apple in her hand. She chewed hard, swallowed, and then flashed a smile.

Jacquelyn wasn't used to sarcasm from Trishita, and wasn't sure of her meaning. She leaned back and closed her eyes. If only she had confided in Arthur instead.

Jacquelyn's eyes popped open. She hadn't confided in Trishita, she'd been caught by her. What would it be like to live free? She looked over at Trishita calmly driving at sixty-five miles an hour, lips and eyebrows as loose as a baby's.

"What's it like to live free?" she asked.

Trishita gave a slight nod indicating she'd heard the question, but she said nothing.

The sun fell behind a cloudbank over the western foothills. It would be dark soon. Jacquelyn closed her eyes and prayed for peace—her own.

"I wouldn't know," Trishita said.

"Wouldn't know what?"

"What it's like to live free."

"Well, goddammit, let's find out!" Jacquelyn sat up straight. She turned on the radio, found some music more rock than country, and turned up the sound.

CHAPTER TWENTY-EIGHT

Trishita put a quarter in the juke-box-like slot attached to the headboard. The bed started vibrating with a jolt, then eased into a quiet pulsing. She compared it to educated foreplay.

"Why on earth would you want to vibrate after driving all day?" Jacquelyn asked when she came out of the bathroom with her face night-cream shiny. "Didn't the car vibrate enough for you?"

Irritated, Trishita wondered what could uncoil Jacquelyn's springs. The "magic massager" felt good, and it was a relief to stretch her legs.

"Hey, don't knock this massage deal," Trishita said. "Try it, it might loosen you up. The medium is the massage."

Jacquelyn gave her a dirty look. She climbed into the other bed and opened a paperback book with a lurid cover. At least the colors looked lurid from across the room.

"What are you reading?" Trishita asked.

"Oh, it's a novel about vampires in a California beach town. My secretary recommended it." Her voice was losing its edge.

Vampires—fitting. The bitch can read after all, Trishita thought. "How much farther is it to your folks' pad?" she asked.

Jacquelyn closed the book over her forefinger. "About seven hours from here."

"What'll we do when we get there?" Trishita asked.

"Get a room off island," Jacquelyn said. "Then, when it's dark, we'll go over and figure out how to break in."

"An island, huh. Do we take a ferry to it?"

"No. It's just a sandbar barrier connected to a smaller island by a bridge. Then there's another bridge to the mainland."

Jacquelyn re-opened her book and continued reading. Heavy trucks rolling by the motel broke the silence outside. Trishita sat up after one extra loud one roared by.

"I guess there's no chance of getting over to the Bahamas."

"My word," Jacquelyn said, looking over at her. "Where did you get a notion like that?"

"My research paper. I just thought—"

"We'd have to fly."

"Yeah. Forget it," Trishita said. "I can read about it, anyway." The vibrations stopped. She opened her textbook, but the words swam across the page.

"Vampires operate in the dark," Jacquelyn said. "I wonder if there's some vampire in me."

"You don't believe in them, do you?"

"Of course not. I don't believe in witches, ghosts, or past lives, either." She turned off the lamp. Flashing neon light from a billboard advertising Jack Daniels sliced through the slats in the mini blinds. "Still, I do believe there's some evil in me. Evil I can't control."

"Everyone knows some evil," Trishita said. The sadness she heard in Jacquelyn's voice softened Trishita. "Course evil is a pretty heavy word for that old dark-side-of-the-moon shit—I think it comes from holding back. It's like stuffing feelings into a stock pot, turning the burner on high and then clamping down the lid. The steam has to escape somehow."

"Funny thing for me is I always feel great after a raid when I should feel scared and guilty. You say everyone knows his own evil. What's yours?"

"Petty shit. Putting things out of reach. Kowtowing to my mother's demands when I know they're wrong. That sort of thing." *And sex at the wrong time with the wrong man.*

"You deliberately put things up high!"

"Now and then."

The covers on the other bed rustled. Trishita listened to Jacquelyn's uneven breathing. What would happen if she knew Trishita was guilty of seducing both Arthur and Ethan? At least she was clean as far as Sylvia was concerned.

"Has it anything to do with Sylvia?" Jacquelyn's voice pierced the dark between their beds.

"Sylvia? You gotta be nuts. Besides, I'm not a member of the church, as they say in Lezland."

"I wasn't thinking about sex, but why is she so crazy about you?"

Trishita reflected on this. It was a good question. "I don't have to judge her," she answered.

Jacquelyn remained quiet. Another truck roared by.

"You remember when you were thirteen?" Trishita asked. "That time for me is etched into my skin. I worshipped the janitor at Clark. He used to take me with him on weekends and let me sit in the classrooms while he cleaned. He listened to me. He was my life."

"Billy—my brother—was like that to me."

"Well, I didn't have any older brothers or sisters so the janitor was it. He was a dry alkie at the time, but after a while he fell off the wagon. Made some mighty rude passes at me. I felt awful and kept out of his way. Later, he drowned in Lake Quinnsigamond. I'm Sylvia's janitor—the dry one. You're her mother for life."

"Not a very tender one, I'm afraid. I get cross with her far too often. Maybe I just expect too much of her."

"You just need to relax around her."

"Relax?" Jacquelyn laughed one note. "Heavens, every time I relax, I start going through Katherine Kubler Ross's stages. You know, when you're facing death. I go through the first three, at least." She sat up and held out one finger. "First, denial: 'Hell no, I won't fall.' Then anger. 'Damn it, I'm going to hang on as tight as I want!' And bargaining. 'If you promise to catch me, I'll let go.' Something like that. I don't remember the other stages except the last one."

"Amazing! Yeah, acceptance is the last one." Trishita turned onto her side and propped her head with her elbow. "Who do you bargain with?"

"God."

"Just for relaxing? Holy crow, you oughta tell that to a shrink."

"I wish you'd get off that kick." Jacquelyn's voice knifed toward the ceiling.

"Hey, I've got an idea. Why not see a stomach specialist while you're in Florida? You won't have to lie about seeing a doctor, since this is why you supposedly came down here, and you can get checked out at the same time. Maybe your troubles with food come from what you said about relaxing."

"I don't have troubles with food—just a nervous stomach. But, you're right. It wouldn't hurt to take home a doctor's diagnosis."

"Good." Trishita rolled onto her back. "It's new moon tomorrow night."

"I don't need to be reminded."

"Dr. McLaren said—"

"Isn't there anyone else at that university you can quote, or is his name constantly on the tip of your tongue?"

"Okay, I've got a school-girl crush on him," Trishita said with a laugh, "but he's married so it goes nowhere beyond the classroom."

"Lots of affairs start in a classroom—especially a college classroom," Jacquelyn said.

"Affairs suck. Only cowards get into them," Trishita said.

"My, aren't we judgmental," Jacquelyn said.

"Takes having an affair with a professor at age twenty to know, I guess," Trishita said, blocking a sigh. "Once you've examined the quality of their shit, though, you do judge."

"As a matter of fact, I'm glad you disapprove." Jacquelyn fluffed her pillows. "Do you think Ethan is sexually involved with Melissa?"

"That's not what I mean by an affair." Trishita was still thinking about her judgment. Cowards? There was more to it than that, actually. "Ethan's screwing Melissa, I'm pretty sure."

Jacquelyn bolted upright. "Oh, my goodness. What makes you think that?"

"No more stained sheets from wet dreams."

"Blunt, aren't you?"

"You asked."

Jacquelyn grew silent. Footsteps moved along the walkway outside their room. Music blasted out of a car radio until the slam of a door cut it off.

"What were you going to say about your precious Dr. McLaren?" Jacquelyn asked when it was quiet again,

"Oh, just that he told me a story about this guy called Tiresias who got to live as a woman for seven years. That gave him a woman's view of things. More grays than blacks and whites. McLaren said men tend to relate to the sun and think in absolutes and women are more like the moon where dark and light meet and meld into gray, sort of."

"Women who think only cowards have love affairs?" Jacquelyn asked.

Trishita groaned and then laughed. "Remember, this is mythology I'm learning about. Universal, primitive stuff. There are nuggets of truth hidden in myths, though. I asked McLaren about it because I wondered what connection you had with the moon."

"What's it to you, anyway?" Jacquelyn asked in a bitter tone.

"I told you. You're my ticket to a downtown career." Trishita released an exasperated sigh. "Anyway, Tiresias was blind but had inner vision. He understood the dark side of life."

"I wish I had some inner vision," Jackie said. "I feel as if all the darkness of my life is risky, yet basically trivial." She shook her head. "Collections—clowns, dolls, figurines, beer bottles. Trivial."

It's funny," Trishita said. "Mickey didn't even notice the broken bottles"

"Well, he had a girl with him and they were both drunk."

"Yeah." Trishita sat up and faced Jacquelyn. "You know, the tiniest mosquito can give you malaria. The smallest insult, thrown at you repeatedly, can boil one hell of a witches' cauldron." She yawned and rolled onto her side, wondering what happened to Flossie.

"I guess trivia can sting pretty bad." Jacquelyn put on eyeshades. "Thank you for reminding me. Goodnight, Trish."

"Goodnight, Jackie."

*   *   *

"This must be a real posh place—beach condo on an island. Are your folks rich?" Trishita was driving; Jacquelyn fiddled with the tuner on the radio, her exuberant mood of the day before back in full force.

"Rich? Ha! Did you hear my father talking? He goes around saying, ad nauseam, 'We're just poor old geezers. Why we're so poor we can't even pay attention.' It's such a tired joke." She smiled, though, as she spoke. "My dad was an auto mechanic in Worcester—worked for other people. Meager salary. They live on his social security now plus what's left of his inheritance."

"Then how did they get ocean-front space?"

"Uncle Roger. My dad's brother built the place in '75, sold some of the units and rented the rest. He asked Dad to manage the whole complex and live there rent free." She gave up on the radio and turned it off. "My folks agreed to move out whenever Uncle Roger and Aunt Mabel wanted in, but that's never happened. They don't like to leave the hotel they own in the Virgin Islands. When the people in the condos leave for the summer, Mom and Dad do, too, and go up to Maine. They do have a rich life, I guess."

"I knew a girl once who had a rich uncle," Trishita said.

"They're nice to have. Uncle Roger gave me Madame Alexander dolls every time he stopped in Worcester on his way to Bar Harbor. Such beautiful dolls."

"What are they? I've never heard of 'em."

Jacquelyn gazed out the window at the sandy, pine-studded land of southern Georgia.

Trishita followed her gaze, fascinated with the changing landscape, the warm, moist air. It took her a while to realize that Jacquelyn had not responded to her question about the dolls. She took her eyes off the road to study her strange companion. Jacquelyn reminded Trishita of a popsicle on a stick, sitting up rigid on the seat, frozen. What the hell had happened to her?

"Jacquelyn? You okay?"

No response.

"Hey, Jacquelyn, come off it. What's the matter?"

"Anybody home?" Immobile, silent. Trishita reached over and shook Jacquelyn's forearm.

"What did you say?" Jacquelyn turned her head toward Trishita and smiled.

*   *   *

The landscape turned tropical green. Highway 95 lay across it like a ribbon rippling down a christening dress. Trishita slowed down each time she noticed the speedometer inching up to eighty.

At four thirty in the afternoon Jacquelyn said, "See that motel up ahead on the right? Pull in there."

"Are we here?'

"Close by."

"I can hardly wait to see the island."

"You'll wait." Jacquelyn went into the motel office to register. Trishita glanced around and saw a small swimming pool enclosed by a chain link fence. She used to swim at the YWCA in Worcester in a lap pool so highly chlorinated her skin stung afterwards. Now she was itching to swim in the natural salt water of the Atlantic. She wouldn't mind having someone like McLaren swim along with her.

"I have a splitting headache," Jacquelyn said when she came out and directed Trishita to a parking spot. "I'm going to lie down for a while."

Trishita wondered about Jacquelyn's headaches. How did they relate to her obsession? To the new moon? And what was that strange trance she went into in the car? Trishita decided that her curiosity was natural, that everybody craves light when the going gets murky.

She carried in their suitcases. The room smelled of Pine sol doing battle with cigarette smoke. Two double beds, covered with brown print quilted bedspreads, faced a television set and a painting of palm fronds. She knew she would have to wait several hours before going to the island and decided that waiting was an acquired skill that took practice. Yet, all of life was simply waiting—doing things to distract from the waiting. Once Sylvia had said that Trishita's meals were so good she could hardly wait to digest and make room for the next one.

Usually Trishita distracted herself by reading. Now, she chose not to. Instead, she went for a stroll in a part of the country where it seemed that no one walked outside of the golf courses, and rarely walked there. There were no sidewalks, nor paths, only highway. Yet the air was wonderfully balmy and the ocean near-by. Though she could neither see nor hear it, she could smell it now and then between whiffs of diesel fuel. Waiting for the next event, she reckoned, wasn't too bad if your senses were operating and you paid attention to them.

CHAPTER TWENTY-NINE

Jacquelyn said she felt better after her nap and dinner. Just before midnight, she dressed in her raiding outfit with the smelly sweatshirt. She, with Trishita, wearing her Clark U. sweatshirt inside out, drove across a long bridge over the Indian River to a small island. Here she parked.

"There aren't any condos," Trishita said.

"Right. People just fish off this island. Hutchinson's Island is over there." She pointed toward a mango grove. "The ocean-front condos are just beyond the mango grove. If it weren't so dark, you could see them. We'll walk from here."

Trishita's skin tingled. This was more fun than it was supposed to be. Maybe that's why she usually found herself involved in other people's capers. She could have the excitement without having to be the loony one.

Jacquelyn pulled up the hood of her sweatshirt as they walked across the next bridge. Then she headed north leading Trishita up the one road on Hutchinson's Island. A streetlight lit a parking lot near her Uncle Roger's eight—story stucco building. Jacquelyn pointed out a path beside an enclosed swimming pool. "That leads to the beach," she whispered.

They sneaked to the front of the building and looked up. There were three units side by side on each floor. Low lights illuminated the middle unit on the fifth floor. The rest were dark. Each unit had a narrow balcony overlooking the beach with a concrete partition between the balconies for privacy.

"Which one is their apartment?" Trishita whispered.

"It's on the seventh floor in the middle. See?" She pointed up. "Two stories above the one that's lit. That one houses security. We have to wait until his lights go out."

"How do you plan to get in?" Trishita acknowledged her fear of heights even as she recognized the irony of it. She hoped Jacquelyn didn't expect her to climb anywhere.

"This," Jacquelyn said as she pulled a card out of her pocket. "It will get us through the gate. But I lost the key to their apartment long ago. Or threw it away."

"Threw it away?" Trishita asked.

Jacquelyn ignored her and moved toward the gate.

"All the units open onto an outside corridor on the west side of the building," Jacquelyn whispered. "That's where the elevator is. Each unit has just one entrance. Probably deadbolted. The only way I know how to break in is from the balcony. A sliding glass door leads directly into the living room and is usually unlocked, at least when my folks are home."

"How the hell are we going to climb seven flights?"

"We're not, silly. That would take stronger arms than I have. We're going to rappel down from the roof."

"Oh boy. Without waking anyone?"

"Lots of these units are vacant until January," Jacquelyn said.

"Which ones?"

"I don't know," Jacquelyn answered. "Most of them. We can take the elevator to the eighth floor. There's a flight of stairs to the roof. If we can find enough projections up there to provide redundant anchors—that means separate ones—I'll show you how to rappel."

"What if the rope breaks?"

"No chance." Jacquelyn's voice was amazingly confident. "I brought along Kermutel, that's regulation rope and a carabiner. We'll make harnesses out of the nylon webbing and run the rope through the carabiner."

"What jargon you speaking in, Lady? What's a carabiner?"

"It's like a figure eight. You feed the one-inch tubular rope through it and toss it over the side. This way, when you rappel down you can brake with one hand and guide with the other."

"Great. Don't you think seeing a shrink would be simpler?"

"Shh. We made it this far. I'm going to do the job, even if I only destroy one trombone." Her soft voice carried the weight of determination.

"How do you know how to rappel?" Trishita asked.

"I don't, but I've watched Ethan practice it."

"Jesus, aren't you scared? My hands are more than just damp from the air, they're wringing wet"

"There's nothing to be afraid of," Jacquelyn said looking up from her tools.

"Okay, what do we say if someone catches us?"

Jacquelyn headed toward the south entrance to the building. "C'mon—let's check out the roof. We've got a built-in alibi. Came to surprise my folks. Flat tire—got here late. Forgot the key."

"And we just happened to have a 'regulation' rope and a carabiner."

"Right. You have a rock-climbing boyfriend currently in the circus in Georgia. It's his rope." Jacquelyn opened the gate with her card, closed it after Trishita, and stepped into the open elevator.

"That makes me feel wonderfully safe." Trishita followed. "All bases covered."

Jacquelyn pushed the button for the eighth floor. She looked up at Trishita with questions in her eyes.

Trishita rolled her eyes. Her supposedly intelligent boss could never read her. The elevator opened onto a corridor and Jacquelyn found the stairway to the roof. Clouds hid the stars and there was, of course, no moon. Trishita was able to make out three projections on the roof, but could see little else.

"Good," Jacquelyn said. "We can tie the rope around each of these air conditioning units. That will give us the redundancy we need and these slats will keep the rope from slipping." She looked at her watch from several angles trying to read it. "I think it's almost one o'clock. We need to wait until two at least. Let's go get the rope and the food."

"Food?"

"Yes, I brought some snacks to fortify us. You warm enough?"

"Sure. It's a lot balmier here than on Ballmans' cupola."

They descended by elevator and ran back to the car on the small island. They giggled like schoolgirls and hushed each other as Jacquelyn opened the trunk of the BMW. She put on her tool belt and handed Trishita a gunnysack containing the rope and carabiner.

"We'll practice on that wall over there." Jacquelin pointed at a twelve-foot wall behind the parking lot.

"What kinda snacks?" Trishita asked.

"Designer bottled water, olive tapenade on rye and some smoked Gouda." Jacquelyn shoved a paper sack at her. "Okay?"

"Party time. I'll carry the gunny sack."

"No, I will. This is my raid."

* * *

Jacquelyn showed Trishita how to make a harness, get in it and rappel down. They practiced for an hour on the wall and then headed down to Huchinson's island.

"This elevator must be well greased," Trishita said when the elevator stopped on the roof. "It sure is quiet."

Jacquelyn led her to a two-foot parapet that enclosed the roof. It formed the upper lip of the building. She sat down, leaned against the parapet and opened the paper bag that Trishita had carried. She handed her a bottle of Evian water and a piece of rye bread spread with olive tapenade.

"Cheers," Jacquelyn said.

"Here's to the last caper," Trishita said, lifting her paper cup as if to click.

"The raid to end all raids." Jacquelyn agreed. They ate in silence for several minutes, listening to the soft lapping of waves on the beach.

"What are those Madame something dolls your rich uncle gave you?" Trishita asked to distract from the waiting.

"Madame Alexander." Jacquelyn straightened her back, sat crossed-legged at the ankles and gazed at the sky. Her arms were thin posts at her side. "They were a precursor of the Barbie doll with lots more class."

"Expensive?"

"Very." Motionless, still gazing up, she said, "None of my playmates had one." She seemed frozen again. Trishita touched her arm. She jumped and then smiled. "My collection made me quite popular."

Collection? The word jarred Trishita.

"It's time." Jacquelyn shook her head and stood.

Trishita hastily packed the remnants of their picnic. Her heart played a riff. "Okay, I'll watch you from up here. What do I do when you get into your folk's condo?"

"When I see the lay of the land, I'll whistle and you can rappel down," Jacquelyn said, animated again. "I'll need your help with the trombones."

"You expect me to destroy them?" Trishita's stomach flipped.

"No," Jacquelyn replied. "I'm the one with the tools—and the burning desire. I just need you to reach up for me. They hang from the ceiling, and I left my ladder at the Lalique figurine raid in Worcester."

Jacquelyn's logic boomeranged around Trishita without connecting. Hell, who could rappel with a ladder, anyway?

"Got it down?" Jacquelyn asked. "When I whistle, you rappel down."

"Roger."

"You making fun of me?"

"No, Jacquelyn. I thought that's what you're supposed to say. Go ahead down."

Jacquelyn put on her gloves, climbed into the harness she'd made, climbed over the edge of the parapet and disappeared.

Trishita waited for her whistle. It was a different kind of waiting this time, rather like a culmination of all her previous practice at waiting. A graduation of sorts.

She heard gentle waves lapping the beach as if there were no tension in the vicinity. If she were trained in meditation, the rate of passing time would make no difference. Then again, she probably wouldn't be on the roof of an eight-story condo in Florida, either.

The night was so dark she couldn't watch Jacquelyn's progress. At least, that's the excuse she gave herself for not watching. All but the sea was quiet, and it told different stories.

A yappy bark from what sounded like a toy poodle broke the silence and lights came on in security unit on the fifth floor. Trishita crouched as she leaned over the side. She saw a man come out onto his balcony and look around. Then she saw Jacquelyn curled against the wall to the left of and just above her parent's balcony.

Minutes passed as if they were hours. The man coughed, spat over the edge of his balcony and then went inside. Soon after, the dog quieted and the lights went out.

Jacquelyn resumed her rappel and made it to the balcony. Trishita strained to hear a whistle. Maybe the sliding glass door was locked.

The excitement of the night's caper passed over that line from the pleasure of feeling alive to the pain of helpless anxiety. Jacquelyn's rope swung in the ocean breeze, in rhythm with the lapping waves. Then Trishita heard a long, sad wail, like the sound of a wolf. But no whistle.

Resigned, she got into her harness and tested the brakes on the carbiner. Her legs shook by the time she reached the edge of the roof. It was so dark she couldn't see the ground if she happened to glance in that direction. She rappelled over the side after one last intense wait and pushed out from the wall with her feet. She braked her descent with one hand and guided it with the other. The rope burned her hands right through her gloves. She felt a sudden rush of hot moisture between her legs when she approached the railing of the Nestroms' balcony. Her pumping adrenaline had brought on her period a week early and with it a harsh, body-doubling cramp. She continued down when the cramp eased. Scared now that she might faint and fall to her death, she began counting to herself. By the time she counted to twenty-seven, she was able to fall onto the balcony. The sliding glass door was open. Where the hell was Dr. Jacquelyn Hyde?

CHAPTER THIRTY

Trishita picked herself up to her knees when her breathing returned to normal. She peered in the open sliding glass door, straining her eyes to see in the dark. Then she heard a soft gulping. A lamp came on and she could see Jacquelyn sitting on a sofa, sobbing.

"Jackie, is that you?" Bill Nestrom stood beside the lamp holding a baseball bat.

Jacquelyn looked up at him and nodded.

"I thought I heard someone," he said. How did you—? What are you—?"

Jacquelyn responded with a wail. He sat beside her and put his arms around her.

"There, there," he mumbled, "Don't cry, my wee Jackie."

Trishita watched, dumbfounded.

"What's wrong, Baby? Is it Arthur?" Bill asked.

Jacquelyn shook her head.

"The children?"

"No," she wailed, releasing such a pitiful sound it brought tears to Trishita's eyes.

Trishita crouched on her knees. There was no polite way out of this scene. Besides, she was bleeding hard and the cramps came in waves. On one strong contraction, she collapsed backwards and hugged her knees.

"Who's that?" Bill shouted.

"Trishita." Jacquelyn jumped up and ran over to her. "I'm so sorry. I forgot to whistle."

"Do you have any rags?" Trishita asked Bill Nestrom.

"Sure. What for?"

"Half way down," Trishita said, "I got so scared, my period started. Early. I wasn't prepared." *He would ask.* She felt blood rushing to her cheeks as well. She was no longer in Russo's Bar.

"Oh my," Bill said, twirling on the balls of his feet. "I should wake Abby."

"Don't wake her." Jacquelyn put her hand on his arm. "I'll find something. Ma may have some Kotex stashed away for guests. Linen closet." She left.

He nodded. White, trimmed hair ringed his bald spot. He danced around in his green plaid cotton pajama pants and striped black and white top,

"Can you tell me how you got onto my balcony? And why?" he asked Trishita,

"How, yes. With a rope tied to the air conditioning units on the roof. I rappeled down," she said, muffling the pride in her voice. "Jackie will tell you why."

"The bathroom's down that hall," Jacquelyn said, returning with a box of Kotex. "I turned the light on for you. Dad, do you have a pair of shorts she can wear? And briefs? Or get some of Mom's." She was in control again, dry eyed, but seemed unaware of her own grungy appearance and pungent smell.

"I'll find something." Bill headed toward the bedroom.

"Don't wake up Mrs. Nestrom," Trishita whispered.

"Don't worry," he yelled back from the hall. "She doesn't sleep with her hearing aids."

"Deaf," Trishita said in awe. "I bet everyone here is deaf. That's why we didn't wake anybody except that yapping dog." She stood, stepped inside and took the box from Jacquelyn's outstretched hand. "Thanks. Hey what's the matter? What got to you so bad?"

"The trombones. There aren't any."

"That's right. Wow." Trishita glanced around the room. "I told your dad how we got in. The why is up to you."

"Oh God." Jacquelyn closed her eyes.

"Here we are, girls," Bill said, returning with a pair of red plaid shorts and men's briefs. "My, it's good to see both of you. Abby will be so tickled. Why it's been a good ten years since you've come to visit us here, Jackie." He peered into her face? "Poor baby. Feeling better? Want a clean shirt?"

Trishita decided this guy had exceptionally good manners or a whole lot of patience.

"I could use a clean shirt." Jacquelyn said, looking down at her sweatshirt and tool belt laden with a ball peen hammer and a hacksaw. Slowly, she removed the belt, dropped it to the floor.

"Be right back." Bill ran off again.

"What happened to his trombone collection?" Trishita asked as she headed toward the bathroom.

"Don't know." Tears again filled Jacquelyn's eyes.

"Here, put this on." Bill returned with a blue plaid shirt for Jacquelyn. "Now, how would you gals like something to drink? Tea? Decaf? Or would you like something stronger? I have some brandy—"

"Decaf with brandy," Jacquelyn answered.

"Same for me," Trishita said. "Excuse me. I'll go clean up."

"And I'll put the kettle on." Bill disappeared into the kitchen.

As Trishita entered the bathroom, she glanced back and saw Jacquelyn tear off her burlap lined sweatshirt and toss it over the balcony. *Step one.*

Trishita put on Bill's briefs after her shower, and felt a little better. The cramps were easing off. She rolled up her jeans and considered tossing them over the balcony, too, but for her, it would be a meaningless gesture. She pulled on Bill's red plaid shorts. They slipped to her hips, but stayed on. She then put on her Clark sweatshirt—right side out. No need to hide the name anymore.

The damp air made Trishita's curls spring tighter than usual. She gave up brushing her hair and surveyed the bathroom to be sure it was clean. Then, not wanting to stall any longer, returned to the living room.

"I put out some crackers and cheese, too," Bill said, handing her a cup of coffee and a snifter of brandy. "It's not much, but we weren't expecting—"

"Thank you," Trishita said. She grimaced, appalled that she had picked up the family habit of interrupting him. Did some people simply elicit interruptions? She glanced at Jacquelyn.

Jacquelyn shrugged. She sat curled up on a floral chintz-covered easy chair wearing a large purple plaid shirt. She looked like the classic waif, big-eyed, forlorn, tiny.

Bill sat on one end of the couch facing Jacquelyn and the balcony. Trishita sat at the other end wondering if she should cut out, maybe go up to the roof and untie the rope.

"Jacquelyn wanted to wait until you came back," Bill said with a cough, "before saying anything about the why." He turned to Jacquelyn. "Well?"

She glanced at the floor, then the ceiling before looking directly at him. "I came here to destroy your trombones.

"My trombones? What on earth for?"

"Trishita suggested it." Jacquelyn lowered her eyes. "She thought it might help cure me, and I agreed."

"Cure you of what?" Even while seated, Bill's feet moved.

"Well, I have this problem. Sort of an obsession. I can't sleep sometimes, especially if I've seen or read about someone's collection. I feel this overwhelming need to break up people's collections of things so I can sleep."

"I sold the trombones," he said. "Two or three a year. That's how I financed our annual jaunts to Maine." Sorrow rimmed his voice.

"Sold them?" Jacquelyn sat up straight. "Oh, no! You loved them." She slumped back into the chair.

"I have one left if you want to destroy it. It's under the bed."

"No, no. Dad. I'm so sorry." Jacquelyn put her face in her hands. "What happened to your inheritance from Grandpa Nestrom? I thought you had enough money from that."

"We invested in you, little girl." He smiled. "Don't you remember? We put that twenty thou where it belonged, in your education. Hell, we'd never had a Nestrom make it through junior college, let alone all the way to a Ph.D." He grinned. "That was our best investment."

"You spent your whole inheritance on me? I knew about the twenty thousand, but I thought you cleared a lot more than that. Grandpa owned a lot of land."

"After taxes and splitting it with Roger, I got twenty and felt damn lucky."

"Uncle Roger's never needed it. He should've given you his half."

"He has. He gave us this place to live. Now hush about the money. Tell me about this—your, uh, obsession."

Trishita recognized how bizarre this scene was. The whole scene. And she had been playing a major role. She sat still, pondering as she watched her tiny employer pace the floor while her father danced in place. Still, if she believed what she read in the newspapers, this was not that unusual. She used to think that drugs and alcohol fueled her mother and her companions' bizarre behavior. Would they, if sober, behave like Jacquelyn? Or dance around like Bill? He looked as if he never once felt the earth under his feet, even in combat during his beloved World War II.

"I don't know where to begin." Jacquelyn paced.

"Anywhere's okay by me," Bill said in a hoarse voice.

Jacquelyn began speaking as if she were confessing her sins to a spiritual father. He listened wide-eyed. She pointed out all her tools, described in detail several of her raids, ending with the raid on Superintendent Ballman's clowns and Trishita's rescue. Then she sat down and sipped her brandy.

Bill reached over to Trishita and touched the top of her head. A blessing of sorts. She smiled at him.

"Trishita's right," he said to Jacquelyn. You need curing. But tonight you need some sleep. Stretch out on the couch or go into the spare bedroom. I'll lower the lights."

"No, we'll go back to our motel room and put on regular clothes," Jacquelyn said, jumping up. "I don't want Mom to see us like this. Besides, we need to untie the rope before dawn."

Trishita stood, turned to leave, then saw Mrs. Nestrom standing in the hall, gray hair combed and pulled back into a bun, hearing aids in place, blue silk dressing gown with matching mules. How long had she been standing there?

"What's the matter?" asked Bill.

"Good morning, Mrs. Nestrom," Trishita said in a soft voice.

"Ma!" Jacquelyn started toward her mother and then stopped dead.

CHAPTER THIRTY-ONE

"Such a sight you all are." Abby Nestrom eyed each of them. "Did Bill give you those Godawful clothes or are you developing his peculiar tastes?"

"Come, sit down, Abby," Bill said. "Shall I get you some coffee?"

"No, I'd like to speak with Trishita privately." Abby turned to Trishita. "Please follow me back to my room."

"How long have you been up?" Jacquelyn asked Abby, releasing herself from her frozen stance. She sat on the arm of the couch.

"Long enough," Abby said. "I don't believe any of it. Why did you make up such a story, Jacquelyn?"

"It's all true." Jacquelyn bowed her head.

"Of course it isn't, but you always did tell strange stories about yourself." Abby moved toward the hall. "Come Trishita. Let her tell her tales to Bill."

Trishita looked at Jacquelyn who nodded at her, and then followed Abby down the hall and into a small bedroom. Abby gestured to a settee and sat on the edge of the unmade bed.

"I understand that you wish to help your employer. So listen to me a little while, for there is little you nor I nor anyone can do. You see, we adopted Jackie when she was two and a half years old, after she'd been severely beaten."

"Wow! She doesn't know? You never told her?"

"No. Just couldn't, somehow. You see, we got this call from the adoption agency—I loved our son, couldn't have any more kids and I wanted a girl I could cherish and dress in pretty clothes. There was a long waiting list for girls at the time." Abby stood, twisted her blue bathrobe around her, and sat down hard.

"Can I get you something?" Trishita asked.

"No, no. I'm fine. I don't know why I'm telling you this."

"It's okay. Sounds like you've been carrying loaded secrets for years."

"Don't you know it!" Abby leaned forward. "You've dealt with kids that weren't yours. I remember you telling me about them when we last went to Northboro. You know what it's like." She straightened and gazed out the window. "We shoulda refused Jackie—her trauma—we shoulda known it would haunt her."

Trishita nodded, decided to remain quiet.

"But no, we had to take her, a two year old so badly beaten we couldn't refuse."

"Wow," Trishita repeated, picturing her troubled boss as a beat up baby girl.

"It's true," Abby said in a soft voice. "Her mother was strung out on meth and booze. Jackie accidentally broke one of her prized crystal elephants. She came unglued and beat the poor baby until she was unconscious. Jackie was still out when the police found her and rushed her to the hospital. It's a wonder she survived."

Bill Nestrom entered. "Abby, stop. It happened a long time ago. Don't talk about it any more."

"She has to," Trishita said as she stood. "And you have to tell your daughter she's adopted."

"So that's it," Jacquelyn said as she entered the now crowded little room. "I once wondered if I were adopted when Ma said, 'when we got you' instead of 'when you were born'."

Bill twirled and then put his arms around Jackie, but she shook him off.

"How come you never told me?" Jacquelyn's eyes blazed. "Not that it matters."

Trishita forced herself to breathe without screaming. No wonder Jacquelyn's stomach was all messed up. Everyone acted as if the floor were covered with fresh laid eggs."

Bill just shook his head and went back to the kitchen.

"He's gone, Abby said. "Now we can all tell the truth."

"Denial," Jacquelyn said, "anger, bargaining. What's next?"

Abby frowned at her from the edge of the bed. "He wouldn't let me tell you. He cried when he first saw you covered with bruises." She lowered her head.

Jacquelyn stared out the window. No one spoke.

"What ever happened to your doll collection?" Trishita asked Jacquelyn, breaking the spell. She wondered what lay beneath this deadening silence.

"I've never had a doll collection." Jacquelyn's shoulders twitched. She stared at Trishita.

"Upstairs on the roof you said that your Uncle—"

"Oh, those awful Madame Alexander dolls," Abby said. "They were broken . . . all of 'em . . . they got broken . . . so I got rid of 'em."

Jacquelyn twisted to face her mother. She stopped breathing and her face reddened. Finally she exploded with a scream—a regular banshee yell. She yanked at her hair and stamped her feet. Abby pulled back onto the bed, looking terrified. Bill rushed back from the kitchen, hopping from foot to foot. He reminded Trishita of a fire-walker who didn't believe.

Jacquelyn showed no sign of letting up. Trishita moved behind her and pinned her arms to her sides.

"Hush, Hush," Trishita crooned, as she had years ago when one of her baby brothers had a tantrum. Jacquelyn stopped screaming and buried her face in Trishita's arms. When Jacquelyn's breathing returned to normal, Trishita let her go and moved back to the settee.

"It wasn't a dream after all." Jacquelyn stood in the middle of the room, staring at her mother.

"What wasn't?" Bill asked. His agitated hopping subsided to a slight, rhythmic bouncing.

Jacquelyn kept her eyes on her mother.

The air was eerily still. Abby put both hands to her ears and began to remove her hearing aids.

"No, you don't." Jacquelyn grabbed her mother's wrists. You're going to listen this time."

"Easy, Jackie. Go easy on her." Bill started to move in, but checked himself.

"It doesn't make any difference." Jacquelyn looked up at him and let go of Abby. "She can hear what she wants without them." She turned to Abby. "I thought I dreamed it all those years—but I didn't. I watched you break the neck on every one of my dolls. The next morning, they were gone. All I saw was that ugly green wall behind the shelves. You told me a burglar stole my dolls in the night. You said they were worth lots of money on the street."

"I remember that," Bill said. "We even called in the police—"

"What I thought was a dream was really vivid, Jacquelyn said. "I saw you come into my room, pick up each doll, curse it, then snap its neck. I thought you were going to break my neck, too. I was scared out of my mind, and played possum so hard I passed out." She shook her head in wonder. "The next morning I thought it was just a bad dream. You told me it was a nightmare." Jacquelyn collapsed into the chintz chair. In a voice scratched from screaming, now soft, she asked, "Why, Ma?"

"Not in front of the help." Eyes wide, Abby looked first at Jacquelyn, then at Trishita.

"She's not the help," Jacquelyn barked. "She's a trusted friend. My *only* trusted friend."

That gave Trishita a glow that worked up her torso and slowly formed a heavy weight across her shoulders. Since her deal with Ethan and dalliance with Arthur, she doubted she could manage a friendship with Jacquelyn.

"You can speak, Abby." Bill said, standing quite still by the door. "You're safe." His deep voice felt soothing to Trishita.

"I'm sorry Jacquelyn." Abby started slowly rocking her torso on the bed. "I hated those dolls for years. Roger kept showing up with a new one. He'd make nasty remarks that you," she pointed at Bill, "would snicker at. You compared that last doll with Grace Kelly and Roger said, 'Wouldn't you like to open a real pair of legs like that?' Both of you were in love with her shapely legs. I saw that look in your eyes. Sick, that's what."

"My room was painted all over in that ugly green," Jacquelyn said in a dreamy tone. "Remember? Dad built those shelves to hold my dolls. The dolls made the room bearable."

"You were jealous?" Bill asked Abby, obviously amazed.

"You and Roger kept smirking around them," Abby said.

"Abby, you were jealous. I never knew I could make you jealous." He moved in closer and stood with his bare feet planted on the carpet. No dancing now. Trishita marveled at the change in his feet.

"Me, too," Jacquelyn said softly, matter-of-factly. "I was jealous of your trombones."

"Am I hearing right? Your mother was jealous of dolls and you of my trombones. Objects! Jumpin' Jehosophat. If you were jealous you must've thought I loved them more than I loved you."

"True," Jacquelyn said, "You were always caressing your trombones."

"Yes," Abby enjoined, "and raving about Madame Alexander's body."

"I never realized either one of you cared." Bill placed his hands on his plaid pajama hips and widened his flat-footed stance. Tears filled his eyes. "I'm going to die a lucky man." He pulled Abby off the bed and hugged her then pulled Jacquelyn into the hug.

"I bet Billy's smiling in his grave right now," Jacquelyn said.

Trishita recalled Sylvia's request to know about her Uncle Billy and felt her eyes fill. She slipped out of the embrace and the room and climbed the stairs up to the roof. A faint light drew a line between the sea and the sky. She untied the rope from each of the air conditioning units, coiled it, and then searched the sky in vain for an outline of the moon. *Step two, Jacquelyn. How many more to go? Sure hope you skip over those steps I took on you last summer.*

CHAPTER THIRTY-TWO

Sylvia ran alongside, grinning as Trishita turned the BMW into the Hyde's driveway. Trishita stopped in front of the house and let Jacquelyn out. With a pang of envy, she watched mother and daughter hug. And she tried to imagine how Flossie felt beneath the protective layer of booze whenever Trishita paid her a visit.

Sylvia gushed. "Everything came out just right. There's some turkey left over but no stuffing and we made two kinds. And three pies. Everybody raved—said it was the best Thanksgiving dinner ever. Dad and Ethan helped cook and clean up. We didn't think we could pull it off, but we did. The only thing we forgot was the butternut squash."

Smiling, Trishita drove around back and parked in the garage. She climbed out of the cramped position she'd held for twelve hours and stretched. All the way home Jacquelyn had talked about telling Arthur, if not the children, everything she'd kept secret.

"Right, you need to tell him," Trishita had said. "Too much to lay on the kids."

"I'm not out of the woods by a long shot," Jacquelyn said. "But I'm ready to go—as you say—to a shrink. Maybe a hypnotist, if can find one I trust."

Trishita stretched again. Then, when she was unpacking the car, someone came up behind her, grabbed her around the waist, and squeezed. She turned and wallowed in Sylvia's hug.

"I'm so glad you're home," Sylvia said. "How's Ma? She looks real good."

"I think she's better."

Sylvia ran away and returned with some wrinkled envelopes. "I hope you don't mind, but I accidentally messed up your mail."

"S'okay." Trishita took two large manila envelopes and one small white one from her and looked at the return addresses. The small envelope came from Clark University; the other two were from the Federal Government.

"Well, aren't you going to open them? I sure wanted to—to find out—I mean look where they're from. Dad said he bet you got accepted plus scholarships. He figures that as long as you live here you can make it without working and get your degree in three years."

Trishita wondered how Sylvia could speak so fast and still make sense. She opened each envelope and scanned the contents. Her guts jumped. Then she jumped and twirled Sylvia around the back driveway.

"You're right, kiddo. I've been accepted at Clark and have two full scholarships." She looked up at the windows of Arthur's office. He and Jacquelyn were looking out. Each gave her a "thumbs-up" and a salute. Trishita decided to hand-wash her Clark University sweatshirt.

*   *   *

For a while, it seemed to Trishita that they had all come to a happy ending. Even Flossie had a new lover who was paying the rent regularly. But, when she turned in her final exam to Dr. McLaren just before Christmas, she felt a heavy weight in her heart.

"Thank you, Trishita," he said. "It's been a great pleasure having you audit my class. After you are officially enrolled and make it to upper division status, I'll change your transcript to credit with an A."

"Thanks. I'll miss seeing you next semester, but I have to take lower division classes now."

"Oh, I'll be around," he said with a slight burr. "Although you won't be in one of my classes, this doesn't preclude your stopping in for a chat now and then. You know my office hours."

"Sure." Trishita managed a smile. "I'll see you next semester then. Have a Merry Christmas." She hurried outside and drove home in a blinding snowstorm wondering what his wife looked like. Although she turned on the windshield wipers this time, they neither wiped away the snow nor cleared her eyes.

*   *   *

Melissa broke up with Ethan in February. He stopped smiling, stopped teasing Sylvia and Trishita, and stopped calling Mickey Carregio. Everyone in the house suffered his broken heart.

Jacquelyn had regular appointments with a psychologist in Framingham. She suggested Ethan make an appointment, but he refused. Arthur tried three times to speak to him about women and heartbreak.

"Forget it, Dad," Ethan repeated every time.

Sylvia tried to get him to play cards. He shook his head and slipped out the back door. Trishita saw him head for the woods, now cold and full of naked, forlorn-looking trees.

"Some hurts stay with you for life," Trishita said one night when she was alone with Ethan in the kitchen. She put her arm around his shoulders.

He leaned over the kitchen sink and cried. She rubbed his back, fighting back her own tears, her own heartbreak.

*   *   *

Jacquelyn came home early on the Ides of March. Trishita was dancing around the kitchen to an Irish jig while preparing corned beef and cabbage and a horseradish sauce.

"Smells good," Jacquelyn said and pulled out a chair. "Mind if I watch?"

"Welcome. How are you? You're looking great all dressed in black and carrying a bright red coat. What did your secretary say about you changing from pastel colors?"

"Thanks, Trish. She didn't say anything but she sure looked befuddled. I can hardly recognize myself. And I have to admit that the shrink, as you call her, makes a lot of sense."

Trishita nodded and stirred. She wondered what she would say to a shrink if she ever had enough money to hire one.

"The new moon still haunts me, but I've tossed my gear and go nowhere—as I'm sure you know."

"I've been thinking," Trishita said as she added yogurt to the sauce, "that everyone has a tough piece of meat lodged in his gut or throat that he can't swallow. Once you find it, you can regurgitate it—pardon my French. I don't think I've found mine yet."

"I'm beginning to agree with you on that." Jacquelyn stood and put on her coat. "I'm going for a walk so I'll have an appetite for dinner. And, by the way, I'm flying to Florida at the Easter break. I'm going to enter the front door and somehow meet my mother."

Trishita danced a jig of joy.

* * *

Trishita, happily enmeshed in five different classes, devoured whatever her textbooks and professors offered. She hadn't gone to see Dr. McLaren, hoping to forget about him. On Friday, just before the April spring break, she came home to an empty house. That in itself was not unusual. But, the note from Jacquelyn on the kitchen table was.

It read, "Arthur and I have gone to see my shrink and then to the Cape for the weekend."

Must be getting serious, Trishita thought, if Arthur's going to the shrink, too. She read on, "The children won't be home until Sunday, either. Before you leave, I'd like you to listen to the tape on the answer phone. It seems Ethan answered the phone just as the tape clicked on. Sylvia listened to it all the way through and said we should all hear it. I agreed."

The note was signed, "Dr. Jacquelyn Hyde."

Since when was she Dr. Jacquelyn Hyde? And what was this "Before you leave," business? Leave for where? *My God, what's happened?* She felt her heart flutter.

The tape player sat on the shelf next to the wall phone. Trishita resigned herself to following directions and sat down to listen.

"Hello." Ethan's deep, bored voice came on followed by Mickey's light one. Trishita realized with fear that Ethan had taped their whole conversation.

"Hey, little fucker, how are you?"

"Mickey, you in town?" Ethan's voice lightened.

"Yep. Came back for spring break. This wild woman from Smith is coming over to see my bachelor pad tomorrow. She's got a friend coming with her. Stacked. Wanting company."

"Yeah. Fine." Ethan's voice sounded as flat as a key on a piano in need of tuning.

"What d'ya mean, fine? Christ, what's with you?"

"I've had it with women. Broke up with Melissa."

"Shit, man, that shouldn't keep you from hustling. I never knew what you saw in her anyway."

"Hang on a minute. I'm gonna snag a coke and can't reach the fridge."

Trishita heard the refrigerator door open and close, followed by the snap of a pop top. She felt decidedly uneasy. And Sylvia had insisted they all listen to this.

"I'm back." Ethan burped, and then said, "I'm laying off pussy for a while. Back to jacking off."

Mickey laughed. That's what you said after Trishita."

Trishita moaned. Her heart fell into her stomach. *After you leave.* Now she knew what that meant. Where would she go? And Sylvia had heard all this? *She must hate me. God, why did I do it? Damn that hole in the pantry wall.*

"Trishita never once claimed she loved me," Ethan's voice said. "We had a deal going."

"You never mentioned a deal. Man, were you pissed at her. Did she renege on it? What kind of a deal?"

"Naw. I taught her how to drive and she taught me how to make love instead of just fuck. She would never renege. Jeez, the stuff she taught me!"

Spare the details, please.

"Like what?" Mickey sounded too eager.

"Oh, all kinds of things."

"Give, you little fucker. Like what?"

"How to save my ching." Ethan's voice was lighter, now. "Melissa loved it."

"Translate please. No capishe Chinese."

"Ching is come, man. You save it by applying pressure with your fingers to a point just between your asshole and balls—for just a few seconds. Keeps you from coming. That way you stay hard a lot longer."

"That's no fun."

"Au contraire. Makes you *feel* like jumping her bones until she comes. Some women are slow, you know. If you do this, you don't have to wait an hour before you get hard again."

"Old Farley says he has to wait a year to get hard again."

"He really needs to save his ching, then."

"Does applying pressure there hurt?"

"Naw. Takes a little practice to get the right timing. You have to do it when you're just halfway excited, not just before you come. Trishita said ripeness was all."

"C'mon, that's from King Lear."

"Really? I thought she made it up."

"Where did she learn this ching racket?"

"Dunno. She reads a lot of weird stuff."

"So, is Trishita still cooking up a storm?" he asked.

Trishita heard Mickey light a cigarette. The snap of the match crackled, exaggerated by the recording of the phone lines.

"Sure."

"I'd like to get a lesson or two from her."

"Forget it," Ethan replied. She's celibate these days."

"How come."

"I think she's in love with her college professor."

"One lucky dude. I wonder if he saves his ching."

Ethan sighed, took a noisy gulp of coke.

Mickey laughed. "Well, I'm gonna have a house full of pussy tomorrow that I'm willing to share."

"Some other time." The pain in Ethan's voice made her wince.

"What happened with Melissa, anyway? You guys were really thick at Thanksgiving."

"She burned me off. Screwed me over royally. Said she wanted to go to U-Mass to a Lambda Chi party with her girlfriend. That jerk Sunshine she hangs out with. They wanted to meet college boys. I told her I'd be a college boy next semester. Shit, after all the ching I saved for her!"

"She's not worth it."

"Right."

"Hey, you sound like you did last summer. You gotta steel yourself, man, then jump a new one every week."

"Yeah, I suppose."

"Say, what did Trishita do to piss you off? She wouldn't tell me."

"Fucked my old man. I saw them going at it in the woods."

"No, no, no!" Trishita cried out in despair. She stopped the tape, dropped her face onto her arms, and wept. The sins of the mother visited upon the children, and you don't recognize them as sins until after you've committed them.

CHAPTER THIRTY-THREE

Trishita packed all her books and loaded down the Rabbit until it almost scraped the pavement. Her plan was to unload at Flossie's, return the Rabbit, walk into town and take the bus back to Worcester. She moved in a leaden daze, noticing in passing that the lilacs were in bloom, yet it was snowing again. Big lacy flakes landed on the violet clusters, blessing them.

Flossie seemed delighted to see her, but looked guarded when she saw Trishita's car full of books. "You plannin' on moving in for good?"

"No, Ma. I just need a place for a week. That okay?"

"Sure, Mija. Henry won't mind. At least, I hope not."

"Fuck Henry."

"Don't you dare."

They laughed. Flossie did look better. Bony as ever, but not quite so poisoned, skin a little less gray.

Trishita trudged up the three flights carrying the same books that Ethan and Arthur helped her with last fall. Well, the bubble had finally burst. She should've known she was caste bound. College was an opium pipe dream. So was cooking for flavor instead of fuel.

"No, dammit," she said to herself the next day. "College is not a pipe dream!" Since it was spring break, she had time to find a night job and a place to live—as long as the owner didn't require a down payment. She was determined to hang onto most of her classes, if not all. One of her scholarships might even cover rent.

She drove back to Northboro Palm Sunday morning, deadened to anything that might happen, anyone she might see. Except Sylvia. She prayed Sylvia wouldn't be there.

No one was home. She let herself in and hurried to the kitchen. On the table, beside Jacquelyn's note, she placed the house and car keys. She headed toward the front door after a glance around to make sure nothing was askew. Then she decided to leave one last meal for them. The least she could do.

Back in the kitchen, she took a Pyrex bowl out of the freezer and a ball of her recently made pie dough. She rolled out the dough and fitted it on top of a veal casserole. Then she pulled a clean sheet from a notepad in the junk drawer and Sylvia's cow-head pen and wrote,

Dear Sylvia, Arthur, Ethan, and Jacquelyn,

Here is my last supper. It's a veal pie I made and froze, waiting for a special occasion. Bake it at 400° for twenty minutes.

I wish I could re-wind my time with you, edit out my peculiar brand of evil. I wish you well. I wish you truth. I wish you the magic to survive truth.

Patricia McCabe

She replaced Sylvia's pen in the drawer and picked up her purse to leave when the front door opened with a burst of cool air. Sylvia blew in with it, rushed toward Trishita, tripped on the threshold into the kitchen and fell against her.

"Dammit," Sylvia yelled and pulled back. Her flushed face changed expressions like an old video on fast forward, covering the range of cold hate, betrayal, trust, anger, love and wonder.

Trishita longed to hold her in her arms.

"How could you fuck my father?" Sylvia whispered in a hiss.

Trishita looked straight at her but did not answer. She knew there was nothing to say. The pain of the moment felt unbearable, yet she knew she would bear it.

"Ethan, I get." Sylvia said. "He taught you how to drive. But my father? Jesus, don't you have any respect? What did you think he would give you? A scholarship? My mother did that."

Trishita wanted to say that it only happened once, that she refused him that time in the woods, albeit reluctantly, but she held her defensive tongue. She knew she had no excuse.

"I'm still a virgin," Sylvia said, gulping between sobs. "You saved me from Harold and then I promised you. I said you could always rely on me—that we'd be friends for life. Now I feel awful.

"I love you, Sylvia." Trishita opened her arms. "I'm so sorry I hurt you. I hope you will forgive me someday. I loved you the most."

Sylvia fell into her arms and screamed, "You never told me what you were teaching Ethan! Now he's pissed that I listened to the tape and made Ma and Dad listen, too."

Trishita held her tight. She felt Sylvia's muscles relax in sporadic, isolated spots, shoulders first and then neck.

"I *am* your friend for life," she whispered to Sylvia. "I will keep in touch, let you know where I am and manage to see you whenever you want. You see, I need you, too, kid." Then she collapsed into tears, herself, releasing her hold on Sylvia.

Sylvia backed into the dining room. She ran her hand along the edge of the table and then entered the mirrored foyer. Trishita saw in the reflections several images of a tall almost-woman moving like a wounded doe. She followed.

"Ethan's out front waiting for me," Sylvia said at the front door. "Our parents don't know we're here. I told them I wouldn't look for you anymore. But I had to." She shook her head. The mirrors fractured her bewildered look.

"Oh God, kid, I am so sorry. I wanted your folks to adopt me. I wanted to be everything to all of you. Tell Ethan, please."

"You *are* everything." Sylvia skipped back to Trishita and touched her cheek. "I've gotta go. Ma and Dad are going through Hell, but it beats the Limbo they were in." She turned and ran out the door.

*   *   *

Trishita took an hour to recoup. As she was heading out, the telephone rang, sounding in her ears like a nuclear disaster-warning siren. Should she answer it? Should she turn on the answering machine? Had Jacquelyn forgiven her?

No. She couldn't forgive this soon, if ever.

Maybe a salesman. Or Mickey, God forbid, wanting a lesson.

Or Ethan, struggling.

"Hyde residence, Trishita speaking," she said into the receiver. At least her voice didn't break.

"Trishita McCabe?"

"Speaking."

"Good. How are you? This is Ian McLaren. I've been trying to get in touch with you, hoping you'd drop by my office."

"I'm sorry."

"I was wondering if you could come in next week during spring break. You see, my grant has been approved and I need a research assistant."

"I'm muddling through a move into Worcester right now." By now, Trishita had slid to the floor.

"Ah, too bad. I had hoped—"

"I lost my job here and have to find a new one."

"That's exactly what I have to offer you. My grant provides ten thousand dollars a year for a part time research assistant. You're the best I know."

Trishita felt struck dumb.

"Trishita, are you still there?" he asked. "I miss seeing you and look forward to working with you."

She managed a throaty gurgle, but nothing more.

"Was that a yes or no?"

"It was a yes." She pictured his shy smile, freckled hands. "I'm stoked. I'll meet you at your office Monday. What time?"

Silence. She imagined him blushing.

"How about ten in the morning?"

"I'll be there."

She hung up and squealed. A job! With Dr. McLaren. Ian. He called himself Ian. She could get used to that name. And she could work with him without seducing him.

No! Wait a dogbone minute. She knew with sudden intensity that she could not work with Ian. She would seduce him because she would want him too much. She knew now that she was a sucker for intelligent, gentle, tender men.

"No! She hadn't seen his wife in the English Department but she remembered her boss saying how generous the McLarens were with the classified help. She wondered what his wife looked like.

"No more married men," she said aloud. "Go back to Russo's and be celibate again. It's easier there."

She looked around the kitchen, and saw that it was not hers and never would be. That cold fact made it easier to leave. Besides, she knew she'd see the Hydes again some day. Vicissitudes come with the territory, especially when you scratch the underbelly of the upper crust and it bleeds, just like Flossie's.

CHAPTER THIRTY-FOUR

Trishita hiked the trash-strewn sidewalks from Flossie's tenement over to the clean paths of Clark University. She dreaded her meeting with Ian McLaren, wondering how much resolve she would need to bid him a final "adieu."

"Welcome. Trishita," he said. He was waiting in the hall by his office, grinning. He opened his office door. "Come in, we have much to talk about."

Not much. She preceded him with a lump in her throat and sat facing his desk. He closed the office door, pulled up a chair and sat beside her. The silence lengthened, but Trishita did not want to be the one to break it, afraid of what she might say.

"You're awfully quiet, Trish. Speak to me."

"I can't accept your offer," she blurted. "And it breaks my heart."

"Why on earth—?" He touched her hand. She felt paralyzed for a minute, and then she moved her hand away from his.

"Because I love you and would seduce you and that's not fair to your wife," she said in one breath.

"But, Trishita, I'm not married and I'm damned glad you love me." His voice rang like cathedral chimes.

"What? What about your wife, Dr. McLaren in the English Department?"

He put his arms around her and caressed the left side of her face. Then he lifted her chin, forcing her to see his broad smile.

"You mean the Dr. McLaren in the English Department who lectures on the works of Robert Henryson, that Scottish Chaucerian poet? That Dr. McLaren whose name is spelled just like mine?"

"Yes, that Dr. McLaren," Trishita whispered, "who, along with you, is generous with the classified employees."

"Well, my beautiful brilliant redhead, that Dr. McClaren is my big sister and she is anxious to meet you."

"Really? She's your sister?"

"I swear on the ghost of Tiresias, she is." He put both hands on her hair and pulled it just enough to raise her face to his. "Believe me, my wonderful red-haired beauty."

"Then," Trishita said, feeling the blush on her face, "I accept your offer as research assistant."

Ian kissed her with a tender passion that floored her. Literally.

Sylvia will be thrilled.

The Beginning